# The Goatman of Guarded Woods

## The Nickelville Novels

Book Two

Tom Barnett

# Books by Tom Barnett

## The Nickelville Novels

*The Haunting of Nickelville Academy*

*The Goatman of Guarded Wood*

*Within the Silver Mirror*

*The Children of Nyx*

# Table of Contents

# Chapter I: Carnival Ancestry

Bruce Grimble hated the song on the radio, and he hated the way that the hot humid air pasted his clothing to his skin. But most of all he hated the way every mosquito in Guarded Wood seemed to think of him as some sort of highly refined delicacy. Furthermore, he'd never been happier in his life.

In the months following the fall of the courtyard wall, life in Nickelville had continued as normally as could be expected when his average ride to school often included flying frogs that waved to him as the bus approached. But now summer break was well underway, and the treehouse had successfully crossed the veil that separated dreams from reality. In fact, the board that he and Megan currently carried should be the last before it was finished.

Bruce tried not to let the way that Megan's hair absorbed the sunlight distract him lest she feel his eyes upon her. Instead he concentrated on the way the awful song's tempo guided her steps, and happily followed her lead.

Megan's mother, Emelia, scurried through the branches overhead. Even from down where he and Megan walked, he could feel the questing tendrils of the woman's magic, searching for weaknesses that might make the impressive structure unsafe. But she wouldn't find any. Of that Bruce was certain. Ever since his abilities had woken, he'd understood the physical world around him in ways that bordered on the arcane.

Somehow knowing that only he would see, Emelia leapt far further than any normal human could have done and continued her survey from another part of the tree. As usual, she wore long sleeves in spite of the heat and looked far younger than she should.

No matter how many times he watched his brother tie knots, the ease with which the rope danced between and around Paul's fingers left Bruce feeling clumsy and awkward by comparison. Oddly enough, the youngest Grimble had known all but the most obscure knots even before he'd become a scout.

"Take it away, Sam," Paul called when he was done. The line went taught as the big man lifted the board with the block and tackle mounted far above.

"What now?" Megan yelled up to where Sam, Mr. Green and Mr. Grimble were already fitting the last board into place.

"I think that's gonna do it," Mr. Green yelled back.

"Let's go look," Jade squealed, grabbing Megan by the hand.

Bruce noticed that his sister's hair had grown over the past several months, exposing almost two inches of the chestnut brown they'd both inherited from their mother before changing to her currently preferred fire-engine red. She seldom kept any color for long, and he wondered what might come next.

The treehouse itself lay cradled in the massive fork of one of the tallest trees that encircled the town, and the enclosed portion could bunk Paul's entire Boy Scout troop. Due to the donations made by Mr. Green, who apparently salvaged building materials from the demolition of the many derelict Victorian homes across Nickelville, it looked more like a mansion than a treehouse. A wrap-around porch surrounded the enclosed rooms, stained glass windows cast multicolored hues across everything (but none of them resembled those used by Jacob Routh in his church) and a single turret tower rose from its center, looking out over the entire valley in which the town sat.

When he and his brother followed the girls up the staircase, which despite its delicate appearance hardly moved beneath them as they climbed, Bruce couldn't help but be a little bit proud of his design.

*You've got every reason to be,* Megan sent.

*Are you eavesdropping on my thoughts?* He sent in reply, not that he really would have minded.

*No,* she answered, still climbing ahead of him. *But your feelings are broadcasting pretty loud today.*

The laughter of the four teens infected the adults as they passed, whooping in excitement as they climbed the tower ladder. From this highest point of the treehouse, the four of them marveled at the view over the tops of the trees which stretched out over to the horizon with no sign of ending.

"I thought you said that the woods were only a few miles across," Megan observed happily.

"They are," Paul answered with a frown. "I could have sworn we could see the big trees that circle the woods on the other side when we were up here before."

"Must be some kind of optical illusion then," Megan said with a shrug.

Down below, Bruce saw his mother and the heavily freckled delivery girl from Gordon's carrying pizza boxes down the path that led from their house. He was struck again by how much older his parents looked than Emelia even though they were almost exactly the same age. Not that either

3

of them had aged badly by any stretch of the imagination. His mother and father both worked in active professions and still turned the occasional head. But each of them had reached the tipping point of having more gray hair than the colors with which they'd been born. Meanwhile, it looked like even Emelia's long black hair dared not risk her wrath by showing her age.

"Bring it on up," Ben Grimble yelled from somewhere below. "Give everyone a call and tell them that we're done."

Bruce had mixed feelings about finishing. Like the rest of them, he wanted to enjoy the tree house without all of the physical labor. But he'd miss the way it had brought them together. He'd miss the stories that Azarich, Tom and Alan told while they out-worked people a quarter their age. Even with Megan bolstering his energy levels, Bruce could barely keep up with those three old men. Only Sam seemed to be their equal.

Emelia had been a wonder in her own right, seemingly everywhere at once. She now balanced precariously on a much smaller branch than he would have trusted were he in her place. Although she looked distracted as she spoke on her new cellphone, she felt his gaze at once and looked down at him.

"Better get down before they eat all the pizza," Emelia suggested in a tone that somehow sounded more like a regal command.

"Thanks Patty," Sam was telling the delivery girl when they reached the main floor. "Tell Dan that I probably won't be in tonight."

"Of course, Mr. Wise," the girl in the Gordon's shirt replied.

"Just Sam," he reminded her.

"Sure…Sam," the girl said, flushing before she fled down the stairs.

Emelia dropped down from above, landing catlike on the balls of her feet and startled Dora so badly that she let out a frightened squeak and almost dropped the pizza she was holding.

"How did you do that?" Jade asked in awe, looking at how far she'd fallen. "Are you sure you're Mom's age?"

"Rumor has it that we have carnie ancestors," Megan interjected, glaring at her mother and exchanging some mental message that Bruce couldn't quite hear. "Probably had a trapeze girl back there somewhere."

"Dad's on his way up," Emelia announced as if nothing had happened, putting her phone into her shirt pocket and giving Bruce a quick glimpse of her badly scarred ring finger. "Mr. Harris and his wife should be over soon as well."

*Actually, how* does *she do that?* Bruce asked.

*I'm afraid to ask,* Megan answered, focusing hard to keep her mother out of the conversation. *I don't think I'm ready to try whatever it is yet.*

Bruce agreed. Emelia had been pushing them hard in their training, and he didn't particularly want to add anything new to the exercises either. As it was, he dreamed about starting fires, honing the shield around himself and moving things with his mind. When she wasn't drilling them, Sam worked with him the best he could on precognition. Although none of them shared this ability with Bruce, the Well of Dreams had given them a place to start.

Mr. Grimble spread the boxes out over one of the picnic tables that Mr. Green had built out of leftover lumber during the construction. Bruce had never realized just how skilled the janitor was with woodworking until they'd started the treehouse. Like a carpenter, Alan didn't need to measure a piece of wood to know its length and could glance at a pile of boards and come up with several things to make out of it without a moment's hesitation.

Just as Bruce positioned himself to fill his plate, the sense he was being watched became almost overwhelming. He glanced around, but only found a big blackbird with red bands across the tops of its wings watching with an inordinate amount of attention. Then Bruce took his first bite and things like birds became much less important.

Later, when hunger had been sated somewhat, conversation replaced the sounds of appreciative eating, and Paul expressed his excitement for the coming night.

"Are you ready to spend the night up here?" he asked Megan brightly.

"As long as you and Bruce don't snore too loudly," she answered.

"We'll make them sleep out here if they do," Jade said, motioning to the deck where they sat.

"Hello up there," Mr. Harris yelled from below where he and Azarich were helping Mrs. Harris up the staircase. "Could someone send down the basket for these cookies?"

"Ooo," Paul said, already feeding rope into the pulley, "No one makes better cookies than Mrs. Harris."

When the three elderly people made their way at last to the top of the winding stairs, Bruce could feel sadness radiating from the librarian, and it didn't take supernatural abilities to know why. Esther's cancer had reached the point where it could no longer be hidden, and Mr. Harris had finally shared the secret with his childhood friends.

"Why Paul Grimble," the frail woman exclaimed in genuine pleasure and a voice that remained strong and clear, "I think you've grown several inches since I saw you last. And Bruce, you've toned up quite a bit with all of this hard work."

"They have," Dora agreed, ruffling Paul's hair affectionately. "I'm almost afraid I'll wake up one day and find that they've grown into adults in the blink of an eye."

"Rub it in," Jade mumbled.

6

"Sorry hun," Mr. Grimble said. "But I think your growing days are over."

"You probably get that from me," Dora said.

"Gee thanks Mom," Jade said.

"Being tall or short doesn't mean anything," Emelia said.

"Yeah," Paul agreed, looking for something to cheer the eldest Grimble, "Look at Megan's mom. She's super short, and just about everyone is terrified of her!"

Bruce suspected that someday his brother would die after saying something as colossally stupid as that, even if it was the absolute truth. But since Emelia didn't want to draw attention to herself in supernatural ways, he was also fairly sure Paul would live to say many more such things.

Emelia looked very stern at the youngest Grimble before the corners of her mouth turned up in a smile and everyone relaxed.

"How can you sound so mature one second, and then be such an idiot the next?" Jade asked.

"Well, given how much you hit me in the back of the head," he answered, quickly moving out of her reach, "it's a miracle I can still talk at all."

"Get as tall as you'd like Paul," Emelia said, "but don't ever let the world take away that beautiful honesty of yours. I'd really miss it if you did."

"So is it story time yet?" Bruce asked, hoping to start everyone's favorite part of these gatherings.

Soon the three old men started talking, and on several occasions, everyone laughed until they cried. Esther even added little parts here and there, or outright steered them away from stories she didn't think appropriate.

7

Bruce had already started to record the ones he'd heard during the construction of the tree house in a journal that Megan had given him for Christmas. As much as he loved the technology that allowed him to capture their words as they spoke, it just didn't feel right that the final copy of these tales from Nickelville's more colorful history should be on anything but paper. Furthermore, somewhere along the way, he'd started to think of them as a family history even though he wasn't actually related to any of them. Particularly since Alan and Tom didn't have children of their own to which they could entrust them. As far as he was concerned, it was an honor to keep these memories alive for the generations to come, for in his young but still wise opinion, the world was better for the retelling of the heroic, the tragic and most of all the funny tales that these people had to offer even if they'd never appear in any history book.

# Chapter II: Megan's Bag of Tricks

"Are you sure that sleeping outside is safe?" Megan asked while she packed for the night ahead.

"I don't really think the treehouse counts as sleeping outdoors," Sam chuckled from where his massive frame filled the doorway to her bedroom.

"You know what I mean," Megan said irritably, continuing to stuff clothing into the bag. She'd gotten over most of her discomfort with Guarded Wood, but that was during the day when she was awake and aware of everything around her with more than just her eyes. Why couldn't it be more like the woods at the school?

"We've lived in apartments that were smaller and had more wildlife to worry about," Emelia reminded her, watching her daughter pack with a raised eyebrow.

"Did you know I used to sleep in this room sometimes when I was young?" Sam asked, looking around the room that was the first place she'd ever felt she could call her own.

"Really?" Megan asked, looking up and noting that her mother was still eyeing the bag with amusement. "So Grandpa was cool about having boys over?"

"He didn't know about it until just now," Azarich said from behind Sam, who stepped inside to let her grandfather pass. "How often was that?"

"Only a few times," Emelia said, picking up the socks that Megan had intended to pack next and whisking them toward the big man who caught them without effort and handed them back to Megan. "I can't take you anywhere."

"Wow," Azarich said, catching sight of the bag on the four-poster bed.

"What?" Megan asked when she noticed the way they were all looking at her, "Am I forgetting something?"

"Not likely," Emelia said, still smiling.

"How long are you planning to stay up there?" Sam asked, looking at the bulging bag.

"One night," she answered.

"And you plan to use all of that stuff in one night?" Emelia asked.

Megan looked down at her bag and realized that the last time she'd packed it was when they were still running from the Wild Hunt. Over the course of the last few minutes, she'd packed all of her old clothes into its familiar interior.

"I just like to be prepared," Megan murmured, feeling foolish.

*It's good to keep in practice,* Emelia sent, *but I don't think you're in any danger at the moment or Bruce would have seen it.*

*He hasn't seen anything, has he?* Sam asked.

*No,* Megan answered, *but he does seem to be preoccupied about something.*

"Be nice to my only grandchild!" Azarich said affectionately and quite unaware that another conversation was in progress of which he wasn't privy. He hugged her and whispered, "Just don't forget you have to lug that monstrosity up all of those stairs."

Since the wall had come down at the Academy, she and Bruce had

10

become better at keeping their minds separate when they communicated. It was a relief to Megan who had never been able to understand the strange feelings he had for her. But with that separation also came the ability to hide things from each other. She knew something was bothering him, but she wasn't sure what it could be.

"Be careful out there," Emelia said with a smile that would have looked out of place on her lips just a few months previous. "You don't want to run into Goatman in the dark."

Megan threw the socks at her. Since Azarich was still smiling at the bag, Emelia swatted them directly back into her daughter's face without moving.

"I don't know anything about Goatman," Sam said in a calm voice though his eyes were laughing, "but my people avoided Guarded Wood. They said the lords of the forest watched over it."

"Really?" Megan asked.

"This whole town is a strange place," he answered, "but whatever is out there in those woods is something altogether different."

"It must be hard to be the only one left," Azarich said, patting Sam on the shoulder. "I know there are so many things I'd love to go back and ask my parents and grandparents about."

Sam nodded in agreement.

"But if you want Goatman stories," Azarich said, "we can get the gang back together on the Fourth. There's a long line of sightings in the McGeehee family. Probably because we've always lived on the edge of Guarded Wood."

Emelia rolled her eyes, but it seemed more out of habit than genuine annoyance.

When they left the room to go downstairs, Megan grabbed the socks and shoved them into the pack… just in case.

# Chapter III: Dancing Lights and Stormy Nights

Bruce frowned at the silhouette of his sister against the darkening sky as she climbed high above. He didn't feel comfortable with her so far up in the tree, but after the things she'd seen Emelia do, there was no talking her out of it. Ever since Megan's mother had become a part of their lives, his sister emulated her every action. But unlike Emelia, Jade didn't have supernatural abilities to bolster the strength of her deceptively fragile body.

"This is going to be awesome!" Paul yelled from the edge of the clearing.

"Do you think Dad will be able to keep Mom from checking in on us?" Jade called down just before she dropped onto the deck.

"I think they're going to see a movie and eat at Gordon's," Bruce answered, frowning at his sister then smiling when he felt Megan approaching. "By the time they get back it should be dark."

"Speaking of dark, we need to start gathering wood for the fire," Paul said with such infectious enthusiasm that even Bruce had to smile. "This is going to be so much fun."

"My gear is already stowed," Jade said, running down the spiral staircase. "So I'll help with the firewood."

"Want me to take your bag up for you?" Bruce offered when he met his friend at the bottom.

"That would be great," Megan said, dropping it at her side and heading off into the woods with his sister.

Bruce grabbed the shoulder strap and nearly toppled over when he tried to pick it up. How had she even gotten it this far? Glancing around to make sure no one would see, he lifted the bulk of the weight with his mind and wound his way up the staircase. Inside the bunkhouse, the smell of freshly cut lumber almost overwhelmed him, a scent that would have irritated his allergies before his friend had come to Nickelville. Like Megan, he suspected he'd packed too much and still managed to forget something important.

*Oh well, it's not like I can't walk back to the house if it's something I can't live without,* he thought.

*Exactly,* Megan whispered in his mind as he dropped her bag on the floor next to the table since he didn't know which bunk she'd want. *Would you do me a favor and go up to the tower? Something feels off with Guarded Wood tonight.*

*Sure,* he sent, moving over to the ladder. He could almost hear Mr. Green explain that the rungs needed to be rough enough for traction but smooth enough to be easy on the hands. As he climbed, he wondered if he should have included all of the janitor's little bits of humble wisdom in his journal. He looked out over the high ledges where they'd made nooks that looked out past the deck. He wasn't sure what they'd be used for in the future, but they'd seemed like a good idea at the time. At the top, he closed his eyes to the spectacular view, and cleared his mind the way Emelia and Sam had taught him. His awareness flowed down over the rail and through the foliage of the ancient tree. Then his thoughts took flight and soared over the treetops.

Megan was right, although he couldn't pinpoint the problem. A restiveness hung over the woods, almost too subtle to sense and too far-spread to find its boundaries.

*It's probably just the newness of the treehouse and the stress it's causing on the wildlife while the animals get used to it,* he sent with a mental shrug. *I don't feel anything sinister in the woods or see anything in the immediate future. But it does feel weird. I'll be down in a second to help with the firewood.*

*Paul wants to have a fire-starting contest,* she sent.

*I know,* Bruce grinned, *I can't wait!*

*No abilities,* she sent, and he could somehow tell she was holding her pinky up.

*You take all the fun out of things sometimes,* he complained, reluctantly hooking the mental equivalent of his little finger on hers.

By the time the last of the setting sun left the sky, a small bonfire burned in the fire pit. A cool breeze that felt good in the aftermath of the hot day fanned the flames higher, giving off a trail of smoke that rose into the night and accented the night sounds with loud cracks as resin pockets within the wood caught fire.

"Don't feel too bad," Paul said with a smug smile in the warm glow of the campfire. "I've had a lot more practice than you guys."

"You're such a pyro," Jade said, throwing a small rock at him.

"So what's in the big pot?" Megan asked, eyeing the cast iron monstrosity in the fire with apprehension. As soon as there had been coals in the fire, Paul had used his hiking shovel to place glowing embers across

15

the lid of the thing as well. Of course, now that she thought about it, she was more curious than repelled. She had, after all, grown up eating her mother's cooking.

"I don't know what it's called, but our troop loves it." the youngest Grimble answered, enjoying this chance to show off his scouting skills. "It's meat and vegetables with biscuits on top."

"So it's a chicken pot pie?" Jade asked.

"Pretty much, except it's got diced ham from last night's dinner in it instead of chicken."

"Won't it burn?" Megan asked.

"Have some faith," Paul replied, still smiling. "Hey Jade, tell the Goatman story while we wait."

"Sam has mentioned something about that a few times now," Megan said, leaning back into the chair Mrs. Grimble had loaned her.

"Oooh, I'll bet he has some good ones to tell," Jade said. "Of course, he could make standardized test questions sound interesting."

"The man has a seriously cool voice," Bruce agreed.

"Alright," Jade said theatrically, "It all started with the witch trials..."

"There were witch trials in Texas?" Megan asked.

"No," Bruce said, "Listen."

"We all know about what happened in Salem," Jade continued, glaring Megan down when it appeared she might speak again, "but local history has it that the only true witch escaped and came here to Guarded Wood to bear her child."

"Did she name it Allison?" Megan giggled, unable to help herself.

"No," Jade said in the same dramatic tone, though she almost smiled.

"It would explain quite a few things though," Paul admitted.

"It was horribly deformed," Jade continued.

16

"Still sounds like Allison to me," Bruce whispered.

"With coarse hair covering the bottom half of its body and horns on its head," Jade said.

"Oh," Megan said, "My mistake. Its name was Chuck then?"

Jade fell silent.

"Okay, okay," Megan laughed. "I'll stop. Tell me the rest."

"That's all there is," Bruce yawned, looking up at the starlit sky.

"What do you mean that's all there is?"

"It's Goatman, not Bigfoot," Jade said defensively.

"So what does he do?" Megan asked.

"People just see him, although I've heard a few local scout stories say that he sometimes helps people who are lost. Of course, that could just be a case of the scouts trying to recruit him," Paul said, pulling the lid of the pot up to look inside. The smell that escaped made Megan decide to hold her judgment until they ate. She had to admit it smelled pretty good.

Somewhere at the edge of her senses, something stirred.

*Do you feel that?* Megan asked.

*No, but the weird feeling in the woods might be getting worse. I can't tell for sure though, it's so faint I can't really get any details.*

"You guys ready to eat?" Paul asked, pulling his flashlight from his pocket to check on the contents of the pot one last time.

Although the nameless scout dish might not have looked like much, it tasted as good as it smelled, and the pot was soon empty. Tired from the exertions of the day and uncomfortably full from the meal, the four of them grew drowsy.

"Hey Megan," Paul said happily, "Put those three logs behind your chair on the fire and see what happens."

Megan did as he asked, though they looked just like the firewood her

17

grandfather used in his smoker. But as soon as the logs began to burn, green flames began to dance across their surface.

"How did you do that?" Bruce asked with interest.

"I doused the logs with a mixture of borax dissolved in rubbing alcohol," he answered proudly.

"Is it safe to breathe?" Jade asked, gazing at the emerald flames.

"It should be," Paul said.

"I have to admit," Bruce said after watching for a moment, "green fire makes a pretty cool special effect."

Either the strangeness out in the woods receded, or they simply got used to it. The flames cast green shadows on the massive trunk of the tree, and for just a moment it looked like they were all dancing to some forgotten melody remembered only by the woodland creatures out there in the darkness.

Distracted by their emerald hue, Megan forgot to avoid looking directly into the flames. She wasn't aware at first when the dancing shapes drew her in, but she wasn't alone this time. Bruce was there in the fire with her, just a wisp of familiar presence on the currents of time. Her friend's ability to see the future influenced the visions, revealing a multitude of threads passing through his hands. Some of them glowed with a wholesome light that filled her with joy. Others seemed to absorb the life force of those around them. It was down one of those darkened paths that both she and Bruce felt something immeasurably old and powerful take note of them.

"Whoa," Jade said, breaking both the silence and their trance, "Are those lightning bugs?"

Megan saw Bruce slump in his chair, mirroring her own wave of lethargy that came with breaking free of the vision. She followed Jade's gaze to what looked like the biggest fireflies she'd ever seen. Even stranger than their size was the oddly rhythmic pattern of their display as they flowed in to fill the clearing at the base of the treehouse.

"Can't be," Paul answered, looking puzzled. "They're too big, and they're also the wrong color."

"Then what are they?" Jade asked.

"I have no idea," Paul said, staring in rapt fascination. "I'll have to do some research tomorrow, I guess."

The wind picked up and carried with it a sweet floral scent she'd noticed before.

Tired from the exertions of the day and the visions from the fire, Bruce shivered in the dropping temperatures and pulled on his sweatshirt. Deep within the woods, a soft rumble of thunder made its way to them and Jade yawned loudly.

"They're cool Paul, but I'm pretty beat," Jade announced, echoing Megan's thoughts. "I think I'm going to call it a night." The eldest Grimble got up, folded her chair and started making her way to the staircase.

"We can't turn in yet," Paul cried mournfully, looking away from the strange insects.

"Come on bro," Bruce said. "We've got the whole summer ahead of us, and the treehouse isn't going anywhere."

"Bruce is right," Megan added, careful not to look into the flames that were already starting to lose their greenish cast. "We were up at the crack of dawn so we could get done in time to sleep here tonight. It's been a really long day. Let's call it a night."

"Suit yourselves," Paul said, pulling off his shoes and stretching his bare feet out in front of the fire. "I'll need to let this burn down enough to bank before we can leave it unattended. We wouldn't want to spend a month on this tree house just to burn it down the first night with an unattended campfire, would we?"

"You're sure you don't mind?" Jade asked from the lowest step.

"Not at all," Paul assured her, watching as they followed Jade up the stairs. "I never get a chance to sit by the fire alone when I'm out with the scouts. Besides," he added, nodding toward the fireflies, "I've only got about half an hour's worth of wood left in the fire before it dies down and one of nature's firework shows to watch while I wait."

*We should stay awake until he comes up,* Megan thought as she climbed into her bunk, too tired to change into the clothes she'd brought to sleep in. She felt Bruce's agreement, though his drowsy mind didn't clarify the thought. She smiled when he started to snore and fully intended to stay awake until Paul returned.

Lightning turned the night into a second of stolen midday sun. It didn't wake Bruce, but the trailing thunder shook the earth in which the tree was rooted and assaulted his senses with such ferocity that it took a moment to understand what it meant. Instinctively he reached out with his mind and found Megan struggling toward consciousness as well.

"Where's Paul?" she asked.

"Doesn't that boy know when to come in from the rain?" Jade asked irritably from her bunk.

*He's not down there,* Megan sent. *I can't feel him anywhere nearby.*

Stretching his own senses out beyond the confines of the treehouse, Bruce noticed that the weirdness with the woods felt much stronger now. At first, he thought the wind was blowing, but then he realized it wasn't a sound at all, but rather his reaction to strong power in use nearby.

A grunt followed by a muffled curse came from the direction of Jade's bunk.

"Damn Megan," Jade exclaimed, "Are you planning to move in permanently? This bag weighs a ton!"

The three of them flew down the staircase as the wind grew stronger, and the first large drops of rain began to splatter against the treehouse roof.

*What's going on with the woods?* Bruce asked.

*It feels like the surface of the land is stretching thin to cover something huge beneath it.* Megan sent, not sounding anything like she usually did, almost as if it were someone else who was speaking through her. *I can feel crevasses forming in the low places as something ancient is pushing its way to the surface.*

"Where is that idiot?" Jade asked, pointing to Paul's chair which still sat next to the roaring fire. "He didn't even take his shoes."

"And his flashlight is still in his cup-holder," Bruce added, shaking off the surprise at the way his friend had sounded and snatching it up to shine around the base of the tree. "There are his tracks!"

"You don't think he'd follow those stupid fireflies into the woods, do you?" Jade asked, looking at the barefoot tracks in the dirt.

"He was pretty fascinated by them," Megan answered. "But why not put on his shoes?"

"We'd better go find him before the storm hits," Bruce advised. "And make sure we get back before Mom finds out, or we'll never get to spend the night out here again."

The trees blocked out most of the wind once they left the clearing, but it still roared through the leaves overhead.

*Can you feel him?* Bruce asked.

*No, whatever is going on here in the woods is making too much*

21

*interference. I can barely feel you, and you're only a foot away. This storm doesn't feel natural either. Something is using a lot of energy around here, and I'm starting to think that we should have gotten Mom before we came in.*

*Not enough time,* he sent back. *And I can't see anything of what's going to happen.*

"We should have run into the bridge by now," Jade yelled over the wind. "Did we take the wrong path?"

"I don't think so," Bruce yelled back, realizing that she was right. "It all looks so different in the dark."

Unsure what else they could do, the three pushed on, yelling the youngest Grimble's name as they went. Focused on the flickering beam of the flashlight, neither Bruce nor Megan noticed the shimmering boundary across their path until Jade passed through. At once, the feel of the woods around them changed, seeming to turn and focus on the three outsiders as they passed.

*That was a ward!* Megan sent. *Not one of my mother's either.*

*How can you tell?*

*Feels older and... different...*

Whatever it was that was different about the ward was cut off by the arrival of Fang, who snarled and growled so loudly that he could be heard above the growing storm. The rain, which had until now only threatened to fall, came down in earnest and Bruce worried about his brother's bare feet.

"Calm down boy," Bruce said, trying to distract the angry wolf as he slowly moved between it and Megan. He'd never seen Fang act that way and understood, for the first time, why most cities had laws about owning wolf hybrids. Focused as he was on keeping Fang away from Megan, he failed to notice that they were no longer alone on the path until his sister

22

gasped in surprise. He felt an instant of hope that perhaps Paul had found them, but it died when Jade turned the flashlight toward the shape and found an old man with white hair and beard glaring back at them.

# Chapter IV: Old Man Biggerstaff

Although Megan felt the old man's anger before she actually saw him, she found it difficult to turn her attention from the snarling beast that clearly wanted to eat her. When Bruce managed to place himself between Fang and herself, she was finally able to look past them to this newcomer. He was a giant in the flash of lighting that illuminated them for an instant before plunging them back into darkness where his eyes reflected like an animal. Most of his body was covered by a patched and ragged cloak, but where it lay open, she could see what looked like the rough-spun garments of the distant past.

"I've tolerated you lot trampling around my land during the day," he growled in a gravelly voice that sounded as if he'd grown unaccustomed to using it. "But Guarded Wood is no place for children when the sun tucks tail and runs. You've got no business here."

Megan could feel his dark eyes on her.

"We're sorry," Jade yelled over the wind. "But our brother wandered off into the woods, and we're trying to find him!"

"Paul?" the hermit asked in surprise. Megan realized that she could hear him clearly even though he wasn't yelling because his voice was also in her mind.

"We think he might have followed those big fireflies," Bruce added.

24

"The wisps came as far as the Sentinel tree?" he asked. Fang stopped growling at Megan and moved over to sit next where his master leaned on a great gnarled staff.

The three frightened teens nodded in reply.

"I know where he's going," the old man said, then looked down at Fang. "Find him and keep her from drawing him in closer to her lair."

Fang sprang to his huge paws and sniffed the ground like a bloodhound before bounding off.

"Go back to the treehouse while he and I find your brother," the hermit growled. "These woods are no place for the likes of you, 'specially on a night like this." Then he turned and ran into the storm with all the wild grace of the wolf he followed.

"Did you see that?" Jade asked, pulling Megan and Bruce close enough to hear her. "It's like Fang could read his thoughts."

"And how did he know Paul's name?" Bruce asked.

Hesitant to trust this enigmatic figure, they nonetheless recognized the wisdom of his words. As they walked, Megan tried to stretch her senses outward, but the rolling energy flows that arced across Guarded Wood made it impossible to sense more than a few yards in any direction.

By the time the three of them reached the safety of the treehouse, wind howled through the leaves, tearing them from the branches and turning them into projectiles that pelted them as they walked. Heavy limbs cracked and fell, forcing them to jump over when they landed directly across the strangely altered path. And when they reached the tree where the treehouse perched, it writhed as if in pain as they hurried up the winding steps.

"Should we go get Mom and Dad?" Bruce asked when they closed the door behind them.

"Not yet," Jade answered, though without her usual confidence. "You know what Mom will be like if we do. Better to wait and see if Old Man Biggerstaff can find him first."

"Is that who he was?" Megan asked.

"Has to be," Jade answered, looking out the window.

"I still don't understand," Megan said, sitting down on the bench, and then immediately getting up to pace off her nervous energy. "Paul never gets lost."

"Paul doesn't seem to be acting like Paul tonight," Bruce observed. "Otherwise he would have told us he was going, taken his flashlight and his shoes."

Lightning flashed and illuminated the treetops over Guarded Wood. The huge tree flexed and twisted in the wind, sending out ominous creaks that worried Megan almost as much as the thunder that shook the glass in the windows and sent shockwaves of energy through the entire structure of the treehouse.

She thought at first that whatever strangeness had settled over Guarded Wood included some slowing of time, because surely the old man should have been back with Paul by now. But when she looked at the antique watch on her wrist, she saw that time still flowed normally, just not as fast as any of them would have liked.

During one of the closest lightning strikes, she thought she could see mountains in the distance. Just a few seconds later, when it seemed the rain might be slowing, they were gone.

"I think I see something," Bruce called from the window nearly an hour later, prompting the other two to crowd in. Fang emerged from the woods, followed by the hermit and their brother.

For once Bruce wasn't the fastest Grimble child. Jade reached the bottom step long before he did.

Paul's feet were bleeding and he had long scratches along his hands and face as if he'd been running through the undergrowth. Although oddly enough, he didn't have any on the upper parts of his arms and legs. He smiled weakly when he saw them, but his eyes were haunted. He had a nasty looking cut across his left cheek that had already begun to clot.

"I guess I didn't have to worry about starting a forest fire after all," he said roughly.

Jade hugged him so fiercely that Megan worried she might hurt him. Then the eldest Grimble let go, returned to herself and punched him hard in the shoulder.

"That's for making me worry!" she yelled.

"If you're quite finished abusing your brother," the old man growled, leaning wearily on his staff, "I'd like to go back to the warmth of my own home. Take your brother in and dry him off before he catches cold. Do you have a first aid kit up there?"

All four of them nodded.

"None of his cuts look serious, but get them cleaned out just in case. Keep an eye on him and make sure he doesn't wander off again, especially if the wisps return," the old man said as he walked back toward Guarded Wood.

"Is there anything we should know about in the woods?" Bruce asked.

"Yeah," the old man grunted, "to stay off my property when strange events are afoot."

*And you, Changeling, stay out of Guarded Wood permanently,* he added where Megan suspected that only she could hear. Then he turned back into the storm and disappeared into the trees. Fang hesitated a second longer, standing on his hind legs and giving Bruce one dripping lick across the face before following the old man.

By the time they reached the top, Paul could walk unaided. He seemed okay, if uncharacteristically quiet.

"How did you manage to cut yourself across the chest without cutting your shirt?" Bruce asked, noticing the blood that had seeped through the otherwise undamaged shirt.

"Just special like that," Paul mumbled. He took clothes with him into the changing room next to the tower's ladder. They looked worriedly from one to the other while he changed out of his soiled clothing. When he emerged, he pleaded exhaustion and promised to explain in the morning.

And though they all took the time to change out of their sodden clothing and settle into what should have been a soothing night of listening to the rain outside, it was a long time before anyone but Paul slept.

# Chapter V: After the Storm

Bruce and Megan eventually drifted off in the predawn hours in spite of their worry for Paul. Perhaps it was the shared need for comfort against the terrors of the night that merged their minds in slumber and allowed them to share the same dreams. It could have been as simple as their proximity to each other or as complex as the supernatural forces at work in Guarded Wood. Whatever the reason, the dreams they shared centered around their concern for Bruce's brother and drew in a multitude of possible futures from Bruce's subconscious.

They woke as one when the dwindling rhythm of the rain reached the threshold that marked the boundary between soothing and too quiet. His drowsy mind surrounded hers, enfolding her thoughts in a warm familiarity that coaxed a smile from her in spite of the lingering exhaustion of the previous night. But before she could enjoy it further, something within her lashed out, ripping her away from him and lacerating her consciousness.

*What's wrong?* he sent, confused by her actions.

The strength of his concern made her head pound, and his thoughts sent a wave of vertigo barreling through her. Forgetting how nice it had been only seconds before, she hardened her shields and basked in the silence that followed until the nausea passed. She began to drift off again.

Were it not for the dampness in her pillow left from the rainwater in her hair, she suspected she could have slept for at least another ten hours.

The sun had already risen, casting multicolored splashes of light through the stained-glass windows. But the bunks on the side where the four of them had slept were still tucked away in their own pockets of darkness.

Jade stirred in the bunk above Megan, threw her legs over the side and jumped lightly to the ground before going to check on Paul. Unaware that both Megan and Bruce watched, she felt his forehead in motherly concern. At her touch, Paul began to hum in his sleep, but it was like no song any of them had ever heard before, somehow capturing the sounds of the storm in which he'd been lost.

"We should probably wake him," Bruce said quietly. "We need to get our story straight before Mom and Dad show up. I'm surprised she didn't come last night during the storm."

"Dad probably gave her the strong allergy meds so she'd be able to sleep without worrying," Jade said, gently starting to shake her youngest brother.

"Have to reach her before...," Paul moaned, thrashing in his bunk.

Bruce rose and joined his sister beside their sleeping brother.

"Paul, wake up," Jade said, shaking him harder.

The youngest Grimble bolted upright, narrowly missing the ceiling with his head. His breath escaped in quick gasps, and Bruce could feel that he was drenched with sweat as he reached out to steady him.

"It was just a bad dream," Bruce said quietly.

"Dream?" Paul asked, frantic. His eyes landed on his hand and he held it up as if he expected to see something different. "But I need..."

"To reach her?" Bruce asked.

Paul looked around, his eyes wild as they slid quickly over them to finally rest on Megan. Then most of the agitation left him, and he came back to himself.

"Yeah," Paul agreed, starting to breathe normally before falling back against the pillow. "It seemed so real."

"Who did you need to find?" Megan asked.

"No one," he answered, too quickly. "It's stupid."

"Tell us," Jade prompted.

"Not gonna happen," Paul said, "Already fading away. No idea who you're talking about. I'm just going to go back to sleep for a few years." He turned his back to them in the upper bunk and looked as if he fully intended to do so.

"Tell you what," Bruce said, sounding extremely tired himself. "We'll drop it if you tell us what happened last night. We need to get our story straight." For several moments it seemed as if he might have indeed gone back to sleep.

"It's sort of the same thing," Paul said at last, his back still to them. "I must have drifted off while I was waiting for the fire to die down."

"And?" Jade prompted.

"Well," Paul continued, turning over and jumping down with a wince of sore muscles to sit on Bruce's bunk. "When I woke up, I heard music coming from the woods."

"What kind of music?" Megan asked, running her fingers through her damp hair before going to sit at the table.

"Violin music," he answered sheepishly.

"Seriously?" Jade asked, shaking her head in disgust.

"Pretty stupid, I know," Paul said with a grin, though Megan suspected there was something more that he wasn't telling them. "Seemed like a good idea to follow the music at the time. It was different from anything I've ever heard before…"

"And you thought it would be a good idea to do it without shoes or a flashlight?" Jade scolded, relieved now that he seemed to be okay. "What kind of a scout are you?"

"Hey now," Paul said, offended.

"Seriously, bro," Bruce continued. "Why did you run off without your shoes?"

"As soon as I heard it, I knew that there wasn't much time, and I had to reach her before she…" He shrugged, shaking his head in confusion.

"Did the woods seem weird to you?" Bruce asked, and Megan had the feeling he was annoyed about something.

"What do you mean?" Paul asked.

"Like they were too big?" Megan prompted.

"To be honest, I don't remember much after I entered the woods," he said. "There were those fireflies everywhere. I remember that much. But then everything pretty much scrambled until the old man showed up. And my dreams must be mixed up in it too, because I remember running through places that couldn't possibly be in those woods."

"We got lost looking for you," Jade said with a frown. "It all looked so different in the rain."

"Rain?" Paul asked.

"You don't remember the storm?" Bruce asked.

"Maybe a little," Paul answered, but Megan suspected he was only saying that to make them drop the subject.

"So what do we tell Mom and Dad?" Jade asked at last.

"Tell Mom and Dad about what?" a new voice asked from the door.

All four turned guiltily to where Mrs. Grimble stood in her housecoat.

33

She had a gallon of milk in one hand and a cloth grocery bag in the other.

"I needed to go to the bathroom last night and got turned around," Paul lied quickly. He might not have been in top shape, but he was still more than capable of covering for them. "I guess I got turned around in the storm and ended up in the woods instead of home."

"Would you believe that it didn't even rain at the house?" Dora said pleasantly, unloading breakfast on the table before turning toward Paul. "How did you manage to get all of these scratches?"

"Got tangled up in brambles," he said, still sounding exhausted. "My feet are pretty bad too."

"Weren't you wearing shoes?" She asked, putting on her glasses to get a better look at the lacerated soles of his feet.

"I really had to go…" he replied with a shrug.

"Why didn't you just go on a tree?" she asked.

"That's not what I needed to do."

"Oh," she said knowingly. "That's odd, you usually only do that right before we leave the house in the morning. Ever since you were a baby, you'd wait until the last minute to fill your…"

"MOM!" Paul roared, sounding at last like himself as he shot an embarrassed look over at Megan.

"So you're saying that it didn't rain outside of Guarded Wood?" Megan asked, looking at Bruce who still seemed to be avoiding her gaze. This sounded suspiciously like what had happened when Jacob Routh had broken their bond.

"I wish it had. We could use the rain," she answered, setting out cups and plates. "Well, eat up. Sounds like you all had quite the adventure last night. Got to keep your strength up!" Then, humming pleasantly to herself, she walked out the door and headed back to the house.

"Okay," Jade said, watching her mother go. "That was weird."

"No kidding," Megan agreed. "Your dad must have piled on the antihistamines last night to make her sleep deep enough to miss that storm."

"No, not that," Jade disagreed. "He must not have given her anything at all or she'd still be out cold. We were out here all night and just gave her proof that we weren't completely safe. She's been looking for a reason to freak out over this for weeks."

"Jade's right," Bruce agreed. "Something strange is going on here."

"Well, I for one am glad that she let it go that easily," Paul said, moving over to the table and taking the lid off of the container. The aroma of scrambled eggs, bacon and biscuits filled the air. And as is often the case with terrors of the night, a full stomach in the daylight can erase most anything.

"You know," Jade said later, trying to take advantage of her mother's mysterious good mood when they returned from the treehouse, "My birthday is coming up pretty soon."

Bruce rolled his eyes and found Megan smiling at him. For a second his traitorous heart beat faster in response to that smile before he remembered the way she'd shut him out only a short time earlier.

She still held her shields rigid, effectively walling him out. He had no idea why she was treating him this way or what he'd done to deserve it. One minute their minds had been merged with a comfortable ease that felt nicer than just about anything else he'd ever experienced. Then, without any warning whatsoever, she'd cast him out, hurting him both physically and emotionally. He'd had a blinding headache ever since, and he really wanted to go back to his own bed and sleep until lunch or maybe even dinner. And that wasn't even the worst part. The ease with which she'd done it suggested things about her feelings for him that left the scales of affection tipping wildly out of favor.

Had he become so addicted to her presence that he could no longer see whether or not she had any feelings at all for him in return? After all, he didn't think it would ever even occur to him to cut her off like this. Yet here he was on the outside, longing to be allowed back in.

Furthermore, he'd noticed that her presence interfered with his precognition. It was much easier to understand situations when she wasn't present. His desire to see her happy tended to skew what he saw concerning her to such an extent that he suspected he was only seeing what he wanted to see. Most of the time it wasn't an issue, but what if they were in danger? What if these Huntsmen found her trail, and he was too busy trying to make her smile to notice?

Bruce shook his head and tried not to think about the day ahead. His dad had noticed a decline in the quality of house cleaning since the treehouse project had begun. Now that it was over, Mr. Grimble believed it was time to rectify the situation. Particularly since it was the first day of his next shift at the firehouse and he wouldn't be there to clean himself.

"Megan," Jade said, handing her an armload of the pillows she'd taken to the treehouse, "would you put these on my bed?"

Bruce followed her down the hall with his own armload of gear. He'd unpack his bag after she left so she wouldn't see how meticulous he was with making sure that everything was put back in its place. He didn't feel like listening to any neat freak comments at the moment.

"Wow," he heard Megan say from down the hall, which was a pretty mild reaction for someone seeing his sister's room for the first time. Their dad sometimes called Jade the anti-Bruce. Her room was as cluttered as his was clean. Combine that with black walls, red velvet curtains, and partially melted candles, and it looked more like an occult bookstore than a teenager's bedroom.

"What are all of the trophies for?" he heard Megan ask. He left his bag next to his bed and took a deep breath before entering his sister's sanctum of chaos.

"Martial arts tournaments," Paul called from his room, sounding more like himself now that they were back in the familiar surroundings of home.

"Jade, I didn't know you were a martial artist," Megan called down the hall to where the eldest Grimble was kicking her bag toward the room.

"Why do you think everyone is afraid of her?" Paul asked, coming in to join them. "She's ranked fifth in her division for state. Right Jade?"

"Something like that," his sister answered, irritated that the bag had gotten caught on something under the dirty clothes in the doorway. "You should try it."

"I might," Megan said thoughtfully. "When are the classes?"

"There's one tonight," Jade answered hopefully. "Want to come?"

"I'll ask my mom," Megan promised. "Speaking of which, I'd better get out of your way so you can start cleaning."

"Joy," Jade said, looking out over her room with a grimace.

"You know," Bruce added, angry with himself even as he said it, but unable to pass up a chance to be with her. "I think I'll come too. With my asthma under control, it would be nice to be able to put Chuck in his place without ending up in the hospital."

Jade looked genuinely pleased.

"How about you Paul?" Megan asked.

"Not even remotely interested," he answered, walking to the door.

37

"I've got a scout meeting tonight to go over the last-minute preparations for summer camp. We're going to Constantin this year."

"Suit yourself," Jade replied.

# Chapter VI: Bruce's New Heroine

"Paul, would you be a darling and pump the gas for me while I go in and pay?" Mrs. Grimble asked, pulling their SUV under the covered awning and up to the pump.

"Sure thing," he replied, climbing down in his scout uniform.

"Hey Paul!" another young man in uniform yelled from the door of the gas station, which he held open for Dora before running up to talk to the youngest Grimble.

"What is that kid's name again?" Jade asked from the front seat.

"No idea," Bruce answered, "John...maybe John."

"How can you guys not know who Paul's friends are?" Megan asked. "It's not like there are that many kids at the Academy."

"He's not from Nickelville," Jade replied. "There aren't enough boys in town for a full troop, so there are quite a few who come from the surrounding countryside."

"Oh," Megan said, watching as the boy related something to Paul with a wealth of exaggerated hand motions. He was dancing around stiff legged in an imitation of something none of them could identify when Mrs. Grimble emerged from the gas station.

On her way back, Dora passed a cargo truck from which the company logo had been removed. She paused, looking in surprise at something hidden from where they sat in the car. Then she hurried back toward Paul and his friend.

O'Toole, the man from both the Jubilee and the chase through the Academy's attic, stepped from behind the truck, watching Mrs. Grimble suspiciously as she returned.

"See you at the meeting, Don," Paul called after his friend.

"What was that about?" Bruce asked as his mother started the car.

"Don's uncle and his neighbor apparently saw Goatman on the edge of Guarded Wood last night," he answered.

"I didn't realize you made it out that far," Jade said to her youngest brother.

"Very funny," Paul said. "Anyway, he wanted me to tell you about it."

"Not that," Bruce said, looking back at the scarred man as they drove away. "Mom, what were you looking at behind the truck?"

"I'm sure it was nothing," she answered nervously. "It was just that horrible man who chased you and Megan last year at the school. He came around from the other side of that truck he's always driving around town and found a man I haven't seen before smoking a cigarette. He slapped the cigarette out of the man's mouth and then pinned him against the truck. Then he told him that if he ever caught him smoking around their cargo again that he'd personally put his eyes out with his own cigarette."

"You're not supposed to smoke anywhere near the pumps," Paul said uncertainly, "but that does seem a bit excessive."

"He's the type to say vile things at the slightest provocation," Mrs. Grimble said, casting a worried glance at the man who was still watching them. "But it certainly did startle me."

40

"He doesn't look too happy that you heard him," Jade added, sizing the man up.

"Let's not talk about this anymore," Dora said, pulling back onto main street. "So, another Goatman sighting? Might be worth it to send someone out to interview them. Heaven knows we could use something to bring in more readers. I know times are tough, but Tribune sales haven't been this low in years."

"You know, Mom," Jade said as they drove away and passed the looming hulk of the Baker Hotel, "if I had my own car, you wouldn't have to take us everywhere."

Mrs. Grimble chose not to respond to that comment.

"I shudder to think of how late I'd be to meetings if I had to rely on you to get there," Paul added.

"Megan," Jade said without looking back, "would you mind?"

Megan slapped him across the back of the head.

"What did I ever do to you?" Paul exclaimed.

"Nothing personal," Megan answered. "But she's going to have quite a few opportunities to hit me over the next couple of hours, and I'd rather she wasn't mad at me when she did it."

"Can't argue with logic like that, can you?" Bruce added absently, still looking back at the gas station.

"Hey," Megan asked, turning to look back down from where they'd just come. "Is that movie theater still open?"

"The Palace?" Mrs. Grimble asked.

"I think that's what it said on the marquee."

"Sort of," Paul replied, glad to change the subject. "It only has two theaters, and one of them doesn't work anymore. So now they can only show one movie at a time."

41

"I can't tell you how many movies I saw there as a kid," Mrs. Grimble said with a girlish giggle. "That's where Ben and I were last night."

"Look what you did," Jade said, glaring back at Megan. "Now she's going to start telling us about the old days."

"Did you hear something?" Mrs. Grimble asked of no one in particular. "Sounds like the possibility of a car getting further and further away."

"Oh golly mother," Jade gushed. "Can you please tell us about the golden age of Nickelville?"

Megan snorted and Bruce watched out the window while Gordon's passed. His mother pulled up into a parking space along Main Street next to the gym. His feelings about trying to learn martial arts were mixed. On one hand, he felt eager to learn to defend himself. He wasn't kidding when he said he'd like to be able to beat Chuck and Glenn if it ever came to a real fight. But on the other hand, he wasn't particularly fond of being hit. Jade came home with some serious bruises on a regular basis, and she was the star pupil.

"Sam said he'd take you guys home after class," Mrs. Grimble said. "I'm going to go check in at the Tribune after I drop Paul off at his meeting. If you need anything just give Emelia or I a call."

"Shouldn't we be in a uniform or something?" Megan asked as the Grimble SUV pulled away.

Bruce felt a deep-seated agitation rise in his friend. But he couldn't understand why she felt so uneasy now when she'd been looking forward to this all the way there. He wanted to know what it could be, but he didn't want to upset her and chance her blocking him out again.

*What's worrying you?* he asked at last.

42

*I hate not being dressed properly,* she answered, and he understood the rest without needing an explanation. He'd almost forgotten about the threadbare shirts and torn jeans she'd worn when she'd first come to Nickelville, because for him her clothing had never been important. However, he remembered not only the memories, but also the feelings they'd evoked on that night in the grove when she'd shown him her past. The only bit of her clothing that had ever really stood out in his memory was the dress she'd worn at Thanksgiving. And even as much as he'd liked the way she looked in it, the memory of it flowing behind her made him uneasy. There was something, perhaps from his dreams, that shuddered unpleasantly beneath the surface of his conscious thoughts when he remembered her in that dress.

"Sam is really relaxed about that sort of thing," Jade said. "I usually only wear my gi pants with a t-shirt unless it's a belt exam or a tournament."

"What does Sam have to do with this?" Megan asked, confused.

"Didn't I tell you?" Jade replied. "He's the head instructor."

Bruce could feel their big friend's presence before he crossed the threshold of the gym, and even though he'd been there many times before, he'd never noticed the way the entire place echoed Sam's awareness. Several ceiling fans circulated the hot, dry air that blew in from the open front and back doors of the gym. Mirrors lined the walls, giving the illusion that the room was much larger than it really was. A worn square mat covered most of the floor and a punching bag hung in the corner, covered in more duct tape than canvas. Chairs lined one wall, presumably for parents to sit while their children trained, but at present all remained empty.

"Besides," Jade said, continuing her earlier conversation, "It's really hot this time of year. As you've probably noticed, the dojo doesn't have air conditioning. My gi is a heavy duty one, which looks great when I compete, but it's too hot for the end of June. Most of the white belts wear shorts though," she added, looking down at Megan's sweats, "I hope you don't get too hot in those."

The dojo was as plain and utilitarian as Gordon's was whimsical, both showing different sides of their friend's personality. Unfinished sheetrock made up most of the walls, but there were also shelves filled with trophies and stands to hold the practice weapons for the advanced classes.

"Hey guys," Jade yelled when she walked through the door. "One line in five, so take care of bathroom breaks now if you don't want to pay for them in push-ups later!"

"Where's Sam?" Bruce asked.

"He usually shows up about the time I finish warming the class up," his sister answered, dropping her bag in the corner.

"Good evening, Miss Grimble," called a little girl in full uniform with a haircut that made her look like a miniature version of Jade.

Bruce turned back to the door, expecting to find his mother.

"Back at ya Ella," Jade called back.

"Miss Grimble?" Megan asked.

"It's a sign of respect to call upper belts by their formal title," Jade said with a shrug as she pulled her black belt out of her bag and tied it around her waist.

"How long have you been training?" Megan asked.

"I started when I was eleven, so that would be about five years now."

"What now?" Megan asked, looking around with nervous anticipation.

44

"I haven't seen you this anxious since the first time we took you into the woods," Jade observed quietly where only she and Bruce could hear. "When I call for one line just follow everyone else. You're both white belts, so you'll be at the end of the line. Bow toward the center of the mat before entering or leaving. Otherwise just follow my instructions and watch the rest of the students. If you do something wrong, someone will correct you. It's not a big deal. We all remember what it was like at the beginning."

The change that had come over Jade when they walked through the dojo doors surprised Bruce. Even though she didn't physically put on the uniform, she still assumed the mantle of authority with confidence.

"Alright everyone," Jade yelled a few minutes later, walking to the front of the mat. "One line!"

Running came easy to Bruce. Sit-ups, push-ups and stretching made him realize he wasn't in nearly as good of physical shape as he'd thought. He managed to stay on his feet throughout the grueling workout, but only because he hated the thought of collapsing in front of Megan. He knew he'd never be like anything resembling a hero, but he'd rather she never saw him as weak now that his asthma was gone.

As promised, Sam walked in through the open back door while Jade finished warming the class up. He stepped into the changing room and returned a moment later in a pair of black gi bottoms and a t-shirt, not even bothering with the belt.

Bruce could feel Megan relax and start to anticipate the training to come. Too bad his own expectations took him in the other direction.

"Good Evening," Sam called out in that soothing voice of his, "As you may have noticed, we have prospective new students tonight. Class, this is Megan McGeehee, granddaughter of Mr. Azarich McGeehee, and

Bruce Grimble, winner of last year's Jubilee Race and brother to our own Miss Grimble." Then he wrung his hands suggestively before him, and with a maniacal laugh he declared, "Now if I can just get the youngest one I'll have the complete set!"

Bruce felt like an absolute fraud being recognized for the race when the class warm-up had so nearly done him in.

"We've got a small group tonight," Sam continued. "Mr. Wallace has come down with a bug, and from the gaps in your line, I suspect others might have as well. Be sure to use good hygiene in your time both inside and outside the dojo. We come into close contact with one another here, and it's easy to pass sickness from one to another. Miss Grimble, will you take the intermediate group through their katas and one-step sparring?"

"Yes, Mr. Wise," Jade said, motioning for several students to follow her.

"And I will take the beginners," Sam announced.

A heavy-set boy with a sour expression and the mini-Jade stayed behind with Bruce and Megan along with a tall, skinny boy who had a mop of curly brown hair.

"This is Ella and Jayden Mickey," Sam said, motioning to the boy and girl. "And this is Andrew Jackson of no relationship that he knows of to the president of the same name."

Bruce and Megan shook hands with the group. Bruce noticed that Andrew seemed to be paying more attention to the intermediate group than his own.

"Let's start off with fore and back balance basics, and then we'll move on to basic snap and spin kicks," Sam said. "Spread out far enough to keep from hitting each other, but don't interfere with the others."

Bruce soon understood why Andrew found the intermediate class so much more interesting. Jade was taking them through a series of drills that looked positively intriguing compared to the repetitive movements Sam taught them.

The oppressive heat of the dojo robbed them of concentration and of any energy that might have remained by the end of his sister's sadistic warm-up. As time slowly passed, Bruce's desire to be there seemed to flow out of him along with the sweat that already drenched his shirt.

*I know it seems unimportant now,* Sam sent, *but everything they are doing over there builds on the foundations you lay here. Both of you are doing well though and will be over there before you know it.*

*Sorry,* Bruce sent.

*Tell you what, we'll end the class by sparring, and I'll let you and Megan try out what you've learned so far.*

*Deal!* Megan sent. *Can we start now? Please, please, please!*

Sam rolled his eyes in mock exasperation.

"Okay," he called out. "Water break! Be seated around the mat with your sparring gear on in five minutes."

"Did you know it was going to be this hard?" Megan whispered in Bruce's ear when they joined the others at the water fountain.

"What do you mean?" he asked enviously. "You aren't even sweating."

"I don't ever sweat," Megan replied with a shrug. "Heat has almost as little effect on me as the cold."

"Of all the cool things about you," Bruce said. "That's the one that I think I envy the most. Are you sure you don't want to make a break for the door?"

"Not just yet," she answered. "I really want to try sparring."

"Masochist," he said while she drank.

47

"I saw my mom fight off a guy who wanted to mug us once," she told him while he drank. "He was twice her size, and she put him on the ground in seconds."

"Are you sure she didn't use something else?" Bruce asked.

"Anything's possible," Megan replied with a shrug while they walked toward the mat. "Don't forget to bow back in when you step on."

"Thanks," he said, watching with great trepidation as Jade walked up with two old sets of hand gear.

"These should fit until you get your own. Why couldn't you have tried this back when I *wanted* to pound on you?" she asked Bruce pointedly.

"Because I wouldn't have made it through the warm ups without having an asthma attack," he answered, flexing his hands inside the padded gloves. "Did I do it right?"

"Yep," Jade said, glancing them both over. "Well, better late than never I guess. You're mine, little brother. Come on up."

"Wait a minute! Don't I at least get to watch someone else first?"

"You've been watching me for years," Jade answered before she put her mouthpiece in. The malicious joy in her eyes chilled him more than his first encounter with the Dark Man.

"Don't I need one of those?" he asked.

"She's actually in more danger of being hurt than you are," Sam said from the center of the ring.

"How do you figure?" Bruce asked.

"She has complete control of her movements. She won't hurt you unless she wants to," Sam explained. "Whereas you are going to blunder around until you figure out what you're doing. You're going to do stuff that a more experienced fighter would know is a bad idea. Until you learn, you're going to be unpredictable and thus, more likely to hurt your opponent without meaning to."

"That's not a very flattering way of thinking about it," Bruce said, taking his place across from Jade.

"Just feel out his defenses," Sam told her. "Let's see what kind of reflexes he has."

Bruce quickly realized that he'd never been on the true receiving end of what his sister was capable of doing. He tried to stay in the fighting stance that Sam had shown him during the first part of the class, but he quickly got distracted by the way Jade kept circling him. Without warning she lunged, striking at the back of his head with the back of her fist.

Just before she started to move, he knew what she was going to do and moved his arm up to intercept it. His arm stung where his block met her wrist, and he knew he'd have a bruise in the morning.

"Nicely done," Jade said with what was probably a grin. It was hard to tell with the mouthpiece.

Feeling better about the whole situation, he didn't realize she was going to kick him in the side until her foot was already sailing through the air toward him. He braced for the impact, but she stopped it when it made contact with his shirt.

"Don't forget that you move faster than she does," Sam reminded him. "You don't have to just stand there and take it."

*Let your mind go blank like you do when you're trying to practice your abilities,* Sam sent.

Bruce found that simple bit of advice more difficult to follow than anything else that night. While it was true that he'd had a lot of experience with clearing his mind to focus over the past few months, he'd never had to do so while someone else was darting in and hitting him. All said, he was able to block most of what she threw at him when she only threw one technique at a time. But if she threw combinations, he got hit every time. And though he tried to hit her on three different occasions, he never even came close.

"That's good," Sam announced after what felt like hours.

"Not bad," Jade said, pulling her mouthpiece out and shaking his hand. "You've got good instincts. With a bit of practice you'd be pretty good."

"Alright, Megan, you're next," Sam called.

Bruce gratefully sat down and Megan crossed the ring eagerly to face Jade. They bowed to one another and the match started.

Megan launched herself at Jade in a perfect imitation of what Jade had opened with in his match. Jade blocked it, but only just.

"Well, well, well," Sam said with a grin. "This might be interesting."

Although Megan might not normally look anything like her mother, when she fought, the resemblance was uncanny. Though Jade was smiling and still in complete control of the ring, Bruce could tell that she'd already stopped thinking of Megan as a novice.

Jade threw a kick at Megan's head, but his friend pivoted under the older girl's leg, swept her ground leg and flowed over her as she fell, ending on one knee with her punch stopped a fraction of an inch from the eldest Grimble's face.

Everyone around the mat burst into applause.

Megan's eyes flew wide, and she immediately began to apologize to Jade for taking her down so hard. The lights began to flicker uncontrollably.

"It's okay," Jade said with a wide grin. "It's my fault for not blocking it since I'm an upper belt. That was really good. Are you sure you've never taken classes before? You didn't even telegraph."

"No," Megan said, still unsettled. "This is the first time. Are you sure you're okay?"

"I have a phenomenally thick skull," Jade assured her. "Just ask Bruce."

"You are so my hero!" Bruce called in support. "Hit her again!"

"Try a few more rounds," Sam said. "Jade, take it up a notch. Intermediate rules. Don't worry about hurting her, Megan. Try to avoid contact to the face though, and don't ever kick to the knees."

"Okay," Megan and Jade said together and started to circle.

Jade was more cautious this time, taking her time to set Megan up and draw her out where she wasn't as well protected. It was pretty clear that Jade would win in a true fight with Megan, but Bruce suspected that they'd both come out hurt if it ever happened.

At the end of the match, the two of them shook hands.

*Did you know you could do that?* Bruce asked.

*No clue,* she answered. *You did pretty okay too.*

*Do you think this ties into our abilities?* He asked. *I'm pretty sure I precogged what she was going to do throughout our match. I knew what she was going to do, but I didn't know enough to stop her. What were you doing?*

*I really don't know. It's almost like there's another me in here that takes over in situations like this, one that knows a lot more about fighting than I do.*

*Like the thing with the throwing knives and pellet guns at the Jubilee?* he asked.

*Yeah,* she agreed, *something like that.*

*Pay attention, you two,* Sam's thoughts interrupted. *You're going to*

51

*pick up this stuff pretty quickly. After you learn to fight hand to hand, Emelia wants me to train you with weapons.*

*I'd love to try Megan on them tonight, but I don't want Jade to get suspicious.*

*I think she already is,* Bruce sent. *We're going to have to tell her and Paul at some point.*

*Emelia and I have talked about it as well,* Sam sent. *Just let us know when the time is right.*

*I will,* Bruce thought and settled in to watch as Sam took Jade's place with Megan in the ring.

# Chapter VII: Summon the Changeling

Megan woke to the metallic clang of her antique alarm clock, wishing once again that she didn't fry electronics when startled. Unwilling to move just yet, she reached out with her mind and flipped the switch. *It would be so nice to wake to music,* she thought drowsily. *It's been a while since I tried one.*

Before she could drift off again, she untangled herself from the covers and threw her legs over the side of the bed. Her exertions at the dojo had left her sore and tight, but that faded somewhat as her awareness drifted outward from her through the quiet house, passing over her mother in the next room (with the mental equivalent of drowsy acknowledgement) and down to the first floor where Azarich already waited.

Likewise, those extra senses guided her through dressing, although she spent several minutes looking for her other pair of sweats until she remembered packing them in the bag she'd left at the treehouse. The lamp that her grandfather left on at the base of the stairs lit the second-floor hallway with a warm glow. After walking quietly past her mother's room, she leapt lightly up to the banister and slid quickly down before dismounting without hitting the knob at the end.

By the time she reached the living room, she'd shaken the worst of the lethargy from her thoughts. She reached out to touch the picture of the grandmother, whom she resembled so closely, in what had become part of her morning ritual before entering the kitchen.

The old coffee pot gave one last rumbling percolation before she filled both of the cups that her grandfather had left out for her, and added a healthy dollop of cream and sugar to each. Then, holding the handles together in one hand, she opened the back door with the other and joined him.

Predawn light outlined the plants and trees that filled the shelves scattered around the porch. The sun would clear the horizon any moment.

"Morning, Sunshine," he said with the same hint of surprise he did each morning. "You know, Megan, you're always welcome to sleep in if you want."

"Why Grandpa," she replied with exaggerated sadness, "don't you like my company?"

"More than anything," he said, happily accepting the warm cup from her as she sat down next to him on the swing. "But I don't ever want you to think that you have to get up every day before the sun rises just to keep an old man happy."

"Good, because I'd be awfully sad if I couldn't spend this time with you," she said, settling in against him. "When Mom gets up I have to share. So what kind of show are we going to see today?"

"Looks like a rerun we've seen a lot lately," he said. "Not a single cloud to color the sun's rays."

"But still beautiful in its simplicity," she finished for him. "What was yesterday's like? We were up so late trying to find Paul that I missed it."

"There were still some wisps of cloud left from that storm you

54

mentioned," he said, putting his arm around her shoulders as they waited. "But it wasn't as brilliant as this one is going to be with you here. I'm glad you were able to find Paul. Guarded Wood can be a strange place at night."

"Have you ever been there after dark?" she asked.

Azarich chuckled and sipped his coffee. The sun cleared the horizon and Megan was struck by how much something as simple as light could be augmented by the sound of laughter.

"Don't hold out on me!" she said, lightly elbowing him in the ribs. "Mom's not here to stop you, and I know that particular laugh is reserved for something you and your friends shouldn't have been doing!"

"To be honest, I've never really been sure what happened that night," he admitted at last. "It was the middle of the summer and Tom, Allen, Carl and I had dared each other to spend a night in Guarded Wood."

"Carl was the one that was lost in the war, right?" Megan asked.

"Yes," he agreed.

"I thought you guys went out there all the time," Megan said, sipping the coffee. "What was so special about camping there?"

"Old Man Biggerstaff," Azarich chuckled again.

"Wait a minute," Megan blurted out, "he was out there when you were a kid?"

"You'd better believe it," he assured her. "He didn't seem to mind if we were in the woods during the day, but night was completely off limits."

"How old was he?" Megan asked.

"Probably about as old as I am now," Azarich answered. "Although the young always see the old as much older than we really are."

"That's not possible," Megan said, confused.

"Oh, I assure you, they do. When I was about fifty there was this kid working at the gas station…"

"No," Megan said, shaking her head and leaning forward to get a better look at his face while she spoke. "He can't have been that old. He helped us find Paul."

"Why didn't you tell us?" Azarich asked, his voice trailing off as the implications of her words sunk in.

"We were afraid Mrs. Grimble would freak out and stop letting us go out there," Megan answered. "But you see what I mean, right? He'd have to be well over a hundred years old by now."

"I'm sure there's a reasonable explanation," Azarich said, recovering from his initial shock. "He probably had a son or some other relative that took over his property when he passed away." But even he didn't sound convinced.

"So what happened?" Megan said, trying to get the story back on track. "You camped out in Guarded Wood…"

"And something happened," Azarich replied. "I remember something about lights, and I think there might have been music. Somehow, we got separated, and the hermit brought us back."

Megan thought about what he'd just told her. She could tell as she watched him that the subject caused him a great deal of anxiety. Had they been lured into the deep woods by what the hermit called wisps just as Paul had? Certainly the memory of music was too much of a coincidence. But to her knowledge, none of her grandfather's friends had shared Paul's fascination with goth musicians.

"I'm sorry I can't tell you more," he said, a little ashamed by the confession. "But my memory isn't what it used to be."

"Which means it's still twice as good as anyone else in this town," Megan said, hiding her disappointment and her eagerness to talk to Bruce. "If you don't remember any more, then there isn't any more to remember.

The magic of the morning was broken, although the two of them still watched the sun as it cleared the trees of Guarded Wood. By the time Emelia came down the stairs, Megan and Azarich had already cooked a large breakfast, and the subject of Old Man Biggerstaff was safely tucked away lest the perceptive woman sniff it out.

As soon as Megan could do so, she slipped out the back door, past the porch that always smelled like fresh potting soil, and down the old fence row to the path that led to the treehouse. The previous day had been full, and she hadn't had a chance to return since the night of the storm. When it rose before her from the underbrush, she realized she'd been expecting it to have changed.

*You should bring him up here to watch the sunrise some time,* Bruce sent down from the tower.

*You were up here alone in the dark?*

*I could feel you at your house.*

*I still don't like the idea of you being alone up here at night,* she sent, climbing the spiral steps and letting him feel her disapproval. She found him leaning over the rail in the tower, staring out across Guarded Wood, which still looked much larger than a few miles across.

"It still doesn't feel right," he said quietly as she joined him.

"All the more reason why you shouldn't be up here alone before daylight," she said. He was right though, she should come up here with her grandfather one morning. The view was bound to be breathtaking.

"I was really afraid of the dark when I was little," he said, still looking out.

"Most kids are," she responded.

"Not like me," he replied. "When I was a kid they tried out an experimental asthma medication on me. It was one that had to be at a certain level in my blood to work."

"And?" she prompted. This was unusual for Bruce, who was almost as close-mouthed about the past as her mother.

"We didn't know it then, but I have a weird metabolism," he continued. "When my body encounters a substance it's not familiar with, it speeds up until it neutralizes it. Anyway, they kept increasing the dose but when they checked my blood, there was none there. "

"What happens when your body gets used to it?" Megan asked.

"It eventually stops speeding up and the medication starts to work normally. That happened one morning after I'd stayed up watching part of a scary movie that had these little monsters that were only hurt by sunlight. I've always been the early riser in the family, so no one was awake when I got up. The sun hadn't risen yet, and the house was still dark. I'd just turned on some morning cartoons when I started to hallucinate the monsters from the movie running around the living room."

"What did you do?" Megan asked, horrified. "And how old were you?"

"I couldn't do anything," he answered with a chuckle, "My asthma was so bad that even the adrenaline from being scared didn't clear it up. I couldn't breathe well enough to scream, and I was too scared to get up from the couch. They were climbing all over the place and peeking over the armrest at me. How old? Probably about six."

"That's horrible," Megan said, putting her arm around his shoulders and hugging him.

"It's no big deal," he said, not looking away from the trees. "I just want you to know why I'm not going to let the dark scare me. I had to sleep with the light on for years after that. It worked itself into a full-blown phobia, and I had this whole night-time terror where I believed the things from the movie were real."

"How did you get over it?" Megan asked, her arm still around him.

"Time and logic," he said. "That's part of the reason why I had so much trouble accepting the Dark Man at first. If he was real, what about my monsters?"

"And the hydrophobia?" she asked.

"That started about the same time that I got over my fear of the dark," he said with a shrug. "It's a lot easier to stay away from water than darkness, though. Believe it or not, I kind of like the dark now."

"Really?"

"Yeah, and with our abilities we can still sense everything around us even in total darkness."

"As long as there's not something strange like the other night in the woods," Megan added, "I couldn't feel more than a few feet in any direction."

"Which brings us to the real reason we're both here," Bruce said with a grimace. "What's going on out there?" They both looked at the woods in silence since there were no answers to be given.

"How is Paul doing?" she asked.

"He had a nightmare last night," Bruce answered. "It wasn't bad, but his room is next to mine, and his anxiety woke me up."

"You didn't try to read him while he was asleep, did you?"

"No, but I was sorely tempted. I think he was back out there in the woods."

"How do you know if you didn't read him?" she asked.

"He was thrashing around on his bed and mumbling about reaching her in time again."

"The violin girl?" she asked.

"That's my guess," he answered. "I'd hoped he'd leave for summer camp soon, but it sounds like they may cancel because of the sickness in town."

"What are you not telling me?" Megan pressed, sensing that there was more and putting just enough force at the edges of his shields to make him look her in the eye.

"That's not fair, you know," he said, pulling away from her arm.

"What?" she asked.

"You keep things to yourself all the time," he retorted with some irritation, "sometimes you even block me out completely."

"Like when?" she asked.

"When we woke up yesterday," he said.

"Bruce," she said, finally understanding. "Our dreams got mixed together and it completely drained me. I hardened my shields to keep everything out, not just you. It was like I had a massive hangover, and your thoughts were just too loud."

"You're sure?" he asked, looking at her hard in the morning light.

"Of course," she answered. "You and I are a team. Where one goes, the other does too."

"Promise?" he asked. She sensed that this meant something slightly different to him than it did her, but she didn't understand what that difference meant or how important it might be.

"Promise," she said, holding her hand up and extending her pinky for him to hook in the childhood oath, "I'd tear this world down to keep you safe and in my life."

"The future is muddy," he said at last, hooking her finger with a sigh.

60

"Lots of rain in the forecast?" she asked.

"No," he said, searching for the right words to describe it. "It's not as clear as it usually is for me. I'm still learning to understand what I see, so it's probably not anything big."

"What are you seeing?" she prompted.

"It's what I'm not seeing," Bruce said in frustration. "Paul's future is so complicated that I can't make any sense of it. It's like there are so many possibilities that the overlapping outcomes are piling up on each other."

"Muddy?"

"As good a description as I can come up with," he said with a shrug, looking back over the trees. "And some of the possibilities look dark."

"Like the ones I saw with you at the fire?" she said, remembering.

"Yes," he said, happy to get out of trying to explain.

"And this started when he got lost in the woods?" Megan asked.

"I'm not sure," Bruce said. "I can't say that I usually look at Paul's future when there's nothing going on. The first time I noticed the problem was when he was lost, but it might have started long before that."

"What does my future look like?" Megan asked, suddenly curious.

"I really can't see yours very far," Bruce said. "I think it's because we're so close that my desire to see a good future overshadows what is really there. I can't see mine with any certainty either. Just the effects my actions have on others."

"Probably a good thing if you think about it," she said. "Major spoiler alerts otherwise."

"One thing that I can see is that Emelia doesn't need to know about Old Man Biggerstaff having abilities quite yet," he said.

"Is he a threat to us?"

"Not that I can tell," Bruce answered. "But they have different reactions to each other at different times. It needs to be just right or they could attack each other."

"What's a changeling?" she asked, not wanting to think about who would win such a battle.

Bruce stared at her blankly.

"He called me a changeling and told me to stay out of Guarded Wood," she said.

"Apparently that was meant for you alone."

"Yeah, I got that part. But what's a changeling?" she repeated.

"A changeling is part of European folklore," he said. "People with bad children often said the Fair Folk had stolen their good, Christian little babies and substituted them with a kind of pod person replica that was evil."

"Oh," Megan said, frowning. "Not very flattering then, huh?"

"Not that I can see," he agreed, deciding to change the subject. "Are you as sore as I am this morning?"

"Yes!" Megan answered, her hand involuntarily massaging her thigh. "I can't believe Jade does that three times a week and still moves the way she does."

"Don't ever tell her I said so," Bruce confessed, "But it was really cool to see how different she was at the dojo. Are we going to keep going?"

"I am," Megan answered. "But you don't have to if you don't want to."

"My body says no, but let's face it. This is something that we could use if we ever get cornered by the Huntsmen."

Megan froze, her eyes finding his once again.

"What?" he asked.

"That's the first time you've ever acknowledged them out loud," Megan whispered, nudging his shoulder with her own affectionately. "But yes, that's exactly what I was thinking too."

"How did your mom react when she found out you're a martial arts prodigy?" he asked.

"Like it was exactly what she expected," Megan answered, "And if you could have seen how overprotective she was before we came here, you'd know how weird that was."

"I might know a thing or two about overprotective mothers," he said, looking happier now that they'd talked.

"Now if there's someone you should get mad at for holding things back and keeping secrets, it's my mother."

As if the thought summoned her, Emelia called her daughter back to the house.

"There is one thing that you need to do soon," Bruce said reluctantly.

"Why do I have the feeling I'm not going to like this," Megan said, pausing on the top rungs of the ladder.

"It's time for Azarich to know about all of this," he said.

"Why would we do that?" she asked. *So much for getting used to laid back Mom.*

"He's going to figure it out on his own in about a week, and it would be much better if it comes from the two of you instead."

"This isn't going to make you very popular with my mom," Megan mumbled, resuming her descent down the ladder.

"This was the path that also held the smallest chance of her turning me into a toad," he called after her. Megan's eyes popped up over the edge.

"She can't really do that, can she?" she asked.

"I don't think so, but where your mother is concerned I don't like to take chances."

Megan was curled up in a chair near the front window of the living room when she felt a presence hovering at the edge of her awareness. She looked up from the book she'd borrowed from Bruce and out across the front lawn, but there was no one there.

*Changeling.*

*What do you want?* She responded, making no attempt to hide her irritation at the name.

*I need you to come at once to your grandmother's grove,* he sent, *we need to talk.*

*I thought I wasn't allowed anywhere near your precious woods.*

*I'd prefer to discuss that in person. It's hard to shield this from your mother at this distance.* Then the presence was gone.

Megan left the book on the chair for later and walked through the house toward the back door. She could hear her grandfather snoring from his room upstairs. He'd recently started to take a nap at midday.

The humidity outside made her hair and clothes stick to her, putting her in a foul mood as she walked toward the back of the property where her grandmother's grove stood. How did he know about the grove, anyway? Combined with him knowing Paul's name, she was starting to suspect that Old Man Biggerstaff was something of a stalker.

She found him standing in the shade under one of the trees that made up her grandmother's grove. The old man no longer wore the old cloak, but if he wasn't wearing the same clothes that he'd had on the night of the storm, they were very similar both in style and in condition. In place of a belt, he held his pants up with a length of rope and his boots had holes in places through which she could see his bare skin. Having been well acquainted with poverty herself, Megan took note of his clothing but didn't stare or judge.

Bruce was already there when she walked up, and Fang was leaning into a good scratching behind the ears when he caught Megan's scent and began to growl.

"Why does he dislike me?" Megan asked, her irritation growing.

"Probably because I don't like you very much," the old man answered, once again sounding as if he wasn't used to speaking any more.

"Why?" Megan snapped, "I've never done anything to you. I don't even like going into Guarded Wood!"

At this, the hermit stepped closer and studied her face. She felt his presence again at the edges of her mind. She was struck again by his dark eyes that almost made it look like it was all one big pupil.

"May I?" he asked at last.

She nodded reluctantly.

Although his manner was gruff, the touch of his mind as it searched the surface of her thoughts was gentle. She didn't give him full access to her memories, but she saw no reason why he shouldn't be able to see what had occurred since she and her mother had come to Nickelville. He was aware of the boundaries, but didn't push. Satisfied at last, he withdrew.

"Do you give me your word that you mean no harm here?" he asked, and there was something in the way that he asked that made her think he knew more about her than she did herself.

"Of course," she answered.

He continued to stare at her, waiting.

"I promise that I mean no harm here," she said, and when she did, something subtle within her changed.

65

Without warning, Fang walked over and dropped his considerable weight on her foot and began to nuzzle her hand. She hesitantly ran her fingers through the long soft fur of his neck, and he wagged his tail appreciatively.

She looked up and found Bruce smiling at this miraculous transformation.

"So you're Josie's granddaughter?" the old man asked.

"You knew Grandma?" Megan asked.

"A long time ago," he said gruffly, and the words hung in the air for a moment where only the sounds of Fang's tail hitting the ground broke the silence.

Bruce couldn't stand having the wolf so close without touching him and sat down on the ground next to Megan, manhandling the beast over onto his back so they could both rub his stomach like a big dog. Fang began to grunt in ecstasy while the old man watched.

"He's always liked you, Bruce," the hermit said. "Thank you for taking care of him that time when he was hurt. I was deep in one of the places where it's not safe for him to go and might not have made it back in time were it not for you and your siblings."

"No problem," Bruce replied.

"Guarded Wood is bigger than it should be," Megan said, happily letting Bruce pet Fang.

"Don't miss much, do you?" the old man asked. "That's what I wanted to talk to the two of you about."

"We knew something was wrong the night of the storm," Bruce said. "Even Jade could tell the woods seemed bigger than they had."

"Did you do anything arcane while you were building your treehouse in the Sentinel?" he asked.

66

"Sentinel?" Megan asked.

"The huge trees that surround Guarded Wood," he said, beginning to walk past through the multitude of yellow flowers and down the path that led to their treehouse. "You built your treehouse in one of them."

"What exactly do you mean by arcane?" Megan asked.

"Anything that used your abilities that was then tied to the tree itself," he said. "Or maybe something you found and removed."

"Not that I can think of," she said. "Of course, Mom or Sam could have done something without us knowing it."

"Can you find out?" he asked.

"I guess," Megan said. "But why?"

"I knew something was wrong about a week before the treehouse was finished, "the hermit explained. "But I had no idea it was anywhere near this bad until that storm hit. In all of my years here, I've never seen anything like that. And now some of the oldest protections on Guarded Wood have become unreliable," he said. "I've been studying the woods for a very long time, and not even I understand most of what is going on in there. The Sentinels mark the boundaries of the wood. As far as I can tell, they anchor it where it is and stand guard over the interior."

"But Guarded Wood isn't that big," Bruce interjected with a frown.

"Not even I know how big it really is," the old man said. Their treehouse rose before them, cradled in the branches of the Sentinel like a babe in its mother's arms. "Until now they've kept most of the dangerous stuff inside so people like you are safe in your beds at night."

"How are fireflies dangerous?" Megan asked.

"Not fireflies," the hermit countered. "Will-o-the-Wisps."

"You're kidding," Bruce exclaimed.

"Wasps of the what?" Megan asked.

67

"Laugh all you want," the hermit growled. "A will-o-the-wisp is a dangerous if rare part of the Old World."

"What do they do?" Megan asked.

"They lure unwary travelers to their doom," Bruce said with a frown that Megan knew meant he'd just put them into context with what had happened to his brother. "They aren't dangerous by themselves, but in folklore they work with other creatures that are. They feed off of suffering."

"Not bad," Old Man Biggerstaff said, pursing his lips and raising a bristly eyebrow. "Those fantasy books must have taught you a thing or two."

"Okay," Megan said, stepping in front of the hermit. "That's gone on long enough. How do you know so much about all of us when we've never seen you?"

"What do you think?" he asked Bruce. "How do I know so much?"

Bruce stared at him, absently rubbing the fur on Fang's head.

"Put it together," the old man said with the first genuine smile Megan had seen on his face. "You haven't seen me, and I'll admit that I wasn't there most of those times in the woods…"

Bruce's eyes flew wide.

"You can see and hear what Fang does!" Bruce exclaimed. "And I'm going to bet you're not limited to him either. You were watching us through that crow when we finished the treehouse."

The old man nodded.

"Okay, that is still completely stalkerish," Megan said, trying to let that revelation sink in. "How do we get rid of the wisp things?"

"As unpleasant as they are, we don't dare," the old man said. "They are part of the natural order, at least the order that once ruled. This may very well be the only place like this left in the world, and I will have no part in wiping out what may be the last remaining members of a species."

"Are there things living in Guarded Wood like the ones in the woods between the Academy and the Jubilee Field?" Bruce asked.

"Are the dryads still there?" the old man asked fondly.

"At least one," Bruce answered, "and I think I saw a pooka."

"Then you saw the Oak Dryad," August said. "She rules the woods that encircle the empty clearing next to your school."

"What about the ones that circle Jubilee Field?" Megan asked.

"Those are ruled over by the Ash Dryad," he answered. "I only saw her once. But as interesting as this might be, it's not why I called you here."

"Okay," Bruce said. "Endangered monsters in Guarded Wood. So what's so different about these woods? What makes them special?"

"It's virgin forest," the old man answered. "Men had more reason than just the need for wood to cut down the old growth. They hunted things like the wisps into their daytime lairs and wiped out whole species that didn't fit their view of the world."

"So this is like a nature preserve?" Megan asked.

"Of a sort."

"And you're the guardian of Guarded Wood?" Bruce asked.

"No," the hermit answered. "Until now it's guarded itself. I'm more of a caretaker. You two are sure you didn't do anything here? Everything I'm seeing suggests that it was something here at this Sentinel that started the chain reaction."

"No," Megan answered. "I'll see if I can find out if Mom or Sam did anything. Is there any chance of us fixing it?"

"Maybe, but I need to know what happened here first. These

69

protections were put here long before I came, and even after years of study, I'm still not sure how they work. Keep thinking about it. It could be something very small."

"We will," Megan said. "Um, Mr. Biggerstaff?"

He grunted in reply.

"What should we call you?" she asked. "It seems kind of rude to call you Old Man Biggerstaff."

The old man studied her for a moment, not quite sure what to make of her.

"Particularly since my surname isn't really Biggerstaff," he growled. "Though I am old and male. I'm not sure why they started calling me that. Tell you what, just call me August."

"Like the month?" Megan asked.

"Like short for Augustus," he said, turning to leave. "Be careful with that information. Names have power. And as far as I know, you may very well be the only two people living who know it."

"August?" Bruce called after him.

"The two of you are starting to remind me why I'm a hermit," he called back. "What is it now?"

"Is Goatman real?"

"Just do me a favor and make sure that no one from your side comes in," he called back. "I've got idiots popping in all over the place looking for Goatman right now, and it would be nice not to have to be everywhere at once for a change.

# Chapter VIII: Bruce Slips Up

"You look tired, Dad," Jade observed as she helped herself to another helping of the dish that Paul was trying out for his cooking merit badge. The family was seated around the kitchen table, and Mr. Grimble had just come in from three days at the station.

"It was a hard shift," he admitted, still wearing the navy-blue shirt and khakis that made up his work clothes and picking at the remains on his own plate without much enthusiasm. "The budget cuts that Jones pushed through during that last city council meeting have reduced everyone's hours and left us shorthanded."

"Any news about Mrs. Gregory and her son?" Paul asked. "You think there's any chance he'll recover in time to come to summer camp with the troop? He was really looking forward to it."

"We had to take them to County General," Mr. Grimble said with a sigh. "So probably not. Four more people called in today with the same symptoms. We just don't have the resources to deal with whatever this is at Doc Soams's office, so we're sending all new cases to county. Especially in light of what happened to your P.E. teacher."

"I still can't believe Coach Beates is dead," Jade said, pushing away from the table. "I mean, she was tougher than anyone I've ever met."

"That means summer camp is canceled for the troop," Paul said, disappointed but still taking it in stride. "As much as we all hate missing out this year, we can't take the chance of spreading this to camp if it does turn out to be contagious."

"It also means every call is taking close to an hour each way," Mrs. Grimble said. "No wonder you're tired."

"Speaking of which," Mr. Grimble added. "Would you be upset if I put in some hours off the clock? All of us got together at the end of the shift and decided that keeping people alive is more important than getting paid. At least until this bug passes."

"Mad at you?" Mrs. Grimble asked, "Not in the least. Mad at Tony Jones for making it necessary in the first place? Absolutely. I still think the whole thing was retribution for forcing Paula out of her position at the Academy."

"The rest of the crew think so too, even though they're too good to say it out loud," he said, resting his face on his hands and talking in an exhausted monotone. "We knew they'd do something like this, but I never dreamed they'd put the safety of the whole town in jeopardy to single us out."

The anger that never really left Bruce these days grew a bit hotter down in his gut. Next door, Megan turned her attention to him in concern. With the merest fragment of thought, he let her know what was happening and turned his attention back to his parents.

"*Tribune* sales are still bottoming out too," Mrs. Grimble continued, rising to start clearing the table.

"I've got that, Mom," Paul said, shoving an entire piece of bread into his mouth and taking the stack of dishes from his mother's hand.

"You're such a dear," she said, drawing him into a weary one-armed

72

hug and sitting back down. "Apparently the *Herald* is going to start devoting a section to Nickelville news."

"You're kidding," Mr. Grimble exclaimed, looking up from his hands in surprise. "They've never been interested in us before."

"I know," Mrs. Grimble said. "It couldn't come at a worse time. We're going to lose subscriptions to them."

"Maybe you should do a piece on all of the people who have gotten sick these past few weeks," Bruce said. "If people knew how much of a strain it's putting the emergency crews under to keep people alive, then maybe the council would restore the funding."

"The Chief spoke about it at the council meeting, and they still voted in favor of the cuts," Mr. Grimble said, "and then they voted to put a new kitchen in at city hall so the chef they hired can be better prepared to cook for the staff should any of them not feel like eating out on the town's tab. Besides, we don't want to start a panic."

"People are already starting to panic," Jade said, starting to rinse the plates. "We're having trouble getting enough instructors to teach classes at Lone Star. How many people have it so far?"

"We're not sure," Mr. Grimble answered. "No one can figure out what it is. It doesn't seem to be affecting everyone to the same extent. It's not hitting the old or the young any worse than any other group, and the people affected don't seem to be having any kind of an immune response."

"Some kind of poisoning?" Bruce asked.

"Not that anyone can tell," Mr. Grimble answered. "We thought it might be contamination of the water supply, but the tests all came back clean. So back to square one."

"How about a piece on Goatman?" Paul asked as he loaded the dishes into the dishwasher. "Goatman always sells papers."

73

"I'm not sure that's a good idea," Bruce said without thinking, "Mr. Biggerstaff said that all of the people coming into Guarded Wood to look for Goatman were causing him a lot of trouble."

It took a moment of everyone staring at him to realize what he'd just done.

"So," Jade said happily, "I guess we're going to tell Mom and Dad about seeing Old Man Biggerstaff after all."

"You actually saw him?" Mrs. Grimble asked, forgetting to be angry about the deception in her surprise. "How can that be?"

"He helped us find Paul the night of the storm," Jade replied, looking at Bruce in disgust. "You are such an amateur when it comes to keeping secrets."

"But there's no way that hermit could still be alive," Mr. Grimble said. "Dora, didn't you say that your mother used to talk about meeting him when she was a girl?"

"Azarich seems to think that it's probably a son or even a grandson of the original," Bruce said, trying to salvage the situation.

"So Azarich can know about a strange man lurking in the woods behind our house," Mrs. Grimble said, her voice rising with each word. "But *I* can't?"

"Paul," Mr. Grimble said, "Why didn't you tell us the truth? Aren't you supposed to be honest and trustworthy?"

"I never said a single thing that was a lie," Paul said defensively, "and by not telling Mr. Biggerstaff's secret, I was being loyal, helpful, friendly and kind!"

"His name is August," Bruce said quietly.

"What?" the rest of his family asked in unison.

"This conversation is obviously going to go on for a while, and it's going to take forever to keep calling him Old Man Biggerstaff," Bruce explained. "Biggerstaff isn't even his real last name."

"You talked to him again after that night?" Jade asked in awe as she walked toward him, "I take back what I said about you not being able to keep a secret. However…" she grabbed a potholder off the table and accented each word of "Don't keep them from me!" with swats about the neck and face.

"What's his real last name?" Paul asked, not at all distracted by his sister's loving affections as he continued to load.

"He didn't say," Bruce said when Jade felt she'd made her point. "Mom, Dad, you're going to have to trust us on this. I'm not sure how we would have found Paul in that storm without his help. He got Fang to track Paul and brought him back. Megan and I met him behind her house and he asked us if we could make sure that people didn't come in from our side. He doesn't like to be around people. That's why he lives out there in the woods. He's just a grumpy old man that looks like a cross between Albert Einstein and Dumbledore."

"But what if he's trying to hide something out there?" Mrs. Grimble said, her imagination flying into high gear. If they didn't shut her down soon, it was going to be the debate over the tree house all over again. Realizing that he was in over his head, he reached reluctantly out to Megan's mom.

"Tell you what," Bruce said, allowing Emelia to work the problem out for him. "Sam is going to go out and check on August to make sure he's okay."

"Sam knows about this?" Jade asked.

"Of course," Bruce lied. "You don't think we'd let everyone live next to a potential psychopath without telling them, do you?"

This seemed to mollify Mrs. Grimble somewhat.

"But no one goes near Guarded Wood until Sam gives the all clear on this August person," Mr. Grimble said.

"But Dad," Jade complained.

"Paul, that was delicious as usual," Mr. Grimble said, raising his hand in what was clearly a dismissal and pushing himself back from the table. "Thank you for cleaning up. I'm going to go and take a very overdue shower."

"But going to the woods is the only thing to do on days like this…" Jade said.

"Not another word on the subject," Mrs. Grimble said. "Your father and I need to talk about some things though, so why don't you call Megan and see if she wants to go to the Palace with you? I think there's a new movie starting today."

"You know," Jade said with a smile, "You wouldn't have to drive us there if I had my own…"

"Now is not the time, Jade," Mr. Grimble said, though he did manage a faint smile at her attempt. "Either I'll take you or one of the McGeehees will."

# Chapter IX: The Forgotten Majesty of the Palace

For the first time since that day at the Well of Dreams, Megan saw the overlapping presence of the past without trying as she walked with Jade and her brothers toward the partially lit marquee of the theater. Spectral echoes of lines long dispersed waited in the finery of bygone days. Children pressed faces against the windows that flanked the ticket booth, and hints of laughter crossed the decades to make Megan smile.

Brass trim edged the glass of the ticket booth, glowing in the light cast by hundreds of incandescent bulbs. Neon tubes swept in graceful lines and curves to spell out the name of the theater three stories tall, and would have easily been the tallest point on main street were it not for the towering presence of the Baker Hotel nearby.

Megan glanced back at Bruce, who as usual looked irritated that he wasn't next to her. He showed no sign of seeing the spectacle around them, and she wondered yet again why their abilities were so different.

Feeling unfriendly eyes upon her, Megan found Mr. O'Toole slowly driving past. He glared at her as he continued on his way to the hotel. He wore a greasy red baseball cap that reminded her of some of the less savory places she'd lived, and she briefly considered blowing out all four of his tires.

By the time she looked back, the echoes of the past had faded, and the Palace's luster had diminished as well, leaving only the husk of its former glory. Half of the bulbs in the marquis were broken or missing. A dull green patina replaced the once bright brass, and the gold leaf disappeared from the ticket booth, though an echo of the adhesive that had once held it there allowed them to read what it had said through the fog of grime that had accumulated over the years.

Inside, an old woman sat on a stool with her hands folded in her lap and her head resting against the wall next to her. Her hair was the bright red of a badly-done dye job, and her roots showed an inch of gray near the scalp. She had the frame of someone who worked too hard and ate too little. Her vintage uniform hung loosely around her and had itself seen better days.

"Excuse me," Jade said politely.

"How many?" the woman asked without opening her eyes.

"Four," Jade answered and slid the money that Dora had given her through a slot edged in silver duct tape.

The woman reluctantly opened her eyes and took the money. Four tickets advanced through the slot.

"Any of you want refreshments?" she asked. When her eyes settled on Megan, she looked momentarily as if she recognized her.

"We're good," Bruce answered respectfully, "but thanks."

"Probably for the best," the woman murmured. "Popcorn's burned again 'cause I'm running the place by myself. Seat yourselves, and I'll be up to start the show in about fifteen minutes.

Inside the tall glass doors, Megan was astonished by how much of the original furnishings had survived.

78

"Bruce, what was that airplane maneuver that the guy at the renaissance festival said they taught to the rehabilitated raptors to help them hunt better?" Paul asked.

"I think it was a wingover," Bruce said uncertainly, "or something like that. Why?"

"I don't know, it just keeps popping up in my head."

The past rose again through the threadbare carpet, bringing with it the laughter and excitement of children. And of course, the place where Nickelville's children had been happiest centered around the concession stand. In delight, Megan watched as her teenage mother and Sam ordered popcorn and fountain drinks from a vibrant redhead behind the counter who was herself smiling enticingly at a surprisingly well-dressed and groomed Alan Green.

Cobweb encrusted light fixtures hung on heavy chains from tarnished copper ceiling panels. Ornately carved banisters rose up each side of the concession stand, though both were blocked by signs that announced that the balcony was closed. Likewise, similar signs nearby read, "GRAND THEATRE CLOSED FOR RENOVATIONS."

The smell of burnt popcorn did little to cover the mingled aromas of decaying fabric and dust as Jade led Megan across the threadbare carpet to a side door marked, "THEATRE II."

"There aren't many of these old movie houses with more than one screen," Megan said.

"I'm not sure I'd say this one does either," Paul said. "The main theater's been closed since I was about two."

"That's when everyone stopped coming, "Bruce said. "The second theater only holds about fifty people, and the screen is really small. The only thing that keeps this place running is the hour-long drive to the next nearest theater."

"I think it's wonderful," Megan said, taking in the golden molding that covered the paneled walls.

"You seem so normal until you say things like that," Jade said, holding the door open for the rest.

Inside, the furnishings were much less grand. Frankly, Megan thought it looked as if it had never quite been finished. Iron light fixtures hung from the darkened ceiling, doing little to dispel the gloom below. Bruce pushed ahead of his brother to make sure that he could sit next to Megan when they finally found four seats together that weren't draped with out-of-order signs. An older boy and girl sat close together in the darkened back row.

The lights dimmed after a few minutes, casting the room into total darkness. The older girl giggled.

Bruce's hand slid over Megan's in the darkness. They didn't need to be so close now that the amulet around his neck linked them, but he still seemed to find it comforting, and she'd decided she didn't mind.

When the screen lit, the image was sluggish, as if the projector were having trouble getting started. Then, like an old mule with a heavy load, it found its gait and plodded along.

To Megan's delight, a vintage concession advertisement played, complete with dancing drinks and popcorn. Beside her, the Grimbles cheered, as did the boy and girl behind them.

*It's tradition*, he sent.

She happily joined them.

Although the story wasn't great, Megan loved the feel of the Palace around her. There had been many good experiences there over the years, and they bathed her extra senses the way she thought a warm breeze on a cool day should feel. When she closed her eyes, she could almost feel her mother sitting beside her in any of the old movie houses they'd frequented since her early childhood. No matter how poor they'd become, Emelia had always found time and money enough to attend movies and carnivals. And though her mother had never explained why, Megan now knew she'd been trying to reconnect with her own childhood.

A woman on the screen played the violin while she danced. Perhaps it was because Megan had just been thinking about her mother, but something about the violinist's movements resembled Emelia.

*Look at Paul,* Bruce sent, snapping her out of her revere.

The youngest Grimble had leaned so far forward in his seat that his chest nearly touched the one in front of him. Longing radiated from him with such force that she could feel his emotions without even trying.

*He really fell hard for that girl,* Megan sent, *didn't he?*

*We only saw her for a few minutes,* Bruce sent back. *How can he be so crazy about her?*

Megan shrugged and went back to watching the movie. Bruce worried enough for both of them, and she'd been looking forward to this for too long to be drawn into Paul's obsession. All too soon, she expected the problems with Guarded Wood and the hermit would intrude, and she intended to get lost in this cheesy movie for as long as she could.

The theater abruptly fell into darkness, and an unpleasant clunk from the projector booth at the back of the room echoed through the theater.

"Oh, not again!" Paul called irritably. "It did this the last time we were here."

"Sorry folks," the lady from the ticket booth yelled down at them from the window above. "It should be up again in a minute."

The lights came back up enough for them to see, much to the chagrin

81

of the couple in the back row who were hurriedly untangling themselves from each other.

In spite of Paul's uncharacteristically angry outburst, Megan was more than happy to people-watch among the phantoms of the past. Here and there among the strangers, someone familiar emerged. To her delight, she saw a very young Azarich finally raise enough courage to put his arm around her future grandmother. Without any respect at all for the concept of paradox, a slightly older version of her grandfather was also sitting with Alan Green, Tom Harris and a boy who she'd never seen before, but still recognized the one who hadn't returned from the war. Then the projector roared back into life and the violin playing dancer continued.

They found the old woman sitting on a chair behind the concession counter when they entered the foyer. Megan didn't need her extra senses to know that the woman was running on reserves and might fall over out of sheer exhaustion if something didn't change soon. But as she looked, for just an instant the years melted away and the old woman became the vivacious girl who'd flirted with Mr. Green behind the same counter.

"Excuse me," Jade said when they passed. "But I noticed that you had a help wanted sign in the front window when we came in."

"Well," the woman said thoughtfully. "I've never had trouble with any of you Grimbles, so that's in your favor. You a hard worker?" the woman asked. "And can you handle the hooligans?"

"Absolutely," Jade replied. The woman gave her a long, hard look in which she took in the eldest Grimble's two-tone hair.

"I'll bet you can at that. You're hired," the woman said, rising to her feet and extending a work-calloused hand. "Call me Kate."

"I'm pleased to meet you Kate," Jade said.

"You've been coming here with your family for years, so it's not like you're meeting me," the gruff woman said with an attempt at a smile. "Come in Thursday and we'll get all of the paperwork squared away before the rush on Friday… not that there's likely to be much of one."

"What time?" Jade asked.

"Any time after five or so," the old woman answered, "Assuming that the projector doesn't give out completely before then. It's held together with bubble gum and bailing wire as it is." With that, she collected a broom and headed toward the theater they'd just left.

Paul remained uncharacteristically quiet while they walked over to Gordon's, but with Jade's animated chatter about having a job and the upcoming Independence Day celebration, no one really noticed.

# Chapter X: Allison's Big Splash

"Are you sure you don't want to wear a swimsuit?" Megan asked her mother. Although Emelia's room no longer looked as if it belonged to a teenage girl, it still didn't look like a place where someone lived either.

"This is a work day for me," Emelia reminded her, checking over the camera equipment spread out over the neatly made bed. "I am looking forward to supporting Sam's new food truck though."

"At least wear a short-sleeved shirt," Megan persisted, walking around the room and taking a closer look at one of the smaller watercolors that her grandmother had painted. This one was an incredibly realistic scene in which two massive trees stood, bringing to mind the ones at the center of the Academy courtyard.

"You know how I feel about the sun," Emelia said, brushing off the suggestion as she always did. Megan couldn't think of a single time that she'd seen more of her mother's torso than when she rolled up her sleeves to the elbow on particularly hot days.

"Is that the swimsuit you borrowed from Jade?" her mother asked.

"Yes," Megan answered, walking over and looking at herself in her mother's mirror. "I would have ordered one when we updated my wardrobe, but I completely forgot about the lake after that first day in

Nickelville." It felt weird having her legs exposed since she usually wore jeans or sweats.

"Most people do," Emelia added. "There's an old quarry about an hour away. That's where most go if they want a day on the water. This one attracts more fishermen than anything else."

"There was a time when Lake Nickelville was all the rage," Azarich called from his room. "I spent more than a few weekends out there with my friends. The fishing hasn't been very good at the lake this year though. There was a big die-off about three months ago."

"Doesn't our water come from there?" Emelia asked.

"Not ours," the old man replied, coming to stand in the doorway. "The public supply line doesn't come out to Beverly Road. There was talk once, but it never came to anything. There just aren't enough people living out here on the outskirts to warrant the work. So we use well water instead."

"Why do you ask?" Megan wondered.

"I always thought the lake had a nasty smell to it," Emelia replied. "I know it's treated, but it's still kind of gross to think about. Might be a story in there somewhere if I keep my eyes open."

"Which is why most people drink bottled water," Azarich agreed. "I know Tom and Alan buy theirs by the case."

"And you're sure you don't want to join us, Grandpa?" Megan asked.

"Not this year. Alan will be here soon along with Tom and Esther. There's not much to draw us there since the fishing dried up. We'll spend the day shooting the breeze inside where it's cool now that the treehouse is finished."

"I'm almost tempted to stay with you," Megan said. "I love your stories."

85

"There will be all the time in the world for you to listen to us ramble on," he said, putting his arm around her shoulders and hugging her. We'll join you for the fireworks when the sun goes down."

Megan tried not to notice the way Paul and Bruce stared at her as they rode in the back of her mother's truck when they thought she wouldn't notice. Even though it was a very modest one piece, and she was wearing shorts too, it still showed more skin than she normally allowed. Maybe her mother wasn't completely crazy in her wardrobe choices after all. Of course, Emelia's aversion to tanning might also be why she looked more like a woman in her thirties than other women her age.

The familiar downtown portion of Nickelville came and went. Although Megan always studied the odd architecture of the Baker Hotel when they passed, she'd never done so from the bed of the truck where she could lean back and look at the upper portion of the building like she did now.

"They say it's haunted," Jade yelled over the wind, noticing the focus of her gaze.

"Really?" Megan asked.

"If you had to haunt some place for the rest of eternity, you could do worse than the Baker Hotel," Paul added. "But I'd rather go to Guarded Wood."

"I'll bet the sunrise from up there is amazing," Megan yelled, thinking about her grandfather. "I think I'd prefer the Palace though."

"Solid choice," Jade agreed, watching her new place of employment pass.

Main Street fell behind them and the ancient trees that surrounded the town rose in the distance. But even though they rivaled the Sentinels in size, they lacked the overwhelming presence of the boundary trees.

Bruce looked away an instant before her eyes flicked in his direction, but she could still feel him looking at her.

*Do you sense anything out there in the trees?* she asked when they entered the woods.

*Sort of,* he answered, closing his eyes to better concentrate. *But they're not exactly like the ones near the school, are they?*

*I don't think so,* she answered, then added, *it's more like they're living memories.*

*Or maybe they're partially here and partially somewhere else,* he mused, opening his eyes again.

*I was scared of them the first time I was here. They were curious about my mother and me. You can see them best by looking at something nearby. They like to tease you by hanging out at the edge of your vision.*

She felt the crowds around the lake before she saw them. It had been a while since she'd been around so many strangers, and her abilities hadn't been as strong back then. She tightened her shields and felt both her mother and Bruce do the same.

Had it really been less than a year since she and her mother had come limping into town with the Wild Hunt hot on their trail? It felt like her life had begun that day, and everything before was just some strange bedtime story. Not that her time in Nickelville had been particularly normal. But like her mother had said on Thanksgiving, she hadn't really been herself until they'd stopped running. And since Megan couldn't remember a time when they hadn't been doing so, maybe her life really had begun when she found her grandfather and the others. When Emelia pulled off into the abandoned parking lot, Megan noticed that the payphone she'd used to call her grandfather that first time was gone. Even though she couldn't explain why that should affect her so, it made her sad enough that Bruce looked over in concern.

"There's a really good spot on the other side of the lake where we can get away from the crowd," Paul offered, slipping over the side of the truck and opening the tailgate to give Megan a hand down. But before she got there, Jade stepped forward and used the top of his head to steady herself as she jumped down.

"And it just happens to be filled with oyster fossils," Bruce said.

"Ammonites," his brother corrected sheepishly.

"It sounds perfect," Megan said. "Which way do we go?"

"It might have come up in a conversation recently that your grandfather keeps a rowboat locked up over next to the boat slip," the youngest Grimble mentioned casually, pointing at the subject of his interest.

"And during that conversation did the combination of yon lock also come up?" Megan asked, already knowing that her thorough friend wouldn't have mentioned it otherwise.

Bruce fell behind them as they walked toward it.

"Is it going to offend you guys if I just run around the lake?" he asked, eyeing the small craft with trepidation. "That thing isn't very big, and there are four of us."

"No problem Big Brother," Paul said, unlocking the rusty chain and replacing it where it had been for when they returned. "I know you don't like the water. But you do have to admit it will be nice not having to lug the cooler all the way around the lake."

"Want me to come with you?" Megan asked.

"No," Bruce said, still eyeing the boat with distaste. "You're looking

88

forward to it, and I don't want you to miss out on the opportunity just because I'm afraid of the water. See you on the other side." He took off at a brisk jog.

"Don't worry," Jade said, loading the aforementioned cooler into the center of the boat where it wouldn't interfere with steering. "He'll probably get there before we do."

"Is it far?" Megan asked, watching him disappear into the trees that surrounded the water.

"Not really," Paul answered. "Megan, you get to sit at the bow and Jade will take the stern."

"Which is which?" Megan asked. "I know nothing about boats."

"Yes Paul," his sister chided, "We are all impressed that you got your rowing merit badge last summer, now speak in English or I'll accidentally knock you overboard."

"You take all of the fun out of life sometimes," he said sadly. "Please sit in the front of the boat, Megan. My sister will sit at the back, where she will likely hit me in the back of the head several times before we arrive at our destination. I'll sit in the middle where the oar locks are so I can row. Is that English enough for you Big Sis?"

"Adequate," she answered. "I'll push us off. I don't like these shoes anyway."

Megan didn't like the way the small craft reacted to her when she stepped into it, feeling almost like something alive in the way it moved beneath her feet. Soon they were afloat, and though Paul didn't look particularly strong, he clearly knew what he was doing. The old rowboat slid smoothly across the greenish brown water.

Megan understood at once what her mother had meant about the lake. A deep-seated, mildewy funk permeated the air, and the blistering sun overhead rendered it into a gritty, transparent fog that made the loose wisps of her dark hair stick to her bare shoulders. Furthermore, although she hadn't been aware that she could feel the presence of the shadowy creatures hidden in the woods around them, she felt their absence as soon as they began to glide across the surface of the lake. She dimly remembered something from one of the stories her mother had told her as a young child about some magical beings being unable to cross bodies of water. Maybe there was something to that after all.

"Did you put on sunscreen?" Jade asked. "Your pale skin must burn easily."

"Everyone always thinks that," Megan answered with a shrug, "But I've never gotten even a hint of a burn or tan even when I've been out in the sun for hours. What you see is what you get. For the most part heat and cold don't bother me either. This humidity is disgusting though."

Paul soon sweated through the back of his t-shirt as he rowed across the still water. Megan looked over the side, but couldn't see much through the murky green algae that floated in the water.

"Is that an eagle?" Megan asked, looking up when she saw the reflection of a large bird overhead.

"Red tailed hawk," Paul replied, barely glancing up at the sky.

"Are you sure?" Jade teased. "It had a library book in its claws."

"Very funny," Paul said, rowing harder.

"Oh, nice boat McGeehee!" an all too familiar voice squealed.

Megan turned to find Allison astride a paddleboard in a scant green bikini likely chosen for the way it contrasted with her red hair. It was clear from the rich girl's expression that she had neither forgotten nor forgiven the events that led to her mother's expulsion from Nickelville Academy.

"Nice suit, Jones," Jade called. "Must be feeling your mom's unemployment pretty bad if you can't even afford a whole one!"

"Just wait," the angry girl began. Then, seemingly of its own accord, the paddleboard stopped as if it had hit a submerged rock or been halted by some giant invisible hand. Whatever the cause, the board stopped and Allison didn't. Arms windmilling as she fell, the girl went headfirst into the smelly water, mouth open in a suddenly terminated scream.

*Definitely front page,* a familiar voice spoke in Megan's mind.

Standing on the shore, Emelia lowered her camera.

"God, I wish I'd seen that," Bruce said when they told him what he'd missed. "It almost might have been worth riding in that deathtrap."

"I thought for a moment that she couldn't swim," Paul said, already eyeing the exposed fossils. "That girl has some seriously healthy lungs."

"I'm sure her lungs were what caught your attention," Jade teased.

Bruce looked confused.

"Allison wasn't wearing much," Jade explained.

"Ew," Bruce said.

"Come on," Jade teased. "She's evil, but definitely not hard on the eyes."

"Neither is Glenn," Bruce prompted. "So you'd be looking at him in the same situation?"

"Ugg," Jade snorted. "You didn't have to take it that far to make a point. How about you Paul?"

"Can't say I want to see any more of Glenn either. As for the red headed wench, let us just say that Allison does not at this time, nor will she likely *ever* meet the minimum requirements for consideration in my personal life," he answered loftily.

"What if she started playing the violin?" Megan teased. Paul, ever the good sport, looked as if he were giving the question serious consideration. "And you don't have to be sad you missed it Bruce."

"Why?" Jade asked.

"You guys were too busy looking at Allison to notice, but my mom was on shore, and I'm pretty sure she got a picture of it. Knowing her, it will end up in tomorrow's edition of the *Tribune*."

Bruce gave her a suspicious look, to which she responded with a barely perceptible nod.

"I just wish it didn't smell so bad," Jade added. Then she started to laugh.

"What?" Megan asked.

"You would have thought Allison was the one that was afraid of water with the way she was screaming when they pulled her out," Jade chuckled. "I halfway expected Paul to pull us alongside and help."

"The water was only about four feet deep," the scout replied. "She could have just stood up if she wasn't freaking out so bad. But yeah, I would have helped her if that high school guy hadn't pulled her onto his paddleboard."

"He never was one of the sharpest tools in the shed where our grade is concerned," Jade added. "Do you really think mom would let Emelia print them?"

"My mom would never do that, even if the Joneses would have definitely done so had our roles been reversed," Megan replied sadly. "The best you can probably hope for is a nice poster to hang on the dojo wall."

"I could live with that," Jade said, nodding in satisfaction as she helped Bruce unload the cooler while Paul pulled the boat ashore. "We forgot to look for Sam's new food truck."

"I'm sure we'll see it on the way out," Megan said, noticing the raised ridges in the limestone all around them. "Are those the things we came here looking for?"

"Great, aren't they?" Paul answered. "I'm not a scout today, so a couple of the ones back under that overhang are coming home with us tonight. That way they don't take away from the beauty of this spot."

Bruce wasn't winded, but it was a hot day, and he'd just run half the circumference of the lake. He soon had a cold soda in his hand as he leaned against the hull of Azarich's boat. Paul was crawling around on the outcrop, looking at each of the fossils with a critical eye before moving over to look under the overhang. Megan sat down next to her best friend, reaching out to steal a drink of his soda as she did so. When she gave it back, the length of her bare leg came to rest against his, sending a familiar jolt of sensation through her, only to fade instantly from her mind.

"Wouldn't it be easier to get one of the ones out here?" Megan asked, shaking her head to rid herself of the impression that she'd just forgotten something important. "Or are the ones under there better?"

"The best is that one close to the water," he said sadly. "But that one is part of this spot's charm. If I take it, the damage to the rock will spoil the view for everyone who comes here in the future."

"You know as well as I do that someone else will try to get it out eventually and probably break it into pieces when they do," Jade said. "You could argue that you're just saving it."

"You know that's a bunch of crap as well as I do. I'd never be able to enjoy it if I did that. These back under here aren't as big, but I can probably make them look better since they haven't been weathered by the elements as much. Now if I can just get this one out without breaking it."

"You need the small hammer and a chisel, right?" Jade asked, pulling

93

both from the backpack that Paul had brought along.

"What happens if you get it loose and it falls down since you're cutting it from below?" Bruce asked. "Here, let me hold it up while you work."

"Thanks bro," Paul said, moving over a bit so his brother could get an arm into the cramped space. "It's going to take me a bit to get it loose though."

"Just in case," Bruce said, closing his eyes in concentration.

*What are you doing?* Megan sent. In response, he invited her in so she could tag along.

Oblivious to what his brother was doing, Bruce allowed his consciousness to identify the edges of the ammonite where the remnants of its shell met the limestone that encased it. For almost a minute, he strengthened that shell, making it much less likely to shatter, even if it would only remain so for a second. Then with a mental twist and an audible pop, the fossil turned loose from the matrix that encased it and it dropped neatly into his hand.

"I know that outcrop," Azarich said, looking over the fossil. "Tom and I caught several good-sized catfish near there a few years back. One of those big trees had washed into the shallows after a storm. It was one of our favorite spots before they dredged the lake and took it out."

"Remember the one we dug out of the creek behind your house?" Mr. Green asked.

"Ours was a lot bigger," the librarian observed, "But I've never seen one with this much crisp detail."

"Is ours still on display in the library?" Azarich asked.

"Yes," Paul answered. "I used to get into trouble with my teachers for sneaking away from class to go look at it. It's what got me interested in fossils in the first place."

"Is that so?" the librarian asked, pleased.

"And it came out of the ground like this?" Ben Grimble asked, having been on more than a few of his son's expeditions. "This one looks better than when you've spent ten hours picking out all of the debris with a dental pick. You can even see the suture marks."

"I know," Paul said reverently. "I sure wish I knew what I did differently this time."

Megan flashed Bruce a smile.

"Would you fine people enjoy some company?" Sam asked, walking up with the heavy-duty camp chair Jade had ordered for him after he killed the third of the smaller ones in as many outings. Most of the world just wasn't made with people Sam's size in mind. He had an unopened bag of blue cotton candy in his hand.

"Did you finally get tired of feeding the whole town?" Mr. Green asked.

"What's the verdict on the truck?" Emelia asked, looking up as he put his chair down next to hers. "Did you make enough off of this to pay it off?"

"At the prices he was charging?" Mr. Harris snorted. "Did you even try to turn a profit, Sam?"

"Profit isn't the only important thing on days like this," Sam answered wearily. "Yes, I earned a profit, but no, I didn't make much of one. Most of the town is either working reduced hours at the factory, or they've got people sick with whatever is going around. We all needed this to make us feel like something was going right. And in my experience, food that is both tasty and inexpensive goes a long way toward fulfilling that need."

"You at least spit in Allison's food, right?" Bruce joked.

"No need," the big man said with a pointed look at Emelia who was smiling up at the stars. "A little bird told me our young friend fell into the lake."

*More like a little squirrel,* Megan sent.

"Our Sam is too good to do something like that," Mrs. Harris said and Megan could feel the pleasure that this simple statement evoked in her big friend.

It occurred to Megan that their big friend had probably been just as lonely as she'd been before coming to Nickelville. After all, she'd always been able to count on her mother to be there when she needed someone. From the sound of it, Sam was the last of his people. His grandfather had died before Emelia left for college, and he never spoke of anyone else.

"As much as I'd like to stay and see the show, I'd better get back to the station," Mr. Grimble said, handing the fossil back to Paul.

"Has it gotten any better since the town started having its own fireworks show?" Azarich asked.

"There are considerably fewer fires," Bruce's dad answered, brushing off the crumbs from the food he'd eaten. "But somewhere out there, at this very moment, some drunk idiot is lighting cherry bombs in his hand and throwing them."

"You're kidding," Mr. Green said.

"I wish I was," Mr. Grimble replied. "I should be home sometime after two. Most of the drunks will either be passed out or out of fireworks by then."

"I can't believe you've still got to go in even though it's not your shift," Jade complained. "If they're not going to pay you, then they can't ask you to work."

"They didn't ask him," Paul reminded her, running his finger along the inner curve of the ammonite. "He's doing it because he won't be able to forgive himself if they need him and he's not there."

"Sometimes you act a lot more like a respectable adult than I do," Mr. Grimble said, affectionately ruffling his youngest son's hair.

Just before the sun disappeared behind what could be seen of the horizon through the trees, the hidden world of the woods broke cover and began to reveal itself. Although only Megan, Bruce, Emelia and Sam could see them, the arrival of the woodland creatures marked the end of their easy banter.

Megan started when she noticed the strange creature climbing up the edge of Sam's chair. Although it looked nothing like the gnomes that people placed in front of their houses, that was the first thing she thought of when she saw it. It had wrinkled gray skin and several inches of white hair growing from its head, and it moved with the slow, methodical movements of a tree sloth. Megan couldn't tell if it was really old or if that was just the nature of such things. She tried not to stare, but her behavior still drew Bruce's attention as well.

Megan realized it was female from the makeshift dress made from mossy bits of tree bark. As she watched, it perched on the top of Sam's chair. Although he hadn't yet looked as if he was aware of his visitor, he reached into the bag of cotton candy in his lap, tore off a small wisp and absently held it up. The thing crawled over to sit on the armrest of his chair and took it before starting to nibble daintily with its sharp teeth.

*What is she?* Bruce asked.

*My grandfather called them helpers,* Sam answered. *If they ever had another name, I don't know what it might have been. As far as I know she's the only one left.*

*That's sad,* Megan sent.

*I'm surprised that she came out with so many people around,* Emelia added.

*She likes the fireworks,* Sam explained.

The helper reached out to tug gently on the edge of Sam's sleeve, and he tore off another pinch of the cotton candy and handed it to her. Then she looked back and made a series of clicking noises that made Paul look up from the fossil in his lap. No one else reacted, and he soon lost interest in what might have caused the sound.

Bruce noticed something moving below Megan's chair and started to get up.

*It won't hurt her,* Sam assured him. *It's just the helper's mount.*

The thing that crept out from under Megan's chair looked like the unlikely offspring of an armadillo and a mongoose. It crept forward, low to the ground like a young dog that knows it's been caught misbehaving. Long, broad ears folded back over its back as it slunk forward.

The helper shook her head in clear disapproval, but smiled anyway, showing a mouth turned blue from the candy.

Taking this as permission to come closer, the mount came to his feet, moving quickly to Sam's leg, which it quickly climbed and came to rest in his lap next to the bag of cotton candy. Then it shook itself and the rustle of the scales across its back made Paul look up again with a frown.

*The mounts only live for five or six years,* Sam explained, giving it some of the candy. *And this one is probably no more than six or seven months old.*

*Can I touch it?* Bruce asked.

*I wouldn't,* Emelia warned. *They only act tame around Sam, and they have extremely sharp teeth.*

When the sun finally set, a group of children ran past along the water's edge, sparklers casting off magnesium cackles that followed after them like will-o-the-wisps. Azarich offered to go and buy some for his granddaughter and her friends, but they'd burned the last of their energy in the hot sun returning from the opposite side of the lake. Now, with stomachs full from Sam's truck, they enjoyed a breeze that came at them from across the still water of the lake, even if it did smell bad. Megan didn't actually see the first fireworks explode over the lake. She'd closed her eyes, allowing the feel of friends and family to saturate her senses. When she did notice, it wasn't the flash of red behind her closed eyelids that told her it had begun. It was the excitement of the children all around her that made her breath catch in her chest and almost cry with the purity of their joy. Even at her young age, Megan knew that there were more kinds of magic than what she and her family practiced, and what she felt now was far rarer and more precious.

By the time they gathered up their things to go, the cotton candy was gone and so were the helper and her mount.

# Chapter XI: Honeysuckle Whispers

"What is that sweet smell?" Megan asked as she and the Grimbles looked out over the oddly ominous expanse of Guarded Wood.

"Honeysuckle," Bruce answered. The breeze had blown strands of her hair across her face, and he badly wanted to brush them back into place.

"You can suck the nectar from the base of the flowers," Jade added.

"Not from those, you can't," Paul said, turning an uncomfortable eye away from the woods. "I don't even like smelling anything that comes from that place."

"Where's that?" Megan asked. It wasn't like Paul to dislike anything except maybe confined underground places.

"You've seen it," Bruce said, turning to look out across the other side of the tower. "See the house on the other side of yours where the road ends?"

"The one that's covered in all of the vines?"

"That's the one," he agreed. "The white flowers on those vines are what you're smelling."

"But why don't you like them?" she asked Paul.

"That place is haunted," he said quietly, looking quickly back toward the woods as if looking at the forbidden place might somehow give it more strength over him than it already had.

"You told me that once before," Megan prompted. "Why do you say that? From what I can see it looks a lot like my house."

"It's a bad place," Paul insisted, heading for the ladder. "But we could go to the dentist's house if you want."

"Where is that?" Megan asked.

"It's the next one down the road after our place," Jade explained. "It's pretty cool, or at least it was. We haven't been in a few years."

"The abandoned houses on this road are the only thing our dad is stricter about than Mom," Bruce added. "He thinks someone should come and pull them all down."

"Why?" Megan asked, "I think they're kind of cool."

"There used to be a lot more of them in town," Jade explained. "But a kid was killed a few years back when one collapsed on her. Ever since then our Dad has been afraid we'll get hurt in one."

"Which of course made Jade and Paul desperate to explore the ones on our street," Bruce said, following Megan to the ladder.

"Except for Honeysuckle House," Paul called from below.

"You've never been inside of it?" Megan asked when they reached the main floor. "Both my mother and grandfather said I should avoid it, too. That still doesn't explain why you think it's haunted."

"It…" he said, looking embarrassed. "It whispers."

Megan looked to Bruce to see if this was some sort of joke.

"I've never heard anything," Jade said with a shrug. "But I trust my brother."

"You've never gone inside either?" Megan asked.

"Nope," Jade answered. "He made me promise not to ever go inside, and the two of us never break our promises to each other."

102

"That's right," Paul agreed. "Promises should never be broken. They help define who we are."

"There you go sounding all wise again," Bruce teased, although something about the subject made him uncomfortable. Perhaps it was the similarities between lies and broken promises. Or maybe it was the fact that in spite of how close they'd become, he still held secrets from his brother and sister.

"You guys seriously can't hear that?" Paul said, looking in the direction of Megan's house and the one beyond. "I swear I can hear a voice whispering just low enough that I can't understand what it's saying."

"All I can hear is your mom's windchimes," Megan admitted. "I've always liked that sound."

The dentist's house wasn't too far past the place where the Grimbles had built their home. It was hard to tell if the paint had been white or if the sun had bleached what little remained to the same featureless gray of the bare wood. Its porch wrapped around two sides of the house like most of the ones on the road, but unlike the McGeehee place and its vine-encased neighbor, this forgotten dwelling lacked any sort of faded grandeurs.

Corrugated iron sheets skirted the crawl space beneath the house. A few of the windows had been boarded up, and Bruce could somehow tell that these had occurred while it was inhabited. A few of the others still held their glass, but most had been broken by the storms that swept in and out of the past like the wheeling flocks of birds that even now passed overhead.

"Come on," Jade said, taking Megan by the hand. "There's a room with one of those old dentist chairs in the center and shelves filled with those jars where they kept medicine."

"Apothecary jars," Bruce said absently. There was an oddly reminiscent emotion coming from his friend even though he was careful not to intrude on her thoughts.

"Dad is always worried that there might be addicts holed up here," Jade added.

"The house is empty," Megan said quietly. "But you do have to worry about addicts in abandoned buildings. An awful lot of mentally disturbed people wind up in such places as well. Especially the old ones who've become lost even to themselves and fallen through the cracks."

At last Bruce understood her feelings and how insensitive they were being toward her. His brother and sister might not know about her past, but she'd trusted him enough to share it, and he should have protected her better than this.

"Maybe Dad is right," he said, stepping in front of Jade and blocking her path to the front entrance from which the door hung open on one hinge.

"Come on," Paul said. "You've been in here loads of times. Besides, without being able to go into Guarded Wood it's not like we've got anything else to do."

*It's okay,* she sent, reaching out and taking his hand. *It's like a history lesson. And I know you don't think less of me for having lived in places worse than this.*

So they walked through rooms where the plaster had fallen in chunks from the ceiling. Dry leaves stood several inches thick on the floor, covering it in a thick layer of crumbly debris. It was worse than Bruce remembered. Or maybe it was the awakening of his senses that told him that this place would soon lose its war with the elements and collapse like several others nearby had already done.

"He was also the town barber," Megan said, when she saw the chair.

"What makes you think that?" Paul asked.

Megan shrugged in response, but Bruce knew she could see the past all around her. He was going to ask her to show him when he noticed a great big blank spot in their immediate future.

*What is it?* Megan asked, feeling his mood change.

*You and I are going into the Honeysuckle House,* he answered. *But I can't see why or what happens there.*

*Paul is right, but the place doesn't just whisper. Something there is calling to me.*

*Why didn't I hear it?* Bruce asked.

*Why do you see the future while I see the past?* she countered.

"This is cool," Bruce said at last, "But something is starting to mess with my allergies."

"No problem," Paul said. "This room was the best part, and I don't like how much the roof has started leaking since the last time we were here. I don't think I want to go upstairs and take a chance of the place falling in on us."

"Yeah," Jade agreed. "I think we already used up all of the adventure this place had to offer. Now it's just sad."

"I couldn't agree more," Megan whispered.

"I'm going over to see Megan," Bruce called down the hall to where Jade and Paul had retreated to clean up some of the rocks they'd picked up before their banishment from Guarded Wood.

"Give her some space," Jade called back. "You seriously just saw her twenty minutes ago."

"She wanted to borrow another book," he lied, again wishing that he could just tell them the truth. When they didn't respond, he slipped quietly out the back door, realizing that he should have at least grabbed a book in case they'd questioned him closer. Then, feeling her already gone from her home, he sprinted all the way to the back of Honeysuckle House, where he found her waiting for him.

"Why did you run?" she asked when he came closer. "I can't go in without you. I promised."

"Where you go," he panted in response.

"We're a package deal," she agreed before turning toward the overgrown structure before her. "Paul is right."

"I can feel it too now," he said.

The structure rose above them, higher than he'd thought now that they were standing in its shadow. It was hard to tell with vines covering most of its surfaces, but he thought it might have one more story than the McGeehee place.

"Can you see anything at all?" she asked, walking toward a place near its base where the back porch should be. Not big enough to be called an opening, the vines thinned there, suggesting a darkened space beyond.

"We come out in about forty-five minutes," he answered.

"I can feel that this place has something to do with my family," she said. "I'll know more when we get inside."

"How do you know that?" he asked.

"There's more than just echoes here," she answered with a shrug. "It's hard to explain. It's like this house has a memory of its own. Two children lived here. They swung on a swing that used to hang from that tree."

Bruce glanced up and could see where the rope had long ago been consumed by the bark as the tree grew around it. He was tempted to lower his shields and let her show him the past that lived on in her visions. But even though he knew they'd come out unscathed, something within the house felt corrupt, like the fetid air of something spoiled. In short, his instincts argued that he should strengthen his shields, not lower them.

Overgrown paving stones led to the opening in the honeysuckle, almost completely reclaimed by the parched grass so that only their centers could be seen. As they drew nearer, the darkened space in the vines parted to reveal steps leading up to the porch, though the bottom one had rotted through and fallen, making the next step difficult.

The back porch had never been screened in like the one where Azarich had grown up, although the curtain of vines served the same purpose to much greater effect. An old whitewashed rocking chair sat next to the door to what Bruce suspected to be the kitchen. But unlike the rotten step, everything enclosed by the curtain of fragrant vines looked like it had been left behind no more than a year or two previous.

"Something is at work here," Bruce said, pointing at a knitted garment that hung from the arm of the rocker. "I think this place is as old as the town itself and has been abandoned for well over a century at least. Rats or moths should have eaten that shawl long ago."

"All of the windows are intact," Megan added. "This doesn't feel like an abandoned house."

Bruce reached out and laid his hand on one of the columns. Through it he could feel the way the house had been constructed, and how well it had held up since its abandonment.

"It feels more like a lair," she whispered.

"This is so weird," he said. "The quality of construction here is much better than it is at your place, even though I can tell that they were both constructed at the same time. They might look similar, but this house was constructed with every luxury of its time. And in spite of the way it looks from the road, it's perfectly sound. I don't even think the roof leaks."

"Let's do this," Megan said, reaching out to open the door. It resisted her at first before giving way. When it did, air rushed in with them as if the interior had existed within some sort of vacuum. Deep inside, a sigh passed through the house as if it were waking.

"You weren't kidding," Megan said as her eyes adjusted, her voice echoing in the vast space beyond. "Our place is nothing compared to this."

An enormous cast iron stove took up one wall, inlaid with ornate ceramic tiles. A heavy wooden table took up the center of the room, lined by two sturdy benches. A huge butcher's block stood off to one side, bracketed by wicked looking instruments for carving and cleaving. An iron cauldron hung on an adjustable crane that was set into the side of the fireplace. The fire that had last burned there remained in the form of the ash and charcoal it had created, once again looking as if it had only been left unattended for a few days at most.

"Look at the wood bin," Bruce whispered, pointing to a space in the wall that was filled to capacity with lengths of wood cut to length for the oven. "That wood should have rotted away half a century ago. This all looks like someone just cleaned up after making dinner and never came back. But where are all of the pots and pans?"

Following a wisp of the past that only she could see, Megan walked over to the corner where a huge velvet curtain that still bore the hooks by which it had been hung covered a lumpy mass. When she pulled it aside, the brass of the missing pots and pans gleamed in the soft light that filtered in from the still open back door.

"Why hasn't anyone stolen this?" she asked, "This stuff is worth a fortune."

A loud thump sounded deeper in the house, possibly upstairs.

"She's trying to scare us off," Megan whispered.

"She?" he whispered back.

"Yes," she answered. "Now that we're inside, I can feel a hint of what she's doing. It's not like our abilities though. I get the feeling what she can do is much more specific."

Beyond the kitchen lay a huge dining room lined with ornate china cabinets, sideboards, and a much nicer table than the one that they'd seen in the kitchen. All of the windows save one were covered in thick velvet curtains, and that one let in just enough light to keep them from needing to create their own just yet. A thick luxurious carpet covered the hardwood floors. Two brass chandeliers hung overhead, still holding the candles that had once lit the room.

*I can't tell if the lack of dust and cobwebs are something she's doing or if she's actually cleaning the place,* Megan sent.

*I have no idea either,* he answered, *I still don't feel any magic here, but something is certainly holding the passage of time at bay here.*

All of the china cabinets stood open, and their contents had been stacked at the far end of the table, though many of the stacks had been knocked over, spilling the shattered remnants of the fine china across the table and floor. As the two of them neared the head of the table, they could see that each dish still held the encrusted remains of some long-eaten meal.

"If she's been cleaning everything up," Bruce said, looking over the mess before them. "Why did she leave this?"

A series of stomping footsteps reverberated through the floor overhead.

*I don't think she likes it when we talk out loud. Those footsteps*

109

*remind me of the Academy. Gross,* Megan sent when they reached the end of the table. *Something bad happened here.*

*Can you show me?*

She reluctantly reached out and took his hand, opening a window into the past for him in which a huge man sat in the ornate chair, shoveling food into his mouth as fast as his hands could move. But even as they watched, he grew thinner and thinner. Plates stacked up around him as his servants tried to keep up. In the end, he was little more than a skeletal husk in soiled finery that hung in tatters from his emaciated frame.

*There are legends about this, especially in Ireland during the famine,* Bruce sent. *This was the punishment for not helping to feed the hungry. I can't remember all of this legend very well. It seems like there was something about grass as well. Let's move deeper into the house, I don't like this room.*

The side door led into a mosaic tiled foyer that in turn led into the main living area. An ornate mirror had once hung on the wall opposite the door, but it had been smashed with such force that only its gilded gold frame and a few fragments of dark mirrored glass could be found on the floor.

Large vases containing mummified floral arrangements stood atop tables, and marble statues filled nooks set into the walls. Framed paintings covered the walls, though it was difficult to see them in the dim light. But like the previous rooms, neither dust nor cobweb hinted at the house's long abandonment.

*She's definitely upstairs* Megan sent, crossing to the exquisitely carved staircase. Carpet muffled the sound of her feet on the treads, but judging from the rustling sounds above, whatever resided up there could still hear her approach.

110

He followed, even though he didn't want to do so. Then something caught his eye.

*Wait,* he sent. *I can feel something weird about the hearth.*

Benches clad in embroidered satin lined the hall leading into the main hall where the wealthy family would have retreated in the evenings after dinner. Ornately styled floral wallpapers clad the walls, but it was the darkened space above the massive fireplace that drew Bruce into the room.

Passing beneath the gallery overlook where the stairs his friend had been climbing only a moment before led, he strode up to the hearth, held his hand up before him and summoned a cold flame to illuminate the shadowed recess. Megan gasped.

At first glance, it looked as if the man and woman in the portrait had been disfigured by the ravages of black mold, but upon closer inspection, mold couldn't have so thoroughly transformed the man into the skeletal image of a living corpse or so perfectly covered the blond woman's mouth as if with a gag. Although her eyes showed no signs of alteration, they brimmed with terror.

*You're right,* he sent. *Something horrible definitely happened here. Are you sure we shouldn't just leave?*

*We can't,* Megan sent. *She's trapped here, and we have to set her free.*

So he followed her up the stairs this time into the cold air of the upper floor that should have been stifling with the heat of the Texas summer.

Just enough green light filtered in through a skylight overhead to reveal a multitude of small portraits along the walls. Megan stopped suddenly, looking back at one and summoning a light.

*I've seen that woman before,* she sent, pointing at a stern-faced woman dressed in the finery of the time. She held a baby in her arms and a young girl sat next to her. *She was in a watercolor painting that was in my room when we first came to Nickelville. I didn't like having her glare at me, so I swapped it for one of the ones with an eagle in it.*

*I think I've seen the man that she's with in this other one before somewhere,* Bruce added. *This is so weird.*

At the top of the stairs, they passed three bedrooms, each as ornate and free of decay as the rest of the house with one consistent exception. The mirrors over the vanities in each had been pulverized like the one at the foot of the stairs.

When they came to the master bedroom, they could both feel the presence emanating from within. Bruce hurried to enter ahead of Megan, knowing even as he did that it was a futile gesture since she had proven herself to be far more capable than he of keeping them safe.

Megan lit the candles in the sconces with a thought to better see what the room held. Once again, nothing within seemed out of place with the exception of numerous broken mirrors. The carvings on the mahogany bed looked too crisp to be real, making Bruce think of the library doors at the Academy. Standing directly over the hearth below, the fireplace likely shared the same chimney and held an odd collection of children's toys on its mantle.

A huge steamer trunk of the sort once used by the wealthy to transport their extensive wardrobes stood on its side in one corner with the door slightly ajar. In the candlelight that Megan summoned, Bruce saw that a long irregular hole had been broken along the leading edge with fragments of wood poking out as if something had forced its way out from the inside. Through that hole, two eyes reflected from its darkened interior.

"Please don't come any closer," a voice whispered from within. "I don't want to hurt you."

"It's okay," Megan said, moving over to sit on the padded dressing bench that stood at the foot of the bed. "You won't hurt us unless you really want to."

"You don't understand," the voice pleaded. "You don't know what I've done."

"Your husband locked you in that trunk for reasons I can't quite see," Megan began.

"I lost our baby, and the doctor said I'd never carry another," the voice whispered with a bit more confidence. "And it was a girl. He didn't want any girls."

"And he didn't let you out," Megan continued.

"No matter how much I begged," the voice added.

"But you didn't die," Megan said.

"No," the voice agreed. "I changed."

"After you clawed your way out," Megan continued.

"It took years," the voice added.

"You saw that he'd grown fat while you starved," Megan said.

"And I wanted him to suffer as I had," she added.

"And then he started to lose weight," Bruce said, making the eyes dart to him.

"No matter how much he ate," the voice continued with a hint of satisfaction.

"In the end he was little more than bones," Megan said. "But you made him do something with papers."

"I made him leave both this house and the servant's quarters to the ones who served us," she explained. "To the only ones who tried to help me. But how do you know these things? This passed from memory long before your birth."

"Megan can see echoes of the past," Bruce explained.

"Truly?" the voice asked. Skeletal fingers tipped in blood-caked nails slipped from the trunk as if she might come forth.

"Yes," Megan agreed. "What was the name of the family who served you?"

"MacGeehee," the voice answered. "And I can smell them in you, and my husband's kin as well. But there is something more…"

For a short time it seemed that they'd run out of things to say until Megan stood and walked over to the trunk.

"I beg, you," the voice pleaded, and the fingers disappeared back into the shadowed interior of the trunk.

"But I have to see you before I can help," Megan said. "You are not the first of your kind that I have met."

"Tell me!" the voice pleaded, and the lid opened another inch.

"He was a child of probably six," Megan began, "or he might have appeared that way because that's how old I was at the time."

"Yes?" the voice prompted.

"A man had taken him from his family and locked him away in a root cellar," Megan told her, "because the boy had seen the man steal from the foreman at the factory where the whole town worked. He left the boy there in the dark to waste away and be forgotten."

"And he wasted away," the voice said, "but he didn't die."

"No," Megan agreed, "Like you, he changed. When he freed himself many years later, it was his captor who began to starve."

"I liked that part," the voice said. "And I think that's why I've been punished to live on like this. Vengeance might have been my right for what he did to me, but I shouldn't have enjoyed it so much."

"I wasn't able to stay there for very long," Megan said. "But he was

nice, almost like a friend."

"You weren't afraid?" the voice asked.

"I've always been afraid," Megan explained, "But I was never afraid of him. Maybe that's why he changed back."

Now the fingers returned and a weathered, skeletal face moved into view though still remaining inside the trunk. The eyes were bright blue even though the hair had mostly fallen out, leaving only a patchwork of blond clumps.

"How did he change?" she asked with longing.

"He became himself again," Megan said, stepping forward and opening the door. Inside stood the living corpse of the woman they'd seen in the portrait over the mantle downstairs. She wore an old gray dressing gown, and the longer parts of her remaining hair had been tied back with a blue ribbon that perfectly matched her eyes.

"Please don't look at what I've become," she whispered, dropping her eyes in shame.

"I see you as you were," Megan said, reaching out and taking the wraith by the wrist and pulling her free of her prison. "Your guilt and loathing have bound you to this form. But I can see who you really are, and you are beautiful."

"No," the wraith said, trying to pull away. "It's my punishment. You shouldn't touch me. I'm unclean. I'll make you sick."

"There is no punishment," Megan said, "because you have done nothing wrong."

"But my husband..."

"Deserved far worse than the judgement you passed on him," Megan said, and something about her words echoed through Bruce's subconscious.

Then Megan took the wraith in her arms and held her close. The woman struggled at first, likely worried that she'd infect her with the same wasting malady that had consumed her husband. But then Bruce felt Megan summon images from the past, images of the woman laughing and smiling.

Bruce wasn't sure when he'd risen from where he'd sat on the padded bench, lowered his shields and taken them both in his arms, bolstering Megan's magic with his own. But when the exhaustion overtook him and he staggered back again, Megan held a beautiful woman in her arms.

It took the woman a while for the worst of the long, infertile sobs to pass through her, but when they did, her eyes opened wide in amazement. She looked first at her hands, which no longer retained the damage of her escape from the steamer trunk. Then she ran her hands in wonder up from her stomach and across the contours of her body to her face. She looked quickly toward the shattered mirror and her face fell in disappointment.

"Here," Bruce said, calling a tarnished silver tray that still rested on the dressing table to him. With a pass of his hand, it gleamed in the light from the cold fire that still hung in the air over Megan's shoulder.

"The woman took it from him and looked eagerly at her reflection. "I'm not a monster anymore," she cried.

"You never were," Megan assured her. "Let's get you out of this place."

"Oh no," the woman said, shaking her head violently. "Guarded Wood will claim me if I set foot outside of this house."

"Not if you've been bound in service," Megan said in that strange voice she sometimes used when talking about things she had no way of knowing.

"Then I freely pledge myself to your service," the woman said quickly. "It's only fitting since it is your family that once served me."

"Can I ask you a question?" Megan asked. "There are pictures down the hall of a stern-faced woman. Who is she?"

"Her name was Crina," the woman answered. "And she was my

mother-in-law."

"I think I'm descended from her too," Megan said. "There was a picture in my house of her. Her name was Kennemur wasn't it."

"Yes," the woman agreed. "And I think it's time I repair my lapse in etiquette. Megan McGeehee and Bruce Grimble, I have heard your names on the wind often while I dozed in that trunk, and I beg you to ask Paul for his forgiveness. It was not my intention to frighten him or Jade. And even though I will never speak the name of my husband's family again, it would please me if you called me Charlotte."

"We are pleased to meet you Charlotte," Bruce and Megan said in unison.

"So what do you want of me, Megan, since I am bound to your service?"

"I want you to go out into the world and find some of the happiness you've been denied," Megan ordered.

"I think I can do that," Charlotte said. "But know that I will never be too far away to return should you have need of me." Then the beautiful woman with the bright eyes turned to dust before them and left her prison behind.

# Chapter XII: Treetop Confessions

One magical morning the three McGeehees went to the top of the tower to watch the sun rise over Guarded Wood. Each sipped the coffee they'd brought up in Azarich's old green thermos. In spite of the heat, a misty shroud that would have looked more at home over some secluded rainforest than in the middle of Texas entwined the trees and on occasion hinted at movements not meant to be seen.

"A man could get used to a view like this," Azarich said, forgetting to drink the hot, sweet liquid for several silent moments after the first light began to color the clouds.

"You wouldn't mind coming up here sometimes?" Megan asked. "There's no swing, but it's still pretty nice."

"Now that I know this view is up here, you might have trouble getting me to leave."

It was a good morning, Megan thought, but she could tell her mother's thoughts never left the discussion that would follow afterward.

"Now that we're up here and the show's over," he said, turning to face them. "Are you two ready to tell me what's been bothering you all morning? Does it have something to do with Guarded Wood looking like it's about a hundred miles across instead of two?"

Megan spit out some of her coffee in surprise, and Azarich offered his handkerchief.

"I guess Bruce was right about him almost figuring it out himself," Emelia said.

"What does the Grimble boy have to do with this?" he asked, raising a white eyebrow in an almost perfect imitation of his daughter.

"I guess there's no turning back now," Emelia said, putting her cup down on the rail. "Do you remember telling me about how my mother often knew things that she had no way of knowing and sometimes saw things that you couldn't?"

"Yes," he said reluctantly. "The women in her family had pretty much always been like that."

"I'll bet there were other things that you never mentioned," Megan said quietly, "weren't there?"

He shrugged and then nodded.

"I'm tired of hiding things from you," Emelia said just before she held her palm up, took a deep breath and then summoned a small cold flame in her palm.

Azarich gasped, stepping involuntarily back against the rail and knocking the cup off.

Without thinking, Megan reached out with her mind and caught it, bringing it speeding back to her hand and sending half a cup of hot, sticky coffee all over the upper part of her shirt. She sputtered in disgust.

Azarich and Emelia stared at the mess in surprise then burst into laughter as Megan tried to regain her composure. But as irritated as she was by what had just happened, she couldn't resist the onslaught of their combined mirth. Even though the pitch was different, their resemblance left little doubt that they were father and daughter.

"That would have been so much more impressive if it had gone the way it did in my head," Megan giggled. "Luckily I have another shirt in my duffle." She put the cup down on the floor and started to descend the ladder.

"I guess you knew what you were doing after all when you packed that thing," Emelia teased.

Megan glared at her in response.

Down below, she ducked into the changing room and peeled off the coffee laden shirt. The only problem with drinking so much cream and sugar in the coffee was that it made a truly sticky mess when you spilled it. She could still hear them talking as she returned.

"I've wanted to tell you for so long," Emelia whispered, holding her father tightly. Feeling left out, Megan quickly joined them. In the years to come, it would be a memory she revisited often.

"So it's not just bending spoons and stuff like that?" her grandfather asked.

"Why would anyone want to bend spoons?" Megan asked, not understanding what that could possibly accomplish. Azarich smiled.

"You can communicate without talking too, can't you?"

"Yes," they both answered.

"That explains quite a bit," he said. "You cover it pretty well most of the time, but lawyers have a good nose for sniffing out omissions. Sam and Bruce are in this too?"

They nodded.

"But what was it you said about Bruce knowing that I was on to you?"

"Bruce can see the future," Emelia said, "Which has proved extremely useful on occasion."

"He's still learning to understand what he sees though," Megan added. "And it doesn't always work when he wants it to. A lot of the time it just leaves him really frustrated and confused."

"I don't know if that's a gift or a curse," Azarich said. "How far can he see?"

"I'm not positive," Megan said. "Maybe a month or so." Azarich seemed satisfied with this line of questioning and moved on.

"Does this have anything to do with why you were gone for so long?" he asked his daughter. Megan held her breath, wanting answers to that line of questions more than anything.

"I don't want to hold anything else back from you," Emelia said slowly, choosing her words carefully, "But as Bruce has become so fond of reminding us, sometimes things have to be done at a particular moment and in a very specific order to get the desired outcome."

"Wait a minute," Megan gasped, revelation washing over her, "You're following some sort of foresight, aren't you?"

"I am so proud of you," Emelia whispered, looking deep into her daughter's eyes.

"That's not an answer," Megan said, hoping that she'd get more, but knowing all the while that she wouldn't.

"I found others similar to me," Emelia answered her father's question at last.

"You were being hunted when you came back," Azarich pressed, making Megan realize just how perceptive the pleasant old man she called Grandfather would have been in a courtroom.

Emelia's lips pressed into a thin line, but she nodded.

"The Wild Hunt," Megan said, making Emelia frown further. "We call them the Huntsmen."

"And who are these people?" he asked. When Emelia wouldn't answer, he looked at Megan, who just shrugged.

"Now you know just about as much as I do," Megan said. "We can feel them when they catch my scent, which is why we've moved all over the country. The only place they don't seem to be able to find us is here in Nickelville. That's why we never leave town."

"Does this have something to do with her father?" Azarich asked, and the way he zeroed in on what Megan most wanted to know made her wonder if perhaps the ability to read minds hadn't come to her from both sides of the family.

"Yes," Emelia answered. "But please don't ask anything else, I won't jeopardize all we've been through up to this point by saying more. Just know that I badly want to share the burden of this knowledge. I don't keep this from you out of spite. It's just the way it has to be for a little while longer."

"So what do we do if these evil huntsmen come here looking for you?" Azarich asked.

"They're not evil," Emelia said, walking to the ladder and starting down. "There was a time when they loved me almost as much as I love them." And then she was gone.

Shortly before Emelia started down the ladder, Bruce and Sam walked down the nearby trail that led into Guarded Wood. Both felt nervous, but for different reasons. Sam took the advice of his grandfather to stay out of these woods seriously, and it was only at the urging of this boy with the gift of foresight that he did so now. Bruce on the other hand, felt as if he were walking across a narrow bridge where one misstep could be disastrous. It was time for Sam Wise and the hermit known to most as Old Man Biggerstaff to meet. However, the big man was almost inseparable from Emelia, and Bruce knew from the visions that it would be disastrous for her to meet August at this time.

As far as he could tell, he'd successfully threaded the needle, and they should be within the safety of Guarded Wood before Emelia lost her focus on the conversation with August and paid more attention to her surroundings.

Bruce felt dishonest about making his friend think that Azarich had to be told now. It would have actually been several more weeks before the old lawyer allowed himself to believe the impossible possible and confront his daughter. But if Bruce waited for things to play out naturally, his own mother would have become an issue and brought Emelia and August together too soon. On days like this, he almost missed when his biggest problem had been avoiding the Terrible Trio.

"Care to share?" Sam asked.

"Just thinking about how complicated it is trying to steer all of our lives onto paths that don't hurt us," Bruce said. "And then thinking that I must have a complete god complex to think that I have any right to do so without sharing everything I know with the people involved."

"You took the words right out of my mouth, my young friend," Sam said, frowning.

"The problem is that the act of telling someone what is going to happen often causes negative consequences that can't be avoided. For example, if I hadn't planned this meeting so carefully, Emelia would have attacked August."

"Why would she do that?" Sam asked, stopping where he stood in the path, unwilling to continue until Bruce explained.

"I have no idea," Bruce exclaimed, throwing his hands up into the air in frustration. "Just because I can see what will happen doesn't mean I always get any information about things like motivations. I just see that one thing somehow leads to another. And in the case of her attacking him, so many different possible futures overlap each other that I've got no idea how to interpret them. I'm just assuming that since there don't appear to be any bad outcomes if she meets him later, it means that it's some sort of misunderstanding."

"That's a lot to keep up with for someone so young," Sam said with concern.

"That's not even all," Bruce said, suddenly realizing that he needed to get all of this off his chest, and that he'd needed this day to happen this way as much for his own sake as for August's. "You know how you can miss something if you're looking the wrong direction?"

"Of course," Sam answered.

"Sometimes big things can slip past because I was focused somewhere else. Like when Paul got lost in the woods. I have no idea when his future went haywire because I never actually looked at him that way. Now it's an unreadable mess, and I have no idea when that started because I was focused on the girl next door."

"You didn't mean to say that last part, did you?" Sam asked, smiling.

Bruce knew his blush was answer enough as he started walking again and turned the corner into the clearing.

"Don't worry," August said from where he was sitting on a boulder. "I won't tell her."

"I still can't believe this was the best future I had to choose from," Bruce muttered irritably. "August, this is Sam Wise. Sam, this is August."

August rose to his feet with the help of the gnarled staff he carried.

"I am pleased to meet you August," Sam said, walking up and extending a huge hand to the hermit who took it without hesitation. "Is there a last name? Our young friend says it's not Biggerstaff, which I admit to having always thought to be an odd surname."

"I'm pleased to meet you as well. Like yours, my people weren't terribly big on surnames, though I could take a page from your book so to say. August Baggins does have a certain *ring* to it."

"Oh, I'm going to like this man," Sam said with a wide grin, glancing over at Bruce.

"He has his moments," Bruce conceded.

"Even if I look like a cross between Einstein and Dumbledore?" the hermit asked.

"Oh my God," Bruce exclaimed, remembering the conversation when he'd said it to his mother at the kitchen table. "You are such a peeping tom! We were inside my house when I said that."

"I know it might come as a surprise, but when you say my name around any of the animals that live in the outer woods it draws my attention."

"But we don't live in the woods," Bruce replied with a frown. "How far out can you reach past the Sentinels?"

"About a quarter of a mile in any direction, why?"

"Just wanted to know how far I had to go if I wanted to gossip about you," Bruce answered.

"The impertinence of youth," August said sadly to Sam.

"I know," the big man agreed.

"Hey," Bruce complained, "I'm standing right here! Sam, you're supposed to be on my side."

"Bruce, I run a pizzeria, and my customers include your Terrible

Trio. I too am often irritated by today's youth."

"Point taken," Bruce conceded.

"But since you're feeling so free of tongue today about your abilities, how is it that you knew so much about what would happen, but not that August would hear your inadvertent confession about Megan?"

"He could see that there was talking, but he cannot always hear what is being said," August answered, surprising Bruce.

"Only the results of what was said," Bruce added. "Sometimes I can hear it too, but not always. How did you know that?"

"Answer one question for me first, and I will tell you."

"Sure," Bruce answered.

"Who is Dumbledore?"

Bruce had never heard Sam laugh so deeply. It was good to hear.

"You can borrow my set of the Harry Potter books the next time I come out," Sam said.

"So how do you know so much about my abilities?" Bruce pressed.

"My wife had the gift of foresight," he answered, "though not as strongly as you do, it seems. Have you also noticed that you cannot see events that coincide with sizable expenditures of power?"

"Is that what causes it?" Bruce exclaimed, realizing that this explained the pattern he'd noticed but couldn't decipher. "That's actually a load off of my mind. Okay, Sam, to illustrate the way this works, you two are about to have a conversation, and it makes you really happy for some reason, but I have no idea why."

Sam looked questioningly at August, who began speaking in a completely unrecognizable language. Sam's mouth dropped open slightly for a second, and then he responded in like turn. This exchange went on for some time, and though Bruce understood none of it, it was still pleasant to hear, particularly the waves of pleasure that were emanating from the big man.

"And now you two are going to make recordings up in the treehouse where the electromagnetic disturbance from Guarded Wood won't disrupt the quality," Bruce said.

"That's what we just said," Sam said. "Well, except for the electromagnetic part. The language of my people doesn't have a word for that. It's been so long since I've heard the language of my childhood spoken aloud. I've been trying to make recordings of myself speaking it, so that it isn't lost, but it's hard when you're the only one talking. It has truly been a pleasure to meet you, August."

"Cool," Bruce said. "So now you can truthfully say that you've met the mean old hermit of Guarded Wood and that my mother doesn't need to barricade the back door?"

"Of course," Sam said. "August, if I can ever be of help, never hesitate to ask."

"Be careful of offers like that," the old man said. "I sense dark times ahead."

"Then I am an ally you can count on," Sam said, reaching out to shake his hand once more.

"And if you ever need anything inside Guarded Wood, I offer the same to you, my friend."

It was a touching moment, and Bruce really wanted to leave on that note, but there was one thing he had to do, even though he knew it wouldn't end satisfactorily. He made it to the tree line before he had to turn and ask.

"Okay," he said, already ashamed, "Does the staff do anything?"

"What do you mean?" August asked, confused.

128

"He means like Gandalf," Sam said, shaking his head sadly at his friend's lack of decorum.

"It's for helping an old man get around all of these woods," August replied irritably. "Maybe you shouldn't read quite so many of those fantasy books of yours after all." Then he was gone.

"Mom," Megan said, "I need to tell you something, but you can't get mad."

"Nothing good ever follows statements like that," Azarich said, coming down the hall to Emelia's room at the sound of his granddaughter's words.

"Does this have anything to do with the fear gorta that no longer resides in the house next door?" Emelia asked, still drying her long dark hair with a towel.

"Is that what she was?" Megan asked.

"There was something living with the Grimbles?" Azarich asked.

"The other side," Emelia elaborated.

"Something dangerous?" he asked.

"Only if you were to go inside," Emelia answered, fixing her daughter with a hard stare, "Which I assume you and Bruce did, even after I told you to stay away from there."

"Yes," Megan admitted sheepishly, "But I could feel that she needed help."

"My friends and I must have explored every abandoned house on the street," Azarich said. "But the first time Josie laid eyes on that one, she made me promise to stay out."

"Sam and I did the same thing," Emelia said. "Let's talk downstairs

129

where we can all sit comfortably. I want to hear all of this."

Several minutes later, the three of them settled around the kitchen table with glasses of cold sweet tea. Megan marveled again at how much more relaxed her mother had become over the past several months.

"How did you know what Charlotte was if you never went inside?" Megan asked her mother.

"I didn't when Sam and I were kids," Emelia admitted. "We could just feel that there was something seriously wrong with the place. I found out about the gortas after I left here."

Megan could tell that her mother was trying to explain without giving away too much.

"And then you befriended one when you were very young," Emelia continued.

"I didn't realize you knew about Robert," Megan admitted.

"I watched over you very closely," Emelia explained. "They have a very unique psychic signature."

"Did you know about the woodland creatures that lived around that cabin where we stayed in the mountains?" Megan asked.

"You're not talking about the deer, are you?" Emilia asked.

"No," Megan said. "The woman that was made out of pieces of wood."

Emelia shook her head, frowning.

"There's one that lives in the woods next to the Gateway Oaks, where they start and finish the race.," Megan explained. "Bruce says she's a dryad."

"Interesting," Emelia said, "now tell me about our friendly neighborhood fear gorta."

"Well, first of all, the inside of that house is perfectly preserved, and unless someone sold it since her husband died it belongs to our family."

"That should be fairly easy to verify," Azarich said. "Although that means we may owe an awful lot of money to back taxes."

"This house was the servant's quarters for that one, and our family used to work for hers," Megan continued. "Charlotte's husband got mad because she couldn't have children and locked her into a big trunk so she'd starve to death and die."

"But she didn't," Emelia said, echoing the words of Charlotte herself. "Gortas are often created when someone tries to imprison and starve someone like that. And then no matter how much he ate, he starved to death, didn't he?"

Megan nodded.

"That's unspeakable," Azarich said, completely disgusted. "And the poor thing has been trapped there ever since?"

"Yes," Megan answered. "But we set her free. It turns out that our family is tied to that one on Grandma Josie's side. Charlotte's husband had a sister, and she's the one we inherited Jacob's church from."

"You did the right thing," Emelia said. "And I'm proud of you for it. No one deserves to go through what that poor woman did. But next time you and Bruce decide to go save someone, would you please take Sam and I with you? We've got a lot more experience than you do with such things."

# Chapter XIII: Disappointed Dreams

"This is great guys," Jade said, trying not to look disappointed about not getting a car for her birthday. But she'd never been very good at hiding her emotions. Sam had dimmed the lights in the room he used at Gordon's for special occasions. But Bruce could still sense his sister's mood through the way she smiled a bit too hard and the way she sat just a little too straight in her chair. He wanted to tell her that he could see her driving a classic from the early forties, but he couldn't do so without explaining everything else.

Seated around the long table were the combined Grimble and McGeehee families, Azarich's childhood friends as well as several people from Lone Star Karate. Although Megan didn't understand why there weren't any people there from Jade's grade at the Academy, Bruce knew that most of her classmates were frightened of her. Sure, Jade would never hurt anyone who didn't deserve it, but that carried little weight with those who feared they might have crossed the line with the oldest Grimble child.

Ella, the young girl who idolized Jade from the dojo, watched intently with doe-like eyes. Her brother, Jayden, kept casting furtive glances toward his mother, who was irate that she couldn't just leave her children there the way she did on the nights when they were training. Rather than join in,

Mrs. Mickey pouted in the corner with her phone, oblivious to the people around her. That was probably for the best since Bruce wasn't sure he had the stomach to watch her berate Ella's every action while praising her oaf of a son.

Bruce's eyes traveled, as they had several times already, to the awkward boy from the martial arts class. He was in the grade above Jade, and his curly mop of brown hair had been carefully combed. He was a bit overdressed for the occasion, though that might be normal since Bruce couldn't recall ever seeing him outside of the dojo. What interested him was the way the young man never took his eyes off of Jade. Bruce was sorely tempted to sneak a peek into what was going on inside his head.

*Don't you dare,* Megan sent.

*Like I'd chance it with your mother nearby!* he sent, casting a furtive glance at Emelia. He was fairly sure that he'd shielded the thought enough so that only Megan heard it, but where Emelia was concerned, it didn't hurt to be careful.

He realized that they both must have been spacing out when he noticed Azarich smiling at them meaningfully. Ever since he'd had his suspicions confirmed, the old man was positively uncanny at noticing when they were talking mind to mind.

*Do you have any idea where the car comes from?* Megan asked. *It looks expensive.*

*Not a clue,* Bruce answered. *I know Jade has a job now, but I don't see her having that kind of money any time in the near future. With* Tribune *sales down and Dad's hours cut back at the firehouse, I don't think the money comes from my parents either.*

*Sometimes I wish we'd just toughed the last few months of school out and left the Jones family alone,* Megan thought, absently twisting her hair around her fingers. *Maybe things wouldn't be so tough on your family.*

*None of us would change a thing,* Bruce sent. *Someone needed to stand up to them.*

*I can't help but feel like this is all my fault.*

*We don't know that for sure,* Bruce argued without much conviction, *maybe it's a coincidence that Jones worked out a deal to bring in our closest competitor to Nickelville at a discount and that he's been pushing to defund the firehouse and hire a private company in its place.*

*And maybe Allison will grow up to be a caring, productive part of our society...* Megan sent.

Mrs. Mickey sighed loudly as if even she found the idea preposterous.

Since several of the Gordon's staff had called in sick, everyone bussed their own tables while Sam went to the kitchen to get the cake. Like everything else he did for the inner circle of his friends, the cake was simply too much. Almost too beautiful to eat, it rose several layers from the cart as the big man maneuvered deftly through the door.

When he sang, the rest of the crowd was reluctant to join in, not because they didn't want to sing to the oldest Grimble child, but because anything next to the rich tones of Sam's voice seemed small and out-of-place. Then Paul slipped behind the keys of the old upright piano bearing the sign, "No, Sam *won't* play it again," and fell into perfect rhythm with the big man as he sang.

*I didn't know he could play,* Megan sent.

*He took lessons when he was younger until something broke in our old piano. I had no idea he could play at all anymore, let alone that well. It's a nice touch though,* Bruce sent, standing with everyone else in the room to applaud when the song was over and his sister was blushing furiously at all of the attention. In the midst of all the activity, Sam still

134

managed to pull his phone out and take several pictures of the crowd.

"Before we begin this magnificent meal that Mr. Wise has cooked for us," Paul called out in a voice that wasn't loud, yet was easily heard across the crowded room, "The time has come to present my sister with her gift." With a flourish that reminded Bruce of something he'd seen in an old movie, Paul presented Jade with a rather plain looking envelope.

Confused, she took it from his hand and looked inside. She was quiet for a moment before she looked up and the whole room waited for her reaction.

"I don't think there is a person in the whole town who doesn't know how much you want a car," Sam said. "It's not enough yet, but it's a good start."

"Thank you guys so much," Jade sniffed.

Cake was eaten, punch was drunk and Bruce thought about ignoring Megan's warnings when Andrew Jackson, of no known relation to the president of the same name, gave Jade a bouquet of flowers since he thought she should have more than one present.

But it turned out when they got home that Jade had two more presents left to receive. A basket sat on the front porch containing a large amethyst cathedral wrapped in linen. It bore a simple note in an elaborate script that read, "to Jade from August." Jade declared this to be the best present ever until Emelia showed up a few minutes later bearing a poster sized photograph of Allison Jones windmilling her arms as she fell into the foul waters of Nickelville Lake.

# Chapter XIV: A Walk on the Wild Side

Humid air hung over the treehouse and sapped the strength from the Grimbles as Megan looked out the window across Guarded Wood. None of them except Bruce had been closer than the Sentinel Tree since the night of the storm, and each of them wanted answers, though each to different questions.

Jade sighed in frustration as she tried to finish the rope hammock Paul had started. She looked meaningfully over at him while he repeatedly maneuvered a paper airplane through the wingover maneuver he'd been fascinated with for the past week. When he'd been the one weaving the strands together, it had progressed with a smooth and seemingly effortless grace even though he said he'd never done it before. When Jade tried there was a great deal of swearing of which their mother wouldn't have approved.

Megan reached out with her mind, feeling Bruce tag along as she went. A restiveness still hung over the trees, but it no longer felt so strange.

*Maybe it's like a strong smell,* Bruce suggested. It's *still just as weird as it was before, but we've gotten used to it and don't notice it anymore.*

Megan gave him the mental equivalent of a shrug and tried to remember exactly where they'd felt the wards during the storm. Past her closed eyelids the treetops drifted below her as she searched.

*What are you doing, Changeling?*

Megan jumped, even though she'd been expecting the touch of the old man's mind.

*Why do you call me that?*

*It's considered rude to answer a question with a question,* he sent irritably.

*So is name calling,* she countered.

*I'm a hermit. We're rude by nature, and need I remind you that it's my front door you're knocking on?*

*Jade and Paul are restless and we wanted to know if the wards were fixed,* Bruce interjected before the two could start to argue. *You have no idea how much mischief they'll cause if they're closed up at the house much longer.*

*It's safe enough,* he sent, *but even Norms will be able to tell that something is different, especially when they've spent as much time in here as those two have.*

*So you don't mind?* Megan asked.

*Just stay out of trouble.*

*We will,* Bruce sent.

As soon as the four of them crossed into the shadows of Guarded Wood, Megan realized how much August had been shielding it from the outside world. Stripped of its old protections, the forest (and there was no chance of mistaking it for a small band of woods anymore) had unfolded like dormant buds, filling in the empty spaces and flowering across her extra senses.

"This is so weird," Jade whispered.

"I know," Bruce agreed, casting an uneasy look at Megan. He didn't sense anything particularly bad in their immediate future, but it was beyond cluttered, and he didn't know what to expect.

"This tree is familiar," Paul said, pointing at a bois d'arc next to the path, "and I could have sworn that one down there came next. But where did these three in the middle come from?"

"This is all wrong," Jade snapped irritably. "Not only are there new trees and rocks, but the ones that are here are bigger than they were before. Something is going on."

*Maybe this wasn't such a good idea,* Bruce sent.

*Nothing to be done about it now,* she admitted. *Maybe they'll get used to it quickly and forget about what it used to be like.*

*You know,* he thought as they followed Jade and Paul, *this is pretty cool. It's like the world we saw when we looked at Guarded Wood was a caricature of the real one beneath. Just enough of the truth showed through to let us interact with it, but not enough to figure out what was really there.*

Fang showed up without warning and fell into step without any form of greeting. With the exception of Megan and Bruce, who could feel the gruff presence of August beneath the surface, no one noticed or said anything about his appearance.

"I've never seen that path before," Jade said, "Let's see where it goes."

*Damn it,* August sent. *They shouldn't have been able to see that. The ward of misdirection that normally protects it must have failed since I passed there last night.*

*Are we in danger?* Bruce asked.

*No, but that path will take you deeper in than any of you have ever been. It's still safe, but there are things there that couldn't be in Texan woodlands.*

*Like what?* Megan asked.

*Things that any person would notice, let alone a scout.*

The change happened almost at once. It wasn't like stepping through a doorway into another place, but there was a place where the air seemed to resist their passage. The hard-packed earth at their feet suddenly gave way to the spongy debris of a forest floor. Massive trees surrounded them, their interlocking branches blocking out the sun high overhead. A thick layer of moss coated the rocks and the tree trunks, painting the world in shades of green. A rotten log lay on its side ahead of them, thick enough that they couldn't see over it.

*How did you get there?* August sent. *That connection has never been there before. Something big is happening. You need to get them out of there.*

"This isn't possible," Paul said, looking at the canopy above. "There's nothing this tall in Guarded Wood or we would have been able to see it from the treehouse. Forget Guarded Wood, there isn't anything like this in all of Texas."

"What's going on here?" Jade asked, peeling back the moss from a rock to see what it looked like underneath. "This is all igneous rock. We don't have anything like this near the surface in Nickelville."

"Wait a minute," Paul said, looking down the embankment of a stream Megan didn't recall having seen before. "Let me get a better look at those tracks."

Fang growled deep in his chest.

"Careful," Jade said, scanning the undergrowth closely. "Could be feral pigs again."

"Feral pigs?" Megan asked.

"They've been out here before," Bruce said wearily. "They're dangerous. We should go back right now."

"Whoa!" Paul said in awe as he knelt over the tracks, completely ignoring both his brother and sister in his excitement. The soil at the edge of the stream was so badly disturbed that it was hard at first to make out a clear print. "If these were made by a pig it would have to be about the size of a rhino!"

"You're kidding," Jade said, walking up to join him.

"Are those claw prints at the edge of the fingers?" Megan asked, curious in spite of the warning.

*That's not helping Changeling.*

*Stop calling me that!*

"Surely not," Bruce said, trying to figure out how to salvage the situation. "They'd have to be close to a foot long!"

*You two need to get them out of there and find a way to make them forget about the tracks,* the hermit's thoughts intruded.

*How are we supposed to do that?* Bruce sent.

*Are you sure we're not in danger?* Megan asked.

*I don't think so,* the hermit answered. *But I didn't think you'd be able to get that far in either. There are a few places nearby that would put you in true danger if the protections on them failed as well. I need to get in there and make repairs before you come back.*

Fang began to growl again, this time facing the woods across the stream.

"I think we should get out of here," Bruce repeated. "I don't think I want to meet up with whatever made those tracks."

"I second that," Megan added.

"There's no way something this big could be living out here without us having seen it before," Paul mumbled to himself. "There's not enough acreage for it to feed from."

"Let's worry about that while we walk," Jade said.

"Yeah," Paul said absently, looking back over his shoulder. "I need to come back with plaster and make casts of them."

"You don't think it was from Goatman, do you?" Jade asked no one in particular.

"No," Paul said. "Those were nothing like cloven hooves. Whatever made those tracks had something more like a hand with claws. But you know, I almost think I've seen them before."

"Where?" Bruce asked.

"Pictures from books," Paul said and then turned abruptly to return.

"Where do you think you're going?" Jade asked, blocking his path.

"I should have taken pictures of them with my phone," he said, almost frantic with the need to explain what was going on. "I need something to put alongside them for a size comparison."

"Not today you don't," Bruce said, taking him by the wrist and leading him back the way they'd come. "Fang still looks like something is spooking him. We need to get out of here."

Back at the treehouse, Paul worked himself into a frenzy, and Bruce wasn't far behind. Megan could feel his concern for his brother, saturating the bond and making it hard to think of anything else.

"What's going on here?" Paul asked, pacing in cramped circles around the room.

"Something seriously weird," Jade added with a pointed look at Megan, "and not just with Guarded Wood."

"It has to be an herbivore," Paul murmured.

"Are you serious?" Bruce asked. "Did you see the size of those claw marks?"

"Lots of herbivores have big claws," Paul explained. "They don't necessarily mean they're used for hunting. What makes me think it's an herbivore is the size of its habitat. A carnivore that size would require an absolutely enormous body of prey to hunt in order to sustain itself. Furthermore, judging from the prints, I think it was more than one."

Megan shuddered.

"You still don't think it could be Goatman?" Jade asked.

"I guess anything is possible," Paul said, pausing to look out over Guarded Wood, "but whatever made those tracks was huge."

"So what do we do now?" Megan asked. "I'm not sure that I feel comfortable going out there anymore." She could feel the hermit listening in at the edges of her senses and suspected that if she looked above the window she'd find an unusually attentive raven.

"We can't tell Mom," Bruce said, still trying to do damage control. "Not if we ever want to go back out there again."

"You've got that right," Paul agreed. "But we have to find out what's out there. Just because it's an herbivore doesn't mean it's not dangerous. After all, elephants and hippos are herbivores."

"But it's like you said," Jade added, "Guarded Wood just isn't big enough to be the home to something that big, let alone a whole herd of them. Sam doesn't even know about it." Her eyes fell on Megan again. "Do you know something about this that you're not telling us?"

"What makes you ask that?" Megan asked, getting up to turn on the radio.

"Let me see," Jade said, ticking off on her fingers. "One, you fight like a black belt the first time you come to class, two, weapons are second nature to you, three, you act like you can read minds or something, and I know you two didn't get all the way to Gordon's that day last year when you went upstairs at the Academy."

Megan felt Bruce's premonition a second before the tremor flowed through Guarded Wood. Less like an earthquake and more like a single ripple spreading outward from the heart of the woods, it caused flares in the visual spectrum as the protective barrier slipped alarmingly toward failure. The Sentinel in which their tree house rested responded by pushing back with such an ancient consciousness that both Bruce and Megan were swept up in its response.

Momentarily caught in the ebb and flow of Guarded Wood settling, she heard Bruce as he called from far away. When she opened her eyes, she found Jade looking back, eyes wide. Fully unshielded, she saw what Jade saw when she looked at her, and in that image she saw that her eyes glowed violet in the shadowed interior of the treehouse.

# Chapter XV: A Problem of Prehistoric Proportions

It had been years since Bruce had seen his sister so angry, and then it had been directed at someone other than him. After the shortest of explanations, Jade had stormed off to the house. At first, he'd been afraid she was going to tell their mother, but no matter how angry she might be, that just wasn't her style. Besides, their mother had run back to the *Tribune* for a last-minute correction and their father was on duty.

Normally Paul would be the one to talk her down, but he was mad too. Bruce feared this might put an end to how close they'd all grown since Megan and her mother had come to Nickelville. He found it hard to believe that he'd disliked his brother and sister so much for so long. Now when he thought about losing that fragile bond, it devastated him.

The phone rang.

Ever the responsible scout, Paul answered it.

"Hello, Grimble residence," he said loud enough to be heard in Bruce's room. "Yes, I'll get her. Who shall I say is calling?"

"Who is it?" Jade asked from her room where she was still sulked.

"It's your boss from the palace," he answered.

Jade hurried to the phone and spoke for several moments before hanging up. When she turned around and found her brothers looking at her, she actually smiled for a second before she remembered that she was angry.

"So?" Bruce asked.

"Kate wants me to come up tomorrow morning and help with some things," Jade said. "I'm still pissed off at you and Megan though."

*Can you bring everyone over to my Grandmother's grove?* Megan sent. *I've been talking it over with my Mom and Sam.*

"Um," Bruce said, "Megan wants us to come over to the clearing behind her house so Emelia and Sam can talk to you."

"Wait a minute," Paul said, "Sam is in on this?"

"That's why he always seems to know what Megan and her mom are talking about without actually hearing what they have to say," Jade said. "So you can just hear her in your head?"

Bruce nodded.

"Wicked," Paul said in admiration. But just as quickly as the excitement had come, the boy became distant as if he were trying to remember something.

"Megan and her mother had to tell Azarich a few days ago," Bruce said, deciding he might as well start bringing them up to speed. As he scanned the immediate future he could see that this information would help Jade forgive. Paul, however, was just as unreadable as he'd been since the night of the storm.

Without another word, Jade walked to the back door, stepped out into the hot summer air and let the door slam behind her. Paul hurried to catch up with her and Bruce was left to feel guilty all over again.

*I sure hope you guys know what you're going to say,* Bruce sent, following behind them. *I'm in over my head here.*

Fang was waiting for them in the middle of the path. But just before they reached him, the big dog caught sight of something in the underbrush and darted off toward it. Bruce caught a flash of an oddly familiar black shape before it disappeared.

"Told 'em have ya?" the hermit said when he joined them on the path that led to the grove. "Probably for the best. Can you two keep a secret?"

"Of course," Jade said, offended that he'd even ask. "You could have let us in from the start."

"We would have liked to do so," Sam said, already standing in the clearing when they walked up. "But the world that you are discovering is dangerous to those who know about it. I'm not at all happy about the two of you being drawn into this. Bruce was bad enough."

"If you have to be angry with someone, be angry with me," Emelia said, walking up with her father. "I forbade them to tell anyone. I assume you are Mr. Biggerstaff?"

"Call me August," the hermit said, turning to face Emelia.

As soon as he did so, Emelia tensed as if she'd been struck. Her right hand made as if to reach behind her back for something in her waistband and Bruce could have sworn he felt something like a force field rise up around her.

"You," she hissed.

"Easy girl," the old man said quietly. "Can't say I'm too pleased to have the Scathlahm herself sniffing around my doorstep either."

Her eyes flashed angrily and shot toward Megan, who looked bewildered by the exchange.

"Why don't we let each other keep our secrets a while longer, you and I," he said quietly. "Does she know?"

"No," Emelia answered, her eyes never leaving his.

146

"I'm prepared to keep it that way if you are," he promised, extending his hand.

Emelia took it reluctantly, and there was clearly more exchanging between them that no one else could hear.

"It's been a long time," Azarich said, also extending his hand to the hermit.

"Not really," August said, his eyes hard to read. "Not so long for me since you and your friends trespassed in my woods that night. I was sorry to hear about Carl. He was a good lad."

"He was," Azarich agreed, as if he were trying to remember something.

"Let's get to the point then," August said, turning to face the rest of the group. "I can't leave Guarded Wood for more than a few minutes. Even this small distance drains me. As some of you saw earlier, boundaries are failing all across the edge of the woods and I can't seem to stop them."

"Huh?" Jade said, not following.

"That tremor you felt earlier was one of the big ones going. You've noticed that the woods have changed since the night of the storm?" he asked.

"Yes," Paul agreed, grateful that he was getting answers at last. "They're bigger than they were before. And there are things that I don't recognize at all."

"Guarded Wood is more than it appears," the old man explained. "Ancient enchantments fold it in on itself and keep the bad things that live at its heart from getting loose."

"At least until we built the treehouse," Bruce added.

"Exactly," the hermit replied.

"Like whatever made those tracks?" Paul asked.

"They're not bad. Follow me," he said, walking toward the tree line. "It's not far."

Everyone walked single file down the same path Jade had noticed just a short time earlier, and once again there was a portion of the path that resisted their entrance to the forest beyond.

"Toto," Emelia said, looking up into the canopy, "I don't think we're in Kansas anymore."

"Well," Paul said. "It certainly isn't Texas. That's for sure."

"It's hard to say with Guarded Wood," August said. "There are pockets that open into every continent as far as I can tell. I'm not even sure if all of them are real places on Earth."

They followed the sound of water to a rocky creek and turned to follow it downstream. A rotten tree stump rose from the earth next to them, covered in mushrooms bigger than Sam's hands. A big gray rodent the size of a house cat popped its head up from the ferns that had hidden it, curious about these intruders to the forest, but not particularly afraid of them.

Overhead, the sound of a woodpecker echoed through the mostly quiet space. The canopy blocked out most of the light from above, but there were beams of light that cut through the understory like spotlights and illuminated patches of the leaf and twig cluttered ground. In one such patch a snake with a head large enough to swallow the rodent whole that they'd seen earlier watched them pass. It was hard to tell how long the thing might have been, given the way it had piled in upon itself to fit within the patch of sunlight. Fang growled softly as they passed, but whether it was to warn them of its presence or signal his displeasure was impossible to tell for anyone but the quiet hermit who led them down the path.

"Is this the same creek we built the bridge over?" Paul asked.

"Yes and no," the old man answered, still plodding along with his gnarled staff thumping against rocks hidden in the leaves. "Water flows through many of these places, but as far as I can tell, nothing actually moves from one zone to another. I've passed through places where you are in summer one moment and then in a blizzard the next. Not even the air seems to mix at those boundaries."

"Is that a waterfall I hear?" Azarich asked.

"I think so," August replied. "That's what should be up ahead if all of this zone moved here in one piece. But this place was much further away yesterday than it is now."

"Are you saying that this whole place just *moved*?" Sam asked.

"It might be better to say that the doorway moved," August answered. "The place where you cross over from the edge of the woods in that spot used to lead to a cliff that overlooked the edge of a desert. I hope that spot hasn't disappeared altogether. I rather liked eating lunch there in the middle of winter."

"But you entered this place from somewhere else in Guarded Wood?" Bruce asked, fascinated by the thought.

"Yes," the old man answered. "I've always liked these beasts. I've been watching over their little family for years."

Up ahead, the path they followed opened into a clearing. At the far side a rocky cliff rose some thirty feet into the air and stretched off into the distance on either side of them. The roar of the water as it fell into the lagoon before them filled their ears with a dull roar.

Bruce resisted the urge to reach out and take Megan's hand as he walked next to her into the woods. He heard the beasts before he saw them: deep grunts and whines punctuated by the sound of rustling branches.

Before them, two of the biggest land mammals that Bruce had ever seen were basking in the sun on a rocky outcrop while one of their young splashed in the shallows. Another juvenile was trying to reach a branch that hung over the spot where the two adults lay. One of them reached up with huge claws to hook the branch and bring it within reach of the impatient youngster.

"I thought they might be ground sloths," Paul said in awe.

"Is that what they're called?" Jade asked.

"They lived here a long time ago," Paul murmured. "Not as far back as the dinosaurs, but still prehistoric."

"Are they dangerous?" Azarich asked, eyeing the size of the claws. "And you say there are other things living in my backyard?"

"I haven't seen anything to suggest that they would be," the hermit answered, leaning on his staff and watching them affectionately. "I couldn't find much about them in the books I've got, but they should behave like any other creature of their size. They don't have any natural predators, so the only thing that seems to rile them up is if they perceive something to be a threat to their young. That's why Fang is staying out of sight and downwind of them."

Bruce hadn't noticed that his friend had fallen behind in his eagerness to see what lay ahead. But August was right, Fang wasn't anywhere nearby.

"How have they survived in Guarded Wood all this time?" Paul asked. "These woods aren't big enough to support a breeding population of ground sloths. They'd strip everything to the ground in no time if there were enough of them to keep the species alive."

"And now we get to the part that I need to talk with you about," August said gravely. "Even now with the boundary failing, most of Guarded Wood is still hidden. I've lived here longer than you can imagine,

150

and not even I know how big these woods are even though I've traveled deep inside for months at a time. Sam, what do your people call this place?"

"Spirit Wood," the tall man answered. "I was told to avoid the woods if possible and never to seek out its heart."

"Better advice has never been uttered," August said. "Most of it isn't too bad, but the closer you get to the center, the worse things get. Something bad lives deep within."

"What is it?" Jade asked, drawn in despite her earlier anger.

"I don't know, and I hope I never find out. The only way to do so would be to meet it, and I suspect that wouldn't be very good for an old man's health."

"So there are ground sloths in this hidden forest which probably isn't a part of this world, and they can just cross over through the woods?" Paul asked, fascinated by the possibilities.

"Or they may be from this world and come from a different time," August said with a shrug. "I've suspected that something along those lines might be happening, but there's no way to know for sure. The boundary usually keeps things like these sloths from getting this far."

Bruce thought his brother might very well explode.

"But now something is wrong with the boundary," Emelia said.

"Ever since you lot built that monstrosity in the Sentinel Tree," he agreed, frowning at the whole group.

"Can it be repaired?" Azarich asked.

"I don't know," the old man said, echoing their previous conversation on the matter. "I don't have any idea how old the boundary is, or who created it. There are definitely some parts of the boundary that feels like your people had a hand in their creation," he said nodding toward Sam,

151

"but there are others that feel alien."

"We're not talking about Yoda here," Paul asked, "are we?"

"I'm not sure who that is," the old man said with an impatient frown, "but I mean not human. The point is that the Sentinel Boundary is the oldest. Everything else is built on top of that. If it fails, then it's only a matter of time until everything unravels and we get some firsthand experience at what really lives in the Heart."

"How do we help?" Paul asked, taking this all rather well for someone who hadn't known magic was real when the sun had come up that morning.

"Think about what you did when you made that treehouse," the hermit said. "We need to figure out what caused the deterioration to start."

"I didn't feel anything out of the ordinary happen when we built it," Emelia said, frowning.

"I didn't either, and I was watching pretty closely myself," the hermit added. "In the meantime, can you help me ward the outer sections that are failing? I've got to make sure that nothing bad gets out and that no one who doesn't belong here gets in."

"Bruce and I haven't learned how yet," Megan said.

"I'll teach them," Emelia said.

"You'd better be quick about it," the hermit said, starting to move back toward his home. "This side is failing faster than the rest. At some point, you may have to hold the entire outer barriers so I can focus on keeping things from the Heart safely tucked away.

# Chapter XVI: Guarded Wood

Even though Jade and Paul couldn't feel the boundary or tell what kind of shape it was in, their knowledge of Guarded Wood made them invaluable. Some of Paul's cockiness returned now that he knew that his inability to navigate the woods had more to do with their supernatural nature than with his wood lore. He'd even started to map the woods while they explored.

"Is it my imagination or is it getting cold?" Bruce asked when they passed another Sentinel and peered out over a rocky valley that looked nothing like anything he'd seen in Nickelville.

"Nope," Jade said, "It's definitely getting colder."

"The rocks in that outcropping out there aren't limestone," Paul said, squinting in the distance. "I wonder..." The three of them watched as he jogged out a ways from the tree line to make sure he was clear of the woods where electronics would work again.

"Not too far," Bruce called after him, drawing a bewildered look from Paul.

"Okay Mom," Paul called back before pulling out his GPS unit and fiddling with the buttons on it for a moment. "This can't be right."

"What is it?" Jade called, starting to move toward him.

"According to this I'm in Northern Wyoming," Paul murmured.

Megan stepped hurriedly back toward the tree line, afraid that she might become visible to the Wild Hunt if she strayed too far from the trees.

"There's no way," Bruce said. "That's halfway across the country from Nickelville."

"I only know what the unit is telling me," Paul said, checking the coordinates against the map he'd pulled from his backpack. "But if this is right, Guarded Wood isn't just in Nickelville."

"This is so weird," Jade said in awe, looking up at the sky. "But it would explain why it's so much cooler here."

Megan closed her eyes and reached out with her extra senses. Something was wrong here that had nothing to do with their location. Bruce felt what she was doing and joined her.

"There's a hole," Megan said out loud, still finding it strange to speak about such things in front of Bruce's siblings. "Let's see if we can ward it ourselves. It doesn't seem to be very big yet."

"Jade," Bruce said, closing his eyes and concentrating. "Keep an eye out for anything out of the ordinary. Remember what August said about things from the Heart being drawn to this sort of work."

"Gotcha little brother," Jade said, scanning the woods.

*I hate it when she calls me that*, he thought.

"Everybody has the rings?" Megan asked.

"Yes," Paul said from behind her, having come closer to watch, "Are you sure Jade and I will be able to tell when the wards you make are broken too?"

"If we do this right," Bruce said. "It should work like my amulet."

"But we don't have any abilities," Jade said with the tiniest hint of jealousy.

"It shouldn't matter," Megan said. "Ready Bruce?"

"Let's do it."

They allowed their awareness to fill the open spaces between the trees and cordon off Guarded Wood from the world outside. As soon as they started, Megan felt the nearest Sentinel Tree turn its attention toward them.

*I wonder what would have happened if we'd been a threat,* Megan wondered. *Let's get this finished.*

"That is so weird," Jade said quietly. "I can feel it now."

"Me too," Paul added. "I think I can hear it a little bit too."

Megan tried not to think about how clumsy their wards were compared to the ancient forces at work around the Sentinel trees. At last their repair solidified and the prickling sensation in the back of her mind faded.

"What is that sticking up from the thicket over there?" Paul asked.

Megan felt a surge of recognition come through her bond with Bruce. She looked at him inquiringly, but he only smiled in return.

*Is that her car?* Megan asked.

*You and I have some work to do*, he replied.

"I don't know anything about fixing cars," Megan said out loud.

"We're going to learn," he said.

"What are you two talking about?" Jade asked, trying to get closer.

"I never got around to telling you that I have some abilities that Megan doesn't," Bruce said.

"Like what?" Paul asked.

"Like being able to see the future," Megan said.

"I've seen you driving that car after it's been restored," Bruce said to Jade.

"You're kidding," Jade squealed with girlish glee. "Help me get back

155

there."

"Hold on," Megan said. "As long as we're showing what we can do, let's do this the easy way. Stand back."

Bruce had trouble holding back his laughter at the open-mouthed looks of astonishment mirrored on Jade's and Paul's faces as the brambles began to uproot themselves and unwind long tendrils from the old car that laid beneath years of growth. The air filled with the pungent green smell of sap as leaves were stripped and vines torn. Creaks and snaps echoed off of the nearby trees.

When it was clear, she and Bruce lifted it free of the earth where it had rested for so long. A rat snake slithered unhappily away from what had until now been its home, disappearing into the underbrush.

"Not much to look at," Paul murmured, eyeing the places where the paint had flaked away and the rusted metal beneath showed through.

"She remembers what she once was," Bruce said, walking over to lay his hand on one rusted fin that rose from the back fender. The rust fell away beneath his fingertips, leaving the chrome shining in the sun.

"Wow," Paul whispered in a momentarily uncharacteristic loss of words. "Can we learn to do that?"

"I'm sorry, but no," Megan said. "You've got to be born to it."

"But what about Bruce?" Jade asked. "He couldn't do it until you came."

"His abilities were always there," Megan answered. "But they were dormant until he came into contact with someone like me."

"So he's like a psychic leach?" Paul asked with a grin. "I've always thought there was something unsavory about him."

"It's not quite that simple," Megan giggled, nonetheless enjoying the look of annoyance on Bruce's face.

"From what Emelia said, my abilities are focused by the presence of another gifted person, but I don't actually take any of their power."

"In fact, he makes me stronger," Megan said.

"And a bigger pain in my backside," a voice noted from behind them.

"I wondered what you were doing to stir up the energy flow of the area so much."

Megan wasn't surprised to find the hermit standing behind them, but she was, however, surprised to see how much the hermit's wardrobe had changed since she'd last seen him. In place of the homespun shirt, he now wore a simple black t-shirt. The patched pantaloons had been replaced by jeans. His feet were encased in a good pair of hiking boots. She could tell he was uncomfortable about how they might respond to this change, and she knew at once that their big friend had something to do with this transformation.

"Do you know anything about this old car?" Bruce asked, hiding his own surprise as well.

"It's the only car I ever owned," the old man said, looking at the rusty hulk with a distant fondness in his eyes.

"I thought you couldn't leave the woods," Megan said.

"Not anymore," he said, "but there was a time when I left Guarded Wood on a fairly regular basis."

"I don't want to sound rude," Bruce said hesitantly.

"Since when?" Jade asked.

"But I've, you know...seen this car with my abilities,"

"Spit it out boy, I won't bite," the old man growled with a mischievous gleam in his eyes, "That's what Fang is here for."

Megan realized that the hermit didn't sound like he hadn't spoken in a long time anymore. In fact, ever since Bruce had arranged the meeting between the old man and Sam, August was becoming positively loquacious at times.

"Can we fix the car up and give it to Jade?" Bruce asked.

"I don't see why not," the old man said. "I can't leave the woods, and it certainly can't be driven in here. It would be nice to know that it's back on the road again. I hope you know what you're getting into, though. I haven't started that thing up since just after the war."

"Which war was that?" Paul asked.

"The second one," August answered, already starting to move back into the woods. "Azarich and his friends had just returned the last time it was driven. But even if you get it working, how are you going to get it all the way back to Nickelville?" the old man asked, looking back over his shoulder and leaning on his staff. "I think you've realized that we're a sizable road trip from home right now."

"Let me handle that," Megan said ominously.

# Chapter XVII: Big Bertha

The next morning Megan came over to the Grimble house shortly after the morning tradition of sunrise, coffee and breakfast to find her friends getting ready to go work on the car. Before they could head out to the woods, the home line rang.

"Yes, Kate," Jade said after listening for a moment and looking extremely guilty. "No, I haven't forgotten. I'll be there soon." She listened for a few more moments. "No, I can probably get a ride from Mr. McGeehee. I'll be there soon. Bye."

"You totally forgot," Megan giggled when her friend put the phone down. "Didn't you?"

Jade nodded sheepishly.

"Let's go see if Azarich can take you," Bruce said, rising from the couch after he finished tying his shoes. "Then the rest of us can go get started on the car."

"Do you really think you can get it running?" Jade asked.

"I've seen you driving it," he answered, tapping his temple meaningfully. She hugged him, which was almost as painful as when she hit him. At least the worst of the soreness from working out at the dojo had faded.

"I'll bring my rock pack," Paul said. "Unless you think there will be something mundane that I can do to help with the car?"

"Not yet," Bruce said. "We're going to need to change out all of the fluids, belts and hoses at some point, but we're nowhere near that point yet."

The four of them locked up the house, which probably wasn't necessary since no one ever came to Beverly Road unless they were lost. The Grimbles teased Megan while they walked, asking her if she needed to stop by the treehouse for a change of clothes. And when they got close to her house, she noticed a black cat in her mother's window. For just a second, she thought it was Mr. Bob, but then it faded out of existence and she realized it must have been another echo of the past.

"Looks like your mom took the day off," Paul said, noticing two extra trucks in the driveway as they approached the front door. "And Mr. Green too."

Inside, the smells of coffee and breakfast still hung in the air.

"Hey Mom," Megan called when they walked into the house.

"She's not here," her grandfather called from the kitchen.

"But her truck is out front," she called, following the sound of his voice past the staircase with Bruce, Jade and Paul. Mr. Green was sitting at the kitchen table with Azarich, drinking coffee and likely discussing the general state of affairs in their fair town.

"Sam must have picked her up early this morning," Azarich said. "Do you fine young people need something?"

"My mom and dad are both at work and Kate just called and asked if I could come in this morning. So I was wondering if someone could give me a ride... or loan me a truck since I've got my license now and you seem to have an extra," Jade suggested, raising her eyebrows up and down in

161

what she might have believed to be an appealing manner.

"I can take her," Mr. Green said with an eagerness that seemed disproportionate to dropping a teenage girl off at work. "You stay here and rest."

"Why would I need to rest? I'm no more tired than you," Azarich retorted. "I can keep up with you any day."

"Nope," Mr. Green taunted, finishing off his coffee and rising from the table with a mischievous grin, "You've gone soft from sitting at a desk and leaching money off the needy while working souls like me made a living the hard way. Come on Jade, I'll drop you off on my way to the Academy."

"I thought they cut your hours," Azarich said with a frown.

"Cut them they did," Mr. Green sighed, "but if I want to get everything done in time for the next school year, I'll have to spend more than two or three hours a day there. What they're paying me for is barely enough to cover the general upkeep. But if I don't take care of it now, I'll be paying for it later."

"Jones wants to shut down the Academy in favor of one of those private charter schools," Azarich said in disgust.

"More retribution for getting Evil Eye Jones kicked out?" Jade asked. Mr. Green found this name particularly amusing.

"I think this might be a bit more complicated than that," Azarich answered. "Charter schools get money from the state just like a public school, but they aren't held responsible for how they spend it. A man with a shortage of scruples and a surplus of money can make a fortune off of our children in a situation like that."

"So he not only gets revenge on us, but he gets richer too?" Paul asked.

162

"Sometimes the world just doesn't seem fair," Jade said. "So one of you can take me?"

"Seriously Azarich," Mr. Green said with a smile. "There's no need to go into town and risk whatever bug is blowing around. I'm going to pass right by the Palace on my way to the Academy anyway."

"Suit yourself," August said.

"Hey Grandpa," Megan asked.

"Yes dear?"

"Have you ever had a black cat?"

"I don't recall ever owning a black one, but I did have a silver tabby named Rambunctious when I was a child. Why?"

"Just wondering," Megan said, almost slipping and explaining what she'd seen in front of his friend.

"If you want a black cat, I'd be happy to bring you Mr. Bob," Alan offered. "Assuming I could catch him, that is."

"Doesn't he belong to Mr. Hamby?" Jade asked.

"Nope," Mr. Green answered. "He just showed up about the time school started last year. No one has any idea where he came from or how he gets into half the places he shows up. You want to know what's really weird?"

"What?" Azarich asked.

"As far as we can tell, he stopped stealing stuff when Bruce figured out what he'd been doing."

"Good, I still get nervous every time someone says something is missing. We're going to explore the woods," Megan said, pausing on the way to the back porch long enough to kiss her grandfather on the cheek.

"Just be back before your mother gets home," he said while reaching an arm around her slender waist for a quick hug. "I'll have something cooked for dinner when you get back."

*Fang found another hole in the wards,* a grouchy presence sent. *Will you two patch it up? I'm going to be doing the same in a section that looks an awful lot like medieval Germany for most of the afternoon.*

*You're kidding,* Megan sent.

*Not completely,* the hermit sent with what might have been just a touch of mirth, *but just in case I'd better do it properly. It takes a while to get there, and it's going to be close to nightfall when I return.*

*No problem then,* Megan sent in reply. *We were about to head out. Just be careful.*

*I'll send Fang to show you where,* he sent, and she could feel that he liked her telling him to be careful.

"Be sure to take some water," Azarich said, giving them the look that said he knew they were communicating again.

"I'm insulted that you'd even suggest I'd let them go out unprepared!" Paul said, covering his own heart in mock-shock. "Just out of curiosity, what are you having for dinner? Dad's on shift tonight and you know what Mom's cooking is like…"

"Don't know for sure yet, but you know there's always room at our table for the Grimbles."

"Mind if I join in too?" Mr. Green called back from where he and the eldest Grimble were going out the front door.

"Our home is always open to you, Alan," Azarich called back. "You never have to ask."

"I'm just making sure you make enough of whatever it is you decide on," the janitor called. "I'll pick up Jade on my way back from the Academy."

"So what's going on that you couldn't say in front of Alan?" the

164

perceptive old man asked as soon as the front door closed.

"Huh?" Paul asked, looking up from the water bottles he'd been filling from the pack.

"They were having a pretty good conversation while we discussed dinner plans," Azarich said.

"There's a hole in the boundary that needs patching, and August is going to be somewhere that, and I quote, looks an awful like medieval Germany."

"Well," Paul said, smiling. "Knowing his royal grumpiness, he was probably there at the time and knows exactly what it would look like."

"Did I ever mention that he can hear and see just about everything up to about a quarter of a mile from the woods?" Bruce asked.

"Oh," Paul said, looking around suspiciously. "Sorry, Your Eminence. I should treat you with the respect due someone of your station."

"If you can hear me, August," Azarich said out loud, "I feel your pain. Young people these days…"

"So what do you think we'll be eating?" Paul asked as they moved toward the back porch.

"Do you ever think about anything other than food?" Megan teased as she herded him out the back door toward the treehouse.

"Well there's fossils," Paul said cheerfully.

"And goth girls with violins," Bruce added.

Paul flushed violently and used Fang's sudden appearance to change the subject.

"If August is right, do you think Guarded Wood could also be the Black Forest?" he asked.

"Now that's an interesting thought," Bruce said and then started searching his immediate future to see how he was supposed to fix the car.

The damaged section of the outer boundary took them further out than they'd had been before. Paul tried to map as they went, but was unable to keep up with the brisk pace that Fang set. By the time they arrived, even Bruce was winded.

This breach in the protections was worse than the one they'd patched before, and it took both he and Megan a few moments to probe the edges of the damage. They worked as one to join the new ward to the ancient ones that surrounded them. Only at the last moment did they remember to tie it to the rings so that all of them could feel an intrusion.

"That's it?" Paul asked, squinting to see anything out of the ordinary. "This one sounds different."

"They seriously have a sound?" Megan asked. Bruce shrugged and they let it drop.

"Anybody know how to get to the car from here?" Bruce asked.

*August?* For nearly a minute it seemed as if he might not answer.

*Follow Fang,* the thought echoed in their minds.

Once again, the wolf took off into the underbrush, and this time Bruce was almost sure he could sense mirth from his four-legged friend, though he wasn't sure if it was the hermit or the canine equivalent of mischievousness.

"You know," Megan panted while they followed. "We should ward the car so we can find our way back to it without doing this again."

*Now you're starting to use your head,* August sent. *You can do it without warding it though. Just anchor your senses there and mark it so you'll be able to find it again no matter where you are in the woods. I have to do the same thing deeper in. Sometimes things change so fast that even I could get lost if I didn't.*

166

When the car came into view, Bruce was struck once again by the contrast between the graceful chromed curves and red panels it would have when they finished and the rusty hulk that stood before them now.

"Is it my imagination, or does Big Bertha not get any prettier with familiarity?" Paul asked, echoing Bruce's thoughts. "Are you guys sure you don't need my help?"

"Not yet," Megan said, eyeing the behemoth unhappily. "I'm not even sure how much help I'm going to be. Bruce is the expert with tech stuff like this."

"Bertha?" Bruce asked.

"A good solid name for such a solid car," Paul said defensively.

"You might want to keep that name to yourself while Jade is around," Megan said, "although it is extremely fitting."

"Point taken," Paul said. "Do you think there's any way I could cross over into Wyoming?"

"I don't think there's any problem," Bruce said, scanning what he could of Paul's immediate future. "As long as you don't go so far out that you can't see the trees you should be fine. You should also turn off your phone so the phone company doesn't wonder how you're jumping from one part of the country to the other and then back."

"What's in Wyoming?" Megan asked.

"They find a lot of fossilized fish there," Paul answered, leaving two water bottles on a fallen tree. "The coordinates I read the first time are in the right formation…"

"Good luck," Bruce called after him.

"Although I can't lie," Paul said, facing them for the last time before turning to look for fossils. "I'm intrigued by the thought of dragon bones in the Black Forest."

"Don't even think about it, or I seriously will tell Mom!" Bruce called after him before adding, "That didn't sound nearly as bratty in my head until I said it."

"Where do we start?" Megan asked.

"I think I can repair the glass," he said. "I'm really glad the windshield doesn't have any holes in it. I can repair the cracks, but I can't replace anything that's missing."

Relying on his visions for guidance, he traced his finger slowly down the length of a long crack that ran nearly the full length of the windshield. As he went, the glass mended with a sound like metal cooling after a hot day.

"That is so cool," Megan said, eager to try. "Do you have to touch it?"

"I don't think so," Bruce said uncertainly. "It just helps me to focus on what I'm doing. The physical contact might help though, now that I think about it."

"Where did you learn this?" she asked, trying with limited success to repeat it.

"I can learn stuff from the visions of what I will do," he said.

"But if you learned from watching yourself..."

"I know, it hurts my head when I think about it too," he agreed, moving over to repair another section of the windshield. "Where did the knowledge come from in the first place, and isn't there some kind of paradox?"

"Well if it makes you feel any better," she teased, "you can think about weapons class tonight."

"Not cool," he said, looking up at her from the glass, "I don't go rubbing your nose in the fact that I'm better at this sort of thing than you.

Why do you think it's okay to remind me about how much better you are with weapons than I am?"

"Oh, I'm also supposed to tell you that Mom wants us to start having weapons practice up on the deck in the tree house where no one can see."

"Why can't anyone see?" he asked, looking up from the car again, a sinking feeling in his gut.

"She's going to join us, and she doesn't want anyone to report flashes of light and loud explosions," she answered, watching his reaction to save for later. She wasn't disappointed.

"I don't think I've ever been more frightened than I am right now," he said out loud. "And of course I can't see what happens with all of the power that's going to be expended."

Paul hummed to himself with a pack full of fossils as he led them down the path to the treehouse. If Bruce wasn't mistaken, it was one of the pieces the violin girl had played the year before at the Nickelville Jubilee. Considering that the youngest Grimble had only heard the piece once and was now able to remember it in its entirety was impressive. Of course, Paul had always been musically inclined. Or maybe he just stood out more because no one else in the family had any talent at all.

It wasn't long before his thoughts turned once again to what Megan had said earlier. He *really* didn't want to train with Emelia. The woman might be almost a foot shorter than him, but as Paul had pointed out, she was easily the most intimidating person he'd ever known. Even before he'd discovered that she had extraordinary abilities, he'd made sure to stay on her good side. It wasn't that he sensed anything cruel in her nature. But she possessed a singularity of determination suggesting that while she'd hate to plow over a person who got in the way of protecting Megan from the Wild Hunt, she wouldn't hesitate to do it anyway.

The stories that he'd heard about her from Azarich, Tom, Alan and sometimes even from Sam suggested that Emelia hadn't always been like she was now. Bruce wondered what could have happened during the years between leaving for college and last year when she'd returned with Megan to bring about such a metamorphosis.

As often seemed to be the case where Emelia was concerned, when he thought about the stern woman she appeared before them on the trail, carrying, of all things, a picnic basket. Her eyes were red as if she'd been crying, but that couldn't possibly be true. He knew from experience that there was a patch of ragweed not far from the path and hoped nothing had stirred it up. He was pretty sure that his bond with Megan protected him from most allergens, but after having spent so many years at its mercy, he preferred to err on the side of safety.

"Hey Mom," Megan said, frowning as if she'd noticed her mother's eyes as well. But if she questioned the fierce woman about it, it must have been with words that he couldn't hear.

"I hope you guys worked up an appetite," Emelia said, taking a knee and holding the basket up to Fang. "My father seems to be under the impression that August has been out on the edges of the known world saving us from medieval invaders and probably doesn't want to cook his own dinner."

The wolf sniffed the basket and immediately began to wag his tail like an overgrown lapdog. He gently took the handle from her hand, careful not to catch her with his teeth.

"There's enough for both of you," she said, scratching him affectionately behind both ears. "And there's a ham bone from the other night. Make sure he shares. And tell him the bottle is exactly what he thinks it is."

With a lowering of the head and a shift of the shoulders that looked suspiciously like a bow, the wolf disappeared into the trees.

"That was nice," Megan said, watching him go.

"It really was Father's idea," Emelia confessed, reaching out and hugging her daughter to her as they walked. Megan shot a startled glance at Bruce, but clearly enjoyed the rare show of affection.

"Did I smell fried chicken?" Paul asked.

"Indeed you did," Emelia answered, reluctantly releasing her daughter. "And fried okra, mashed potatoes and cornbread. Everything a southern boy like you could want."

"I'm so glad I invited myself to dinner with you guys," he said, his eyes rolling back into his head in anticipation. "Is it okay to give Fang chicken bones though?"

"Oh, he has the rest of the ham along with the bone," Emelia said. "Not that I think he would choke on chicken bones like a regular dog. I don't think August's consciousness ever completely leaves him."

"So August sort of possesses him?" Bruce asked.

"No," Emelia explained with a faint laugh. "It's more like August tags along with him in the back of his mind. It's a symbiotic relationship as far as I know, beneficial to both of them. Anyway, there's going to be a full house tonight. Alan already brought Jade home from the Palace, and she's had her hands full keeping Sam out of the kitchen. I don't think he's eaten a meal he didn't cook since we all got together at Christmas."

"How about Mister and Misses Harris?" Paul asked.

"Sorry, but there won't be any of her cookies for you tonight," Emelia said, knowing exactly where his mind had gone. "She's not feeling very well. Sam said he'd take them a care package on the way home."

"It's the cancer, isn't it?" Megan asked.

"I'm afraid so," Emelia replied. "I wish healing was one of the gifts we possess, but that's not a part of our line. I'm still surprised that you have the ability to help Bruce with his asthma." At this, she turned to look at Bruce, narrowing her eyes as she looked.

"What?" he asked.

"You don't have to be so worried about weapons practice with me," she said simply.

"I thought it was unethical to read someone without their consent!" he complained.

"Bro," Paul laughed. "Even I can feel the worry drifting off you and I *can't* read minds."

The rest of that uncomfortable line of discussion was cut off by their arrival at the back porch where Sam was happily rocking back and forth on the same swing where Megan drank her morning coffee with her grandfather.

"Did you find anything of interest young Grimble?" he called, avoiding discussions of subjects to which some of their guests were still ignorant.

"A lot of gastropods, a couple of loose shark teeth in a gravel bed from a dry creek and part of a fossilized fish. I left it though since it wasn't complete. It's my first time to that area though, so it was fun just poking around. There was one exposure that looked really promising, but I'd need to bring climbing gear to get to it and another experienced climber to belay me while I did." Paul reached into his pocket and pulled out the shark teeth to show the big man when they approached.

"I can go with you if you'd like," Sam said, looking with interest at the teeth. "I've never been that far away from Nickelville."

"If that's an offer, you've got a deal!" Paul exclaimed, grinning more than Bruce had seen him do in a long time. It was nice. The scout helped Sam up from the swing even though the big man didn't need it, and they joined the others inside.

Soon the table was set, drinks were poured, and it was confirmed that Dora would soon be there with a bag of ice for the tea. Azarich clearly loved having everyone together again. Emelia, who normally stayed at the edges of the crowd or hid behind Sam, seemed to be everywhere at once. One minute she was hugging her father, who looked almost as surprised as Megan had been just a short time earlier, and the next she was actually encouraging Alan and her father to tell another one of their stories from the days before the war.

When Dora arrived it was more like a party than a weekday dinner and became even more so when Emelia broke out bottles of mead that she'd apparently fermented herself in one of the neighboring deserted houses sometime over the past months. The adults all raved about how good it was and even the kids were allowed to taste it. Bruce frankly didn't understand what all the fuss was about. For lack of a better description, it made his eyeballs itch.

Their combined laughter chased away their worries, and for that short time at least, all was well on Beverly Road.

# Chapter XVIII: Battle in the Treetops

Unfortunately for Bruce, his worst fears about the blank spot in the future came true not long after they'd returned home after the impromptu feast. Just as he kicked off his shoes and began scrolling through a list of shows he'd intended to watch, the summons came.

*Come on up to the tree house,* Megan sent. *Mom and Sam are setting things up for our first augmented weapons training.* The eagerness in her thoughts was inversely proportional to his own.

*We just ate,* he sent half-heartedly. *Aren't we supposed to hold off for at least half an hour after eating?*

*That's swimming,* she sent. *Unless you'd rather go swimming. I'm sure she'd have you cliff diving in no time.*

His stomach lurched at the thought even though he knew she was teasing him.

*You're a cruel woman. I'll be there in a bit.*

Although it wasn't far, it took Bruce a long time to make his way up to the main deck of the tree house. As much as he enjoyed his abilities, this was the one area that didn't come easily to him. But he hadn't been kidding when he'd said he wanted to be trained in combat for when they encountered the Wild Hunt someday.

When he climbed the last steps of the spiral staircase that wound its way around the trunk of the sentinel, he saw that Sam and Megan were training in the same clothing they normally wore at the dojo. Emelia was wearing a pair of jeans and one of the same loose fitting, long-sleeved blouses she always wore, regardless of the weather.

Megan was running through one of the staff forms they often practiced.

"Okay," Emelia said. "Now that we're all here, I'd like to see what you've got. Megan, attack me."

"But you're unarmed," Megan managed to get out before her mother pivoted inside her daughter's defenses, wrenched the staff from her hands and used it to sweep the girl's legs out from under her. It happened so fast that Bruce hardly had time to register what was happening before his friend was disarmed and falling.

But as unexpected as the attack had been, his friend was already turning her fall into a controlled roll. It seemed however, that Emelia had anticipated this response and was swinging the staff toward her daughter's unprotected side.

Emelia wasn't the only one pushing the boundaries of what he'd thought possible though. In the instant before the staff struck her, Megan drew the other staff to her from the table where it had been faster than his eyes could follow. The sound of wood striking wood echoed across the woods.

"You can't win a fight like this by staying on the defensive," Sam advised.

In response to his words, Megan pivoted on her knee and rose to step

175

into

Emelia's attack before her mother's weapon could build enough
momentum to do any real damage. But the woman put her weight behind
the staff and shoved her daughter back off balance and swung her staff
high toward Megan's head.

Bruce was already coming to her defense when Megan blurred for just an instant during which her mother's weapon whistled through the space where she'd just been, then solidified with her own staff swinging toward Emelia.

"Excellent," Emelia yelled, easily blocking her daughter's attack before lowering her guard. Unlike Megan, she was barely winded. "I was hoping your instincts would kick in with a bit more stimulus."

"A bit more stimulus?" Bruce shouted, for the first time raising his voice to this intimidating woman. "You could have killed her!"

"Do you really think I'd do anything to put my daughter in danger after spending every waking moment of the past decade and a half keeping her safe?"

"I have no idea what you would and wouldn't do," he retorted, still angry and if he admitted it, more than a little frightened about what might happen next.

"I would never allow one of my students to be hurt," Sam assured him, completely calm.

"But they were going at it full force," Bruce said, feeling outnumbered.

"Emelia is much better than I am and has the control to match," Sam explained. "At any point she could have pulled her strikes if it looked as if Megan wasn't going to be able to defend herself."

"Are you sure about that?" Bruce asked quietly.

"I'm okay," Megan panted, still trying to catch her breath. "I don't know how to explain it, but this stuff comes naturally to me. I felt really competitive, especially there at the end, but I never felt like I was in danger."

"Good for you. I think I may have ruined a perfectly good pair of

177

underwear," he confessed.

They were kind enough not to laugh, but their smiles were contagious.

"I think I know how to get you past the worst of your nerves," Emelia said.

"Let me run away?" he asked hopefully. "I'm really good at running."

"Hey August," She called loudly. "I know you've been watching."

A raven flew down from where it had been perched on the tower balcony overhead.

"Feel like giving Mr. Grimble a hand?"

The raven elegantly bobbed its head in a clear gesture of agreement. Then Bruce felt the old man's awareness brush against his shields.

Bruce lowered them and immediately felt the hermit's presence intensify.

*Just relax and let me take the wheel. You could easily kick me out, but I wouldn't advise it while you're squaring off against Emelia. She's quite a piece of work, isn't she?*

*You can say that again,* Bruce answered. He felt better having the old man with him in this.

*Open your mind to the immediate future so I can read what she's going to do.*

*But I can't see anything around all of this,* Bruce warned.

*That's because she knows about your blind spots and is intentionally using so much energy that she interferes with your foresight. I'm going to keep her so busy that she won't be able to keep it up.*

*So I take it, you know what you're doing?*

*I wasn't always an old man. But don't forget this is a learning exercise. Watch and learn. This is going to be so much fun!*

Then before Bruce could respond, power began to build within him in a way that he'd never felt before, and for lack of a better description, he threw a fireball at his best friend's mother.

It dissipated harmlessly about an inch from her skin, and before she could recover, August used Bruce's abilities to snatch up the staff from Megan's hand and swung it directly at the woman's unprotected flank. Her own staff rose to meet it and the recoil of the impact traveled the length of the wood and left his wrists throbbing. Then, moving faster than he ever had in his life, he exchanged a flurry of blows he feared might wake his own mother next door from her meal induced slumber. More eerie than having his body used like a puppet was the banter that the two experienced fighters kept up for the entire duration of the fight. The match finally ended with both staves shattering on each other and spraying the deck with splinters of wood. They both fell heavily to the wooden surface, panting with laughter.

"By the gods woman! I haven't had that much fun in centuries," Bruce heard himself say. "I'd forgotten what it feels like to be this young. Thanks, by the way, for the meal. Fang was appreciative too."

Then he was gone, and Bruce realized he missed the grouchy old man's presence.

# Chapter XIX: Excitement on the Boundary

Megan woke when something crossed the boundary she'd repaired with Bruce. She could feel her mother stir in the room next to hers and knew that her friends next door had woken as well. She hurriedly pulled her shoes on and tied her hair back to keep it from catching in branches once they entered Guarded Wood.

The moon wasn't full, but after a few moments, their eyes adjusted and they were able to see their surroundings well enough. By the time they arrived at the treehouse, the mosquitoes had found them.

"This is so cool!" Paul whispered. He had the headlamp he took camping with the scouts strapped to his forehead.

"Maybe you should stay here," Bruce said quietly.

"What is up with you?" Paul whispered urgently, rounding on his brother and bathing Bruce's face in light. "You're not that much older than me, and I've got years more experience in the woods."

*I'll stay close to him,* Emelia sent.

"Well," Bruce said quietly, "You did remember your shoes this time. Just tell us if you hear music or see any of the wisps."

"Come on," Jade said, almost as eager as Paul. "Let's see what tripped the alarm."

*Let me know if it's anything you can't handle,* sent the hermit from deep within the woods. *Fang is on his way.*

Guarded Wood was actually much louder at night than it was during the day. The birds might be gone, but the deafening drone of the crickets, cicadas and frogs more than made up for their absence.

Although they weren't running, they moved quickly enough to remind Megan how sore she was from her match with her mother. She thought she could see a certain amount of stiffness from Bruce's movements as well.

The silhouette of the sentinel trees near the newly repaired boundary rose into view above the smaller trees of the interior. Megan cast her senses around, looking for what had tripped her wards.

"Uh," Paul said with his usual irritating cheerfulness, "Is there something going on here that I can't see?"

"Not that I can tell," Megan answered, scanning her surroundings with all of her senses. "Mom?"

"Looks like a false alarm," Emelia said, and even though it was too dark to see, Megan knew her mother was frowning. This shouldn't have happened. "I guess we can go back to bed."

"Oh well," Jade yawned. "At least we know the alarm works. I wouldn't have minded staying in that dream a while longer though. We'd just gotten my car running, and the whole Jones family was crossing the street in front of me..."

181

# Chapter XX: Cleaning Up a Dust Storm

Bruce moaned and covered his head with his pillow when his mother stuck her head into his room and told him that breakfast was ready. After the first three false alarms, Megan and her mother had told the Grimbles to stay at home while they tried to sort out what was going on out at the boundary. But he still waited anxiously for their return each time throughout the night. As a result, he hadn't slept much either.

"When am I going to stop being so sore?" Bruce moaned when his sister passed the open door to his room.

"Ah yes," Jade said with a malicious grin as she poked her head back through his door. "Tell me more of your suffering. It is music to my ears!"

"You are such a...." Bruce muttered under his breath.

"Finish that statement and I might just have to kick your ungrateful behind!" Jade called on her way to the kitchen.

"I'd rather it happen now when your feet are padded by the Elmo slippers than later," he called after her before he pulled on a shirt and followed her down the hall.

"You're going back to the Palace again today?" Mr. Grimble asked as he heaped pancakes up on Jade's plate. From the way everyone was loading up, it was safe to say that the family was happy to have him back home again.

"Nope," she answered sadly, eagerly pouring syrup over the whole thing. "Kate said she wasn't feeling up to opening today and didn't feel comfortable asking me to run the show after so little training."

"And everything is going well there?" he asked after several silent moments filled only with sounds of appreciation.

"It's so cool getting to check out all of the places where she doesn't let the patrons go," Jade mumbled around a mouthful of food. "I just wish we could fix the place up. I knew it was falling apart, but you've got no idea."

Jade froze in the middle of her next bite, eyes wide as she looked at Bruce.

"What?" Bruce asked. "Do I have syrup on my face?"

"The Palace is not going to open today or tomorrow, and you're really good at *fixing* stuff," she gasped, leaving no doubt in Bruce's mind that she was thinking about what he was doing with Big Bertha.

"Are you sure Kate would be okay with that?" Mr. Grimble asked with a frown. "I'd hate to do anything that would upset her."

"Oh no," Jade assured him, her food temporarily forgotten. "She told me I was welcome to fix anything I was capable of when I asked. What if we could get the other projector working?"

"What projector?" Paul yawned, finally joining them at the kitchen table in his old man pajamas.

"Are you feeling okay?" Mr. Grimble asked, "I hope you three aren't coming down with something. I mean, I know it's summer and all, but none of you ever sleep this late."

"We're fine, Dad," Jade said, turning to Bruce. "So what do you think? Are you up to a day at the Palace?"

*Want to spend the day fixing things at the Palace?* Bruce sent.

*Finally woken up have you?* Megan sent in return. *Of course I'd like to go. Mom would probably come too if she wasn't out with Sam again. I'll be right over.*

"Sure," Bruce said. "Megan will want to come too."

Jade jumped up, ran around the table and hugged Bruce so hard it hurt before sprinting toward her room to get dressed, all signs of her previous exhaustion lost.

"So I assume I'm taking you guys to the Palace then," Mr. Grimble said. "Can we even get in if Kate isn't there?"

"I've got keys," Jade yelled from her room.

"And here I thought things were going to quiet down now that the tree house was finished," Mr. Grimble said with a shrug as he drained the last of his coffee and started to load the dishes into the washer.

As soon as Mr. Grimble drove off after making sure that Jade's key did, in fact, open the front doors to The Palace, the four of them headed straight for the unused theater. The door wasn't locked, but the stiffness of the hinges suggested that it hadn't been opened in a very long time.

Although the Grand Theatre might not have been quite as cluttered as Mr. Green's storage shed at the Academy, it was easily three times as big with the balcony. Cobweb encrusted chandeliers hung from long brass chains, worn velvet curtains hung half closed across the screen, and the small wooden stage was littered with boxes. Why couldn't all abandoned places be as clean as Honeysuckle House?

"I'm not sure you're going to be able to stay in here, Bruce," Paul said, brushing a thick layer of dust from the back of one of the worn velvet seats.

"I think I can help with that," Megan said. "Paul, would you go back and prop the front door open?"

"Sure Megan," Paul replied, running back toward the front of the building.

"Jade, can you open the fire exit at the back of this theater?" Megan asked.

"Probably," Jade said, reaching into her pocket for the keys. "It should be the same as the front door."

"Fire exits aren't supposed to be locked from the inside," Bruce called after her. "Stand guard but don't stand in the doorway. We don't want to hit you."

"I can probably do this by myself," Megan said. "I don't want to mess with your asthma."

"I'll be fine," he said, trying not to think about the way her smile made him feel. "Just try not to let a static charge build. I don't want to fry the electronics any worse than they probably already are."

"Gotcha," Megan said, turning her thoughts toward the boundaries of the theater.

Linking hands, they reached out and began to push the stale air out the fire exit. At first, it felt like little more than a faint breeze, but as they became more confident the air flowed faster and faster.

*I've got this part if you want to move closer,* he sent.

Megan released his hand and walked down the center aisle, sending stronger bursts into the individual seats and their contents. With each mental swat, the seats belched forth a cloud of dust which the negative air pressure in the room carried out to the alley behind the Palace.

185

"No wonder your room is always so clean!" Paul exclaimed over the dull roar of the air's passage.

Bruce allowed himself to be swept up in his brother's excitement and started to push harder. Unfortunately, the extra pressure was too much for the stacks of paper that littered the cavernous space. Without warning, they took flight.

With a level of finesse that she hadn't possessed a few short months before, Megan began to pluck each of the pieces of paper from the air and deposit them into a big empty box near where she was standing. When the last of the dust was cleared, they allowed the air to still, leaving the cool air of the theater replaced by the hot, humid air of a Texas afternoon.

"Think you could do anything about the heat?" Jade asked.

"Not if you want us to fix anything," Bruce said. "We could heat it pretty easily, but even though I think I understand how to cool it, that's a lot harder than making the air move."

"Oh well, can't blame me for trying," Jade said. "I'm going to go clean the popcorn popper. I'm pretty sure there's nothing wrong with it that some elbow grease wouldn't fix. You want to help, Paul?"

"Sure," he agreed, following her back toward the lobby.

"Let's have a look at the projector," Megan said, rubbing her hands together eagerly.

"Um," Bruce said, choosing his words carefully. "I don't want you to take this the wrong way, but I should probably handle the projector by myself."

"Why?" she asked, looking more puzzled than hurt.

"It runs on electricity, and…"

"I still tend to fry electronics when I'm excited," she finished.

"You're probably right. I'll go see what non-electrical things I can work on.

Bruce breathed a sigh of relief. He'd worried that she'd be upset with him for making the suggestion.

Able to control his eagerness no longer, he returned to the lobby and found his way up to the projector rooms which were located above the Grand Theatre's single balcony. Jade and Paul looked up as he passed, but he could feel the layout of the theater with his extra senses and knew what was wrong with the projector even if he didn't know what to call it. It only took him a few moments to fuse the broken pieces of a small internal gear back together before he flipped the power switch and the projector roared back to life.

"Oh my God!" he heard his sister scream from downstairs. "I can't believe it! You actually got it working again!"

*Pretty impressive,* Sam's thoughts whispered in the back of his mind.

*Don't tell me you can hear Jade all the way over at Gordon's?* Bruce sent. *I know she's loud and all...*

*No, I'm just about to walk in the front door of the Palace. I've got a couple of pizzas for you hard working children. You wouldn't know anything about a big cloud of dust that blew down the alley on this otherwise calm day, would you?*

"Oops," Megan said, when she and Bruce met him in the foyer.

"We posted a lookout," Bruce said.

"No harm done," Sam said with a good-natured grin. "Just be careful not to let anyone else notice. And don't accomplish too much too fast or people will begin to wonder how four teenagers cleared up twenty years of clutter and neglected maintenance in one afternoon."

"It's definitely going to take more than one afternoon to get the main theater usable again," Paul said with relish as he took the pizza boxes from Sam. "You wouldn't believe how much junk is stored in there."

"I've got a business of my own," Sam replied as he followed them to the break room, "and I know exactly how much accumulates at Gordon's. I can only imagine how much junk I'd have if we had this many places to

188

stick things before we had to start throwing stuff away."

"And we have to be careful not to throw anything away that would upset Kate," Jade said with a frown that lasted only as long as it took her to eat her first bite. "This is getting harder and harder by the moment."

"Hey Sam," Megan called out, "Is Mom with you?"

"I haven't seen her today," the big man answered.

"I thought she left with you early this morning," Megan said, frowning. "Her truck was still there, but she was gone."

"That is a question I cannot answer for you," he replied.

"Anybody home?" Mr. Green's voice drifted from the foyer.

"We're back here," Megan called.

The janitor walked into the break room with his old battered toolbox in hand.

"You're going to be my favorite person next to Sam and his pizza if you're going to help us with repairs," Jade said.

"If the town council doesn't want to pay for my services, then the Academy can do without me for the day," he said, putting his toolbox down next to the table before taking a seat and helping himself to a piece of pizza. "And frankly I'd love a chance to look around this place."

"I know what you mean," Bruce said. "It's amazing. I'd do it for free just for the chance to see all of this stuff."

"You are doing this for free," Paul said. "Unless my sister is taking advantage of my scoutly service…" The youngest Grimble stopped in mid-bite, which given his near insatiable appetite gave some indication to the magnitude of his thoughts.

"What?" Megan asked.

"Do you guys see any reason why I couldn't send out word to the rest of my troop?" Paul asked quickly, his voice breaking in his excitement.

189

"I'm sure some of them need service hours, and the rest are just as curious as we are about this place."

"I'll be here if anyone has a problem with them being unsupervised," Mr. Green added.

"And I will too," Bruce's dad said from the doorway of the break room, having just arrived to check on the progress. "I think it's a great idea. This place is a Nickelville cornerstone, and we need to help preserve it. The scouts wouldn't be doing anything dangerous, and who knows, maybe some of their parents will come to help too."

"Can I ask the scoutmaster to bring the climbing gear?" Paul asked his dad.

"What for?" Mr. Grimble asked with a frown.

"I found several crates of those clear light bulbs that go on the marquee," Paul said, "And as I recall more than half of them are burned out. It would look a lot better if I could rappel down from the roof and change them."

"Doesn't Kate usually rent a cherry picker for that?" Sam asked.

"Yeah," Mr. Green answered. "But they're pricey."

"We have several harnesses and more than enough rope," Paul said. "Both of us could do it. And Sam said he wanted to learn how to climb and repel just yesterday."

Bruce smiled to himself. Paul knew their father loved to rappel and didn't get a chance to do it very often. Throwing in Sam was a stroke of genius since everyone was always looking for ways to pay the big man back for everything he did.

"We'll see," Mr. Grimble said, also smiling at his son's blatant attempt to manipulate him.

"So I can call the troop?" Paul asked.

"Knock yourself out," Mr. Grimble answered.

"Well," Sam said, getting up reluctantly, "as much as I'd love to stay, I've got a restaurant to run. Are you guys going to be here as late as dinner?"

The four teens looked at each other, surprised that the adults were letting them call the shots.

"Probably," Jade answered at last.

"Then let me know how many show up before dinner, and I'll send over something besides pizza," The big man offered. "And if you give me a yell," he looked pointedly at Megan and Bruce, "I'll come learn about the arts of climbing and repelling."

"You don't have to do all that," Mr. Grimble called after him.

"Oh, I consider this an investment. If the Palace starts to draw a steady crowd again, it will improve my business as well. And I've always thought climbing looked interesting."

Now that the projector was working and opportunities for his "special" skills were diminishing, Bruce thought he'd put his organizational talents to use. Borrowing the spiral notebook that Paul always kept in his "ready for anything up to but not excluding an alien invasion" backpack, Bruce began to take note of the clutter and work out what to do with it all.

Much to his surprise, the storage rooms at the top of the stairs next to the projector rooms weren't as full as he'd feared. In view of how much was stored in the main theater, he suspected Kate had decided it was too much work to carry things up the stairs when there was such an easy alternative available on the first floor.

*Come up here, would you?* he sent.

Within seconds Megan was at his side.

191

"What's up?" she asked.

"I know we don't want to upset Kate by throwing away anything she might want to keep," he started. "But I think most of the stuff in these two rooms can be condensed to make room for the stuff we're not sure about downstairs."

"And you want me to help you go through all of it," Megan said.

"Bingo," Bruce said distractedly as he opened a box at the top of a stack.

Inside were a mismatched collection of movie trinkets that he could dimly remember his mother mentioning from her childhood. As he moved it aside, he noticed a promotional poster from an old movie he'd seen hanging on the wall at the Palace when he was a child.

"My mom loved that movie," Megan said from behind him.

"Some of this stuff is really collectable," Bruce said. "We need to store it in a way that won't damage it.

Over the next hour, the two of them combined and consolidated until the original contents of the two storage rooms took up the corner of one, thus giving them someplace to store the stuff from the main theater.

"Wait a minute," Megan said, taking one last look at a pile of movie posters. "Why don't we see if Mr. Green can make displays out of these for the reopening? If we picked a wide range of titles from past years, it would make people of all ages happy to see them."

"Good idea," Bruce said. "We should move these down to Kate's office then so they don't get buried at the back of the room when we bring everything else up."

No sooner had Megan left with the stack of posters than a boy Bruce recognized from Paul's troop peeked around the corner.

"Your sister wants to know if you're ready for us to start bringing stuff up," the boy asked.

"That's perfect," Bruce answered. "I'll be right down."

"No," the boy said, "We're bringing it all up to you. Your Tetris skills are legendary."

In the hours that followed, the air of abandonment faded to be replaced by something of the Palace's former glory. Nothing could replace the worn fabric of the curtains or seats, but metal shone, and glass surfaces gleamed for the first time in decades. By the time Mr. Green finished repairing the broken seats, any scout interested in completing the welding and woodworking merit badges had done so.

With all of the extra help, no one suspected anything supernatural about the transformation, though Bruce and Megan still made repairs when necessary. Paul's scoutmaster had already hauled off two loads of trash to the dump, and both Paul and his father were hanging down in front of the marquis, replacing lights as they descended while Sam and the Scoutmaster belayed them.

*Can you spare Jade for a few minutes?* Emelia sent from somewhere nearby, making Megan jump.

*Sure, why?* Bruce replied.

*I'm going to interview her for the* Tribune, she sent. *If it's not too much trouble, I'll get a picture of everyone together and maybe some candids of people working. If we let the town know what's going on, we can generate more interest in the Palace and raise our own lagging sales at the same time. Everyone wins.*

*That sounds great.* Bruce replied. *I just had an idea for how to pay everyone for helping today.*

*Is Sam with you?* Megan asked, masking her emotions as she did so.

*No, do you need anything?*

*No, I'm good.* Megan sent, quickly shifting her thoughts away from her suspicions about her mother's absences. *I was just wondering what he was making for us tonight. I'm starved!*

"Everyone listen up!" Paul called over the assembled scouts, family and friends at the end of that long day of cleaning. In spite of the general exhaustion that hung over the crowd as they took seats in the newly restored Grande Theatre, weary smiles greeted the youngest Grimble as he spoke. "Jade has something to say."

"On behalf of Kate I'd like to thank all of you for coming together and helping us restore The Palace to at least part of her former glory," she said with the air of authority she usually saved for teaching at the dojo. "As a token of our appreciation we thought you should be the first audience in the Grande Theatre in over a decade."

Cheers broke out over the cavernous room and became louder when Bruce and Megan pushed a cart down the center aisle, passing out bags of popcorn and bottles of water as they went.

In a rare, unguarded moment, Bruce felt unbridled joy emanating from Emelia as she passed popcorn down to Azarich and his childhood friends. When her eyes met his, she gave him the first genuine smile he'd ever seen on her lips.

*You guys did well,* she sent.

*The whole town needed this,* Sam added. *We are so proud of you.*

Worried that something might go wrong in spite of his thorough testing of the ancient projector, Bruce reached out with his mind and dimmed the lights before starting the movie. As it roared to life and the concession reel filled the screen, everyone in the theater erupted into applause, all exhaustion forgotten.

# Chapter XXI: Josie's Hidden Treasures

The next morning Megan woke to the sound of rain and distant thunder. Her immediate feeling was of disappointment, because on mornings like this, there wasn't much point in going out to watch the sunrise because the heavy clouds would block out even a hint of what was going on above them.

She thought briefly about staying in bed a while longer, particularly in light of all the times she and her mother had been out to the boundary during the night. But the possibility of more of her grandfather's stories while they sat around the kitchen table drinking their coffee was an awesome way to start the day as well. She had just gotten dressed when the darkness outside exploded with light and thunder shook the glass in the window frames.

She felt her mother come awake just as the power cut off.

Megan walked to her door through the darkness, not needing light to know her surroundings. She walked down the hall to her mother's room, where the woman was pulling on her own clothing.

"Sam says the whole town is blacked out," Emelia said. "That one probably struck the power station."

"You ladies okay up there?" Azarich called from below.

"We're okay Dad," Emelia answered, then repeated Sam's message.

"Bruce says his mom is going to call you in a second on the landline to tell you not to bother coming in until they get the power back on, which he adds, won't be until just before lunchtime," Megan added.

"Maybe he should think about being a weatherman," Azarich said from the base of the stairs where he was holding a lit candle. "At least the coffee finished before the power went off. We've got a camp model I could use on the gas stove, but I'd be hard put to tell you where it could be. I don't think I've used it since before you were born, Emelia."

"My guess would be that it's in the attic," she suggested. "Isn't that where just about everything ends up eventually?"

"You're not wrong there," he admitted, smiling up at them as they came down the stairs.

"You know," Megan said, looking down the hall toward the other set of stairs. "I've never gone up there."

"You're not missing much," Emelia said, following her nose to the promise of coffee. "Of course, you might like it better than I did at your age. It reminded me of the Academy at the time, and that wasn't exactly my favorite place."

"What's up there?" Megan asked, following them into the darkened kitchen.

"The clutter of about a hundred and fifty years of McGeehee history," Azarich said. "I always say I'm going to clear it out and organize everything, but let's be honest. I've been saying that since Josie and I got married."

"Want us to help?" Megan asked, sitting down with the cup.

"If you want," Azarich said. "Don't feel like you have to though."

197

"I think it would be fascinating," Megan said. "I want to find out everything I can about where I come from."

"And soon you will," Emelia said, reaching out and placing her hand over her daughter's.

"That's not what I meant," Megan said quickly.

"I know," her mother said, taking a long drink from her cup. "Coffee really does make everything better, doesn't it? Anyway, I'd love to spend the morning stirring up dust and mold with my two favorite people. Want me to whip up something for breakfast?"

"No!" the other two said far too quickly.

"Have it your way," she said loftily. "I'm going to go put on some shoes before we go up there. I still haven't forgotten about that spider the last time."

"What's that about?" Megan asked after her mother had left the table.

"She was playing hide and seek with Sam once when they were still young enough to do so, and she thought she'd hide in the attic. She stepped on a big spider barefoot, and I'm pretty sure the people in town heard her."

"Ew," Megan said, wrinkling her nose in distaste. "I can't say I blame her for that one. I don't mind spiders, but I wouldn't want to step on one of those big wolf spiders Paul is always pointing out."

"I'll scramble some eggs for us, and then we can tackle the attic afterward," he said, pulling eggs out of the darkened refrigerator.

A short time later Megan saw the attic for the first time, or at least as much as she could by candlelight. She wasn't quite sure what she'd expected, but in spite of her mother's description she hadn't expected it to be quite that cluttered.

The soft roar of the rain on the roof above reminded her of that day when they'd found Jacob Routh's journal. She knew it had only been a few months ago, but it seemed like a lifetime had passed since then. An odd assortment of clutter poked here and there from boxes, trunks and rafters. Some of the stuff could be readily identified, while some could have ranged in origin from recreation to torture.

"We can never let Bruce know that this exists," Megan whispered in horror. "It took us weeks to clean out the school storage shed, and even though this place is a little bit smaller, I think there might be four or five times as much stuff."

"See what I mean?" Azarich said. "This is what happens when one family lives in the same place for multiple generations. I don't think I've ever made it more than about ten feet in any direction before I give up and go back downstairs. Josie used to come up here sometimes though."

"And do what?" Emelia asked, trying to make sense of the sheer volume surrounding her.

"I don't know," Azarich said. "I'd catch her coming back down the stairs sometimes. If I asked what she was doing, she'd just say that she'd been exploring."

*Sam is coming with us to the Wyoming boundary so I can show him how far we've come with Big Bertha. Then he and Paul are going to teach us how to climb. The weather is nice there. Want to come?*

"The Grimbles are going rock climbing out past the Wyoming boundary," Megan said, looking over from where she'd been thinking about starting her exploration. "It's not raining there and Sam is going too."

"Dora is letting them go out in a storm?" Azarich asked.

"They have rain gear," Emelia answered, likely already

199

communicating with Sam. "Paul and Jade go out fairly often when it's wet. Something about the moisture making it easier to see some kinds of rocks and fossils."

"And Bruce says his mom will call you around eleven and tell you that the rest of the staff can finish the layout without you," Megan said. "It looks like you've got the day off."

"Then I'd say the day's plans are up to you," her mother said. "Dad, are these the letters we looked at back at Thanksgiving?"

"Yes," the old man answered. "Some of them go back to the early 19th century. I have no idea who most of the people who wrote them are though. Quite a few of them mentioned their dealings with an old hermit in the woods."

Megan thought about it for a moment and then told Bruce they'd take a, pun intended, rain check on the outing. She'd like the day to spend with her family. While the other two looked through the letters, she noticed an old soap box race car sitting on top of another trunk.

"Did you build this, Grandpa?" she asked, moving it down to the ground so she could get a better look.

"My dad and I did," he said fondly. "They used to have a yearly race where the road into town dips down toward the lake. I only raced it once, but it was a lot of fun just building it with him."

"What was your father like?" Megan asked.

"He was a quiet man, but a hard worker," Azarich said, looking up from the letter he'd been reading. "I was a lot closer to my mother than I was to him though. I mean I loved them both, but that's one of the only times that I can really remember us doing something where it was just the two of us. Most of my childhood memories center around my mother and my friends."

"That's funny," Emelia said, getting up to look at something else. "All of my memories center around my father, his friends and a certain tall boy who had this weird habit of talking to trees. My dad was pretty cool though."

Azarich reached out with his free arm and hugged her around the hip when she passed by. She ruffled his thick white hair affectionately.

"It sounds like the storm might be passing," Megan said, noting that the roar of the rain had diminished to the point where she could hear the water running down the gutters to the ground below. "I think there's light coming from back there," she said, pointing toward the front of the house.

"There's a window set into a dormer over there," Azarich said, "Although I've never seen it from the inside."

"You can climb back if you want," Emelia said. "Just use your abilities to steady things if you need to."

Needing no more encouragement than that, Megan flattened herself as best she could and slipped between an old wardrobe like the one in the school library and a bookcase full of really old books. The light grew brighter as she approached the place where the roof beams began to slope downward toward the wall.

"Those belonged to your mother," she heard her grandfather say. "And that was her wedding dress."

"I want to see that when I get out," Megan called. It looked like there might be a fairly large open space up ahead. Giving up on moving what appeared to be a canoe, she ducked down and crawled under it into the lit space.

Were it not for the odd entrance, she would have thought it was a separate room. Old trunks and crates made walls that rose from the dusty floorboards and continued up to the rafters. Covering these makeshift walls

201

were hundreds of watercolor paintings. In the center of the space where the light from the window would best land, was an easel and stool.

"Grandpa," Megan called.

"Yes, Darling?"

"Where did Grandma do her painting?" she asked, although she already knew the answer.

"I'm not really sure," he said after a moment. "I'd just come home from the office sometimes, and there would be a new painting on the kitchen table. Now that you mention it, I never even considered where she might have done her painting. Why?"

"I think I just found her studio," Megan called. "You guys might want to hold your breath for a moment. There are a lot of pictures back here and I want to get the layers of dust off of them so we can see them."

"Okay, Megan," her mother called. "I'll try to shift some of this so we can get back to you."

"She had to have had a way to get back here," Megan called back. "Give me a minute before you start. After hanging around with Bruce for so long, I'm pretty sure I can feel how it opens. Just let me take care of the dust first."

Refining the method they'd used to clear the dust from the Grand Theatre, she used the air to lift the dust from the paintings without damaging them. But unlike what they had done with the dust before, Megan took off both of her shoes and used her socks, one inside the other, as a filter to channel the soiled air through before turning it loose again. It didn't work perfectly, but at least they'd still be able to breathe while they looked.

Getting out was as simple as realizing that the canoe had a pocket of space into which it could be moved. But as far as she could see, it was only

202

possible if you had the ability to move large objects with your mind, for there were no places to get enough leverage to do it otherwise. The other obstacles had all been put in place by Azarich himself over the years since as he'd tried to organize the space and were easily moved away from the entrance to Josie's hidden space.

All three moved through the room in silent reverence, looking at these forgotten treasures. In the first that Megan studied, she recognized the Academy, but not as it looked now. It was clearly a church in the image her grandmother had captured on the thick paper.

"I had no idea she'd painted this many," Azarich said, reaching out to touch one in which a much younger version of himself was throwing his head back and laughing.

"Megan," her mother called from further down the wall.

Megan walked over and was greeted by an incredibly accurate rendition of Jacob Routh. Next to it was a picture of him in what was clearly his wedding to their ancestor. She'd seen the pulpit and cross from the picture in the attic at the Academy when they'd found the journal. The memories he'd given her that day stirred and tried to bring themselves to the surface of her thoughts. But as always, they remained disjointed and impossible to understand.

"She has two bridesmaids," Emelia noted.

"We're descended from that one," Megan said, pointing to the stern woman she'd seen before. "Her name was Crina, and she was Charlotte's mother-in-law."

"But who is the other one?" Emelia asked.

"It's like it's on the tip of my tongue from the memories he gave me," Megan said, trying to call it forth. "But I never can get any of it to clear itself."

"That's okay," Emelia said. "This is all ancient history now, anyway. It would have been nice if we'd known all of this back when he was trying to get us to clear the graves."

"I don't know what to make of these," Azarich said, pointing to two paintings that were quite different from the others. The first was a night view of his wife's grove. A full moon lit the space within the trees in such beautiful detail that it almost looked like a photograph. But that's where the realism ended. Dancing around the spring in the moonlight were several half-goat half-human shapes that looked like something from a book on mythology. In the second, Megan recognized several of the woodland creatures she'd seen as a child. "Before this summer I would have said she was just having fun with her art, but now I'm wondering if she saw the goatmen from local legend."

"Welcome to my world, old man," Emelia said, walking over to the easel. "I wonder how many hours she spent sitting here." Her fingertips caressed the dried tubes of paint and the cups that had held water. There was a palette tray with dried pigments still in the cups and a brush resting next to it as if Grandma Josie had only put it down a moment ago. She moved around the easel to sit on the stool then looked at the drawing surface. A quick intake of breath was all it took to bring both her daughter and father to her side.

An unfinished piece was still clipped to the front of the easel, with only a quarter of the paint filling the faintly drawn sketch that Josie had been using to guide her strokes. It was Emelia's room, because they could see the corner of the driveway where it met Beverly Road through the window. The vanity with its silver brushes and mirror was in a different spot than where it stood now, and in place of the four-poster, there was a much smaller crib. It was this crib that was the focal point and most complete part of the painting. Across the head of the crib ornate letters read, Emelia.

"Alan built that crib for us when Josie first picked your name," Azarich said, his voice thick. "I can never thank you enough for finding this Megan. It's like reaching out and touching her again for the first time in all of these years."

It was a long time before they left the attic, and it was even longer before they thought of anything other than what they'd seen there.

# Chapter XXII: Opening Day

That Friday night, in the dusky gloom above an anxious crowd that stood in line all the way down main street, hundreds of newly replaced lights banished the darkness as the Palace's marquee burst into life. A sprinkling of masks dotted the crowd. However, the city had announced that there appeared to be no evidence that the strange illness, unofficially named the goat flu to coincide with all of the recent Goatman sightings, could be transmitted from person to person. However, the fact that it only seemed to affect people while they were in town left health officials baffled.

Since Kate still remained too sick to come in, Jade took over ticket sales, and Megan could feel both the eldest Grimble's stress and happiness all the way from the concession stand. Given the number of times they'd been woken by something crossing the boundaries at Guarded Wood, they were all running close to empty. Paul ushered the crowd toward the correct theater, though he'd been instructed to let people look into the newly renovated Grande Theater even if their ticket wasn't for that movie. Bruce, of course, ran the projectors in both theaters.

"Make sure you keep your ticket stubs," she heard Jade say over the rising din of excited patrons. "It's worth ten percent off of your next meal at Gordon's."

*He really didn't have to do that,* Megan sent.

*He knows what he's doing,* Bruce sent in return. *He's going to make a lot more in increased revenue tonight than he's going to lose with that discount.*

Even with an extra batch of popcorn precooked and bagged, Megan was soon overwhelmed by the number of customers. As her stress grew, she noticed the lights overhead start to flicker and forced herself to relax lest she ruin all of their hard work.

Upstairs she could feel Bruce's relief when the projector roared into life without any mishap.

"Oh my heavens," Mrs. Harris said, walking up to the antique counter in her best Sunday dress and hat with her husband at her side. "I haven't seen the Palace look this grand since I was a teenager myself! I'm sure Kate is as happy as can be."

"Well," Megan said, glad that she was finally getting the hang of the register, "She's not feeling well tonight."

"Oh no," the school librarian said with his hand on the arm of his frail wife. "It's not that horrible sickness that everyone in town seems to be getting, is it?"

"We hope not," Megan answered, touched by their concern.

"Have they taken her to the hospital yet?" Mrs. Harris asked.

"Not yet," Megan answered. "We've been talking to her frequently to make sure she's still okay."

"That's good," the pleasant woman said, nodding and taking the popcorn with a hand that shook slightly. "You have a good night now, Megan."

As the librarian and his wife turned to leave, Megan heard hacking coughs near the entrance to the Grande Theatre. When she looked, she found a middle-aged man with a receding hairline coughing into the crook of his arm.

"How is it going?" Jade asked when she walked up.

"I thought you were selling tickets," Megan said, taking money from a teenage boy she'd seen at school.

"Andrew came in and I put him to work," Jade answered pleasantly.

"Andrew from the dojo?" Megan asked, thinking about the awkward boy who always seemed interested in what Jade was doing.

"That's the one," Jade said with the hint of a blush. "It won't be for long, we're almost sold out for the night."

In spite of the festive atmosphere, people were moving away from the coughing man with worried glances. As Megan and Jade watched, the man swayed on the spot and collapsed against the wall next to one of the vintage posters that Mr. Green had mounted.

Paul had apparently been watching as well. Within seconds he knelt by the sick man's side.

*Sam, call Mr. Grimble, someone just collapsed at the Palace,* Megan sent.

Jade reached for her phone, but Megan reached out and stopped her.

"Your dad is already on his way," she said, tapping her temple with a finger. Jade nodded in response.

"I'd better go take his spot," Jade said, casting a worried glance toward her younger brother. Even though he'd completely recovered from that night in Guarded Wood, they all still felt overprotective of him.

To make matters worse, Megan could hear the shrill voice of her least favorite person as she argued with poor Andrew. Megan glanced over at Jade who, by the suddenly sour look on her face, had already spotted the

Terrible Trio as well. Judging by their swaggering gait as they made their way to the concession counter, they were over their humiliation at the Academy the day of the storm.

Megan knew she should be professionally polite, but couldn't manage it. There was simply too much animosity left over from the previous year. Worse, she could feel the hunger deep within her stir as Allison drew nearer in her designer jeans, having already fed on the foul girl's fear once before.

"And here I'd heard that this place had taken a turn for the better," the red-headed girl said in a lofty imitation of her mother's. "I'm not sure if I want to eat anything that's been cooked here."

"Then you're free to go enjoy your movie," Megan said, wanting very much to set the girl's hair on fire.

"But I'm *thirsty*," Allison whined.

"What would you like?" Megan asked, breathing deep and slow. A slight tremor ran through the glass concession top.

"Hmmm…" the spoiled girl murmured. Glenn giggled to himself, but Chuck looked uncomfortable. "Do you know if the ice is made with water from the public supply?"

"No," Megan said, losing patience. "We pour bottles of purified water into the ice machine with a funnel. Of course it comes from the public water supply."

"Then I guess I'll take bottled water," Allison pouted.

Megan passed her the bottle of chilled water and took the girl's money. Chuck and Glen either didn't want anything or didn't have money. Either way, Megan was glad to see them turn and leave.

"Behave yourselves," Jade said in her most solicitous voice as she took their tickets. "You know how much I'd hate it if I had to throw you out."

"I'd be careful if I were you," Allison said in an almost perfect imitation of Jade's warning. "From what I hear, your parents may be out of work soon, and then you'll need this one to support your family."

"Yeah, yeah," Jade said with an insincere smile, "They can stand in the unemployment line with your mom. Please enjoy your movie, and don't feel like you ever need to come back here again."

A few moments later Megan put the "sold out" sign on the counter. Sam had already helped Jade put in orders for increased inventory, but they were worried that the order might not arrive in time for the Saturday matinee.

They were all lucky to have the big man in their lives, Megan thought. Everyone took it for granted that he would drop everything to come to the aid of his friends if they needed him, but what did they really do for him in return? Most people would have said that running their own business was enough, but here he was spending hours pouring over the Palace's finances to help Kate keep the place. He even agreed to loan Jade his car once a week so she could go get groceries for the sick woman and bring her the paperwork that needed to be signed. If Megan was honest with herself, she wished he had been her father instead of this mystery man her mother had met in college.

Of course, thinking about her mother and honesty brought her back to wondering what it was that the woman was doing during all of those times that she'd said she was with Sam. However, as Megan had learned over the years, it was pointless to ask her mother outright. She'd have to wait and watch if she wanted to know what was really going on.

# Chapter XXIII: Secret or Prophecy?

Bruce got up early the next morning in spite of the continued night-time alarms at the boundary, knowing that if he wanted to get anything done on the car before his taskmaster sister had him back at the Palace for the Saturday matinee, he'd need to get an early start. Next door Megan was rising up out of sleep to start her morning time with Azarich. He looked forward to seeing her, but he knew he should try these new repairs without her there to distract him. Sometimes it was hard to concentrate with her presence hovering at the edge of his senses.

Movement caught his attention as he walked slowly down the path. Remembering what Sam had taught him, he stilled himself instantly, both physically and mentally.

Coming away from the woods, Emelia took the path that led to her own home. Wrapped in her thoughts, she didn't notice Bruce down the side path.

*What is she doing out this early?*

With his mind stilled as it was, he felt the tiniest hint of premonition involving the formidable woman. Lacking anything like vision or sound, it was just a feeling of unease as if there were something he'd forgotten nagging at the back of his mind. But like so many recent events, he saw that the only outcome from mentioning this was more problems than they already had. He filed it away, but felt uneasy just the same.

In the pre-dawn glow he could see that all of the broken glass was whole again. It hadn't been terribly difficult to mend, but it was tedious and time-consuming. Hopefully removing the dents in the roof would be more fun. The hard part would be popping them out without making the paint fleck off. Perhaps he could make the paint go somewhat back to a liquid state.

By the time he'd removed several of the smaller dents caused by hail storms and felt confident enough to move on to the big one in the roof, Megan had entered Guarded Wood.

*We've got to find out what's messing with the boundary and giving the false alarms* she sent when she was still several minutes away.

*I know, what was it? Six or seven times that it woke us up last night?*

*I lost track after four,* she answered.

The biggest dent rose with a groan into its original shape and the sixty-year-old paint, which had become a liquid again for a few short seconds, dried almost instantly. He stepped back to admire his work.

"Wow," Megan said when she saw the roof of the car.

"Is it the light from this angle or does the paint change color when I do that?" he asked.

"Hmm," she said, moving to the other side and looking at it closely. He couldn't help but notice that one strand of her hair had pulled free of her ponytail. "I think it does, but not much."

"Oh well," he said with a shrug. "I guess I'll have to do the whole car anyway."

"You know she won't care," Megan said.

"But I would," he said, moving on to one of the smaller dents.

212

"How are you doing that?" Megan asked, frowning.

*Tag along,* he sent, dropping his shields in invitation. *If you can help it would speed things up tremendously.* Her thoughts meshed with his and he worked through another dent.

*Whoa,* she thought after a second, *that is a lot more complicated than it looks from the outside. I'm not sure I can do that without making things worse.*

*That's what I was afraid of,* he sent. *There are a lot of things that come easily to you that don't to me. I guess we just have different skills.*

Her thoughts disengaged from his and he felt a moment of emptiness before moving on to the next dent. In less than an hour the roof of the car was free of dents and Bruce felt like he'd spent ten rounds on the mat with his sister, or worse yet, Emelia.

"Didn't we bring trash bags at some point?" Megan asked, looking for something to do while he worked.

"I think they're in the front passenger seat. So how was sunrise with Azarich this morning?" he asked, taking a break for a moment and laying back on the still-dented hood to rest. He'd learned the hard way that if he kept working without breaks he made mistakes that were much harder to fix than the original problems. It was already starting to warm in the early morning sun.

"Good," she said, climbing up on the hood with him, apparently deciding that this was more fun than cleaning out the inside of the car. "We won't dent this more than it already is, will we?"

"I doubt it," he said, rapping the hood with his knuckles. "The steel they used back when they built this is thicker and better quality than what they use now."

"Kind of like Mom's truck?" she asked.

213

"Exactly," he said. "Maybe we should fix that one up after this one."

"She won't let you," Megan said quietly.

"Why not?" he asked. "That would be one seriously cool truck if it was restored.

"Exactly," Megan said. "When we leave, we can't have anything that would draw attention. It would make it easier for the Huntsmen to find us."

Suddenly the morning wasn't so pleasant.

"But an old truck like that is going to draw attention anyway, isn't it?" he asked, turning to look at her profile as she lay next to him, still staring up at the cloudless sky.

"Old vehicles don't have modern electronics, and the layers of steel help hide me while we're moving," she said.

"Oh," he said, understanding at last. "You probably get pretty upset when you're being chased…"

"And it would be mucho bad if I fried the vehicle we were using to escape," she said. "Mom seems to think I'll eventually be good enough at walking between the shadows to escape that way."

Bruce shuddered. His memory of last year's escape was one he'd rather not ponder at any length. "Hasn't that always been an option? I mean, you took both of us through. Surely your mother…"

"She can't do it at all," Megan said, still staring off into the sky. He could tell this subject bothered her.

"Then why can you?" he asked.

"And there we run into that big filing cabinet filled with all of the stuff she knows but won't tell me," Megan answered bitterly. "It must have something to do with my father."

"It would almost have to, I guess," he replied, wishing he could do more to help.

"I haven't had a chance to tell you about what we found in the attic," Megan said, changing the subject "By the way, how did the climbing trip to Wyoming go?"

"Jade loved it, I hated it, and Sam was a natural. He's never been that far from Nickelville before. He loved climbing too. I think it had more to do with the sense that someone else could hold him up than anything else though."

"What do you mean?" she asked.

"I think he gets tired of holding everyone else up in one sense or another," he explained. "What did you find?"

Megan spent several minutes describing the pictures, even going as far as showing some of them from her memory. He was particularly interested in the implications that Josie had possessed abilities like theirs and by the picture of the goatmen in the clearing.

"Do you think she actually saw them there?" he asked.

"Like Grandpa said, before the ground sloths I would have said no. Now I'm not so sure. I did find out more about my father than I knew before when we told him about all of the supernatural stuff we can do. Mom actually told us several things that I'd never heard before," she said. "Apparently he can ask questions and get answers."

"Like what?"

"Evidently the Wild Hunt isn't bad." she answered. "She said they used to love her and then she even implied that she still liked them."

"Then why have you been running from them all these years?" Bruce asked, flabbergasted by this information.

Megan spread her hands in a gesture of frustration. "She also said that she couldn't tell us anything else yet without jeopardizing the outcome."

"Wait a minute," he said, raising up on his elbow to see her face while they spoke. "That sounds like we're dealing with foresight!"

"That's what I thought, but when I asked, she avoided answering."

"I never even suspected that she might have the gift," he said, laying back on the hood again. "But why is she always asking me about the immediate future if she can see it herself?"

"I don't think she can," Megan answered. "There are too many times in the past when we almost got caught by the Huntsmen for her to have been able to see what was coming."

"Maybe it's like you and me," he said, thinking out loud. "We share many of the same abilities, but we also differ greatly in others. Maybe she can't see the immediate future. Oh man," he paused, his eyes darting across the sky as he worked something out.

"What?" Megan asked, rising up to see him better. "You'd better not start keeping things from me too."

"You've been on the run from the Wild Hunt for what, fifteen years?"

"More or less."

"When predictions come as detailed as hers would have had to have been from that far out, you don't call it foresight. That's a bonafide prophecy."

They both lay there quietly, looking up at the clear sky and seriously thinking about taking a nap to make up for the sleepless nights.

"I'm so tired," she said at last, echoing his thoughts. "I need to get a full night's sleep without running out here every hour."

"And when I do sleep, I have bad dreams," he said.

"Premonitions?" she asked.

"Maybe," he said, starting to wish he hadn't said anything. "But they're probably just nightmares."

"Want to talk about them?" she asked.

"No, I'd rather not relive them while I'm awake."

"Think it has anything to do with what Allison said about your family on opening night?" she asked, and he could tell that she'd been looking for an opportunity to broach the subject.

"No," he answered without having to think. "The financial problems are going to sort themselves out over the next month or two. I haven't seen how yet, so don't ask."

"So it's just bad dreams and a general lack of sleep," she said. "I really wish I could figure out what's been tripping the wards."

"Why don't we spend the night out here?" Bruce asked, "That way we can see firsthand what's happening!"

"That's not a bad idea," a gruff voice agreed from nearby, making Bruce lose his balance on the hood of the car and slide precariously backward toward the edge before Megan reached out and grabbed him.

Fang ran up to the edge of the car and began to lick the side of his head enthusiastically. Megan laughed and suddenly it was all okay again.

"Not bad," August said, surveying the progress they'd made on the car. "I was sad when the tree fell on it and broke the windshield."

"Why didn't you fix it?" Bruce asked.

"I couldn't leave by then," the hermit answered, "and as you may have noticed, there aren't any parts houses here in Guarded Wood."

"What?" Bruce asked. "I mean why didn't you mend it like I'm doing?"

At this the old man laughed. Even the dog seemed to think it was funny.

"Um," Megan said, looking back to Bruce. "I get the feeling I'm missing something here."

"I've never seen *anyone* do what Bruce is doing with that car," he

217

said after a moment. "Did Emelia teach you how to do it?"

"No," Bruce answered, still confused. "Now that you mention it, we haven't seen her do anything like this either."

"Good," he replied. "I'm not particularly fond of the idea that the Dan…" The old man stopped in mid-word, his eyes flying toward Megan. "That's not what I came here to talk about."

"What was that?" Megan asked, suspecting that it had something to do with the recognition that the old man and her mother when they'd met.

"No time for that now," August said irritably. "I came to talk to you about changes in the Wood."

*I don't know what that was about, but he's not going to talk about it now,* Bruce sent, hoping that only she could hear.

Megan grudgingly let the moment pass.

"The problems with the boundary are getting worse," the old man started, relieved. "In addition to the outer perimeter that you've been helping me patch, there are wards that guard the thin spots where it is possible to move from one of the inner realms to another."

"Like the one down the path that leads to the waterfall," Megan said. August nodded.

"And some of those are starting to fail?" Bruce asked.

"Yes," the hermit agreed. "And that's why I want you to be careful tonight. I'll leave Fang with you just in case, but I want you to promise not to go wandering around like you did the night Paul got lost."

"We know better than to follow the wisps," Megan said.

"The siren is just one of the things here that the parents of the past used to scare children into staying in their beds at night.

"We'll call you if anything happens," Bruce assured him.

"Good," the old hermit said. "And under no circumstances should

218

you separate. Many of the night creatures are illusionists. The easiest way to get to either of you would be to get you apart and make you think that the other one was in danger. Individually you're both smart enough to know when you're out of your depth and call in for reinforcements. But if either of you ever thought the other was in immediate danger, I'm pretty sure you'd make poor decisions on the fly to try and save each other. So stay together, and stay away from small bodies of water as well. There's a bog hag fairly close who would love to pull tasty young flesh like the two of you into her underwater lair."

"Ha ha," Megan said.

"I really wish I was kidding," the old man replied.

# Chapter XXIV: Carrier Tone

*Come on in, I'm in my room*, Megan sent when she felt Bruce at the front door. Her mother had remembered that she wanted to see Grandma Josie's wedding dress after the surprise of finding her hidden studio. Now it was spread out on her bed, and even though she could imagine what its simple, lace-edged hems and sleeves might have looked like at their wedding, the dry heat of the attic had taken its toll on the dress. Both the satin and lace had yellowed with age and the once-supple fabric bore traces of dry rot in several places.

"That looks really old," Bruce said, walking in to stand next to her.

"It was my grandmother's," she explained. "We stumbled across it right before we found grandma's studio. I wish it had been stored better. It's almost falling apart."

"Want me to fix it?" he asked.

"Can you?" she asked. "I mean, it's not like a car."

"No, really?" he asked sarcastically. "As long as it's complete and not missing any pieces I should be able to restore it."

"How?"

"It remembers what it was like before," he said, reaching down to run his hand, palm down across the old fabric. As his hand passed, the color and texture returned to what it had been like when it was new. The fabric regained its sheen and when Megan touched it, it was pliable again.

"Oh my god," she whispered and gave him a spontaneous hug that left him blushing. "I wanted to try it on so badly when I saw it, but I knew it would tear. Do you mind?"

"Knock yourself out," he said. "I doubt anything will hit the boundary for several hours yet, so it's not like we're working against the clock or anything. I'll go down and see how Azarich is doing."

As soon as he closed the door, she changed into the dress. It fit her perfectly. She turned around several times in front of her mirror to see how it looked.

"Hey Mom," she called, stepping out into the hall, knowing even before the sound faded from the second floor that Emelia wasn't in her room.

"We're down here in the kitchen," Emelia called.

"You won't believe this," she called from the stairway. "Grandma and I were exactly the same size!"

She stepped into the kitchen in her bare feet and twirled once in girlish glee. Bruce grinned broadly at her and something passed through his eyes that she couldn't quite define. Her mother's look was one of pleasant surprise. But when her grandfather turned from the sink with suds still clinging to his hands, Megan realized how cruel her foolish act had been. For just an instant his eyes filled with joyous surprise and his smile radiated hope. But then his shoulders went rigid and confusion clouded his eyes. Even though he didn't move at all, he seemed to crumple inward upon himself as if something vital had drained from his heart.

"Grandpa," Megan whispered. "I'm so sorry, I wasn't thinking about how much we look alike."

"No harm done," he lied, somehow holding on to a smile that no longer held any joy. "Wait here a minute," he said, wiping his hands on a towel and walking past her to the living room, pausing to kiss her lightly on the peak of her forehead.

*It's okay,* her mother sent. *There's no way you could have known that it would hit him that hard.*

"Come here for a minute, Bruce," Azarich called from the next room.

Bruce walked past, reaching out to squeeze her hand as he did. When she and her mother followed him, the old man was pointing to something in one of the many photo albums that lined the shelf next to the fireplace.

"That's uncanny," Bruce said, looking repeatedly from the picture to Megan.

"How did you get the dress to look so much better?" Emelia asked, reaching over to touch the fabric.

"I just told it to return to what it had been," Bruce replied with a shrug.

"You could make a fortune working for museums," Azarich mused.

"And here I thought Megan was probably just packing another duffle bag for your night out," Emelia teased.

Megan stuck her tongue out at her mother and went back upstairs to change back into the clothes she'd wear into the woods.

The scent of honeysuckle filled the air as she and Bruce walked down the path to the tree house, and she wondered how Charlotte was doing. The moon had been full the previous night, and though it was waning, there was still plenty of light. Fang fell into step with them a few minutes later.

When at last they reached the clearing where Big Bertha still slumbered, Bruce took out a sweatshirt from the backpack he'd brought, hopped up once again on the hood, and put it behind his head for a pillow. Megan did the same, though she'd brought hers more out of the habit to look like cold affected her than actual need. She laid down next to him on the faintly warm metal and stared up at the stars.

"That was funny," he said.

"What was?"

"Her comment about the duffle," he chuckled.

"You guys are never going to let me live that down, are you?"

"As Paul would say, it's extremely unlikely that what you wish will come to pass."

"Where did he get that?" she asked. "None of the rest of you talk that way."

"Beats me. Why am I the only one who has abilities? Doesn't your mom say that it usually runs in families?"

"That reminds me," she said, reaching over and pulling something from the backpack she usually carried to school. "You said you wanted to see this."

"So this is your father?" He said, summoning a cold flame so he could see it better.

Megan nodded.

"Emelia really looked happy," he said. "Have you noticed these patterns on her dress and on your father's suit?"

"Knotwork," Megan answered. "I used to draw them all over my books when I was a kid. Mom noticed and made me stop."

"They're often associated with the Celts," he said thoughtfully. "And the Celts are often associated with the Wild Hunt. I need to do some research on that."

She put the picture back into her pack and laid back on the hood next to him.

Fang chose that moment to jump onto the hood with them. Then he

224

nosed his way behind their heads and lay down like a big furry pillow that breathed.

"By all means," Bruce laughed. "Make yourself comfortable."

*He is more comfortable than my sweatshirt,* she sent, absently running her fingers through his fur.

*Definitely,* Bruce agreed.

*You said that everything is going to work out with your parents and their jobs,* she sent, dropping into silent conversation since she felt like they should listen for what was crossing the boundary.

*I can sense a future in which everything turns out fine, but I can also sense varying levels of disaster in others,* he sent. *There is something that I'm going to do that determines which one comes to pass, but I don't know what it is or when it will come.*

*I'm sure everything will turn out okay,* she sent. *But that does put a lot of pressure on you.*

All around them the boundary wards flared into life. Bruce and Megan slid from the car and took to their feet almost as fast as Fang. Even as they ran, Megan hardened her shields the way her mother had taught her and felt Bruce do the same. After all of the training they'd had with her mother, she felt like they should be able to handle just about anything.

Both of them scanned the darkness, looking for danger.

As soon as Megan saw the armadillo, she knew what she'd forgotten to do. In her inexperience, she'd forgotten to define what could pass the wards unchallenged. So for the past several weeks, she and the Grimbles had been woken every time a mouse, frog or insect as far as she knew, had crossed through this part of the boundary.

She could feel the mirth in August's thoughts as he approached. Further away, back at her house, her mother knew too.

"Don't feel too bad," the old man chuckled when he came into view a while later. "At least it wasn't something from the heartwoods testing for weaknesses like I feared. This can be remedied readily enough. It won't be pleasant for you when we take it down though."

"Why?" Megan asked, trying to hide her embarrassment.

"The only way to take down a ward without having everyone present who is tied to it is to overload it," he said. "You're going to shield this area from the others so we don't wake them up. There's no point in making them think that the end of the world is about to bash in their back door. It's probably going to take both of you to pull that off."

"We can't just turn it off?" Bruce asked.

"Not with it tied to the rings," he said. "If we brought everyone out here we could probably take it down, but there's no point in making everyone lose sleep over minor varmints tonight."

Reluctantly, Megan and Bruce meshed their thoughts and wrapped the clearing in a web of containment. They'd never attempted anything quite like it before, and they were unsure if it would work.

"Not bad," August said, closing his eyes and probing what they'd done. "That should hold long enough."

Without further warning Megan felt something start to build within their protections. With all of her attention focused on maintaining the shield, she hoped that it was whatever August was doing. Then in an instant of blinding pain at the base of her skull, everything August had built came crashing into the ward, sweeping it away like a tent in the face of a hurricane.

Both Bruce and Megan faltered, then lost their hold on the shield. It disintegrated around them, but not before it contained what had happened to the ward. The section of the boundary stood exposed once again.

226

"Sorry about that," August said, rubbing his hands together in anticipation for what lay ahead. "But aside from the definition problem, it was a good ward and nothing less would have taken it down. Now let me show you how to do it right."

It took a second for Megan to realize that the old man had lowered his outer defenses and expected the three of them to work together. She knew how it was done. After all, it was what she did with Bruce and sometimes her mother. But for August to allow them to do so suggested that he'd decided to trust them completely.

The two of them learned more in the time he spent creating the ward than they had the entire time Emelia and Sam had taught them. There was also something familiar about the flavor of his magic that Megan couldn't place at first.

"You created my grandmother's grove!" she blurted out in recognition.

He didn't answer for several minutes, and Megan suspected he was going to just ignore the comment the way he always did when they tried to steer the conversation in a direction that he didn't like.

"Suppose I should have expected you to figure it out," he said at last. "You're a very observant person. Just like she was."

"You told me before that you knew her," Megan prompted, hoping that the old man might tell her more.

"I never met her in person," he said.

"But you watched her through the animals," Bruce said.

"Her abilities were strong," August said, moving beneath a tree where they lost all but his outline. "Just like they always have been with the women in your family. She reminded me of my wife when she was young even though they didn't look anything alike."

227

Megan waited for him to continue, eager to hear more, but knowing how his mood could change in an instant. She didn't want to miss what he had to say.

"She was drawn to that grove," the hermit continued after a while, with a thick quality to his voice. "Especially after she was with child. For her it was just a quiet place where she could try to make sense of the amazing and sometimes confusing world her extended senses showed her. So one night, while she slept, I came to the edge of Guarded Wood near what became her grove. I worked from dusk until dawn, shaping the natural energy flows of the area, including Guarded Wood, into a nexus where her abilities could mature in time. It was a source of wonder for her. I didn't intend for the spring to break surface there, but it did after that night."

Here he paused again, and she was sure that he was finished. He left the shadow of the tree and headed back the way he had come.

"It was there in her grove that she started the labor that ended her life," he whispered gruffly.

"And that's why you called me a changeling," Megan said. "Because I looked so much like her. And part of my power is like hers."

She could feel his agreement, though he didn't answer.

"I was confused at first," he explained. "I'm an old man who has lived alone longer than anyone here in Nickelville has even been alive. Even among my people, diseases of the mind that bring about the loss of memory still occur. And then I saw your eyes change and knew what you must be…"

"Please…" she begged.

"If it were up to me I would," he said sadly. "Your mother must choose the hour when that burden is laid upon you. But know this my

228

young friend. Your childhood is almost at an end. Enjoy what hours are left to you before you must confront the truth."

Bruce had taken her hand at some point during the hermit's reminiscence.

"How would the two of you like to see my charges?" August said brightly, clearly wanting to change the subject.

With his defenses lowered and his feelings still raw from what he'd said about her grandmother, Megan could feel how fond he was of the ground sloths. How lonely must he have been out there in the woods for so long? To hear her Grandfather talk, the hermit must be well over a hundred years old. She suspected he was much older than that.

August moved like a wraith through the dimly lit woods, making almost no sound as he went. She and Bruce, on the other hand, seemed to step in the middle of every dry twig in their path.

At last they came to a small clearing through which ran a slow-moving stream. Near its edge, beneath a massive oak tree, slept the sloths.

Megan could hear the deep breathing of the adults from where the three of them stood.

*This is probably as close as we should get,* August sent. *Like I said before, they don't have any natural enemies. But they like to be the ones to choose how close we get. I've spent entire days walking through Guarded Wood with them. They make for pretty good neighbors.*

August's head swiveled toward the deeper woods, tracking something that only he could hear.

*Damn it,* he sent irritably. *Never a moment's peace. Three men just crossed the boundary into Guarded Wood. They're looking for signs of Goatman, and the protections are weak there. I'd best go warn them off lest they end up as dinner for something in the inner woods.*

229

Then he was gone with little to show that he'd been there except for his footprints in the pre-morning dew.

Megan settled down at the base of a tree to watch the sloths for a while. She wasn't sure, but it almost sounded like one of the juveniles was snoring.

Bruce lowered himself next to her and closed his weary eyes.

*Have you ever really listened to the night sounds?* He asked.

*You mean like the crickets and the frogs and stuff?*

*Yeah,* he sent. *Do you feel how there's an undercurrent to the sound? It's almost like a highway or the carrier tone when one of those old computers communicated.*

*Okay, I think I can hear that.*

*These are the only woods I've ever been in, so I'm not sure they are all like this, but it's like everything here in the woods is joining in this one sound that permeates everything. It's like something here in the woods uses that carrier tone to communicate. I wonder if that's why Paul was the one who wandered off? He seems to hear a lot more than the rest of us do.*

*Maybe,* she answered, relaxing now that the worry of what might be testing the boundaries had passed.

*Can I ask you something?* Bruce asked.

*I have no secrets from you,* she replied, rousing herself.

*Why don't magical creatures frighten you?*

*What do you mean?*

*Charlotte terrified me, and I get the feeling that she terrified your grandmother, your mother and Sam as well,* he answered. *Yet you took her into your arms like a long-lost sister.*

*You did too,* she reminded him. *And in a way she was.*

*But I only did it after I'd seen you do it first. And you apparently did it when you were only six years old. How can you be so brave in the face of what most people would consider to be monsters?*

*Many would consider me a monster as well,* Megan pointed out, *but you have never once hesitated to hold me.*

*That's not the same,* he insisted. *And what about the creatures from the woods near the Academy and the Jubilee?*

*That wasn't the first time I've seen things like them either, although I have to admit until quite recently I thought they'd just been imaginary friends.*

Apparently satisfied by her answers, his thoughts grew silent.

Listening to the rhythmic breathing of the sloths, Bruce's carrier tone and the sound of his thoughts in her mind, Megan drifted off to sleep, her head slowly coming to rest on his shoulder.

# Chapter XXV: Strange Bedfellows

Bruce woke when he felt Emelia brush against his shields. He knew she stood several yards away to his right before he opened his eyes. His back still rested against the tree, but Megan now slept with her head on his leg.

*Don't make any sudden movements.* Emelia sent, a certain amount of amusement in her thoughts.

Bruce opened his eyes to find that at some point in the night, not only had August returned with the blanket that now covered Megan, but the juvenile sloths had woken and come to investigate their visitors. Both were now nuzzled next to Megan sound asleep.

His surprise woke Megan, whose eyes traveled to the furry beast next to her, roughly twice the size of a Great Pyrenees. Slowly she reached out and touched its fur.

*It's really coarse,* she sent.

Unable to help himself, he reached down and ran his hand gently across the shoulder of the nearest sloth.

*Your Grandfather will understand if you miss a morning,* Emelia sent.

Moving slowly lest she wake the young ones, Megan untangled herself from the blanket and rose to her feet. Bruce, stiff from leaning against a tree for most of the night, followed her across the clearing to where Emelia waited.

They left the blanket folded in Big Bertha when they passed. Bruce wasn't sure, but he thought the sky was already growing brighter. By the time they came to the tree house, the worst of his aches were behind him, and he wondered how they'd spend the day.

"Will you be able to get in without being noticed?" Emelia asked. "We don't need you to get grounded again."

"I've got it under control," he answered. "My room is warded. No one's been in there to discover I'm gone or I'd know."

Emelia nodded, pleased that he'd applied what she'd taught him. He wanted to hug Megan goodbye, but felt awkward doing so in front of her mother. So instead he waved awkwardly when they branched off the path and walked toward their own house.

Inside all still slept. He could sense the dreams of his siblings as he passed their rooms. A night without warnings from the boundary had been a welcome relief.

He only planned to rest his eyes when he crawled into his bed…

"To what do I owe the honor of having both of the ladies in my life join me this morning?" Azarich asked when both Megan and Emelia walked up to the porch.

"I just couldn't resist your magnetism this morning old man," Emelia said waspishly, "I'll get the coffee."

This brought a deep chuckle from Azarich. Beyond the porch, the sky was a washed out white with only the faintest hint of blue. As usual lately, there wasn't a cloud in the sky.

Emelia came out a few minutes later, juggling all three cups and the door at the same time like the waitress she'd been on so many occasions. All three of them fit on the bench, even if Megan was a bit squished in the middle. She didn't mind at all though as they watched in silence. It was Emelia that noticed Azarich's mood.

"What's wrong, Dad?" she asked.

"Oh, nothing much," he answered.

"You know it will be easier if you just tell her now," Megan said, trying to lighten the mood. "She'll get it out of you eventually."

"Something strange is afoot," he said reluctantly.

"You're going to have to be more specific than that," Emelia prompted.

"This sickness," he said after a moment. "And the Jones's."

"Bruce's dad is working half the time off the clock trying to get people to the hospital," Megan said.

"And Jones is contributing to our competitor at the *Tribune* to drive us out of business," Emelia said, sipping her coffee. "At this rate, he may succeed."

"That's just it," the old man said, still staring off into the horizon above Guarded Wood, "The whole town is worried. I've never seen the townsfolk this downtrodden."

"They're watching what's happening to the Grimbles, who supposedly didn't rely on the Jones family for its survival," Emelia said.

"And they're realizing that if the Joneses can reach people who don't work for them," Azarich added, "How much easier would it be to come after the ones that do?"

"Isn't there something legal we can do?" Megan asked.

"Tony Jones is evil, but not stupid," he replied. "Since the town meeting last year, he's retained the services of an entire law firm from out of town to represent him. They've looked at everything he's doing from top to bottom to make sure he's not vulnerable from that direction again."

The three of them sat in silence for the next few minutes, sipping coffee and for the first time finding no comfort in the sunrise.

"That reminds me," Emelia said, "I was wondering if you and Bruce would like to come up to the *Tribune* today? You've never been, and his mother says that he used to practically live there in the summer."

"I'd like to," Megan said regretfully, realizing that she would like to see where her mother worked, "But I told Jade that I'd go with them to the grocery store and help buy food. Kate's been at home sick for quite a while now and we want to make sure that she's holding up okay."

"And they're sure this sickness isn't contagious?" Azarich asked, looking worried.

"No one in the neighboring town has caught it when we send the sick there," Emelia answered. "They thought it might be something environmental, but they had the water supply, soil and air checked and nothing seems to be amiss. In short, no one has a clue about what is causing it."

"I'm still not too fond of you going into the home of someone who is actively sick," Azarich said, taking Megan's hand in his own. "But I also know that we have to help each other when we can. You'll be careful, won't you?"

"Of course Grandpa."

# Chapter XXVI: Adopt-a-Grandma

"I need to get Andrew to come over and mow again," Jade observed when they pulled up in front of Kate's tiny home.

"You seem to be staying in rather close contact with the boy of no known relationship to the president of the same name," Megan observed.

"I have no idea what you're talking about," Jade said, getting out of Sam's car and watching in amusement as Bruce and Paul extricated themselves from the back seat. "Don't forget the groceries in the trunk."

"Yes, your highness," Bruce muttered.

"I've always wondered what it would be like to be royalty," Jade said, ignoring his tone.

The moment Kate opened the door in her faded purple housecoat, Megan knew Jade hadn't warned her that they were coming. She looked much older than she had when they had last seen her.

"Hey Kate," Jade said pleasantly, pushing the door open further and carrying her bags past the surprised woman, "We brought you groceries."

"Jade," the woman said in weary irritation, "I told you the last time that I don't need you to come over like this."

"You've been here for two weeks," Jade countered, still pleasant, "And it's been a week since I brought you fresh food. So here we are."

"If I'd wanted…" She started again, not knowing how to handle this determined girl.

"And at the risk of being rude," Jade continued, ignoring the growing irritation from her employer, "It smells in here. We're going to put up the groceries, cook you some soup and tidy the place up."

"Give me a good reason why I shouldn't fire you right now," Kate said, losing her steam and sitting down on a threadbare couch.

"I'll give you two," Jade replied, still as pleasant as ever. "One, I'll still keep going to work because I'm the only one left who isn't sick. Two, I've adopted you as my new grandmother. You see, both of mine died when I was quite young, and I've come to realize that it might very well stunt my emotional growth if I don't have one. So tag, you're it."

"Trust me," Bruce added. "Once you're family there's no escaping her."

"Why thank you my dear delinquent sib," Jade said. "Now where is your broom?"

Flabbergasted by her impertinent employee, Kate fled to take a shower while they cleaned. The first thing Jade did was open all of the blinds to let in light.

The inside of Kate's home reminded Bruce of one of the old sit-coms his parents watched. From the green recliner to the couch that sported log cabin inspired upholstery, it heralded back to the sixties or seventies. It was pretty clear that Kate normally kept things clean, but was simply too weak to worry about it at the moment. Paul immediately started to collect dirty dishes from the bright yellow formica table and take them to the sink, where Jade rinsed and loaded them into the old dishwasher. Megan heated some of the soup that they'd brought, and Bruce swept the worn hardwood floors.

"Do you think she's okay in there?" Paul asked. "She's been

showering for a really long time."

Megan turned her senses in that direction.

"She's getting dressed," she answered, grateful that they wouldn't have to invade her privacy to help her.

"Look at all of these," Paul said, drying his hands on a dish towel after cleaning up the kitchen.

Megan followed his gaze to the wall opposite the kitchen where hundreds of photos made a huge collage. Each had been taken at the Palace, and some of them were quite old.

The door to Kate's bedroom opened, and she emerged, holding on to the door frame for support.

"These pictures are amazing," Megan said when the old woman settled into the recliner. Bruce and Jade joined them to look. At the very top of the display an old green Wrigley's Gum wrapper had been tucked behind one of the pictures.

"Like them, do you?" Kate asked in a weary but pleased voice. "You're looking at my life there child."

"They're older the further you go up the wall," Bruce observed. "The oldest ones…"

"Are from before I worked there," Kate explained, leaning her head back and closing her eyes. "That was before the war. My mother used to take me before she passed away. My father was always too busy after that, and I knew the only way to go back was to get a job there."

"When did you start?" Jade asked, studying a picture of the old woman as a teen.

"It was a couple of years after your grandfather and his friends were drafted. It was a quiet time at the theater when they left…"

"Do you remember them from when they were younger?" Megan

238

asked, coming to sit near the sick woman.

"Girl, everyone in town knew those four," Kate laughed and then started to cough. It took her a moment to continue. "Back in those days when mischief came a callin' it was usually them that answered."

"Four?" Paul asked, perplexed.

"Carl died in the war," Megan said quietly. "Grandpa talks about him sometimes. He still feels bad about never having had a chance to say goodbye."

"Killed in combat?" Paul asked.

"Missing in action," Megan replied. "His body was never recovered. He disappeared while on patrol and was never found."

"That must have been hard on his family," Bruce said.

"It was hard on the whole town," Kate replied, starting to get drowsy. "Nickelville never had that many people, and the enthusiasm of those four brought laughter to us all. They were never quite the same once Carl was gone."

"Kate," Jade said, bending over the woman and feeling her forehead. "Are you sure you don't need to go to the hospital?"

"There's no point sitting in a hospital bed so they can charge me thousands a day to tell me they don't know what's wrong," Kate said, rousing herself at the thought.

"But most of the people are getting better once they get to the hospital," Paul said.

"Furthermore," Kate said in a tone that made it clear that her mind was made up, "I prefer to keep this wrinkled backside of mine completely covered at all times. None of those open back gowns for me, thank you very much!"

Megan laughed. Kate might be a few years younger than her

grandfather, but it was clear they were from the same generation.

"Now, if you don't mind, I'm going to bed now that I'm clean and fed," she said in her usual gruff tone. "Jade, take the extra key from the peg by the back door if you're going to be my granddaughter."

When the four of them started toward the door, Paul froze.

"Is that a violin?" he asked, having noticed a closed case sticking out from behind the sofa.

"Yes, it is," Kate said. "Why?"

"I've been wanting to learn," he said. "Do you mind if I look at it?"

"Knock yourself out," she said. "Believe it or not, I fancied taking students once upon a time."

"Is there any way I could talk you into teaching me?" he asked, lovingly touching the strings.

"I 'spose there wouldn't be any harm during the week when the Palace is closed," she answered. "Assuming this crud doesn't kill me, that is. Now get out of here and let an old woman get her beauty sleep!"

# Chapter XXVII: The Future Down Memory Lane

"Maybe another week," Bruce said wearily, "but probably less." He was sitting in the front seat of Azarich's truck while his sister drove.

"But it looks perfect!" Jade said, "Doesn't it Megan?"

"Don't get me into this," Megan said watching the *Nickelville Tribune* approach.

"I've barely gotten into the engine," Bruce said, speaking slowly like he would to a small child. "The engine is a lot more complicated than the projector at the Palace. You're going to need most of your money to get a new battery, replace all of the rubber hoses and belts, and buy oil and gas. I can't create those out of thin air, and most of the originals either rotted away or evaporated years ago. You're lucky Alan had tires that would work. I swear that man has just about everything in that garage of his."

"So it will be a lot like this, won't it?" Jade asked, her excitement getting on Bruce's nerves. "I mean they're both about the same age."

"They're both Fords," Bruce interjected, "But they're not the same age. This is from 1955 and the car is a 1940."

"I've driven this truck quite a few times, and the controls look pretty similar," Megan said, looking over. "I think the truck has a bigger engine than Bertha though."

"Bertha?" Jade said, hitting the brakes in surprise and making the car behind them honk angrily. "You named my car Bertha?"

"Actually it's Big Bertha," Bruce answered, wishing they could hurry up and get to the *Tribune* so they could stop moving. "And it was Paul that started calling it that, not us."

"I'm going to have words with that boy," Jade said irritably. "I was thinking of calling her Christine."

Megan snorted a laugh and covered her mouth to stop herself.

"Let me get this straight," Bruce said, leaning forward against his seat belt so he could look around Megan at his sister. "We find an abandoned car in supernatural woods that are trying to lure us in and eat us, and you decide to name it after the possessed car from a Stephen King novel?"

"No," Jade said, "I'd never do that."

"Good," Bruce said, leaning back in his seat.

"I'm naming it after the car in the movie," she said before adding, "You know I hate to read."

Megan made no attempt to hide her laughter this time.

*Come on,* she sent. *That was funny! What's wrong? You're making August look positively cheerful by comparison this morning.*

*There are a lot of possible futures merging over the next few hours,* he sent, staring out the window. *The choices I make today have serious repercussions, but for the life of me I can't figure out what is so important about this afternoon.*

*I don't understand,* Megan sent. *If you can see what's going to happen, how can you not know what to do?*

He placed his hand over hers, lowered his shields and allowed the images to flow.

*I think I'm going to puke,* Megan sent, hurriedly pulling her hand away from his. *That feels like when the Dark Man tried to explain everything that was happening in one big burst. No wonder you're in a bad mood.*

*And her driving is making me sick,* he sent. *There's so much in the visions that I can't sort them out. I don't know which action leads to which outcome. And the whole town depends on me making the right one!*

At last the truck pulled up to the *Tribune.*

"I'll be back in a few hours after I check in on Kate," Jade said.

"Thanks," Megan replied before following Bruce out the door and up the steps.

Inside, Bruce found a modicum of peace in the familiar sounds and smells from his best childhood memories. He hadn't realized how much he'd missed them until that moment.

"Hey," someone yelled, "Bruce is here!"

Megan faded into the background, uneasy with the crowd of people that surrounded him at these words. Even the presence of people he considered extended family did little to expel the confusion that continued to build inside him. Now that he was inside the *Tribune,* the images were coming even faster as if they were all trying to navigate the bottleneck of his mind.

"What?" the assistant editor said, "You get a girlfriend and forget all about us?"

Bruce glanced quickly at Megan who suddenly became interested in one of the awards framed on the wall. She'd turned about three shades redder than normal.

"So how has it been?" he asked, trying to change the subject.

The responses proved almost as confusing as his precognitions. Most

243

seemed to be upset that his mother wasn't letting them run any stories about Goatman. But there were a few brave souls that were talking about what the Jones's had been doing to their family.

"Thanks guys," Bruce finally said when he could take no more hugs and back slaps. "Is Mom in her office?"

The small mob gave assent, and Bruce was finally free to save Megan from the awkwardness of the situation and escape to his mother's office. He saw Heather from a distance, the same intern he'd spoken to so often the year before, and realized he no longer dreamed about getting away from Nickelville. He cast a cautious glance at Megan.

He felt his mother's anguish before he opened the door, and realized that he'd always been able to feel her emotions to an extent. She looked older than he remembered, sitting there with a newspaper clenched in her fists and her eyes closed as she attempted to calm herself. She opened her eyes when she heard him close the door behind Megan.

"What's wrong, Mom?"

Unable to speak, she shoved the newspaper across her desk to him.

He realized at a glance that it wasn't a copy of *The Tribune*, as he'd first thought. It was their competitor. Across the top of the page in bold type was the heading, "Jones & Jones Industries: Creating a Stable Economy in Nickelville for Generations."

"Surely no one could take that seriously," Megan said.

"I don't recognize any of these people they've interviewed about how wonderful it is to work for the factory," Bruce said.

"They probably don't exist," his mother said, running her fingers through her graying hair.

"Surely that's not legal," Megan said.

"That's the least of our worries," Dora said. "Bruce, do you

244

remember Margaret Crump?"

"Aunt Margaret?" he asked.

"She's not really his aunt," Dora told Megan, "But he's always called her that. Well, she's leaving the *Tribune*."

"Why?" Bruce asked.

"Her husband works at Jones & Jones," she said bitterly. "He was made aware yesterday that there are going to be some layoffs. All of them are workers with family that work for the *Nickelville Tribune*."

"Now I know that's not legal," Bruce said. "Mr. McGeehee…"

"Can't help us," Dora said quietly. "They've all been harassed by the management since Mrs. Jones resigned. They've all been given poor performance reports in spite of their real actions. When they're let go, there will be a paper trail justifying their termination. There's no way to fight it in court. Besides, the judge is in Jones's pocket. He'd rule against us no matter what the evidence proved."

"I'm so sorry Mrs. Grimble," Megan said. "I wish we'd just…"

"I wouldn't change a thing," Bruce's mother said, pulling her into an awkward one-armed embrace. "What we did was the right thing to do. Besides, they're helping me out even if it is unintentional."

"What do you mean?" Bruce asked.

"With sales so far down, it was only a matter of time until I had to start letting people go," she answered unhappily. "This way we can hold off on that for a bit longer."

"But don't you need those people to keep the *Tribune* afloat?" Bruce asked.

"Yes," Dora admitted, closing her eyes again. "What other choice do we have? But this isn't why you are here! Bruce, take her on the tour."

Bruce gave his mother a hug and led Meagan out the door and back into the *Tribune* proper.

"Where is this window you fell out of when I came to Nickelville?" she asked.

"Over this way," he said, leading her toward his childhood roost. He found a certain amount of comfort in the sounds and smells of his earliest memories and lowered his shields so Megan could sense them the way he did. Lost in his senses, she jumped when a stray piece of newsprint, carried by the big ventilation fans, blew across his bare leg.

When he reached down, he recognized the daily stock report. As he looked at the page in wonder, the future solidified, and he knew at long last which path to take.

# Chapter XXVIII: Roc of Ages

"Hello up there," a familiar if cranky voice called from down below. For the past half hour, Bruce had been sitting in one of the tree house's many nooks, transcribing one of the stories Azarich had told them the night before from the recording on his phone.

"Hey August," he called back. "Come on up!"

"Why would I want to do that?" the hermit yelled back. "I'm old, and I get more than enough exercise climbing things in Guarded Wood."

"Good point," Bruce said, laughing at the seriousness of his friend's tone. He stowed his journal and favorite fountain pen under the mattress where he'd slept on the fateful night when they'd met their infamous neighbor.

He thought about trying to walk the shadows to the old man and avoid all of the steps, but that seemed like something that could seriously shorten his lifespan if he did it wrong. And while he could still see his future on the other side of such an exercise, he was cautious by nature and liked to take his time and plan things out.

Megan, Emelia and Sam came walking down the path toward them as Bruce reached the hermit.

"Do mine ears detect the dulcet tones of our most venerable of neighbors?" Paul called from the direction of their house, which of course meant that Jade wouldn't be far behind.

"You do know that no one ever talked like that, not even when Shakespeare was alive," the hermit grumbled at Paul when he showed up. "You sound ridiculous."

"And how exactly would you know that?" Jade asked, more out of curiosity than disrespect.

"Because I was there," the old man snapped.

"So why did you call us?" Emelia asked, apparently not surprised by this revelation. "I was just about to take a well-deserved shower."

"Mom," Megan said, leaning toward her, "What is that smell?"

"I had to do an interview at the water treatment plant," the stern woman answered. "The site manager insisted that we tour the *entire* facility to show that the rumors of contamination are unfounded."

"Sounds like Mom is mad at you about something," Jade observed. "I've been on the receiving end of her passive aggressive revenges before. Trust me, you got off easy."

"One of the internal boundaries failed and allowed a herd of extinct animals to enter the hunting grounds of two huge predators," August announced. "And to make matters worse, there's a big cliff at the edge of the area that drops into the sea. It's only a matter of time before they stampede off the edge."

"What do the extinct animals look like?" Paul asked eagerly.

"Weird wildebeest things that make strange trumpeting sounds," the hermit answered. "They're dumb brutes, but I don't think we should let anything in the woods go extinct, and that's exactly what I'm afraid will happen if we don't do something about it. I caught it before more than a few hundred or so got loose, but I don't know how long my patch on the

248

wards will hold."

"What are we waiting for?" Jade asked.

"Yeah," Paul added eagerly. "I have no idea what those things could be, and that alone intrigues me."

"You're not going," the hermit said.

"What do you mean, we're not going?" Jade asked. "Do you really think you could stop us from following you?"

"I don't have time to put this nicely," the old man said. "The two of you don't have anything that will help us, and we're already going to have our hands full. At best you'd be useless in what we're doing, and at worst you'd distract us and put us in more danger than we're already going to be in."

"But I'm sure my knowledge about prehistoric animals and hunting skills would help," Paul said.

"What hunting skills?" Jade asked. "You've never hunted anything in your life!"

Paul looked startled by this remark, almost as if he'd thought for a moment that he had indeed done something like this before.

"We don't have time for this," August said. "Fang, keep them from following us."

The wolf sat down in front of them, watching them closely.

"I'll take pictures of them for you," Sam called back, hurrying to catch up to the hermit who was already halfway to the edge of the woods.

August moved surprisingly fast for a man who'd just suggested that he'd been around during the Elizabethan Era, taking them through turn after turn and down paths that were often only apparent when he turned onto them. They quickly gave up on trying to remember their way back, since any sane analysis of their path would suggest that they were moving in an increasingly convoluted series of circles that shouldn't be taking them anywhere.

But their wildly evolving surroundings suggested otherwise. They walked from woods to jungle, from jungle to the crest of a mountain ridge complete with some very angrily vocal goats. For a few moments they passed through the mouth of a cave that opened into the melting underside of what must have been a glacier. After the sixth or seventh question about where they were and their guide's responses of, "There's no time to dawdle right now," they gave up and saved their wind for walking. At one point, even the old man seemed to be stumped.

"Damn it," he mumbled. "This way is closed off too. I hope you all kept hydrated. We're about to get a little warm."

In an impossible transition from meadow to desert crevasse, they passed single file down a rocky defile with the walls of the chasm worn smooth with the passage of time. Within seconds everyone except Megan was drenched in sweat. The steep walls of the slot canyon towered above them and blotted out most of the sun from above in irregular jutting ledges. When a breeze passed through, it whistled eerily past them.

"It's not much farther from here," the hermit assured them. "Just watch your footing on the downward slopes. There's not much of anything you can hold onto if you start to fall."

"How long did it take you to learn how to navigate this place?" Sam asked, winded in spite of his constant martial arts training.

"A lot longer than your standard lifetime," the old man answered, then froze.

"What is it?" Emelia asked.

"Hush!"

All three of them looked at each other in concern for the man's safety. No one in their right mind hushed Emelia.

Then Bruce heard it too, a dull roar far behind them.

"That's not possible," August whispered in horror. "It never rains in this place. Another boundary must have failed where it borders the ocean. Run!"

The realization of what that sound meant in the narrow confines of the crevasse turned Bruce's bowels to water, and he took Megan's hand, dragging her along behind him until she finally understood that she needed to run, faster than she'd ever run before.

August hadn't been kidding about the downward slopes. Both he and Megan took a tumble down the first, but managed to scramble back to their feet without major damage.

*What about the others?* Megan sent, worry starting to overpower her sense of self preservation.

*We're right behind you girl!* August sent. *Don't stop for us or we'll accidentally bowl you over. Just a little bit further.*

*We're not going to make it,* Bruce realized, feeling the future bear down like the flood waters at their heels.

Then the miracle happened. With a deafening burst that coincided perfectly with a massive surge of energy behind them, Bruce and Megan suddenly found themselves on a flat piece of land nestled between two ranges of snowcapped mountains. Trees ranging from deciduous yellows to deep cypress greens climbed the distant slopes except for the open expanse directly opposite them. In that vast open space stood several thousand honking herbivores that seemed surprised to see them.

Looking back the way they'd come, both Emelia and Sam, each looking as terrified as Bruce felt, barreled down the chasm toward them. Further back, his back turned toward them with his shoulders rigid in concentration, August held the mounting flood waters at bay so the rest of them could escape.

"We have to do something!" Bruce yelled, casting about frantically for any future path that would give him a way to save the old man. But in the shadow of the hermit's sacrifice, he couldn't see anything.

Suddenly Megan disappeared from his side, only to appear next to August, where she wrapped her arms around his waist and walked the shadows back with him to safety. The hermit dropped to the ground, gasping for air and bowing his back in agony. His fingers curled into claws and guttural sounds escaped past his clenched teeth.

The four of them gathered around him in concern, unsure what to do.

"Don't ever do that again," he gasped when the worst passed. "I know you meant well, but you have no idea how close you came to killing me with even that fraction of a second out of Guarded Wood."

"I couldn't just let you die," Megan whispered, hugging him tight. Then his face broke into an exhausted smile.

"I've been to Tyr Sgodl and lived to tell the tale," he said.

"Indeed you have, old man," Emelia said warmly, kneeling next to him.

"Guys," Bruce said uncertainly. "I know we all just had a big moment and all, but maybe we should pay more attention to the big duck cows."

"They aren't the ones you've got to worry about," August said, allowing Sam to help him to his feet.

"I'm still going to worry," Megan whispered, looking out over the sea of honking wildlife. "Just a little bit."

Bruce cast his eyes everywhere, but couldn't sense anything that resembled the large predators that the old man had brought them there to deal with. His senses told him that there were indeed cliffs on the opposite side of the herd, and now that they had moved a short distance from the flooded crevasse, it had disappeared. In its place a mountain rose into the sky.

"Damn it," August mumbled, looking out over the oddly swollen-faced beasts. "My patch didn't hold. The whole herd is on this side now."

Sam pulled out his phone and took several pictures of the herd and captured a moment of their strange trumpeting call before putting it away in his pocket again.

"I promised Paul I'd do that," he apologized.

"So good so far," August said, scanning the mountains above. "If we're lucky, we can try to get them moving back to their side of the boundary before Huginn and Muninn notice that they're here."

"Seriously?" Megan said. "Anything within ten miles can probably hear that honking."

"Where's the hole back to their home?" Bruce asked, starting to have a bad feeling about this whole situation.

"About halfway between the tree line to the right of the mountain and a big rock that looks like Fang's left ear."

"Wow," Megan said. "It does look a lot like that now that you mention it."

"How exactly are we supposed to make all of these creatures move in a particular direction without making them stampede?" Sam asked.

Before the hermit could answer, something huge came plummeting down out of the sun where they couldn't look directly. But even when Bruce could finally see it clearly, his brain refused to accept it as real. With feathers so black that they seemed to absorb the sunlight, the largest raptor he'd ever seen caught up one of the honking beasts in its immense claws, barely slowing as it climbed through the air toward a neighboring mountaintop.

That was enough for the herd. In a series of high-pitched nasal whistles that pierced the air before passing blissfully out of the range of human hearing, the strange horned beasts wheeled away from the place where their brethren had been taken.

The five ill-prepared humans ran for their lives... again.

*I don't think we're going to be able to do anything to help these creatures,* Sam sent. It was hard to believe that someone so large could run that fast.

*Make for the opening,* Emelia sent, dodging between two of the bucking beasts.

*Why didn't I think of that?* Megan thought wildly. *Should be a piece of cake.*

*Look out!* Someone sent.

One of the huge beasts turned toward Megan, hooves flashing toward her unprotected back. She faded into a wisp of shadow, solidifying when the danger passed.

*That was too close!* Megan sent, glancing Bruce's way with a triumphant smile just as another of the beasts hit her head on and sent her flying through the air like a rag doll.

"NO!" he screamed, already sprinting to where she lay motionless.

The beast that had hit Megan disintegrated before him, and another bearing down on her motionless body flew across the field as if a giant had decided to make a field goal.

Emelia wasn't playing any more.

*They're afraid of fire,* August sent, his voice strangely calm in a world exploding with sound. *Sam, wall us in on your side and I'll take this one. Then we can get Megan and carry her out.*

254

It was a sound plan, and just hearing it made the terror coursing through Bruce a little more manageable. At least until the other raptor swept his unconscious friend up in its claws and headed directly toward the cliff and the open water beyond.

Reaching out, he tried to ensnare the bird and force it to return, but although he could feel his friend, the bird evaded his extra senses.

Running faster than he ever had before, he slipped between the stampeding animals, using his abilities to supplement the power of his body, leaping and landing as he'd seen Emelia do at the Sentinel tree. Emelia took care of the ones he couldn't dodge. But fast as he was, the monstrous bird easily outdistanced him.

Acting on instinct alone, he began to walk the shadows in rapid succession, flickering in and out of existence across the plain. Then the monstrous bird's shadow disappeared over the rocky edge just as the choppy waters came into view. Stretching out to the horizon, the white-capped swells broke against the rocks below. He had just an instant of clarity in which he tried to analyze how something so beautiful could evoke such debilitating terror within him. Then he let out a breathless groan, sounding like an extremely worn whoopie cushion and walked the shadows to the shrinking silhouette so far above. He appeared too far above and behind the bird, barely able to focus past the thought of what those massive claws might be doing to Megan. He appeared much closer the second time, but realized that he was starting to fall. Were it not for his intuitive grasp of the laws of physics even in the midst of utter fantasy, he and Megan would have certainly died.

As it was, his third jump brought him down directly in the center of the roc's shoulders, knocking the wind out of him with the impact. The bird shrieked in pain and its forward momentum, so much greater than that of its unwanted passenger, spun Bruce backward. Reaching out in desperation, Bruce managed to plunge his right hand into the feathery mass and catch hold of the base of one of the foot-long feathers. But even with the added strength of his abilities, he was barely able to hold on. His shoulder exploded in agony.

The roc roared in pain as the feather pulled free, and it released its prey to better flee from this strange creature that pursued it through the air.

Bruce appeared next to Megan and drew her back against his chest with his good arm while the other trailed uselessly behind him. Then, unable to look at the water rushing up toward them, he hooked his leg around her so he could free his hand to cover her mouth and pinch her nose shut. Then he walked the shadows with her to the water's surface before they picked up any more life-threatening momentum.

In the instant before they struck, the combined magic of Emelia, Sam and August cloaked the two in a protective cocoon of power and shoved them out past a jutting spit of rock that rose like a dark iceberg from the water's depths. Even so, the forward momentum that he and Megan had carried from above sent them skipping inside their protections across the turbulent waters like a stone cast from the shore.

By sheer force of will Bruce held onto consciousness while he waited for them to stop, still holding on lest Megan breathe in water when they sank. When they did, he used the last of his strength to walk the shadows with the girl he loved, taking a perfect sphere of water from the ocean around them to the edge of the cliff where his friends waited. There he finally allowed the pain to drag him down into the darkness, but not before making sure that he could still feel her next to him where they'd landed.

Bruce woke from dreams of a dark place that stank of mildew and forlorn longing to the sound of his shoulder slipping back into its socket. It hadn't been a particularly pleasant dream, but he definitely preferred it to the reality of what Sam was doing.

"Is she okay?" Bruce croaked, his mouth tasting of bitter saltwater. He wasn't quite ready to open his eyes, so his ears were sharpened to the absence of honking bleats. He took that as a good sign until he remembered Odin's damn birds and how the only way to sense them was with his eyes.

"I'm fine," Megan said from above him, and he realized his head was in her lap.

"Azarich is going to need a bigger smoker," Bruce said, trying to lessen the severity of the moment. "I'm going to kill that thing and serve it for dinner next Thanksgiving."

"You can't," August said, sprawled out on the ground with far less decorum than he normally exhibited.

"Supernatural game preserve or not," Bruce said, thinking he should try and sit up, but liking the closeness to Megan too much to move. It would be over all too soon without him doing anything to end it prematurely. "That goose is cooked."

"I've never seen one of these particular creatures die," the old man continued. "But in my experience, enchanted creatures disintegrate when they pass. That's why no one ever finds their remains."

"How are you feeling?" Bruce asked, looking up at Megan's face. She had a nasty bruise already blooming across her jaw. He thought it might be on the right side of her face, but looking up at her upside down made the world lurch unpleasantly.

"From what I hear, I have you to thank for being alive to feel anything at all," she answered softly.

"I don't know what you're talking about," he mumbled. "You totally had the situation under control."

258

She shifted her weight, and he thought it was time to get up, but instead he felt her lips on his forehead.

It was the best second and a half of his life.

# Chapter XXIX: Phantom Queen

Bruce lay on his bed, looking at the printout he'd downloaded of specs for Christine's engine. He felt confident that he could fix it, particularly since it was mainly just locked up from sitting in the same place for so long. In fact, if he understood what was wrong well enough, it would only take a few minutes to solve the problem. Sam had already picked up the fluids and rubber parts he couldn't repair, so in short, Christine's resurrection was almost at hand.

From the direction of Megan's house, he felt a surge of excitement. Without waiting to find out what it was about, he got up and stuck his head into Jade's room where she and Paul were trying to identify a strange rock that they'd picked up at the boundary the previous day.

"What's up bro?" Paul asked, resembling a giant bug as he looked at him through the jeweler's magnifying glasses.

"Megan's excited about something next door," Bruce answered. "Want to find out what it is?"

"Mom said you can't go out until the sling is off of your arm," Jade said. "Of course, you could share what really happened out there and we'd ignore her instructions."

"I fell," he answered yet again. "And I dislocated my shoulder when I caught myself."

"And Paul is only a little fixated with goth violin players," Jade replied.

Bruce reached up and pulled the obnoxious thing over his head and dropped it on the floor next to him.

"Look at that!" she said with feigned surprise. "Not only is he shirking responsibility, but he's littering as well. He's come so far from that wimpy little rule follower..."

"Can't you just do the psychic radio thing?" Paul asked. "Or look into the big old might be?"

"Okay," Bruce admitted. "I'm bored, and this is a good opportunity to get out of here and do something. As for looking into the future, my brain still hurts from all of the weird stuff that's going on. And sometimes I like to be surprised like everyone else."

"And you're missing her," Jade said. "Perfectly respectable reason to get out of the house. Think we're going into the woods?"

"Probably," Bruce said. "If nothing else, I can put on the new fan belt and replace the coolant hoses on Christine."

Paul pulled out his phone and consulted it for a moment.

"There's a cold front in Wyoming right now," he said. "I'm definitely in favor of hanging out there instead of in the Texas heat today."

"That's settled then," Jade said, always eager to go work on her car. "Think today might be the day?"

"It might," Bruce said with a smile, knowing that patience had never been his sister's strength, "I'd say two more days at the longest. But that's only if some major problem turns up. I really think it should be today or tomorrow. I'm just not looking forward to lugging all of that antifreeze or the battery out to the car."

He moved his arm gingerly, testing to see how much it still hurt.

"What tools do you need?" Jade asked.

Bruce rolled his eyes.

"Oh, right," she said.

Armed with the parts he would need for Christine, they left the house and tried not to gasp as the oppressive heat descended on them. Bruce noticed that Emelia's truck was pulled around to the back of their property, and there was a long cattle trailer hooked up to it.

He felt Megan's elation just before she rounded the house astride a pale horse with a black mane. Without reins or saddle, she had it at a full gallop and looked like she'd been born there.

*I didn't know you could ride,* he sent.

*It's my first time!*

*I'm glad Emelia isn't here,* he sent, *I don't think I'm up to riding bareback.*

*Don't worry,* Sam sent, *I've got saddles for everyone. I don't want any of us to have to limp home injured again.*

"Look at her go," Jade squealed in delight. "Think she'll let me ride?"

"Sam has several horses for us to use while we're patrolling the barrier."

"Well hurry up then," Jade said, taking off at a run toward the back of the McGeehee property.

It wasn't easy running with the coolant hoses in hand, but he managed in spite of the heat. Sam already had the other four horses saddled when they walked up.

"So you're coming in with us?" Paul asked, noticing the extra horse.

"Not this time, but I do have a package for you to take to our reclusive friend." Sam said, placing several hardback books into the saddlebag. "The extra horse is for August."

"He looks fast," Paul observed.

"The fastest of the bunch," Sam agreed. "I didn't realize you were so interested in horses."

Paul shrugged, looking a little bit confused about why he'd asked.

"August is about to find out who Dumbledore is, isn't he?" Bruce asked, and Sam nodded.

Bruce could feel August's interest from where he watched them through a squirrel that perched in a tree overhead. Could that actually be excitement?

*I haven't ridden a horse in decades!* He sent. *Hurry and bring them back to the grove!*

"You guys go ahead," Bruce advised. "I'm going to load up these parts. Sam, do you think it would be too much if I put a jug of antifreeze in each of my horse's saddlebags?"

"I doubt she'll even notice it," he said. "They're used to carrying me around. I'll come back later and carry in the battery myself. You guys should probably get a little more practice before you try to ride without both hands."

"Good idea about the horses," Bruce said.

"I can't take credit for it," Sam said. "Paul called me last night and suggested it."

Grateful for the family friend who had taught them to ride, Bruce loaded the parts and mounted the nearest horse after waiting for Jade to pick hers first. Paul followed, and the horse with the books turned its head as if hearing something and trotted off in the direction of Guarded Wood.

"This is awesome," Megan said, guiding her mount alongside his. "I'm naming her Phantom Queen. I've never gotten to name anything before!"

"Are you sure you don't want a saddle?" he asked.

"Nope," she answered, leaning forward over the neck and hugging her horse contentedly.

"You guys take it easy until you get used to them," Sam called after them.

*Hey Sam,* Bruce sent on a whim. *What would you do with an obscene amount of money?*

*Get this town back on its feet,* Sam replied at once. *What did you have in mind?*

*We'll talk soon,* Bruce replied, encouraging his horse to catch up with the others.

August had already mounted his horse when Bruce caught up, and the glee on the old man's face truly transformed him.

"I've never seen you look so happy," Megan called out.

"Smiling makes you look younger," Jade agreed.

"I mean you could pass for a hundred right now," Paul said, unable to help himself.

"You have no idea how much of a compliment that really is," the hermit called back as he took the horse into the trees.

# Chapter XXX: The Stairmaster from Hades

"I'll get it!" Megan called to her grandfather when his ancient rotary phone began to ring. "McGeehee residence."

"Megan, you've got to help," Jade's frantic voice came over the line.

"What's wrong?" she asked.

"Kate's unconscious, and I can't get her to wake up. Her breathing is really shallow, and her pulse is weak. I called Dad, but he's already in the next town. It's going to take an hour for him to get here. What should I do?"

"Let me get Grandpa," Megan answered quickly, putting the phone down next to the cradle before running down the hallway to the kitchen table where her grandfather was placing several of his wife's recently discovered paintings into frames.

"What's wrong?" he asked as soon as he saw her face.

"It's Kate," Megan blurted out in a rush. "She's unconscious, and Jade can't wake her up. Mr. Grimble is in the next town, and their mom is out of town on *Tribune* business."

"I'll call Sam and see if he can bring that new food truck," Azarich advised. "It won't be the most comfortable ride for Kate, but at least we'll

265

be able to lay her down. Tell Jade that we're all on our way and then call Alan. His number is in the notebook next to the phone. You might want to get Paul over here too. Without Bruce's dad, Paul's first aid training might be useful."

"Okay," Megan said, relieved that he was there to take over and make decisions. She relayed Azarich's instructions to Jade and then called Mr. Green and summoned her friends from next door.

"Okay," Azarich said, taking his keys from the bowl by the front door. "Let's get going."

Bruce and Paul came running up and jumped into the back of the truck just as Azarich started the engine. Soon they were breaking the speed limit on their way into town.

*How did Jade sound when you talked to her?* Bruce asked from the bed of the truck while they sped past the deserted houses at the head of Beverly Road.

*Understandably freaked out,* she sent back. *She sounded relieved that Azarich was taking over and getting everyone coordinated.*

*I'm with her there,* Bruce sent. *What is causing this? Dad says everything points to it being an environmental reaction, but if that's the case what is it and why isn't everyone getting sick?*

*Any hints on the prediction horizon?*

*I wish. I can't look backward to see causes, and as far as I can tell, none of the people close to us that I keep tabs on are going to get sick. I didn't look at Kate until the day we brought her groceries, and we already knew she was sick, so there wasn't much to see.*

*At least that's in our favor. I'd hate to have my grandfather or one of his friends get it at their age. I just hope Kate makes it out okay.*

When they pulled up, Mr. Green had already arrived since he'd been at the Academy when they'd called. Jade was talking fast and moving her hands to emphasize points so quickly that she sounded like she was speaking another language. Paul, of course, remained calm and went in to assess the situation.

Sam pulled up in the food truck. He'd already cleared out as much equipment as he could to make room for their sick friend and several passengers.

"Luckily she doesn't weigh much," Paul said, coming out and calling for help getting Kate out of her house. "She passed out on her bedspread, so we can use that like a stretcher to get her to the truck."

It was cool to watch the way Paul took charge, directing each of them on how and where to hold the bedspread to best support the sick woman. Within moments, Kate had been moved to the back of the food truck with pillows tucked in around her to make sure she wouldn't move. Though Mr. Green didn't say anything, the way he hovered around the unconscious woman made it clear he had no intention of staying behind.

"Should we call the police for an escort?" Bruce asked.

"That's the first thing I did when we couldn't get Dad," Jade spat bitterly. "I don't know what I was thinking. The sheriff is Mrs. Jones's brother, and I found a letter from Mr. Jones offering to buy The Palace. Needless to say, I was informed that it is not the place of the Nickelville Police Department to take up the slack when the fire department falls behind."

At that moment the wards that protected Guarded Wood flared, and not one of the portions that Megan or her mother had patched. This was a section of the ancient protections that were still intact. Something had broken free, something massive.

"Azarich," Sam said when they were ready to go. "I'd love to go, but

Patty is the only one of my staff who showed up today, and she can't cook and wait on tables at the same time. Would you guys mind if I headed back to Gordon's before the lunch rush. I'd really be in trouble if Patty quit on me too."

"Of course," Azarich said, catching the keys when the big man tossed them to him. He'd noticed their reaction when the boundary broke and knew something needed their attention. "Jade can drive everyone else home. Alan, I assume you want to ride in the back with Kate?"

"You couldn't stop me," the janitor said absently, his face twisted with worry.

"I call shotgun," Paul said, climbing into the front seat along with Azarich. "Just bang on the wall of the cab if you need us to stop."

"So what's going on?" Jade asked.

"Massive failure at the boundary. And Azarich just took the keys to his truck too. No matter," Bruce said, reaching out with his mind to manipulate the tumblers in the steering column and start the truck.

"That's a trick that could come in handy," Jade said, walking over to the passenger side of the truck. "Shotgun."

"Where are you going?" Sam asked. "You're driving."

Delighted, Jade lost some of the worried look she'd had since they arrived.

"I hate that you had to lie," Megan said. "Sorry about that."

"What lie?" The big man asked, pulling out his phone before he took the passenger's seat. "Patty is the only person who showed up today, and she can't run the restaurant by herself, even with the number of people who are staying in to avoid the goat flu. But in the last few moments I've decided that we should shut down early today instead of returning."

Megan and Bruce jumped back into the bed of the truck, and they were soon underway.

*Do you have any idea where your mother is, Megan?* He sent, as he talked to Patty on his phone. *I can't reach her mentally, and when I call her cell it bounces back as unavailable.*

*She was gone again before Grandpa and I got up, but her truck was still at the house. She's done this several times now. I'm not sure where she goes.*

*Maybe she's out making more mead,* Bruce suggested. *We didn't know she was doing that until the other night.*

*Perhaps,* Sam sent, clearly puzzled himself. *I'm sure she has her reasons for not telling us.*

*She always does,* Megan sent, immediately feeling guilty for thinking it. Bruce's anxiety rose suddenly as Jade skidded around a turn, apparently changing directions based on something Sam had said.

"Worried about her driving?" she yelled over the wind. He shook his head in response.

*Between the three of us we could almost pick this truck up if we needed to move it to safety. I've been trying to pinpoint where the breach happened, and from what I can tell, it's near the rich part of town.*

*Well if it's a dragon, I say we let it eat Allison before we send it back where it came from,* Megan sent.

Bruce grinned in spite of himself.

As expected, the hermit's thoughts settled about them when they got closer to Guarded Wood.

*What took you so long?* He sent, worry saturating his thoughts.

*We were on the other side of town,* Megan sent. *What happened?*

*My sloths left the boundary while I was busy elsewhere,* he sent. *Once they were outside, I couldn't bring them back. I can't move past the Sentinels and the sloths completely ignored Fang when he tried to herd them back*

Relief flooded through Megan. She'd been afraid it was something dangerous.

*You've got to hurry and get them back into the woods before someone sees them! No one can know about them or people will be flooding into Guarded Wood by the hundreds. I can't protect that many people!*

Jade turned down the road that led to the gated community where Nickelville's wealthier citizens lived. When she found the pavement suddenly smooth and devoid of the potholes that plagued the rest of Nickelville, she sped up.

As if attempting to show her that he wasn't afraid of his sister's driving, Bruce turned toward the cab of the truck and rose to his feet, holding onto the roof to steady himself.

*What are you doing?* Megan asked.

In answer, he reached out to the security gate, which after only a few seconds began to swing open. Then he made a gesture with his hand as if crushing a wad of paper. The security camera still smoked when they passed.

Luckily, the wealthiest neighborhood in Nickelville was also one of the smallest. Huge multi-level homes passed at even intervals, sporting private tennis courts and ornamental gardens. Tall fences surrounded luxury pools, and in spite of the mature trees that suggested the neighborhood to be as old as the rest of the strange town, nothing showed any sign of decay. The wealthy apparently shed their skins often, while their underpaid servants cleaned up the mess.

270

It didn't take long to find the sloths, or rather the swath of destruction they'd left through the well-manicured neighborhood. A few yards sported fruit trees, and from what Megan could tell, these were what had drawn the big beasts. However, their desire for the fruit hadn't stopped them from eating whole flower beds and potted plants.

To her surprise, Emelia had already arrived by horseback and was trying unsuccessfully to herd the prehistoric mammals away from a peach tree that was now almost devoid of fruit. In spite of her darting in and yelling along with Fang's barking, the prehistoric beasts remained largely uninterested in her presence.

"How are we supposed to get them back to the woods?" Bruce asked, jumping down from the bed of the truck. "And how are we supposed to hide that they've been here?"

"Paul and I don't even do this much damage!" Jade exclaimed in admiration.

"They're almost invulnerable to my abilities," Emelia yelled over the sound of Fang barking and nipping unsuccessfully at one of the adult's legs.

"I think I've got an idea," Megan said. "Hopefully it doesn't piss them off."

"Yes," Sam agreed, "I think we can all agree that angering the prehistoric monsters would probably be bad."

"At least they aren't too far from the woods," Megan said, drawing energy from the area around her.

Standing behind the parents, Megan lifted one immature sloth several inches off of the ground and started him moving toward the woods. It felt like trying to pick up a small child who didn't want to be carried. At the first sensation of movement, the juvenile sloth suddenly became much heavier. Then after a moment it changed its mind. With a squeal that sounded suspiciously like glee it helped her out by "galloping" through the air as it went.

Both of the adults and the remaining juvenile began to follow, grunting unhappily as they went.

"Man she's heavy," Megan muttered as she walked to keep up.

Bruce fell into step with her after he got over the initial shock of seeing a flying sloth and took her hand in his. The familiarity of his thoughts meshed effortlessly with hers, and together they herded the animals toward the boundary.

*Thanks,* she sent, noticing the odd thrill he always felt at being this close to her.

*You can put her down,* August sent when they were a few dozen yards from the nearest Sentinel.

Megan and Bruce happily complied.

*Now go back and erase any sign of their passing before anyone finds out they've been there!* the hermit sent anxiously.

"Yeah, about that..." Bruce said when they headed back. "Half the people in this neighborhood have security cameras."

"Oh no," Megan said, looking hastily around and finding several.

"You know what that means, right?" he asked.

"You can't possibly want me to fry the whole neighborhood!" she stammered.

"I think it's the only way. We're just lucky that the ones on this street aren't storing remotely. I'm not sure that I could do anything about an online recording." he said, pulling out his phone and handing it to Megan's mother. "Everyone give their phones to Emelia. Hopefully she can shield them from the pulse. If not, I'm happy to say the past year has taught me to

272

keep everything important backed up and to buy the best insurance on my devices."

"Sorry," Megan said wearily.

"Oh, I don't mind," he said. "I kind of like having you around."

"We need to do this together so everything works out time wise later," Sam said. "Megan, you pulse and blow out everything in the neighborhood. This is going to need to be stronger than what you did at the Academy last year."

"Something in the range of an EMP?" Bruce asked.

"Yes," Sam said. "Bruce, you need to make that transformer at the end of the street have a catastrophic failure."

Bruce's eyes took on a distant look. "Shouldn't be too hard," he said. "The outer housing is new, but the components on the inside are at least forty years old."

"Really?" Emelia asked thoughtfully.

"Emelia and I are going to start at the transformer and burn everything where the sloths have been to destroy any evidence," Sam said, taking a deep breath and looking around with regretful trepidation.

"And what do I do?" Jade asked eagerly.

"Sorry," the big man said, "But this requires skills outside of what you possess."

"We'd better do it now," Bruce said uneasily. "I don't feel anyone here now, but I can see someone coming to that blue house with the ugly sculpture in about thirty minutes. This is going to be cutting things close if we want to finish and be out before then."

Having learned to trust Bruce's premonitions, Megan closed her eyes and prepared to pulse. Given how much of her childhood had been spent trying to keep from having energy leak out like this, it was the equivalent of intentionally wetting herself.

When she released it, a wave of electromagnetic chaos rolled out from her, causing car alarms to chirp mournfully and sprinklers to come on as the circuitry in their timers disintegrated. Carrying so much power, it bled over into the visible spectrum, and they could all see its path of destruction.

"Whoa," Jade said as it moved past her, making her hair rise off of her head for a second. "That felt awful!"

It turned out that Bruce had no need to sabotage the transformer since it blew on its own when the pulse hit it, sending a shower of sparks into the dry grass below.

"Damn it," Bruce grunted, going rigid with concentration.

"What's wrong?" Emelia asked.

"Can't let...rest blow...burn whole neighborhood down," he grunted.

"Change of plans," Sam said, moving quickly. "Control the fire."

"You can do that?" Jade asked, impressed.

"Don't know," Emelia answered, "Never had a reason to try before."

*This is going to take out the whole neighborhood if we don't stop it within the next fifteen minutes,* Bruce sent when he'd finished protecting the rest of the neighborhood's neglected transformers.

Megan took one tendril of the fire, closing her eyes to keep from trancing as she watched it within her mind's eye. Trusting her instincts, she intensified the flames, making them her own and sending them roaring down the sloths' paths. When she was satisfied with this bit of artistic arson, she slowly quenched the fire to make sure it looked like it had gone out naturally.

"Megan's got the way of it!" Sam yelled. "We've got to feed it in order to make it ours!"

"Ten minutes until we have to be out of here!" Bruce yelled, surging the flames to take out a tree that had too much sloth damage to hide. "We can't be seen by anyone on the way out or they'll say it's arson and then

Emelia won't be able to print anything about it!"

Rushing through activities that required so much fine control quickly sapped Megan of her strength. Before the last of the evidence was destroyed, she and Bruce steadied themselves by holding on to one another. Megan didn't even realize Jade had retrieved the truck from where it was parked until she pulled up alongside them.

"Less than three minutes," Bruce mumbled weakly as everyone returned to their places.

"I'll meet you guys back at the house," Emelia yelled, swinging up into the saddle and heading off at a gallop toward the tree line.

"You have totally got the coolest mom in the world," Megan heard Jade say through the open window. She barely managed to lean her head against Bruce's shoulder before falling asleep.

Bruce could feel the hermit at the edge of his shields before Megan's house came into view, and judging from the way Megan stirred against his shoulder, she could too.

"I feel like I just ran a marathon," Megan mumbled groggily. "That little runt was *heavy*."

"You're telling me," Bruce said, his shoulder still warm from where her head had lain a moment earlier. It was nice, and if he wasn't mistaken, his shoulder wasn't as sore as it had been before either. Not a kiss on the forehead nice, but still pretty good.

"They're at my grandmother's grove," Megan told Jade, who she knew couldn't hear or see what was going on.

Emelia was unsaddling the winded horses so they could properly graze when the rest of them walked up. Then she crossed the bridge, laid down among the yellow flowers and closed her eyes against the sky overhead. August crossed the bridge and sat heavily on one of the stone benches with a weary sigh.

"That was so awesome!" Jade exclaimed, drawing irritated glares from everyone present.

"I can't thank you enough," August said as the rest dropped into exhausted heaps on benches and in the shade of trees.

"Any idea what happened?" Megan asked. "I thought the wards were supposed to keep them in."

"Until now, they have." August answered, running a gnarled hand across his right knee as if it hurt. "Either that's starting to fail too, or maybe they can sense the things locked away at the center starting to get restless."

"What kind of things would that be?" Jade asked, actually doing a passable job of not sounding excited by the possibilities. If she and Paul ever learned about the rocs, Bruce thought, they'd probably be out there trying to ride them.

"The kinds of things that are only remembered in mythology and quite a few that weren't written down because no one who encountered them lived long enough to tell the tale." When that didn't get the reaction he wanted, he turned to the oldest Grimble. "What do you know about sirens?"

"They're loud," she answered.

"The ones from the myths," Bruce prompted.

"Oh," she said, thinking for a moment. "Like Odysseus?"

August nodded.

"Women whose voices lure men to their…" she cut off, realizing what the hermit was saying. "That night in the woods?"

277

"The wisps work with it to lure people close enough for its song to drive them wild. Then…" he clapped his hands suddenly, making them all jump.

"So if you hadn't found Paul that night?" she asked.

"Our house would have been much quieter," Bruce agreed.

"Boys and their hormones…" Jade said.

"Not just boys," Sam interrupted. "If you'd been there alone that night instead of Paul, there's a good chance that you would have heard someone calling to you. Maybe a member of your family or a boy you've taken an interest in…"

"Point taken," Jade said quickly, turning almost as red as her hair.

"And that's just one of the lesser things near the edge," the old man said.

"Why can't you leave Guarded Wood?" Megan asked.

"My life is tied to it," August said.

"Has it always been like that?" Jade asked.

"No," he answered. "I could still leave as late as the early sixties. But I've outlived the days I was allotted. Even people like me don't live forever."

"Wait," Bruce said, "There are others like you?"

Megan felt something pass between her mother and the old man.

"You're going to have to tell her eventually," August said.

"The hour is drawing near," Emelia replied cryptically, "but not yet."

"And while we're on the subject of things you aren't telling me," Megan said, likely tired of being lied to, "Where have you been going all of those times that you said you were with Sam?"

"She was helping me in the woods," August answered quickly, cutting off any other discussion. "We've been working on something

278

together."

"How old are you?" Bruce asked, not wanting to sit through another one of the tense moments between Megan and her mother. "The stories from generations past aren't about other members of your family, are they?"

"No," the hermit answered. "The only other member of my family who ever lived here was my wife."

"Everything I've ever heard about you suggests that you lived alone," Bruce said.

"She was shy and never left Guarded Wood. So no one could have spoken of her. Well, that and the fact that the only people here back then were your people," the hermit added, nodding toward Sam. "The Spaniards hadn't come this far yet."

The group went silent, letting the implications of that simple statement sink in.

"That can't be right," Emelia said, clearly trying to speak without giving too much away. "Your kind lives a long time, but surely not that long."

"Unlike your friends," he explained, "Longevity wasn't bestowed on us uniformly. Some of us live lives comparable to normal folk. Others, like me, are cursed to live much longer."

"How is that a curse?" Jade asked.

"I watched my wife grow old and die," he answered. "She was dying when we came here. I was something of a scholar, and I knew that this was a special place that could extend her life if it chose."

"But it didn't," Emelia whispered. "It chose you instead."

August nodded.

That was too much for Jade, for even though she had a hard exterior, she was likely the kindest of the three children. She stood up, walked over to the hermit and gave him the first hug he'd probably had in centuries. She was still doing so when Megan spoke.

"You're wrong," she said.

"About what?" August asked, trying to act as if he didn't like the attention.

"About not having family," she answered.

"In case you haven't heard, I'm adopting grandparents this week," Jade said, her voice thick with emotion. "You don't want to stunt my emotional growth by saying no, do you?"

"I guess I can live with that," the hermit said. "Would you guys promise me something?"

"Of course," Megan said.

"Will you make sure there's someone to take care of my woods when I'm gone?"

Bruce stiffened, his eyes losing focus, and his thoughts going somewhere Megan couldn't follow.

"What is it?" she asked him.

"I can see a young dark-haired woman who is going to follow you as the caretaker of Guarded Wood," he answered, his voice sounding distant.

"Who?" August asked eagerly, reluctantly breaking free of Jade.

"She looks familiar, but I can't place where I've seen her before," Bruce said, shaking his head. "But it's like she *belongs* in Guarded Wood. It's like she's a part of it."

"You're sure?" August asked.

"It's one of the strongest premonitions I've had yet."

"Good," the old man said. "That also suggests that this all gets straightened out at some point. Or did the woods seem strange?"

"No, I guess that means we'll survive this," Bruce said, then added, "Unless we all die and someone else comes in to fix it."

The sound of Jade hitting him could be heard far into the woods.

"Well," August said, starting off toward the trees. "As long as you're all taking up more responsibility for Guarded Wood, I should probably start sharing some of her secrets. There is someplace I need to show all of you, but it's one of the places that is only accessible at certain times. Will you all come back just before dusk? Paul and Azarich should be back from the hospital by then. They should probably see this as well."

"Cool," Jade said, "a field trip. We can tell Mom and Dad that we're staying over with you guys so she doesn't check up on us."

"Now if you don't mind, I'm going to go and see to my charges. Maybe I can figure out how they were able to pass the boundary," he added. "You should all probably get some rest. It's a bit of a journey, and we can't take the horses through most of it. Bring good hiking gear so that you can add layers and remove them as the temperature changes. A coat is too heavy to carry, but you'll wish you had one at times." Then he disappeared into the trees as if he'd never been there without addressing any of the questions to which they immediately wanted answers.

Light faded from the horizon as August led them into Guarded Wood. Each had tried to follow his advice to dress for a changing variety of environments. This challenge had, of course, sent Paul into a positively ecstatic burst of scoutly planning and packing. Night sounds closed in around them as they walked, and shortly before the darkness released the shadows from their daytime prison, August summoned a tongue of cold blue flame like the one Emelia had used to initiate her father into this strange new world. It hovered, just above the gnarled top of his staff as they walked. With a brief finger pressed to his lips, he indicated that they shouldn't speak.

The wisps found them first, drawn by their presence in these dark places where only the hermit belonged. Soon the air was thick with them, and for the first time Megan realized that the dancing lights looked nothing like fireflies up close. But what she had originally taken for a swarm of individual creatures was actually a single, malignant entity that dwelled where light never reached.

As if crossing some threshold through which the glowing lights could not pass, the path widened and eventually ceased to have meaning as they entered old growth forest. Jagged stumps the width of the sentinel trunks stretched up into the darkened sky, and if day still came to this forgotten land, it wasn't often enough to keep more than the hardiest scrub alive. Over the course of the next half-hour, the air turned bitterly cold. Everyone except Megan held their arms across their chests and balled their fists into the warmth of their armpits as they walked through a light sprinkling of snow.

Paul pulled a thin thermal blanket out of his pack and handed it to Jade, who shivered as she walked.

Ice soon encased the bare branches of the trees overhead, giving them the illusion of a world spun from glass, reflecting the light cast by the flame that burned atop the hermit's staff in a hundred thousand pinpricks of blue light.

Domed shapes emerged from the darkened edges of the circle cast by the blue flame. As they approached and details became apparent in the improved light, Paul ran ahead in excitement.

"It's okay," August chuckled, his breath steaming in the air as he spoke. "We're going to stop here and rest for a bit. The path becomes difficult up ahead and some of us could use a chance to warm up. I keep firewood in that dome nearest the fire pit."

"Oh my god!" Paul whispered loudly enough to carry through the trees for hundreds of yards in any direction. "Do you have any idea what those are?" he asked, then continued before anyone had a chance to answer. "They're glyptodon shells! They were like giant armadillos. They think primitive man hunted them and used their shells for dwellings, which looks exactly like what they've done here!"

"You'd better go start that fire, " Emelia told Bruce, watching the youngest Grimble run around. "I think we've just found the point where the rock hound eats the scout."

Soon the small company stood around the blazing fire, minus Paul who continued to crawl in and out of the small dwellings around them. Its reflection in the ice-encased surfaces flickered and danced like the flames of a thousand candles around them and overhead.

Another burst of excited dialogue sounded from within one of the shell dwellings of which the words *tail* and *club* were understandable.

"Where are the people who lived here?" Sam asked. "This camp looks like it's been abandoned for a very long time."

"They didn't abandon it," the hermit replied, not taking his eyes from the fire. "There were about thirty of them when I first came to Guarded Wood. They left me alone, and I did the same for them. I found it fascinating to see how much their day to day lives mirrored what everyone else does. People are people, I guess, no matter where or when they lived."

"And?" Jade asked, almost burning her hands in her distraction while trying to warm them. "What happened to them?"

"I wasn't here when it happened," he continued at last, "but I came through not long after. It never gets very warm here. So when winter comes, it takes a long time for the environment to start producing food for all of the different layers of the food chain. I think that's what brought the wolves. Big ones from the look of it. You could put all four of Fang's feet in one of their tracks. That's why I don't bring him here." The hermit drifted off in thought again for a few moments during which the popping of the fire seemed dangerously loud. "There's a bluff that looks out over a lake that never completely thaws. It must have been important to them because that's where they buried their dead in rock cairns. I buried what was left of them there."

"How long ago was that?" Jade asked.

"It was around the start of the Great Depression."

"I'm glad we finally met you, August," Azarich said quietly. "You're a good man."

"I don't know about that," the hermit replied gruffly. "We'd better see if Paul wants to warm up before we head on. We've still got a long way to go. And make sure you don't leave anything behind that we brought with us. I've never been able to figure out if this is a part of Guarded Wood or if we've actually gone to the past."

"Although it might be interesting to see what someone would make of a pocket knife in the middle of a prehistoric settlement," Paul said, hearing his name and reluctantly coming over to the fire. "Sorry I geeked out on you guys," he added sheepishly. "Nice fire by the way."

"I think we all enjoyed watching you even if we didn't share your excitement," Sam said and everyone else nodded.

"We'd better get moving," the hermit said, looking back in the direction from which they'd come. "Something out there has noticed us, and I'd rather not be here when it comes to investigate. Most of the things from this time period seem to be fairly safe, but the ones that aren't are bad."

Megan extinguished the fire with a thought and fell into line between Bruce and Jade. Paul looked back with longing.

"Maybe you can take something with you when we come through here on the way back," she offered.

"As much as I'd like to, it isn't safe," he said sadly. "A fossilized glyptodon tail could pay my way through college, but one that's not fossilized would bring the entire scientific community down on our heads if it fell into the wrong hands. It would look like there's a pocket of them living in Guarded Wood, and they'd tear everything apart looking for it."

"Hey August," Bruce said. "Should we be worrying about carrying prehistoric diseases and bacteria back into the modern world?"

"You've got a quick mind," the hermit observed, still walking. "It took me a long time to worry about that. All I can say is that it's never happened yet, and I've been coming here for several hundred years."

"Did you just say several hundred?" Jade asked.

"I thought we'd already established that I was really old," August said, starting to sound irritable.

"It's just a little bit shocking when you come out and say it like that," Megan explained.

"If you don't mind my asking," Paul said, "Exactly how old are you?"

"Let's just say I was here after Columbus but before the Mayflower," he answered. "And I was well over a hundred before that. I really couldn't tell you much more than that. We didn't consider things like dates all that important, and for a very long time Sam's people were the only ones I saw."

"So they were here that long ago?" Sam asked with interest.

"They were well established and their customs felt ancient," August answered. "Their language was peculiar. I've never found anything similar before or since. And I've traveled most of the world several times over."

A braying call sounded off to their left, and a huge herbivore that stood at least twice as tall as Sam and had antlers a dozen feet across sprang across their path to disappear into the distance just seconds after it appeared.

"I think that was an Irish Elk," Paul yelled, jumping up and down in excitement. While there were indeed many times when he seemed much older than his years, this was not one of them.

"We're going to start climbing pretty soon, so you'll want to save your breath. After that it's going to warm up, but be too windy to talk normally. There's a lot to see, so you might want to keep your mouths closed and your eyes open for a while."

"In other words, stop making him wish he hadn't brought us along," Emelia said.

"You always were a perceptive girl," the hermit observed before leading them out of the trees.

As they walked, the winter forest began to thaw. The spaces between the trees grew until they fell behind the silent travelers altogether.

The hermit continued to lead them across the peak of a ridge that split two valleys like the spine of a book. Although the crest wasn't treacherous, it was still quite a way down.

The sky grew brighter and the darkness gave way to crimson hues unlike Megan had ever seen. Her grandfather smiled at her, likely thinking as she did that they were about to be treated to a bonus sunrise.

A herd of buffalo that looked different from the ones that had roamed the American plains filled the vast valley to their right almost to capacity. Even in the dim light, Megan could tell they were too big. Paul could hardly take his eyes off of them, and Bruce scanned the sky for what might be hunting them.

The wind carried scents that defied recognition, and Megan wondered if Bruce should be here with his allergies. But he seemed to be okay, so she soon let her mind wander to other things, like the fact that she'd never seen a place so big and so completely devoid of human presence. Although she knew there should be people somewhere, this was likely long before humans had begun to shape the world to match their own vision of perfection.

"Is that a staircase?" Sam asked, pointing toward a fault in the side of the mountain before them.

"It is," the hermit answered. "And before you ask me who made it, I don't know for sure. After you see what's at the top, you'll know as much as I do. And you'll probably have as many unanswered questions as well."

Paul lost his footing at one point and his sister had to steady him.

"Keep your eyes on your feet," she chided. "We'll get to see it up close soon enough."

"Sorry," he murmured, trying to do as she suggested without much success.

"Be careful," August called back when at last, they reached the steps that disappeared somewhere on the mist-shrouded peak above. "They're better than no steps at all but they're still treacherous. Jade, Paul and Azarich should go first. There's nothing dangerous up there, and we can help you if you lose your footing. It's easier if you use your hands too and sort of crawl up the mountain." Then he leaned his staff against the stone face where the steps began, implying that it wouldn't be of any use from this point onward. "Paul, you'd better leave your pack."

The first thing Megan noticed was that the steps were too shallow to accommodate her full foot. With only the first two thirds of her shoe finding purchase, the back hung off. Furthermore, the rise of each step was extremely short as if they'd been made for some ancient race of children.

"This is going to be fun," Sam said, eyeing the steps warily.

"You're just jealous that something in the world is finally my size, " Emelia said.

It took a while to reach the top, and Megan only made the mistake of looking down once. Once they reached the cloudy portion, it became difficult to determine how much more remained. It helped that she could use her abilities to hold herself safely against the stairs, but hated to think about what it must be like for her grandfather and the two Grimbles ahead of him.

Paul let out a whoop of surprise when his eyes cleared the top. Megan admired the fact that he had enough wind left to make any sound at all. Next, Jade cleared the top and paused for just a second for whatever the view provided, but quickly moved on so Azarich could get off the stairs as well. In a short time they all stood at the summit, and in spite of their exhaustion, not a single one of them sat down.

Stretched out before them on the broad mesa were the ruins of a lost city. It stretched out before them as far as the eye could see, but the ravages of time had reduced the structures to little more than fingers of stone. The sky overhead churned in hues of red and purple, eclipsing any that Megan had witnessed with her Grandfather.

A stone path stretched out before them, flanked on either side by tall stone pillars from which blue witchfire burned.

"Why is the sky so beautiful?" Megan asked aloud. "I thought it was

pollution that made the modern one pretty."

"This might be in the aftermath of a really big volcanic eruption," Bruce answered.

"It's always like this," August said with a shrug. "But we've still got a long way to go."

"At least it's flat," Azarich said thankfully.

A few of the decayed structures that could be seen from the path while they walked still had recognizable doorways. Like the stairs, their proportions indicated that their builders had been much shorter than humans, perhaps only three or so feet in height. But while the height of the openings was too short, the stepping stones were spaced too far apart for any of them except Sam. Faded markings that might have once been runes of some sort etched the worn surfaces of the flame-topped pillars that lined the edge of the path, but they'd been all but obliterated by the passage of time.

By the time they reached the intact structure at the end of the long path, the sun had fully risen and the world looked a bit less like a surreal painting. However, the architecture of the building itself suggested that its builders were something other than human.

"I found this a few decades before the American Revolution," the hermit told them. "It's nice to finally share it with someone."

"Wow," Paul whispered.

At first, Megan thought that trees had grown up the sides of the roughly conical tower, leaving their roots to cling to the elaborately carved surfaces. But as they drew closer, she realized that they too were carved from stone and a structural part of the building itself. Vines had wrapped themselves around the sculpted roots, climbing all the way to the top where their leaves gave the illusion that the stone branches had indeed sprouted in the air high overhead. Beneath these, sculptures of small creatures could be seen. Although none of them were close enough for her to be sure, she thought they might have legs like those of a goat.

While everyone else looked on in silent wonder, Bruce strode up to

its

base and laid his hands on one of the root-like protrusions that covered its surface. When he did, several hundred birds that Megan couldn't identify took flight from within the crevices that covered its surface.

"I think it's been carved from one solid piece of stone!" he cried out.

"Can we go in?" Jade asked eagerly.

"Of course, but I'm afraid we're all going to have to crawl through. It's a long way to the end and you'll wear your back out if you try to hunch over. Probably hit your head a few times too. And don't forget, we've still got to climb back down after this is over."

The ground near the entrance began to glow as they approached, and the sky overhead rumbled in irritation, sending out tendrils of lightning.

"Are we sure this is okay?" Sam asked.

"It always does that," August chuckled. "It scared me off the first hundred years or so."

"You say things like that just to freak us out, don't you?" Jade asked.

The hermit smiled in reply.

In spite of the open entrance, the debris of the outside mountaintop ended at the opening's threshold. When a ward of unknown purpose sent feather-soft tendrils across Megan's skin she looked at Bruce in surprise.

They came to the point where light no longer reached from the entrance, partially because the tunnel curved as it climbed the tower, and partially because Sam nearly filled the entire passage behind them. In the darkness, however, they became aware of a faint blue glow ahead, and they continued toward it.

"We're sure this place is secure and won't fall in on us, right?" Paul asked.

"It's solid," Bruce answered. "You guys know what? I think this place is similar to the pyramids in Egypt."

"Maybe that's where they got the idea for this place," Azarich mused.

"Or maybe this is where they got the idea for the pyramids," August countered.

After a long uncomfortable crawl that had come far too soon on the

292

heels of that climb, they finally reached the end. Four of the small stone columns that they'd seen outside stood in the corners of the room. Blue flame danced above three of them, casting the runes with which they'd been carved into sharp relief. But even in the dark recesses of the fourth corner, they could see that the markings had been thoroughly obliterated from the last, leaving only a hint of what might have once been there.

A dais rose from the floor at the center of the room, surrounded on three of its four sides by the finely sculpted statues of three women. Each stood facing inward with the fingertips of their outstretched hands just touching, leaving only one side unoccupied. The first, cut from the same stone as the rest of this strange place, was that of an old woman with long flowing hair and a simple, wind-swept garment. The veins on the backs of her hands could be traced across the surface of the stone, as life-like in their detail as they'd likely been in life.

The second was a woman somewhere between youth and the onset of middle age. Her garments were slightly more ornate than her elder, but still of a similar style. When they looked closely, they could see the weave of the fabric carved into the hard surface. Unlike the older woman next to her, her gaze was not directed toward the dais before her, but rather directly across to the empty side of the dais.

The last statue was of a woman barely crossed over from childhood, and even though the moment of her sculpting was motionless, something about her hinted at a ceaseless potential for dance and revelry. Her clothing was simple, but her hair was plaited with wildflowers.

But in spite of the skill exhibited in this discovery, it was the occupants on the dais itself that drew the gaze of Megan and the others. There rested the mummified remains of two creatures that they'd only heard of from myths and local lore. When alive they had probably only

293

stood three feet tall at most. Their lower halves were covered in black fur and their legs bent backwards at the knees and ended in cloven hooves. Their heads and torsos were vaguely humanoid, though the facial structures were elongated with eyes that looked out at angles, suggesting that these creatures were herbivores. In spite of the name they'd been given, the one on the left had small horns on his head that resembled more the ones found on a first-year buck than those found on a goat. The female at his side did not.

"So Goatman is real," Jade said casually with a hint of hysterical laughter flavoring her words.

"Is that a satyr?" Bruce asked.

"More like a faun," August answered. "Satyrs are bigger and have ram's horns."

"Oh," Megan heard herself say, "Of course they do."

"So I assume you've been studying this for a long time," Sam said. "What do you know about them, and are there anymore?"

"I've never had any luck deciphering their language," August said, gesturing toward the rune-covered walls, "but I do know that the wards that keep this crypt clean are of the same origin as the ones that protect Guarded Wood. I'm pretty sure that the ancient protections were set up by these creatures. As for if there are more, I have no idea. There are times when I feel like I'm being watched, and there are definitely presences within the woods that I can't identify. But if it's them? I can't be sure."

"I don't think they are," Bruce said, unable to take his eyes off the dais and its ancient occupants.

"Why not?" Emelia asked, fascinated by the creature as well.

"It stands to reason that if they were still around," Bruce said, "that they'd come and fix the boundary."

"Grandma painted a picture of them dancing in her grove," Megan said.

"Really?" August asked. "I'd like to see that if you don't mind."

"There's something missing here," Bruce said, moving to the side with no statue.

"I wondered if you'd notice that," August said

"What do you mean?" Megan asked.

"There was another statue here," Bruce said. "The fingertips are rough on these two next to the opening. Everything else is perfect in its detail, but these two were reshaped after the fourth statue was removed."

"Look down at the floor," August advised. "You can see where his feet were."

"What makes you think it was of a man?" Azarich asked.

"The discolored places on the floor are several sizes larger than those of the three women," the hermit explained. "And I suspect the height of the ceiling was chosen to allow him to be carved standing."

"Everything else in here is perfect except for the damaged column which incidentally coincides with the same side as the missing statue," Emelia said. "And someone maintains the enchantments that protect this place. I don't see them allowing anything to happen to this tomb or its contents. That rather suggests that they removed the statue themselves."

"The question is why." August said. "This concludes your first lesson on Guarded Wood, where long-awaited answers are always accompanied by several new questions."

When at last they'd had their fill of these mysteries, they started the long trek home. There were no more conversations as they walked, although Paul did look longingly at the prehistoric camp as they passed. And though they made it back to the McGeehee home before the morning light, none of them were able to sleep.

When the Grimbles returned to their home the next morning, their silence convinced their mother that they might be coming down with goat flu after all, and she kept them inside for the rest of the day.

# Chapter XXXI: Driving Through the Shadows

After the Grimbles convinced their mother the next morning that they had not, in fact, contracted the illusive illness, Bruce and Megan spent the morning in Guarded Wood. When they returned, they could feel Jade's irritation long before they climbed the stairs up to the treehouse where they found the fiery young woman peering out over the trees toward the distant profile of the Baker Hotel. Paul was lying on the top of one of the picnic tables, staring up at the sky deep in thought.

"Are you sure you can't heal her?" the eldest Grimble asked when she noticed them.

"We're not even sure which one of us controls my asthma," Bruce replied regretfully. "I have to be bound to her for it to go away, but is it her healing my lungs, or is she giving me the power to do it myself? We're still just figuring this out as we go."

They sat in moody silence for a while in which Bruce admired the craftsmanship of the tree house. In the ruckus of the past few weeks, they hadn't had much time to enjoy it. It also took his mind off of the second day soreness of the stair workout. His shoulder gave only modest twinges, and the dark bruise on Megan's jaw had already faded to yellow against her alabaster skin. He pulled his mind away from that memory. He'd already rehashed it too often during his confinement to his house and wanted nothing more to do with it.

"I take it that the news about Kate isn't very good," Megan said.

"They're hopeful," Paul answered.

"Let's go for a walk," Bruce said, taking his sister by the hand and dragging her toward the stairs.

"I don't feel like walking in the woods today," Jade grumbled.

"Humor us," Megan said, taking her other hand.

Now that they'd started to unravel a few of the secrets held within Guarded Wood, they could no longer see it as they once had. Furthermore, August no longer needed to hide it from them in light of more pressing matters.

"I can't even identify half of these plants," Paul said, eyeing a large fern. "And now I'm wondering if these are just not from this area or if they're extinct. One part of me thinks we could bring these things back and undo some of the damage man has caused. Then another part says we have no idea what would happen if these were reintroduced. Would they just die out again? Would they completely take over because they've no longer got any competition and mess the world's ecology up even more than it already is?"

Fang fell into step with them at a fork in the path, nudging Bruce's hand for a quick scratch.

"We missed you the other night," Megan said, taking advantage of the opportunity to run her fingers through his fur.

For the first time since any of them had started coming to the woods, they heard the sounds of wolves howling from deeper in the forest. Fang's ears perked up, and he paused for a moment, looking in that direction.

"It's okay boy," Bruce said, taking a knee beside him. "I wonder if he's concerned or if he wishes he could be with them."

*Those are the wolves I told you about in the village. He doesn't want anything to do with them.*

Bruce relayed what the hermit had said.

"I don't think I want to encounter live dire wolves," Paul said. "Things like that make me worry about what would happen if the boundary completely failed."

The bridge that the Boy Scouts had built still spanned the gorge, but the drop was now much deeper, and the water rushed below with more volume and velocity than it had done even during heavy rains. For some reason this didn't bother Bruce as much as it once might have.

"I remember we came here the first time you brought me into the woods," Megan said.

"That's when you suggested that Bruce should run in the Jubilee," Jade said. "That seems so long ago now. I mean I know it was only a few months ago, but wow."

"A lot's happened since then," Bruce agreed.

"I finally got to tell someone about the weird world I live in," Megan said.

"I got to find out what it was like to really breathe," Bruce added.

"Girls with violins," Paul said with a wistful grin. Fang chuffed in what sounded suspiciously like a chuckle.

Once they started talking, the walk became easier. For although the woods around them had for the most part altered beyond recognition, their friendship had weathered all.

At last they came to the clearing where Big Bertha stood, chrome shining in the afternoon sun. Jade looked at it longingly, then realized what the absence of parts must mean.

"Is it?" she asked.

"Sam brought the new battery and a five-gallon gas can out this morning," Megan answered. "That's what we were out here doing before you got up."

Bruce tossed her the keys.

"Have you tried to start it yet?" Paul asked, running his hand down the spotless red paint.

"Nope," Bruce said. "We thought Jade should have the privilege."

Jade climbed behind the wheel and turned the key with the fingers on her other hand crossed. The big engine roared into life, almost drowning out Jade's squeal of delight. Over the next few minutes there were infectious bouts of spontaneous dancing around Bertha/Christine and even Fang joined in with whining barks that sounded suspiciously like an old man laughing.

"Everybody in the car," Megan yelled.

"Why?" Paul asked. "It's not like we can drive it back to the house."

"Oh ye of little faith," Bruce said, pushing his brother into the back seat and climbing in with him, letting Megan sit up front with Jade. "Can Fang leave Guarded Wood for a little while?" he called out.

*It shouldn't be a problem,* August sent. *He isn't bound here by the same restrictions that I am.* In response, the wolf hybrid happily jumped into the open door, filling the back floorboard almost completely.

"What do you say Bruce?" Megan asked. "Do you see any major catastrophes in our immediate future?"

"Not a blip," he answered, excited by what they were about to do. Fang's musky odor filled the confines of the car. "Jade, pull forward slowly."

With Jade driving no more than a few feet per minute, Megan reached out to that cold place where she and Bruce had gone to escape O'Toole that day at the Academy. At first Bruce wasn't sure that she could part the shadows carrying so much mass, but when he added his power to hers, darkness descended upon them. They could hear the wind howl past the newly renovated seals along the edges of the doors, but it wasn't nearly as cold in the car as it would have been outside.

Fang whined in concern, unable to feel his master any longer.

A patchwork of ice crystals formed snowflake patterns across the glass. Then, just ahead of what Bruce suspected to be a bolt of lightning forming between the unevenly charged sky and the car, Megan pulled them back into the bright sunlight they'd just left. They'd come out onto the road next to the ruins of the general store that Sam's Uncle had once run.

Jade and Paul sat in wide-eyed silence when they rolled to a stop in the middle of the road with the frost already melting from the car. Bruce slumped down into the seat, almost losing consciousness until Fang began to lick his face.

"What the hell?" Paul asked.

Jade made an unintelligible sound that made Bruce and Megan start laughing weakly.

"Seriously," Paul added when they showed no sign of answering on their own.

"We just walked, well in this case I guess we drove between the shadows," Bruce explained, and then added when he sensed their confusion, "Megan took Bertha into what I suspect to be a parallel universe. Emelia said it was called walking between the shadows."

"Is it dangerous?" Jade asked, finally regaining the ability to speak.

"Incredibly," Megan answered with a grin. "And something about that place really didn't like Christine. I think it had something to do with all of the metal. Anyway, we're here, the car still works, and it's out of the woods."

"And we didn't die," Paul added, still shaken. "That's always a bonus."

Bruce rolled down his window so Fang could stick his head out.

"Just follow the road down a ways and then turn left," Megan advised, settling back into the seat for a brief nap. "That will take you back to the main road. You'll know where you are by then."

*He's really enjoying that,* August sent. *Come by your grandmother's grove when you get back. I've got something for Jade.*

"You have no idea how smooth she handles!" Jade squealed. "They just don't make them like this anymore. Thanks guys."

"Don't get all sentimental on us," Bruce mumbled from the back seat. "It was the only way to get you to stop hinting that you wanted a car every few minutes. Park at Megan's place. August says he wants to give you something."

The man in question was standing in the circle of trees at the back of the McGeehee property when they walked around the house. In his hand was the original paperwork for the car.

# Chapter XXXII: Senior Omission

The Palace continued to draw crowds, although never quite as well as it had those first few days after the renovations. Money came in and bills continued to be paid, but it became clear all too quickly that the theater, though revitalized in the image of her better days, was still not going to be able to pull out of the financial hole that she'd fallen into over the past few decades. This wasn't for lack of trying. Megan and all three Grimbles worked as if they could overcome financial woes simply through an act of will. However, when the gradual loss of novelty combined with the continued presence of the unexplained illnesses, the results were depressing.

Still dressed in her sweats and t-shirt from the workout at the dojo, Megan was restocking popcorn bags in preparation for the next evening's show when the front door opened to admit Mr. Green, who seemed to have reversed the aging process some twenty years over the past week. Gone were the stained coveralls he wore when working at the Academy. In their place he wore suspiciously new looking jeans and a western shirt. None of them had ever seen him so neatly groomed.

"Hello," he called out happily. "Anybody home?"

"Hey, Mr. Green," Paul replied, appearing shortly from the doorway of the newly-restored main theater, pushing a mop and bucket before him. "What brings you in?"

"I thought I'd stop by and see how things were going, so I can update Kate when I go visit in a bit," he answered, grinning contagiously.

"It's all good," Jade said, coming out from the office to join the conversation. "It's slowing down a bit as the newness wears off, but we're still taking in more than we're spending. And if we're lucky, sales will pick up again when the goat flu passes."

"Does that mean you can start paying us soon?" Bruce called down from the projector room where he'd been setting up everything for the next night's premier.

"Silence peasant!" Jade yelled up at him. "It's an honor to live and die in service to the Palace!"

"He did just fix a car for you," Megan reminded her, knowing where this would lead.

"You haven't seen my car yet, have you?" Jade squealed, grabbing Mr. Green's surprisingly clean hand and dragging him toward the alley where Christine was parked. Everyone gave up on trying to work and followed as Jade marched her reluctant prisoner toward the alley.

"Isn't she something?" Jade asked when the car came into view. "I wish it was daylight so you could see her better."

Although he smiled, his breath caught somewhere in the pit of his stomach, and his eyes lost their focus. His neck twitched ever so slightly to the right, and then he stood still, staring at the vintage automobile.

"I know, she's a beauty," Bruce said uneasily.

"I've seen that car before," the old man whispered, more to himself than to the young people around him. "Back when the four of us were still young…"

Paul walked up to him and made sure that he was between the old man and the car. As soon as Mr. Green lost sight of the car, he came to his senses with a start.

"Sorry," he mumbled, "bit of a senior moment there." He looked confused and shaken.

"Are you sure you're okay?" Megan asked. "Do you want to sit down and have a coke before you head back to the hospital?"

"No," he said, sounding almost like himself when he thought about the theater's owner. "I don't want to keep Kate waiting." He gathered Jade and Megan into a sudden bear hug and squeezed them soundly to prove that his condition was good.

"Wait a minute," Jade said, standing on her tiptoes to get a better smell. "Are you wearing *cologne?*"

"What if I am?" he growled.

"I think it's wonderful," Megan said, looping her arm into his as they walked toward the front door. "It's about time something went right in Nickelville."

"I take this to mean Kate is getting better?" Bruce asked.

Mr. Green nodded, grinning once again.

"But just so you know, you still have to pay full admission," Jade said. "Even if you are dating the owner."

It wasn't possible to tell if Mr. Green was blushing or not, his skin being what it was after so many years of working in and around the Academy. But his eyes shone and the deep-seated contentment he exuded was a balm for the scars the summer had left on Megan's soul.

"I'm hungry," Paul announced, following the school's janitor to the front door.

"You're always hungry," Megan observed, but followed anyway.

306

"I'll bet Sam would take pity on us poor unpaid serfs," Bruce added. "He'll be closing up pretty soon, though. We'd better hurry."

Jade ignored the remark, but grabbed the keys off the counter and locked the door so they wouldn't have to worry while they ate.

"That's weird," Paul said, looking down the street. "There are lights on in the ground floor of the Baker."

"I'm sure it's that O'Toole guy," Jade muttered. "But you're right, it's weird. I didn't even know that place still had electricity."

"Don't forget to tell Kate we miss her," Megan called across the street to Mr. Green as he opened the door to his truck.

"Hold up a minute," he called over to them. "Now that you mention it, I have been forgetting something."

They crossed to where he'd parked.

"I found this when we were working on the tree house, and I keep forgetting to give it to you guys," he said, handing over an old leather bundle to Bruce. "It was tucked into a crevice of the tree. Looks like the kind of stuff Paul and Bruce would be interested in."

The leather was of a type that they couldn't identify, though he thought it looked vaguely reptilian. Inside was what could only be a partially fossilized sloth claw, a lock of strangely iridescent green hair, and a wooden carving of one of the creatures that they'd first seen in Josie's painting and again at the shrine on the mountain.

Megan could feel the dormant power it held from where she stood and knew at once that this was the missing element of the failing protections around Guarded Wood.

"That's really cool," she said quickly, before they'd have to explain their excitement. "Be careful on the drive over and give her a hug for me."

"I might do just that," he said, his eyes going a completely different

307

kind of distant. "Enjoy your pizza."

"We will," all four children said at once.

"Sam says he'll meet us there," Bruce said as soon as they were out of hearing, heading back toward the Palace and Jade's car.

Just before she reached the Palace door, Megan felt someone watching them. She turned toward the source of the feeling, scanning the deserted main street but found nothing amiss.

"You okay?" Bruce asked.

"It felt like someone was watching us," Megan said.

"You mean the guy that looked like he was trying out for a part in that vampire movie dad always makes us watch?" Paul asked.

"The one where they ride motorcycles?" Jade asked.

"Yes," Paul said, also scanning the street, then he pointed at one of the shops. "He must have gone into that store."

"You're saying a guy who was wearing a black trench coat in the middle of July went into the quilting shop?" Bruce asked. "Did he strike you as an avid quilter?"

"How do you know it was a black trench coat?" Megan asked.

"Everyone in that movie was dressed like that," Bruce answered. "Dad loves that show."

"Should we go check?" Paul asked.

"No," Megan answered, "We've got to get this thing to August."

# Chapter XXXIII: The Pitter Patter of Small Cloven Feet

"It really does handle great," Jade repeated yet again, taking the turn onto Beverly Road much faster than any of her passengers would have liked. Abandoned houses flew past, and Bruce reminded himself that they should probably ward Honeysuckle House now that it wasn't protecting itself any more. For that matter, they needed to get the vines off of the house before they pulled the place apart.

"It's not a race," Bruce reminded her once again.

"Of course it is," Jade replied indignantly. "We'll definitely be first unless Emelia does that teleport thing." With this she looked suspiciously at her companion in the front seat.

"As far as I know she can't," Megan said. "Unless she's been keeping secrets from me."

"Which is pretty much guaranteed," Bruce added, not sure if it made him more nauseous when she hit the numerous potholes or swerved around them.

"Faster then," Jade urged.

They were relieved a few seconds later to see that the McGeehee driveway was empty: Jade because she'd won and the rest because they'd survived. Bruce deeply regretted fixing the car.

*You've got it with you?* August sent as soon as they came close enough.

"Someone's impatient," Megan said out loud where their friends could hear as well.

"I knew I drove too slow," Jade said mournfully as they jogged down the darkened path back to the grove.

"Emelia and Sam are right behind us," Bruce said, carrying the bundle with him. "I can't believe Mr. Green had the missing element the whole time!"

"Now we just have to fix the interdimensional security system and start on the summer reading so we don't fail English," Paul said.

"Already read it," Bruce bragged, daydreaming about what the rest of their summer could be like without constant problems from Guarded Wood. For some reason, all of those dreams centered around the girl in front of him on the path.

August waited impatiently at the furthest point from the grove that he could safely travel. His horse grazed nearby but looked winded. Apparently, they weren't the only ones who wanted things to go back to normal.

Bruce handed the bundle to the old man as soon as they approached. It felt good to be rid of the strange package which seemed to breathe with a life of its own. When it passed from his hands he also realized that it *wanted* to be reunited with the Sentinel tree.

"This is definitely what we've been looking for," the old man whispered reverently, slowly unwrapping the bundle. "I'm pretty sure this is chimera hide… ground sloth claw and…" he cut off abruptly. "Did any of you touch the hair?"

"No," Bruce answered uneasily. "I'm the only one who has touched the bundle and the hair didn't look very wholesome."

"What is it?" Paul asked.

"This is what was calling you that night in the deeper woods," August answered grimly. "I don't have any idea how they got close enough to get hair from a siren."

"And the figurine suggests that the whole thing was put together by one of our little friends from the ruin," Emelia observed. "So how do we do this?"

"Any suggestions Bruce?" Sam asked.

"Why me?" Bruce asked.

"You've seen how to do things before you've done them several times now."

"Not like this," Bruce exclaimed, suddenly feeling his inexperience. "Those things were all small." He searched for a better way to explain. "When I try to look at this, it's just too…"

"Powerful to see past," August explained.

"Exactly!" Bruce exclaimed, gesticulating wildly.

"Of course, seers can't see past their own deaths either," August added.

Bruce looked horrified.

"Well that turned unexpectedly dark," Jade said. "So what are we going to do?"

"You and Paul should probably stay here," Sam answered. "I'm sorry, but this might indeed be dangerous. Neither of you have abilities that could help us, so there's no point in putting you in harm's way without cause."

"Forget that," Jade said angrily.

311

"Yeah," Paul added, "There's no way I'm going to be the one to tell Mom that her favorite child is dead. Or killed by a rampaging rusingoryx."

"A what?" Megan asked.

"The honking cows," Bruce said. "He's been telling me all about them."

"We're coming," Paul insisted.

"But if you die with us you won't be able to see Violin Girl at the Jubilee this fall," Bruce teased.

"Uncool Bro," Paul said, though he grinned when he said it. "It's a chance I'm just gonna have to take. Besides, if I don't find her in this life then I'll just have to catch her in the next."

"Whatever we plan to do, I think we should start soon," August urged, turning to walk toward the tree house. "Something terrible is starting to wake in there, and I don't think we want to find out what it might be."

Even for the short walk to the tree house, they could all feel what August meant. Guarded Wood looked and felt dangerous in ways that it hadn't just a few days previous. The shadows looked deeper, and the sounds from within were both louder and yet more ominously quiet.

"If we finish before it's opening time," Jade said. "You guys are so coming to help me run the Palace even if Bruce does die."

"I'm right here," Bruce complained.

"And I'll let you off the hook tonight if you do," Jade said, pointing her finger in his face. "But don't expect any more time off or I'm docking your pay!"

"You don't pay me now!"

"Totally irrelevant," she mumbled, shooing him onward.

In the fading light over the woods, it looked as if the Sentinel might

312

be starting to wilt. None of them said anything though, as if speaking it aloud might doom them all. Soon they ringed the substantial trunk of the tree, each wondering what to do next.

"Any idea where Alan found it?" Sam asked.

"All he said was that it was in a crook between some branches," Paul answered. "Which must mean it came from the place where the main supports for the tree house connect. I don't think we can even get to that spot now."

"What if we cut a hole…" Jade started.

"Don't even think about it," August warned.

"Are those fireflies?" Sam asked, looking back toward the tree line.

"Oh crap," Paul said, looking where Sam was now pointing.

"Jade, you keep an eye on Paul," August advised. "We're likely to be very distracted before this night is over. Fang will help you." The wolf hybrid trotted up from the growing shadows just as Emelia started a roaring fire in the pit with a wisp of thought.

"No sitting on me this time!" the eldest Grimble ordered, holding a finger up to the wolfy face. He licked her hand in reply.

August took the leather bundle, wrapped it tighter and then pressed it firmly to the trunk of the ancient tree. Though nothing happened, it did *feel* as if this were a step in the right direction.

"It must be reset," Megan said, though she didn't know from where the words were coming. "Focus on what we want from the Sentinel tree and then lend it the power to do so."

"How do you know that?" August asked.

"I don't know why I even said it," Megan answered even as the internal voice told her that she needn't explain. "But it's what we should do."

313

"I sure hope you're right," August said. "This feels like something that could get out of hand."

"Yeah," Bruce agreed. "And I really wouldn't want to miss my next installment of child labor at the Palace."

"Okay," Emelia said, taking the bundle from August with an air of confidence that suggested she'd done things like this in the past. "Megan and Bruce, you hold this against the tree. Bruce, we're going to be feeding power through you to Megan. You've never amplified the power of five gifted people before, and I'm not sure what it's going to feel like since none of us share your gift. We're dealing with non-human power structures here, and as you know, that can be tricky."

"We knew that?" Paul asked from nearby.

"Totally," Jade agreed, laughing hysterically.

*No time like the present,* Megan sent and felt it reverberate through the bond that was forming between them. She opened her mind to Bruce and his mind merged with hers with a painful intensity.

August shaped the purpose of what they wanted from the Sentinel, gathering the lines of power they could now sense radiating out from the tree to its brethren across the entirety of guarded wood. Building upon what remained of its original purpose, he began to breathe life back into the strange structures created by their cloven-hoofed predecessors so far in the past that they'd since been lost in legend. As he did so, Megan took the power the others provided, added it to her own and felt the sum magnified through the lens of Bruce's gift. When the hermit first released what he'd shaped, its delicate complexity settled over them. Until the first tendrils of combined power flowed through it and into the Sentinel, she thought it wouldn't hold. But then it shuddered with the promise of being, budded, and began to grow.

314

The sky overhead heaved with newly formed thunderheads as Megan channeled more power than any of them had ever summoned. Wind tore through the trees as the weather responded to their workings.

Although nothing of what they did yet showed in the visible spectrum, Paul and Jade knew they'd begun. Something deep and instinctual stirred within them all from far back in time when mankind was still in its infancy. And the message that instinct sent was a warning, a warning that something infinitely old, powerful and hungry had noticed them.

In the first seconds of its life, their creation awed them with the purity of its purpose, but like all newborn life it needed to feed. Megan concentrated so hard on making sure that she provided it with a constant flow of power that she didn't notice when it stopped receiving the energy they freely gave and started to take without their consent. The power blinded them to anything but the supernatural forces moving within and around them.

*What should I do?* Megan asked, panic filling her thoughts. *Should I stop?*

*This is what I feared might happen*, August sent. *See if you can gently cut it off from our power.*

Megan tried what he'd suggested, but it was like trying to turn a river aside with a single stone. Almost as if it understood what she was trying to do, it responded by opening new conduits through which it could drain her strength. She could no longer pretend that they were in control of what happened to them.

*It will be okay,* Emelia sent, armoring them with calm. *We will live past this day.*

"Do you hear someone singing?" Paul asked from far away.

*What happens if we can't break free of it?* someone asked.

In the maelstrom of energy, it was becoming hard to keep any sense of self, as if they were being fused together. But when their weakest link broke, it would be the end of them in spite of what Emelia thought. At the moment, even though he was physically the strongest among them, that weak link was Sam. If something didn't happen within the next few moments, he'd be drained to a husk.

With a nauseating wrench, Emelia shunted the conduits that threatened to kill her childhood friend into herself and thrust him out of the circuit, tossing him away from the tree as if he'd weighed nothing. Angered, the conjuring tried to reach out and ensnare Sam once again, but the small woman held firm, and no path remained open to him past the iron of her will.

When all seemed lost, a vast alien presence brushed the edges of their senses. Nothing about it felt human, though they could feel within it the keen intelligence and wisdom garnered through ages of watching and waiting. Too desperate to deny any offer of help in that hour, Megan reached out and drew them in.

*They've come!* August sent.

*Who?* They all asked, but before he could answer, the presence embraced them.

*You have done well,* a multitude of voices whispered in unison, *but it is our responsibility to maintain this boundary. We would have intervened before now, but we could not retrieve the talisman once it moved beyond our lands. Now rest, and we will finish what you have begun.*

The conduit through which the talisman had fed died away, and Megan collapsed at the base of the Sentinel along with the others. But even so, the package clung to the tree as if she was still holding it.

Emelia and August lost consciousness at once, but Megan and Bruce managed to hold on. From the edges of the clearing small forms crept toward the tree. At first, they might have been mistaken for human children, but something in the way they moved spoke of a different heritage. Their legs bent the wrong direction at the knee and ended in hooves rather than feet. Like the mummified remains at the ruin, their heads were crowned with the nub-like horns of a young deer. But it was only in their size that they seemed young.

Bruce wondered where his siblings had gone.

The fauns circled the Sentinel as if preparing for a massive game of Ring around the Rosies. But there was no laughter or stirring at all. Three small forms separated from the rest and walked up to the base of the tree where Megan and her friends still remained.

Just shy of the trunk and the talisman that waited for its purpose to be fulfilled, the two creatures on either side released their grip on the one in the middle. In turn they each spent a short time, heads bowed forward, their horns touching.

Then without hesitation, the single faun stepped forward and placed its hands on the talisman, which flashed bright and melted into the trunk of the giant tree, taking its willing sacrifice with it.

At once Guarded Wood began to roll around them, thrashing as if something alive, which of course, it had always been. The Sentinel began to writhe within its bark, and for a while it seemed as if the tree house would come crashing down on top of them. But the combined strength of Bruce's design and Mr. Green's craftsmanship held it firm.

Guarded Wood began to fold inward upon itself, tucking away the places where the unwary were never meant to tread. As exhaustion overtook Bruce and Megan, their dreams must have risen into their

317

conscious minds because just before the fauns left, they all bowed their heads to the youngest Grimble in respect.

# Chapter XXXIV: Bad Dreams Are Made of These

Megan sat quietly next to her grandfather, taking in the glorious colors dancing across the sky. She'd slept poorly, visited repeatedly by visions of that small body disappearing into the trunk of the Sentinel. Sometimes it was alone, sometimes it rode in on one of the ground sloths. Sometimes it had iridescent green hair. But it always ended the same way, and it was their fault for building a stupid tree house.

"You're quiet this morning," Azarich said. Emelia had already filled him in on the events of the previous night, so there was no reason to rehash the whole thing this morning. What Megan really wanted was to have a normal day.

"This is one of the special ones," she said, nodding toward the place where the sky met Guarded Wood.

"It sure is," he said happily. "It's been a while since I've seen one with this many colors. So what are you and the Grimbles up to this morning?"

"Bruce wants to go over and see Sam about something he's been cooking up in that head of his. I'll go over when he gets back."

"Are you ready for the start of a new school year?" he asked. "Just a few more weeks left of summer."

"You know what," she said, looking away from the sunrise to her grandfather's handsome face. "I think I am. I'm anxious to start a completely Jones-free year."

"So Allison's not coming back I take it?"

"Nope, her daddy is sending her off to some prep school up north. I hope for their sake that they don't use water from the public supply like they do for us mere mortals. Now if we could just get him and his wretched excuse for a wife to leave too."

"Ah," he murmured, taking another sip of his overly sweetened coffee, "We can always dream I suppose. Alan and I are heading out to the hospital to check on Kate, so I'll probably be gone until dinner."

"Does she seem as happy as he does?" Megan asked.

"I'm honestly not sure why I'm going," Azarich chuckled. "Once they lay eyes on each other, I could probably strip naked and practice alligator mating dances without them noticing."

"That's oddly specific, Grandpa," Megan observed, raising an eyebrow.

"I'm an oddly specific person," he replied. "Be careful today."

"Careful of what?"

"Driving with Jade for starters."

"Okay," Bruce said, taking a deep breath and opening the browser on his computer. "Now that the problem with Guarded Wood is sorted out, I think I can see what I need to do to help the town."

"This sounds good," Jade said, wandering in and plopping in the middle of his bed, Elmo sans nose slippers and all. "But even if you do save us all, you can't have the day off."

"In our defense, we were nearly eaten by a sentient tree last night," Paul said, then to Megan, "Jade almost let slip what happened at breakfast this morning."

"That would have made for some lively discussion," Megan observed. "So what is it that we're doing?"

"This one isn't so much a we as a me," Bruce answered, taking another deep breath. "The vision showed us all here when I did it the first time though, and I don't want to jinx something this important by changing anything."

"How can you say so many words without saying anything?" Jade asked.

"Right down to you saying that," he added irritably, "I saw Sam first thing this morning and helped him open a trading account."

"As in stocks?" Paul asked, standing directly behind his brother.

"Yes," Bruce replied. "And now we find out if his trust in me is well placed."

"What do you mean?" Megan asked from the doorway, starting to move closer.

"Nothing personal, but please don't come any closer to my computer," Bruce advised, glancing over to make sure she didn't move. "I'm nervous enough about doing this with Sam's entire life savings without worrying about you going thermonuclear and frying half of the town."

This got Jade's attention.

"Knowing how to make a ton of money isn't the problem," Bruce said, starting to navigate the unfamiliar sites as if he'd been doing it for years. "I could make him a million before the day is out. Knowing what

321

investments would call attention to him is the problem. As it is, I'm going to have to remember to make some choices that I know won't pan out in order to make it less suspicious. And we're going to have to sit on Mom to keep her from doing a story about how a local business owner does good when he makes slightly over half a million in his first two weeks of trading. Ugh..."

"Hey, no Ugh's when playing with Sam's future," Jade said protectively. "What's this Ugh for?"

"Starting the process solidifies it in the future and lets me see more. In about a month I'm going to have to intentionally lose a quarter of a million to throw off suspicion. This is *so* nerve wracking!"

"Making Sam rich is great and all," Paul said, whistling as their friend's portfolio immediately began to grow in value. "But how does this save the town?"

"For starters Sam is about to become a silent partner in The Palace and pay off all of the past due loans Kate had to take out in order to keep it running. She, just like everyone else in town, loves Sam and will jump on the chance to get the place out of the red. Without loan payments bleeding out profits, The Palace should be stable for years to come. Then he will move on to start renovations on some of the abandoned houses where he grew up for reasons I still can't completely understand. Maybe someone is coming? Anyway, this will put a sizable portion of our unemployed population back to work and get money flowing back into the local economy. That, in turn, will start opening the shops back up along main street. Up until now a few families like the Jones's have been sucking up all of the loose cash and hoarding it. Sam won't do that."

"Sam is such a good person," Jade said with such seriousness that she missed Bruce rolling his eyes. "Maybe I could get a raise and hire some

322

real help. Maybe even Andrew!"

*Which is why you're starting off with The Palace first?* Megan sent.

He glanced away from the screen long enough to nod.

"Can I go tell Kate?" Jade asked, bounding up off the bed and nearly knocking Paul aside in her haste to go get dressed.

"Sam doesn't have the money yet," Bruce called after her. "And don't you think he should be the one to make the offer first? Until then you can go look at online catalogs for the updated equipment he's going to buy for the dojo," he called after her, glad to be done with investments for the moment.

Her squeal of delight somehow made it all worth it.

"Want to go horseback riding?" Megan asked. "Phantom Queen needs some exercise."

"You know," Paul said, "I'm a bit tired of Guarded Wood for some reason. And I've been thinking about what Bruce said he saw during the race. Do you think we could check out Ringed Woods instead? We've never really had much opportunity to look around there."

"You do know that she's not going to be there," Jade said. "She's probably halfway across the country getting ready to play at some town's toe jam festival or something."

"Gross," Bruce complained. "I'm in, but I'm not sure that the two of you are going to be able to see anything."

"I could feel that the woodland creatures were close," Megan added, "but even I had to concentrate in order to do that much."

"It's okay if we can't," Paul said. "But now that Jade can drive us to new places, I think we should take advantage of it."

Jade slowed down when she noticed the sheriff driving behind them. Given his relationship with Mrs. Jones and the animosity between their two families, it seemed like a good idea to be the most law-abiding citizen that she could.

"What if he follows us all the way to the woods?" Paul asked. "I'm not sure we can legally go in there when the Jubilee isn't going on."

To their great relief, the sheriff's SUV pulled off next to the Baker Hotel. By the time they reached the road that led to the festival parking lot, no one else was around.

Jade parked her beast of a car near the Gateway Oaks. It was the first time any of them had been there since he'd ridden out in his father's ambulance. But when they paused to consider all that had happened since, Paul became impatient and started toward the woods without them.

At first, the woods felt perfectly normal to Bruce, and he started to wonder if maybe he had imagined it all. Then he started to feel like he was being watched.

"Anything?" Paul asked.

"I can feel them," Megan said, looking around and smiling. "But apparently they don't want to show themselves right now."

"I've never been here in daylight," Jade said. "But these are the cleanest woods I've ever seen that were this close to where people live."

"You're right," Paul said absently, his head turned toward the festival field.

"Go ahead," Bruce said. "She's not here, but you might as well look."

With a sheepish grin Paul took off at a trot, careful not to turn an ankle on one of the numerous tree roots.

The longer they stayed, the more Bruce could feel. Sounds too faint to hear teased him with whispered laughter, and movements drew his eyes to shadows that might or might not have been his imagination.

"They're definitely here," Megan said happily. "The ones in the mountains showed themselves fairly quickly, but that might have been because the place was so isolated or maybe it was because I was so young at the time.

Even though he knew it was foolish, Bruce still felt a twinge of jealousy at the thought that she'd had friends before she'd met him.

When they came to Jubilee Field, it was much as it had been the day of the race. The air felt as if it were lacking some vitality Bruce couldn't identify. Even the colors seemed faded and two dimensional.

"I had no idea they left this many of the rides and booths here during the off season," Jade observed.

The trash of the previous year had been removed in the wake of the memorable race. Rides had been tarped in preparation for their long sleep. Booths had been shuttered, and the whole place held the disused echoes of a ghost town.

"I don't get it," Bruce said at last. "I think almost everything is still here. Why didn't the carnies take it with them when they left? Is the Jubilee seriously the only one that they run?"

Paul stood under the trees that covered the stage where he'd begun his goth musician fixation and sighed deeply.

"We should probably go soon," Jade said, looking at him with mild concern. "I have to teach class tonight."

"Wait…" the youngest Grimble said, turning toward the unused part of the clearing. "I hear something." Then without warning, he took off through the silent rides.

"Do either of you hear anything?" Jade asked, hurrying after him.

"Nothing at all," Megan said. "Has he ever been fixated on something

325

like this before?"

"Just knots and rocks," Bruce answered.

When they caught up to Paul again, he was standing in the middle of a bunch of stakes that appeared to have been driven at random intervals into the ground. Eyes closed, he ran his outstretched hands into the emptiness before him as if expecting to find something.

"It's coming from right here," he whispered when he heard them approach.

"Paul," Jade said sternly. "None of us can hear anything. Are you feeling okay?"

"I'm fine," he said, frowning. "I just…"

What he would have said was soon forgotten in the angry arrival of a man from a small shed at the end of the field.

"Get away from there!" he yelled. "You're not supposed to be there!" The startled teens watched as he approached them. He didn't look to be more than twenty or so, and the misbuttoned shirt he wore suggested he'd put it on quickly.

"We're sorry," Megan said when he came closer. "We haven't done anything except walk around. We were about to leave."

"You didn't move that, did you?" he asked, pointing to the stake driven into the ground at Paul's feet. It had the number one painted on its head.

"I didn't touch any of them," Paul answered. "What does it mark?"

"Nothing," the man snapped. "I need the four of you to leave right now. This place isn't safe during the off season. No one is supposed to come here except on the night of the Jubilee and then on the day of the race."

"We're sorry to have disturbed you," Bruce apologized, taking his

326

brother by the shoulder and guiding him back the way they'd come.

"But there's something there," Paul said, looking back over his shoulder at the stake.

"We're trespassing," "Bruce reminded him. "If he follows us to the car he could call in a complaint. Bertha isn't exactly inconspicuous."

"Christine," Jade said and slapped him across the back of the head.

"Whatever," Bruce said irritably. "Is he still following us?"

"No," Megan said without turning to look. "He's still standing next to that stake as if it were the most valuable thing in the world. Something seriously strange is going on here."

A wave of nausea washed over Bruce.

"Are you okay?" Megan asked, reaching out to steady him.

"A big blank spot just opened up in the future around us," he said, urging Paul to walk faster. "I want to get out of here."

They made it to the place where Chuck had been waiting for him before a premonition pierced his mind's eye, plunging him into a vision so strong he lost all sense of himself.

*A cloud of noxious fumes belched forth from the foundations of the Baker Hotel as it slid at an angle across the previously quiet street to bury The Palace. His father ran without protective gear into Gordon's where the dinner rush had drawn a decent crowd. But it was in vain. All of them, including Sam and Andrew, died within seconds of breathing the fumes. Had he taken the time to put on his respirator, he would have survived... Flames consumed the dojo and Bruce could hear his sister screaming inside.*

"Can you hear me?" Megan was screaming when she and Paul swam back into focus. Bruce tried to sit up, but between the nausea and bone-weary fatigue he just couldn't. His entire body hurt as if he'd gone an entire class sparring with Emelia without pads. He tried to speak, but his mouth wasn't forming words.

"Hey bro," Paul called loudly. "Blink if you can hear me."

That at least remained within his current abilities.

"Good," Paul said, relaxing a little. "I think you just had a seizure."

Bruce shook his head and tried to speak again. This time it sounded like a really drunk Tasmanian Devil. This struck him as funny, and he almost threw up.

*Don't try to speak.* Megan sent, her thoughts warm with her concern. *Can you talk this way?*

*Yes.*

*What happened?*

Rather than try to explain the urgency of what he'd seen, he joined his thoughts with hers and was rewarded with an anchor that let him realign himself within her framework. He let the images flow into her mind and hoped that they wouldn't trigger a similar response in her.

Eyes wide, she sat back hard and would have fallen over if Paul hadn't steadied her.

"What the hell?" Jade asked.

"Had vision," Bruce managed to say, "Help me sit against the tree."

"Of what?" Paul asked, still holding Megan upright.

"The Baker is going to blow up and take half of downtown with it," Megan answered.

"There are elephants with iron tap shoes having a hoedown in my head right now," Bruce said, finally able to speak properly and closing his eyes against the light through the trees above.

"Are you sure he's the one?" an unfamiliar voice came from a branch overhead. "He seems to fall down an awful lot."

Following the voice, Bruce found the flying frog looking down at him.

"Don't be rude," chided a raspy voice that seemed to come from all directions at once. Then the dryad he'd seen the day of the race rose from the debris of the woodland floor. "We've merely come upon him on particularly difficult days."

"You are incredibly cool," Jade said, looking up into the wood-spirit's swirling autumn eyes.

"Why thank you," the creature answered before turning to Bruce. "You and the others must prevent this vision from coming to pass. And once again, I must apologize that my dominion ends where the furthest oak root reaches."

"You look different than before," Bruce observed.

"My physical body is only temporary," she explained. "It's made up of whatever happens to be on hand when I rise."

"What is your name?" Paul asked.

"It's not one that any human could hope to pronounce," she answered. "But you may call me Oak for the trees that give me life. My sisters are Ash and Laurel, though the latter has not been seen in many years. Now I must send you off poorly prepared once again, and for that I am sorry."

Then she dissolved into the things from which she had formed herself and the frog flew away with wishes of good luck.

"Jade, can you drive us to The Palace without making me puke all over your upholstery?" Bruce asked.

"Shouldn't we hurry?" she asked in reply.

"It's not supposed to happen for several hours," Bruce assured her. "It was dinner time, and Gordon's was full. Someone needs to call Sam and Emelia. I'm too weak to call that far and I'm pretty sure I'd spazz out again if Megan tried to reach them while she's this close to me. Man, that vision *hurt*."

"And nothing at all before that?" Paul asked.

"Everything was clear before that," Bruce said, rising to unsteady feet to head out to Jade's car. "Something must have changed that leads to this. It almost feels like buying the stock for Sam somehow caused this."

"But no one knows about it but the four of us and Sam," Jade said.

"It's all a big jumble now," Bruce complained in frustration. "I can't see anything at all ahead right now, and before anyone makes comments about my death, I'm really not in the mood right now."

A short time later, the Grimble children, Megan, Emelia and Sam stood together in the lobby of the Palace, trying to make sense of Bruce's vision and what exactly they should do about it. Predictably, he hadn't been able to see anything in or around the disaster since the vision itself, and it felt like everyone was waiting for him to produce information he didn't possess.

"Gordon's and the dojo are shut down due to illness," Sam said, getting off of his phone. "That at least is something we can prevent."

"Good," Bruce said. His brain kept supplying irrelevant information about the Palace since he'd spent so much time repairing things there lately. He was going to be really pissed off if someone blew it up after all that they'd done to bring the place back from its deathbed.

"Any idea what starts it?" Emelia asked.

"None," Bruce answered, looking out the window at the looming outline of the hotel. He'd actually found a place that would replicate the original gold leaf inlays that framed the window. "I think we're just going to have to go in and find out what's going on. There's too much interference for me to see more than I already have."

"That's what I think too," Sam said. "We just have to make sure no one sees us going over there. As unsatisfactory as Sheriff Pullen has proven with almost every other aspect of his job, he does seem to take an inordinate amount of interest in preventing trespassing at the Baker."

"Which is in itself interesting," Emelia said, "given who his in-laws are."

"We saw him earlier, and that's where it looked like he was going," Paul added.

"I don't understand what could possibly be that explosive," Bruce said, "I mean, the city doesn't store dynamite down there does it?"

"Not that I know of," Sam answered. "And you said the fumes that came out of it were the worst part."

"Yes," Bruce agreed. "Do you think Jones is in on whatever it is, or is it just O'Toole?"

"I can't see Tony letting anyone poke around one of his properties without knowing exactly what was going on there," Emelia answered. "He was always something of a control freak."

"By now Grandpa should have the Harrises at our house," Megan said. "And Alan is still at the hospital so we don't have to worry about him."

"Jade," Sam said, putting his big hands on her shoulders.

"Don't you dare tell us we can't go," she growled. "We can help."

"I know you can," Sam said in that soothing rumble. "But as much as it pains me to say it, you don't have the skills necessary for what we are about to do. Where we need you and Paul to be is at the newspaper. If this goes wrong, you're going to need to get them to safety. The prevailing winds are heading that direction."

Jade would have argued with anyone else, and it broke Bruce's heart

332

to see her shoulders slump when she finally nodded.

"If we don't hear anything from you, I'll pull the fire alarm at the *Tribune,*" Paul said, his voice husky and his eyes overly bright, "That should get Dad and the other fire fighters there. Then we'll get them to an interior room, shut off the air and stuff wet towels under the doors. But what about everyone else?"

"Jones controls everyone we could contact," Emelia answered. "The best shot we have is for the four of us to go in and stop whatever this is before it happens. And don't forget, we're actually very well suited for this kind of situation. What we're asking the two of you to do is just our insurance policy."

They huddled together there in the lobby of the theater, hoping that they'd see each other again and trying not to think about the devastation it would cause for the people they loved if they didn't. Then Jade and Paul walked out into the Texas heat and got into Christine.

"And here I thought the hardest part of the day was going to be making Sam rich," Bruce said, waving to them as they pulled away.

"How did that go, by the way?" the big man asked with mild interest.

"Splendidly," Megan answered. "You've got a real head for the stock market."

"Just one of the many things that makes Sam Wise," he chuckled.

"Please, no dad jokes until you're actually a dad," Emelia said.

"Is that an offer?" he asked softly.

Bruce and Megan pretended that they hadn't heard that last bit. Each would have rather detonated the building themselves than look over to see what exchanged between Emelia and her oldest friend.

"Megan," Emelia said, "I'm going to show you a spot inside the fence at the back of the hotel. I want you to walk the shadows with me there.

Bruce, you're going to take Sam."

When they did so, something about the transition affected Sam more than it did the rest of them. Even though Bruce was already holding onto his arm, the big man suddenly reached out with his other hand and grabbed hold of him for support. Bruce was not sufficient to the task. With a surprised yelp, they both tumbled to the ground.

"That felt awful!" Sam groaned.

"Are you okay?" Megan asked, kneeling next to her big friend.

"Sorry guys," Sam apologized, looking embarrassed. "I haven't had vertigo like that in years."

"We've got this if you can't go down there," Emelia said quietly.

"And let you guys have all the fun?" Sam asked, levering himself to his feet. "I'm okay. I just need a few seconds for the world to stop moving."

While they waited, Bruce scanned this hidden area behind the abandoned hotel. An overgrown chain link fence surrounded a courtyard that contained not only a partially completed tennis court, but also what must have been a truly sophisticated swimming pool for its day.

Megan spun around, looking wildly about.

"What's wrong?" Emelia asked.

"That's the second time I've felt someone watching me when there wasn't anyone about. The other time was down the street at The Palace. I didn't see anyone, but Paul said there was a guy who looked like he was trying out for an old vampire movie his dad likes to watch."

"Lost Boys?" Emelia asked Bruce, who nodded.

"Does that mean something to you?" Megan asked, but her mother only shrugged.

"There's a service entrance down those stairs," Sam said, rising to his feet and pointing toward a break in the stonework.

"How do you know that?" Bruce asked.

"We snuck in here a few times when we didn't want to be found," Emelia said with a nostalgic grin. "We even went swimming in the pool at the back of the property before it went stagnant."

"You actually wore a bathing suit?" Megan asked, then immediately regretted it when Sam grinned in response. "You know, you can't really get mad at me for all of the trouble I get into. It's practically printed on my DNA."

"When have I ever gotten mad at you for trouble?" Emelia asked. "Frightened for your safety, of course, but never angry."

"We should probably stop talking out loud when we go down," Sam whispered, leading them over to the door. "Creepy van guy is probably down there somewhere, and noise travels far in those concrete passageways."

Bruce suspected that the lock on the door had been broken for a long time given the way Sam reached for it as if he'd already known it would open. With a faint creak it opened into a metal utility stairway, designed more for function than for beauty. He hoped the rest of the place proved to be more solid than the staircase. A dislike of tight underground spaces was something he shared with his brother, and he tried not to think about what it would be like to be under the place if it were to collapse like it had in his vision.

The door at the bottom of the stairs was both locked and extremely rusty. With a brush of Bruce's hand the red flakes fell away. It took him only seconds to manipulate the tumblers in the lock and open the door.

Sam summoned a small globe of red light that hovered a short distance over his open palm. This gave them enough light to see metal steps leading downward without casting shadows that could give away their presence.

*Please don't let this be a meth house,* Bruce sent. *Those are really explosive and toxic.*

*But strong enough to take down a building this solid?* Sam asked. *This is old construction.*

*True,* Bruce conceded, *and from what I can feel from here it may look like a ruin, but there are no structural problems at all. Everything you see is cosmetic. But what could account for something like what I saw?*

It was dusty and dank in the corridor, bringing back an unexpected memory of the isolation room at the Academy. As much as he didn't want to, he closed his mouth and breathed through his nose. There was so much humidity down there that he could almost taste the mold in the air. There were also puddles several yards long where water had been allowed to form and dry up in repetitive cycles of intensifying stagnation over the last century.

*How is your breathing?* Megan asked, likely aware of his thoughts even though she wasn't actively trying to read his mind.

*Good. This would have killed me before you came, though.*

*And now we can die down here together in a big explosion,* Sam sent.

*There are worse ways to go,* Bruce sent.

At last the corridor ended in another door, and Bruce repeated his impromptu restoration on it. When Sam quenched the flame, they could see faint light coming under the door from the room beyond.

*I can feel two people on the other side.* Emelia sent. *Let me go in first, I've got the most experience at fighting if it comes to that. This is the basement and it's huge. There are columns every fifteen feet or so and another staircase on the other side that leads up to the maid quarters. I*

336

*think there's an elevator to the left, but I'm not sure.*

*That's right,* Sam sent. *We go in slow and quiet. If we're lucky the light source is on the other side of the room and we might even come out in the shadows.*

Bruce reached out and squeezed Megan's hand in the dark for good luck. She clung to it for a few seconds and then let him go.

Emilia turned the handle and pushed it slowly open, giving them a few seconds to adjust to the light on the opposite side of the room. A noxious stench filled the otherwise stale air of the basement, and Megan worried that it might trigger Bruce's asthma. For that matter, it might make the rest of them have an attack as well. Whatever it was making that smell should definitely come with a hazard warning on the label. They moved slowly into the room and took in what lay on the other side.

"We should have respirators for this," a deep yet still unpleasant voice complained. "There's no telling how many brain cells we're losing being down here like this."

"For what I'm paying you, you can spare a few," a familiar voice retorted. "Now hurry up, and get the last of those detonators online so we can blow this from a safe distance."

*That's definitely the van guy, Mr. O'Toole, but who is the other one?* Bruce asked, unable to see the men because of the barrels that were stacked, floor to ceiling with only small walkways between them.

*Our favorite politician and businessman,* Sam sent. *Have you guys noticed the labels on the barrels?*

*My eyes aren't as good as yours,* Emelia sent. *Can you make out what they are?*

337

*No, but most of them have a biohazard symbol on them, and judging from the smell I'd guess many of them are leaking. If so, I'd say there are several hundred of them and given the age of this place I'll bet the floor drains go straight into the storm system.*

*Which would take it to the lake,* Bruce added.

*Think this could be the source of the goat flu?* Megan asked.

*It couldn't be,* Bruce answered. *They've checked the water supply for contaminants.*

*Ah, but who would have collected the samples?* Emelia asked. *Who would they have sent them to, and is there any reason to think that they wouldn't have been on Jones's payroll?*

*Remember when Allison came to The Palace and wanted to know if the ice came from the public water supply?* Megan asked.

*I'll take out our friend from the Jubilee,* Emelia sent. *Tony doesn't seem to be doing anything that could set off an explosion so I'll leave him to you guys.*

Without waiting to see if they were ready, Megan's mother stepped into the light and walked calmly up to the scarred man who was busily working on something attached to one of the stone columns.

"Good evening," she said when he looked up. Then as if there were nothing at all strange about her presence there in the basement of an abandoned building, she added, "I'm a reporter from the *Nickelville Tribune* and I'd like to interview the two of you for an upcoming article about life incarceration."

"What the hell," O'Toole exclaimed in surprise. "You seeing this, Mr. Jones?"

"No one will find her in the rubble," Allison's father answered with a shrug.

To Megan's horror, the scarred man pulled a buck knife from a sheath on his leg and lunged toward her mother with ill intent. Megan could feel her mother draw power, apparently not caring if either of the men saw her work magic. That didn't bode well for the chances of either being allowed to live. But before O'Toole could close with her, a dark blur broke from the shadows, and Sam was on him, his huge hand closing over the man's wrist.

Megan thought it was over, but it turned out that the man with the buck knife had been through more than a bit of training himself. Using his free hand to help him, he rotated his arm hard in Sam's grip, breaking through at the thumb.

Having attacked from an odd angle to reach O'Toole before the man reached Emelia, Sam couldn't have been at a worse angle to attack. Giving up on technique, he grabbed the man by the neck and threw him back into the column where the man had been working, slamming his head against the concrete pillar and crushing the explosives into his back.

Sam released him, stepping back and probably hoping to move the fight away from the potentially deadly column. O'Tool came down on the balls of his feet and lunged into Sam, knife extended before him. When he pulled away, it was slick with blood.

"Sam," Emelia called back as she stepped between them and advanced once again on her attacker. "Are you okay?"

"He didn't hit anything important," the big man answered, placing his hand over the wound in his abdomen. Light flared between his fingers, and the smell of burning flesh filled the already foul air as he burned it shut.

"You're like them!" O'Toole spat, before moving toward Emelia again.

"Oh, I'm going to enjoy hurting you," Emelia purred, pulling a wicked looking knife from behind her back. Megan had just enough time to realize that there was something wrong with her mother's weapon before she advanced. It seemed to absorb what light there was in the darkened basement. Furthermore it was invisible to her other senses. "I've missed this," Emelia added.

Clearly upset to discover that his high-school classmate wasn't alone, Tony Jones snatched something that looked like a small walkie-talkie from a nearby desk and tried to run for the staircase.

Emelia's laughter as it echoed around the underground space was a bit disturbing for them all.

"Where do you think you're going?" Bruce asked as he reached out with his mind to pick up the town leader and bring him back. *I always wanted to say that!* he added.

Still distracted by her mother, Megan sent the device spinning to the floor from Mr. Jones's hand instead of bringing it to her own as she'd intended. Cursing, she glanced over to find her mother dancing past her opponent's attack, drawing a line across his shoulder with the strange knife.

Bruce brought Jones to his knees and Megan crossed the distance to slap him hard across the face.

"What were you thinking?" she asked.

"Who the hell do you think you're dealing with?" Jones spat. "I'll have you behind bars before the day is out, and you'll all take the blame for this as well."

"He's right," Sheriff Pullen said, coming down the stairs with his sidearm already drawn.

"You can't fire that down here," O'Toole growled, still trying to find a way past Emelia's guard.

340

"You know," the man with the unpleasant resemblance to the former ninth grade teacher drawled, "I'm pretty okay with my chances. I'm not that attached to any of this." Then he took aim at Megan and pulled the hammer back with his thumb.

Before anyone could react, a hand reached out almost calmly from the darkened wall next to him, taking the gun from his suddenly limp fingers and pushing him against the stair rail.

Bruce recognized the long blond hair and slight form as the sheriff looked into the impossibly blue eyes before him. Surprised by her beauty, he smiled at her, hardly noticing when his flesh began to wither under her touch. Then Sheriff Pullin folded in on himself until his desiccated corpse fell the rest of the way down the steps and broke into a cloud of ash that settled to the floor.

Megan grabbed Tony by the throat and felt the hunger within her come alive as it had with his daughter just a few months before. But this time she didn't try to hold it in check. She drank in his fear as his face reflected the harsh violet glow of her eyes. As had happened before, images began to flood her mind: images of him watching her mother at the Academy, knowing that it would infuriate his girlfriend and make Emelia's life even harder than it had been. She saw him as he inserted himself in every aspect of business in Nickelville, slowly draining the resources its population needed to survive. She saw the deal he made with O'Toole to store toxic byproducts from his business here beneath the hotel where no one would ever find them. How was he to know that they'd leak? Or that it would end up in the municipal water supply? Like the retrofitted infrastructure that he'd substituted for new upgrades in the town's electrical grid, his father had signed off for a company that was supposed to have rerouted these old drains. But now all of that had caught up to him.

341

He'd received word that morning that someone from the EPA would be out any day now to run real tests, and that simply couldn't be allowed to happen. He'd already sent his family on vacation outside of the blast radius, though to be honest, he'd thought about cashing in on their insurance policies as well. After all, if he was going to take his wealth and start new somewhere else, why not start with a completely fresh canvas?

Megan could feel his understanding of what was happening, and she reveled in his fear. Oddly enough, Tony Jones had a past understanding of magic. It wasn't an evil that demanded atonement, so it didn't cross through judgment well, but Megan could see that he knew about the supernatural aspects surrounding the Academy. He also knew that the graves had been hidden as an attempt to hide Jacob Routh as much as the graves of his wife and son. She wanted to know more, but the hunger would no longer be denied. His life force drained from his body into hers. Nothing she'd ever experienced felt as good as this feeding. In that moment, she realized that her life had been nothing but a shadow cast by the potential of this. All too soon the spark of life left his eyes and she allowed him to fall at her feet.

"NO," Emelia yelled, distracted by her daughter and realizing too late that her opponent had given up trying to beat her and lunged toward the device that his dead accomplice had dropped. She hurled the strange knife, which passed through the scarred man as if he'd been nothing more than vapor to imbed itself in the stone foundation, but not before he reached the remote.

"There are explosives on all of the columns," Bruce said, reaching out with his mind. "We've got less than a minute. I can't shut them all off in time."

Time slowed as Megan instinctively used the power she'd harvested from Allison's father to speed her reactions. She didn't think before she acted. She simply reached out with this glorious newfound strength and used it to save the ones she loved. Without even touching them, she gathered her people up and cast them through the shadows into her grandmother's grove where they'd be safe. In time she hoped they'd forgive her.

The device flew to her hand, and she used its connection to reach out and ensnare the detonators along with the explosives they controlled. Her senses were alive in a way that stretched an instant into an eternity, and she knew she'd made the right choice.

"Goodbye Megan," Charlotte whispered in her ear.

Somewhere at the edges of her senses, she felt Bruce bending the world around him to return to her side. She had only an instant left to act before he reached her, so she walked the shadows one last time. The cold ripped away her warmth as she crossed with the deadly charges trailing behind her like lost children. The explosion threw her far into the barren landscape, and when her bond with Bruce broke, she hoped that her mother would find a way to keep his asthma in check.

Something within her wove the stolen power she'd consumed into a cocoon of raw power much like the one her mother, Sam and August had created at the cliff. But even so, the force of her impact cast her into the oblivion beyond.

# Chapter XXXV: Arrivals and Departures

In the week since Bruce had found himself thrown into the grove at the back of the McGeehee property, he'd spent a lot of time at the treehouse looking out over the treetops. Jade and Paul had come with him at first, but even his sister had finally realized he just wanted to be alone.

*Alone*, that was a word that meant so much more now. He thought he'd been alone before Megan had come. But then he'd just been a child with no true understanding of what his life lacked. Now that he knew, now that he understood what he would miss for the rest of his life, he finally understood.

He wasn't in mourning. He wasn't sad or angry. Any of those would have been better than what he didn't feel. As far as he could tell, Megan had taken the part of him that could feel with her, leaving him nothing but an empty husk where hopes and dreams had once grown. The time they'd spent together felt like something he'd read in a book, not something he'd taken part in himself.

Sam and Emelia had both tested his ability to amplify, and on that front, all seemed to be functional. However, he didn't take on their abilities like he had with Megan. He supposed nothing was ever going to be like it had been with her again.

He'd been forced to take his asthma medication this morning instead of spitting it out like he usually did. It interfered with his abilities, but maybe leaving that world behind would be best.

The state police had been called in once it became clear that Mr. Jones was involved with the contamination of the water supply. Further exploration of the Baker Hotel's basement had revealed not only a black-market disposal site, but signs that explosives had been produced in large quantities. The current location of said explosives was the source of much speculation, and some suggested they might be with the missing sheriff. The entire Jones fortune had been frozen, and his family was currently believed to be hiding with relatives. Many wondered what might have happened if he hadn't suffered what appeared to be an embolism after murdering his associate. The only real mystery, as far as the officials were concerned, was how a strange knife found at the scene had disappeared from the evidence locker.

But none of that mattered to Bruce. It had rained on him yesterday while he sat there, lost in her memory, and he never noticed it. His clothing was almost dry by the time he returned to himself.

Somewhere in the distance he felt something stir.

"She's coming home," he heard himself whisper.

A young man in a black trench coat picked through the boulder-strewn landscape. He held a glowing orb of light before him as he searched. He was tired. This had taken far too long. He only prayed that the heir had inherited her father's hardiness.

Then something caught his eye, and he rushed over to the still form.

The dark-haired girl showed no sign of life. Her clothes were singed from the explosion that had thrown her this far, but that was to be expected. The force of the explosion had hidden her from the others who'd come to investigate the strange anomalies within the shadow realm as of late. They'd come when they first felt the presence of the heir, but they hadn't lingered because she wasn't their only charge as she was his. So while they had returned to home and hearth, he had stayed. For over two weeks he'd stayed here, though he knew nearly a year had passed in the world where she lived. Then it had happened.

She returned again, passing back so quickly that it was clear she had begun to come into her power. He wasn't able to follow her back that time, but he'd be ready when she did it again.

But when it happened, several times in rapid succession, it wasn't the heir who passed through, but a boy who shouldn't have been able to walk the shadows at all. When he passed through at last with the heir and a great deal of water, the young man followed, only to be cast back from the place where they traveled by enormous amounts of iron. Frustrated, the young man sat back to wait yet again.

Then, not only had she returned, but she'd had the audacity to bring an antique automobile into this place where even a needle would have been noticed for the disruption it caused in the energy flows. With her concentration focused on the strain of moving it back through to her own world, she'd never noticed him when he followed her back. And a good thing it was that he had. Since his predecessor lacked the ability to walk between the shadows, there was no way for her to rescue her daughter once the girl had brought the explosives here.

Likewise, the previous scathlahm was lucky that his oath bound him to his charge and not to the will of his liege. What he did now would be

346

considered treason to most of his clan. But his oath meant more to him than ties of kinship, and now that he'd found the heir, he had no intention of letting her die. That she'd survived as long as she had spoke a great deal of her power.

He'd hoped that their first meeting would be under better conditions, but alas that would not be the case. He gathered her unceremoniously into his arms and took her back to her own world.

Bruce's senses came alive in a rush, and he sprinted to the grove where they'd found themselves so unceremoniously dumped a week previous. Her skin smoked in the warm sun, and were it not for his ability to feel her thoughts as she slept on one of the stone benches, he would have thought her dead.

Something in the sight of her lying that way in that place triggered the first premonition he'd had since she'd saved them all. But that was nothing in the face of her here, here and alive! He ran to her side.

Curled against her was Mr. Bob.

"Is she okay?" Emelia asked, walking up behind him.

"I think so," he answered, placing his hand over hers. "I think she's just unconscious, which means she probably didn't make it here on her own. Any idea where she's been?"

"I think she's been in the place where she goes when she walks between the shadows," Emelia answered, coming over to sit on her daughter's other side. "It's cold there."

Mr. Bob purred loudly as she reached out to stroke his fur.

"It's a good thing she doesn't feel cold," Bruce said. "I've never been that cold in my life. It wasn't as bad when we were in Big Bertha though."

"You took that car through the shadows?" Emelia asked, alarmed.

"Yes," Bruce answered, reluctantly looking up. "How did you think we got it out of Guarded Wood?"

"I had my mind on other things," she answered cryptically. "I'll bet that didn't go unnoticed."

"How did he get here?" Bruce asked, nodding toward the cat.

"I suspect he goes wherever he wants," Emelia said. "Her mind may still be traveling. We need to call her back."

*Megan,* they sent together, trying to rouse her from wherever it was that she'd gone.

For an uncomfortably long moment, she didn't respond, but then Emelia reached out, took his hand, and placed it over her daughter's. *Call to her and bring her home.*

When he did, Megan's presence solidified at last and rose to the surface.

"Did anyone get hurt?" she whispered.

"No," Emelia answered, gently brushing her daughter's forehead with her fingertips. "You saved us all."

"Good," Megan mumbled. "Totally not doing that again anytime soon."

"You knew she'd come back," Bruce told Emelia. Aside from spending more time with her father, the woman had been oddly unconcerned about Megan's absence.

"Yes," she answered.

"But how?" he asked.

"The time for secrets is almost over," the woman replied with a sad smile as she absently reached out and stroked the cat's dark fur, making him purr again. "Soon you'll both know everything, though you'll probably miss the days when you were innocent of it all."

"Promises, promises," Megan whispered, finally opening her eyes. "Has it always been this bright here? How long have I been out of it? Do I have a cat attached to my head?"

"You've been gone for over a week," Bruce answered. "But you just came back a few minutes ago. I don't know how Mr. Bob got here. Was it your grandmother again?"

"No," she answered. "The last thing I remember is being thrown by the explosion. She guided me the last time, but I'm the one who brought us through. I don't think she could have brought me by herself."

"What do they think happened with Mr. Jones?" Megan asked

"Brain aneurysm possibly brought on by the fumes," Bruce said. "But that's not the best part. With the cash Sam earned from his investments, he bought the controlling shares of the factory and is in the process of setting it up to run as a non-profit. He's already started raising salaries and hiring back the people who were laid off. Word is that he might just run for mayor when the next election comes."

So it was that Megan was carried inside to sleep for the remainder of the day and night with a big black cat purring at her side. Her dreams were often troubled by the things she'd seen in Tony Jones's mind, but in others she traveled far away where people with pale skin and violet eyes lived.

When she woke, she went in search of her family and friends, eager to start what was left of the summer. She found her grandfather downstairs, sitting at the kitchen table with a note and an odd rune-marked stone in his hands.

"Your mother left sometime last night," he said, stricken, and handed her the note.

*Azarich and Megan,*

*I'm sorry to leave like this, but it has come to my attention that there are some things outside of Nickelville that I need to take care of. I'm going to be gone for a while, but I don't want you to worry. I will be back when all of this is settled. In the meantime I want you to know that I love the two of you more than anything, and that I would be there if I could. Take care of each other. Megan, take this stone to August. He will show you what to do with it. Until then,*

*Emelia.*

# About the Author

Tom Barnett was a sick kid who escaped into fantasy books at a young age. As he grew, his asthma got better, but his love of reading never diminished. After three decades of leading teens toward a love of reading in which the stories of Nickelville have been percolating in the back of his mind, he's finally set them free.

Tom currently teaches middle school English in the Dallas area where he lives with his wife and children. He is also owned by several cats, one of which may or may not be the oldest creature in the universe.